CW00484742

JULIET & ROMEO

JULIET & ROMEO

David Hewson

THE
DOME
PRESS

Published by The Dome Press, 2018
Copyright © 2018 David Hewson
The moral right of David Hewson to be recognised as the author
of this work has been asserted in accordance with the
Copyright, Designs and Patents Act 1988.

This is a work of fiction. All characters, organisations and events
portrayed in this novel are either products of the author's imagination
or are used fictitiously.

A CIP catalogue record for this book is available from the British Library

ISBN 9781912534050

The Dome Press
23 Cecil Court
London WC2N 4EZ

www.thedomepress.com

Printed and bound in Great Britain by Clays, St. Ives PLC

Typeset in Garamond by Elaine Sharples

Contents

Foreword by Richard Armitage

This is a story about a woman who is bound by her time. Juliet and Romeo are at odds with life, at odds with their parents. They recognise that in each other and enjoy that about each other. Ultimately it becomes yet another thread that pulls them together and enables their love.

I love that this version takes the essence of Shakespeare's words and creates modern dialogue that makes such an incredible character out of Juliet. You can understand her perspective within a family that is at odds with one another. Her sensibilities are very much those of a modern woman though the people in this story very much reference the era in which is set. There is a powerful atmosphere of the Renaissance, the time of Leonardo da Vinci, and the discovery of the New World that gives you a sense of that burning desire of opportunity as they are about to step into the 1500s. It's one of the most familiar stories we have, but this retelling makes it read as something fresh and new.

Richard Armitage

Preface

It was Monday, July the tenth in the year 1499. A restless moment in a restless world. Rodrigo Borgia reigned as Pope Alexander the Sixth, a pontiff as fond of corruption and debauchery as he was of pomp and ritual. In Florence a brief republic was struggling to emerge from the ruins left by the rule of the apocalyptic priest Savonarola, hanged and burned in front of the Signoria the year before.

The din of war rang over the rival city states of Italy. A mighty French force had invaded Lombardy. To the east an Ottoman fleet of almost a hundred galleons had embarked for the Adriatic from Constantinople to do battle with Venice.

Nowhere did mankind seem still, settled... or in the least incurious. Seven years before, Columbus had discovered a new world for his Spanish masters, turning the eyes of Europe from east to west in search of riches and fresh territory to colonise. Fearful of the coming French, Leonardo Da Vinci had fled Milan for Venice to design new military emplacements that might save the city from the impending Turkish storm. Michelangelo had returned to Florence after Savonarola's fall and was slowly working on the slab of Carrara marble that would become the statue of David. While in Rome a young cleric named Nicolaus Copernicus spent his evenings stargazing, quietly becoming convinced of the heretical notion that the sun and not the earth lay at the centre of the universe.

Four hundred years later, hindsight would dub this era the beginning of the Renaissance. But the sweep of history is invisible to those who live through it. For the actors on this restive, panoramic stage there was no name for the state of their particular world, only a shared sense that it stood on the brink of fateful change, as full of peril as it was opportunity.

Tense times without were mirrored by tense times within. The walled city that was Verona, an outpost of the threatened Venetian Republic, possessed a violent enmity of its own, one generated by nothing more than a breed of grape.

Luca Capulet owned the monopoly of production for the variety known as Garganega, grown throughout the flat lands towards Venice. Andrea Montague, maintaining estates to the west, had inherited the licence for the rival Trebbiano vine. So Montague and Capulet had become enemies, bitter ones, when it came to shipping barrels to the great houses that desired them. A vendetta was in a place, one so deep-rooted few recalled the argument that had started it nor cared much to question this small war's origins.

A feud was a feud, one that of late had increasingly brought violence and bloodshed to the streets of fair Verona.

On the other side of Italy, in the corridors of the Signoria in Florence, a thirty-one-year-old clerk named Niccolò Machiavelli was beginning to believe this bold new world required a handbook, a set of rules through which it might be well and ruthlessly governed. It would take another fourteen years for his ideas to emerge with the publication of *The Prince*. But for those who led this fragile, edgy realm, Machiavelli's lessons were old news. They'd learned early: a stable state required a tame and subdued populace. Riots, dissent and civil commotion only served to aid the enemy. They were to be put down in every instance, with all the force required.

Then summer came, with all its fiery heat, and met head on the unpredictable, random spirit called human nature.

Part One: To Borrow Cupid's Wings

The Marangona bell in the Torre dei Lamberti had just sounded the hour. Nine of a busy Monday morning in what was once Verona's imperial Roman forum, now its marketplace, the Piazza Erbe. The square thronged with shoppers bargaining at stalls selling meat and fish, cheese and fruit and vegetables, cheap wine and cheaper beer. In the shadows of the colonnades two youths lurked, Samson and Gregory, both servants of the Capulets. The first a skinny seventeen-year-old kitchen boy, the second a priest's bastard from Padua, a tall and hefty stable hand shuffling on his big feet as he caught the glint of metal in Samson's grubby hand.

They wore the clothes of their class – rough wool jerkins, baggy britches, sandals held together by thread and nails. This poverty extended to the weaponry they took with them on to the streets. The sons of fine families were in the habit of carrying daggers and rapiers forged in Florence and Milan. The lower orders snatched at anything they could lay their hands on, sharp or blunt. They fought with fists and boots and punches to the balls. Died that way, too.

A crude swagger stick sat on a piece of rope round Gregory's fat stomach, a mallet handle with a spiked iron ball on the end. The blade Samson owned was nothing more than a paring knife stolen from the kitchen, the edge honed carefully until it gleamed. He held it now, low by his side so that only his companion might see.

'There's that fat Montague pig Abraham with his mate. Time to put that stick of yours to some use, Gregory. Go over and wallop him. He wants it.'

Across the piazza, just visible beyond the stalls, two figures moved through the market. Much the same age as the two Capulets. Much the same size: one short and lean, one tubby and daydreaming. Samson and Gregory wore a scarlet feather in their caps. The Montagues a blue one. Not that any of these were flesh and blood of the Montague or Capulet lines. Just servants, sharing the same borrowed hatred and never asking why.

Gregory kicked a fish head and stuck his fists deep into the pockets of his britches.

'I don't know. We're getting hard looks from those blokes on the stalls. They don't like trouble when they're trying to sell stuff.'

'I reckon it was them Montague lads who had that kitchen girl of ours last week.'

Lucia. An orphan who worked the ovens. She'd gone out for a walk by the river. Came back in tears and rags, telling tales the soldiers of Escalus, the city's current military master, didn't want to hear.

'That hare-brained lass should have been in the kitchen stirring the pots, not hanging round down them dark alleys in Sottoriva. Could have been anyone had his way with her. Besides the watchmen reckoned she was up for it. Plenty been there with that daft cow. You for one.'

'Scared are you?'

'Just thinking it through.' The Montague pair had spotted them but they hadn't moved their way. 'I don't see you in a rush either.'

Fights were fine so long as the numbers were on your side. And you had the right comrades. Samson liked to whine. It was his principal pastime. Action always came last.

'It's only fair. They had one of ours. A bit of gravy on their chops and then we leg it.'

Gregory pulled a stick of dried sausage out of his pocket, bit off a chunk and waited.

'Master sent us out to buy grub for his ball tonight. He won't be happy if we come back empty-handed.'

'We whack them round the head a bit. Then go hunting round the back of their palazzo. First girl that comes out of the kitchen's mine. Unless she's hideous — then you can have her.' Samson had a sly and cruel face and it was turned on Gregory. 'With a bit of luck we might get a virgin if the Montagues have got any left. You all right with that?'

'I'm all right with the girls. Escalus ain't so bothered about them. It's the walloping bit—'

'They got to know who's boss. You with me or not?'

Gregory patted his pocket. He had a stable knife with him as well as the swagger stick. Short, a bit blunt. But he was strong enough to hold a struggling stallion when he had to. The thing would do.

'I hate the buggers, too, you know. But like I say. Escalus has got that one wicked eye on lads like us. Same way his bosses in Venice have got their eyes on him. The Marshal hates riots. They get him in trouble too. I don't fancy jail or worse just for giving one of them scummy Montagues a few bruises and a sore head.'

'Then let's get clever. Make them start the scrap. I'll look at them funny. Get 'em going. That way we're just… defending ourselves. Which is every man's right, and Escalus is bound to uphold us in that.' Samson grinned, displaying a remarkable absence of teeth. 'As to the kitchen girls... well... everyone knows what they're like. I want first go though. This'll do it.'

Samson winked, grinned and bit his thumb. The oldest, stupidest gesture any of them knew. Someone said the Romans used to do it when they fancied a brawl.

'Go on then,' said Gregory and didn't move.

Samson looked up at him. 'You first.'

'When we get around to the girl, you mean?'

'No. The fight. You're the big one. You lead. I'll follow.'

Gregory slapped him hard on the shoulder.

'Ow,' Samson whined. 'That hurt.'

'Oh sorry, friend. We're supposed to be buying stuff for the evening ball. There'll be trouble if that goes wrong. Capulet will do the walloping himself and we both know what he's like with that whip of his.'

Samson went quiet. He'd had enough of Capulet's beatings.

'Tell you what,' said Gregory. 'We'll skip the girl. Next week. When we've got more time. And...'

A shape they recognised was moving through the crowds, a tall youth around their own age. But he was an aristocrat; it showed in his clothes, his manner, the haughty way he held his head above the swarms of common folk around him as if he couldn't stand the stink of them.

'Well, well,' Samson murmured, gleeful all of a sudden. 'If it isn't our master's well-loved nephew. Just the chap you'd want at a time like this.'

'I suppose,' Gregory agreed, though the sight of the young man across the Piazza Erbe gave him pause. 'I heard the noble Tybalt crippled a clerk who'd done nothing more than bump into him in the street a month or so ago.'

'Dead right he did. I was there and he paid me well to keep quiet. Back last winter he ran a cheeky cart boy right through down by the brothels in Sottoriva.'

Gregory didn't like those dark and dangerous colonnades by the river. 'Our Tybalt got caught hanging round the tarts down there?'

'The only kind of girl that one beds are the sort you pay for. Expensive business. The old man had to dig deep to keep him out of Escalus's clutches after he murdered the poor little bugger.'

Tybalt was bloodthirsty, vicious and short tempered, always armed with the latest weapons, forever spoiling for a quarrel and a chance to use them.

'Nothing stopping our Tybalt,' Samson added. ''Specially when there are Montagues around.' He clapped his grubby hands. 'This will be fun.'

* * *

Juliet was the only child of Luca and Bianca Capulet, sixteen years old, bright and forthright, a catch the locals said, the prettiest girl in town. Her straight blonde hair ran loose to her shoulders, framing an alert and intelligent face that switched easily from angelic to mischievous in a moment.

'When can we go to Florence?' she asked, as her mother fussed over the state of her bedroom.

Verona sat in a sharp bend of land enclosed by the broad, grey waters of the Adige which rose high in the German Alps and ran two hundred and fifty miles south to the Adriatic. It was a place of fortalices: compact residential castles built behind martial barbicans, with towers and battlements ready for conflict against distant enemies and neighbours alike.

The palazzo of the Capulets occupied a sizeable estate to the east of the government buildings in the Piazza dei Signoria. High stone walls stood on all four sides, three facing narrow streets, the last against the grassy bare bank of the river, all of them composed of hefty rusticated blocks. On top sat lines of brick merlons, like inverted swallows' tails, a few with military arrow slits. The palace occupied the centre, with a courtyard to the front, a long garden and an orchard running to the Adige at the rear. Like all good Verona fortalices, the Capulets' was surmounted by a tower, in this case the fourth highest in the city. The third tallest belonged to the Montagues. It was Luca Capulet's intention to do something about that one day.

'Did you hear?' Juliet demanded.

Her mother sighed. 'We'll see.'

'"We'll see" usually means no.'

'This room…' Their daughter had her own apartment overlooking the gardens at the back, with a view of the river from the balcony. Her parents occupied the top floor on the opposite side of the palazzo. Bianca Capulet sometimes wondered if they couldn't find somewhere a little further away. 'This room is evidence of a deeply disordered mind.'

'Florence.'

'We're only three days back from Venice! These books we bought you. Everywhere.'

From the door to the window they lay like fallen leaves. Pocket-size octavos from the Venetian press of Aldus Manutius, some closed, some open, a few already marked with scrawls of ink. These recent inventions were cheaper, more easily carried than the big volumes of old. In Venice the booksellers couldn't find enough of them. Reading was all the rage, especially among the educated young.

'You must tidy them up, Juliet. I can scarcely cross the room without treading on an old Greek philosopher or some dubious Roman historian.'

'It may look a bit chaotic but it's not. The books are like this for a reason. I know where everything is.'

'Really?' Her mother put her foot over the nearest title. 'In that case what's this?'

A quick glance and then, '*The Letters of Pliny the Younger*. You should read the bit about the eruption of Vesuvius. Very exciting. Flames shooting up into the sky. Terror and death everywhere. His uncle perished. Probably gobbled up by molten lava.' She shuddered. 'What a way to go. Quick though.'

Bianca Capulet removed her foot and looked at the title page. The girl was right. As usual.

'Florence. There are these frescoes I've been reading about. Adam and Eve. The Brancacci Chapel. Everyone's been to see them and they say they're wonderful. You see the pair before the Fall. Then after, entering the world we know—'

'One thing at a time. Have you thought about the paintings we took you to see in Venice?'

They'd hardly left her head. Her father had busied himself with commercial discussions in the great palace of the Doge by the Piazza San Marco. While he sold wine and all the other goods the Capulets handled, a local guide had led Juliet and her mother through the streets of Castello to a *scuola* dedicated to Saint Ursula. It was housed in a large, airy and impressive building, and was not a school as Juliet had expected but a charitable brotherhood, one of many in the city competing in their patronage of the arts.

The artist Carpaccio had decorated the walls of its main chamber with nine canvases depicting the tale of their chosen saint, executed with such a colourful and vivid imagination Juliet felt she'd witnessed a piece of theatre performed by real people, not stared at stationary paint. Ursula was said to have been a Christian princess from Britain, betrothed to a pagan lord from France for the benefit of her father's politics. The panoramic canvases covered the diplomatic missions before the marriage, a visit to the Pope in Rome, the eventual meeting of the couple and a fateful dream in which an angel came to the sleeping girl and gave her a palm branch, a symbol of her coming martyrdom. Then, in a final scene so graphic Juliet could scarcely thrust it from her imagination, Ursula and her followers were massacred in a forest by savage, though often rather handsome, heathen warriors.

'I think they were very striking. But to be honest the whole thing doesn't make a lot of sense.'

'It's a love story—'

'Not quite. More a story about love. Which is rather different, don't you think?'

Bianca Capulet stepped daintily through the sea of books, took her daughter's hand and led her to the balcony. There'd been good rain the previous winter. The garden had never looked more beautiful. Roses and lilies bloomed in the manicured borders. The scent of orange blossom came to them on a breath of wind along with the buzz of happy bees and the chatter of song thrushes flitting through the orchard.

'As I think I've mentioned… I'd like to teach Nurse to read,' Juliet said.

'And as I've said already… for pity's sake, why?'

'Because everyone should be able to. What's the point of books if only a few like us can benefit from them?'

'Nurse wants nothing to do with books. She told me so herself. Stop pestering her.'

'We could begin today. It may take a while. I doubt she'll be… quick.'

'Daughter!' Seventeen in a few months. A quiet, shy child when she was small. An awkward, inquisitive adolescent, forever arguing but always with charm, wit, good humour and a smile that could disarm the fiercest fury. It had never been hard to love her, even when she was at her most exasperating. 'Stop trying to avoid the subject. You know why we took you to Venice. Don't pretend otherwise.'

Her mother's voice veered from soft and kindly to harsh and dictatorial so easily sometimes. A crow squawked in the garden. A horse neighed from the lane by the river. There was no avoiding this conversation.

'I don't want to get married. To anyone. I don't think Ursula did either. Hardly surprising given she ended up in bits and pieces scattered across some foreign forest.'

Bianca took her daughter's slender fingers. 'We all find husbands. A girl as pretty as you… Well, I can't imagine you in a nunnery.'

'That's a relief I must say.'

'Please–'

'Parents are just a little version of God, aren't they? He furnishes us with the faculty to form questions then slaps us down if we have the nerve to ask for a few answers in return. While you give us life, then, when we want to own that life, you say… oh, no. It's ours. You belong to us. We made you.'

Do not argue, Bianca told herself. That never ends well.

'There's a count called Paris. A rich and well-connected aristocrat with properties here, in Florence, everywhere. He's seen you from afar and I think will soon declare his love and fond devotion–'

'He hasn't met me! What's he found to love?'

'Your beauty. Your innocence.'

Juliet removed her hands and stabbed a finger at her breast. 'None of those things are *me*! I'm not some imaginary saint in a painting. I'm flesh and blood. *My* flesh and blood.'

Bianca Capulet struggled to contain her temper. 'This is the way of the world, child. Round and round it goes. Twenty years from now you'll be sitting in a room like this somewhere, having the same conversation with your own daughter. If it pleases God you'll find me in the corner listening. I'll give you a wry wink then. Just a reminder–'

'They say there's plague in Vicenza. I could be dead before the week is out.'

Juliet's young voice was usually so light and pleasant. At that moment it had taken on a gloomy and sullen tone her mother hadn't heard before.

'And why would a plague in Vicenza choose you?'

'Why not?'

'Because you're young. You've everything ahead of you.'

There was a bleak look in the girl's eyes at that instant. Fear. Or resignation. Or both. 'You mean the young don't die? '

A sudden breeze rustled the drapes. Juliet looked around her at the room. The books. The bed, a four-poster too big for a girl in truth. The desk where she worked. The quills were there and the lead inkwell in the shape of a frog they'd bought her as a little girl, encouraging her to write. The silly portrait her father had commissioned. All familiar things. Part of a childhood that was safe and happy in a way. Yet a whiff of the river lay behind the orange blossom on the air. Stagnant water and decay.

'Juliet–'

'While we sit here time eats at us. Every moment. Every breath we take brings us closer to... what? A robber on the highway, too quick with his knife? The plague? Some horror in childbirth?' She closed her eyes. 'If we could silence every bell in Italy. Every clock in every campanile...' She scowled. 'But still the sun would rise. And set. And rise. And set–'

'Stop it...'

Bianca took her daughter in her arms, the way she'd done on the rare occasion – following a graze, a fight, the death of a beloved pet – they'd found her crying as a child. Juliet had inherited her German grandmother's hair, straight and blonde. Bianca Capulet was plainer in face, the lines of age marking the passing difficult years. All the beauty the Capulets possessed seemed to find itself in their only living child. Perhaps, as a mother, she should have suspected this came with a price. They were close. They were distant. They were the same blood. But separate too. Before Juliet had blessed their lives they'd lost a son who never reached the age of one. That still cast a shadow over everything, especially for her husband.

'Every day...' Juliet murmured.

'Hush! We all have dark thoughts from time to time. I never realised...' This sudden outburst had shocked her. That their only child harboured such black and secret fears seemed so out of character. 'You should have told me. I had grim thoughts when I was your age too. We all do.'

'Of what?'

'Night terrors. Monsters coming for me in the dark. While I was alone in bed.'

There was a long pause. Then the girl pulled away and there was a bright smile back on her face.

'And so you married. It happened, didn't it?'

'I beg your pardon!'

'A joke. Nothing more.'

From charming to infuriating then back again in an instant. That was Juliet through and through.

'Your father may have a temper from time to time. But he's not a monster. There's much worse out there.'

'It's not my fault I'm not a boy.'

This was a refrain they hadn't heard for a week or two.

'Don't start that again. He loves you. But a father's love for a daughter is different from that he might feel for a son. He's bound to have more... limited expectations. That's all.'

'I'm sorry, Mother. You're right. They're just silly dreams. Let me hug you.'

They embraced. They kissed. Bianca Capulet wiped away a tear from her daughter's clear blue eyes.

'This is an imperfect world. But it's the only one we have.'

Juliet raised her finger and said, 'Which is why I must teach Nurse to read. To make it better one step at a time.'

Her mother laughed. She could always win her over in the end. But that was the charm of a child. It couldn't last.

'My poor precocious daughter. You think too much.'

'Is that possible?'

'It is. Now... I promised your father I'd accompany him to the market.'

There was shopping to be done, and a fateful meeting later, not that she had any intention of mentioning that.

She picked up a book, found the page she wanted and handed the volume to her daughter. 'Tidy up the rest, please. And find something nice to wear for the banquet this evening. Silk. White in there somewhere. A scoop neck but not too low. Leave your hair loose the way a maid should. The silver diadem we bought you. I never see that and it was expensive.'

'It's uncomfortable.'

'Good jewellery often is.'

'I still don't know why we're having a banquet. Has Tybalt killed someone or is it something else? Are we celebrating?'

'Leave your cousin out of this. Does there need to be a reason?'

'Usually.'

'Well, there isn't. Now. You know what you have to do.'

* * *

Her mother left. Juliet closed her eyes and listened. The palazzo was made almost entirely of stone, floors and walls, scarcely a tapestry anywhere to deaden the sound of footsteps. She'd grown up in this place, could picture who was walking where just from the noise they made.

'Courtyard,' she murmured and dashed from the apartment to the staircase window at the front. There she hid behind the wooden shutter and peered out. Her parents were at the fountain and deep in serious conversation. Her mother shook her head, unhappy. Her father was florid-faced, wagging his index finger the way he loved. When she was small they'd been closer. He'd taught her how to ride out in the vineyards. Together they'd fly around the hills of the lower Alps on their mounts. But he didn't take to his horse any more. Too old, he said. Too busy. Now angry voices rose through the hot summer morning, too faint for her to hear the words.

'My life,' Juliet whispered. 'Not yours.'

She tiptoed back into her rooms, through the piles of books on the floor, and went to sit on the balcony with the title her mother had suggested.

It was the one volume her parents had chosen for her in Venice, the last Juliet would have picked. *The Golden Legend* by Varazze, a collection of strange and fantastic fairy tales about saints she suspected never even existed.

The page was open at the chapter on the doomed Saint Ursula, the inspiration for Carpaccio's spectacular cycle of paintings. Varazze was bleating about the saint's obedience to her father and how she would happily submit to marriage for the betterment of the nation without a single thought for herself.

That's the beginning of the story. Not the end.

Three pages on she found the place she wanted and read the passage out loud, her index finger following every word.

'When all ten thousand virgins were beheaded in the forest the heathen warriors came to the blessed Ursula. There the prince of them, seeing her marvellous beauty as on her knees she prayed, was ashamed of his slaughter and sought to comfort her for the deaths of her companions.'

Juliet hesitated over the next paragraph then spoke it anyway, in a firm, determined voice.

From the courtyard came the angry, bellowing voice of her father, shouting, 'That's enough, woman. She'll do as I say. As shall you.'

Juliet waited a moment then continued.

'At which the warrior prince vowed to take her as his wife. Yet Ursula refused this chance to save her life, declaring boldly she despised the villain and everything he stood for. Furious, at close quarters, he drew his bow and, with his arrow, pierced her through the heart. So the blessed Ursula accomplished her martyrdom.'

The Marangona bell in the Torre dei Lamberti began to toll. She dropped the book and placed her hands tight over her ears.

'We'll see,' she said in a whisper so soft it mingled with the morning chimes and the bird song in the trees.

* * *

'Oi,' a hard, cold voice bellowed as the two youths from the Capulet house crossed the square. 'You. Yes, you pair. I want a word.'

Close to the colonnades a muscular and hairy arm reached out to stop Samson and Gregory in their tracks. He was an ugly man, blood all over his loose white shirt and leather apron. Cleaver in one hand, the half-skinned body of a young kid in the other.

'Don't like goat,' Samson said straight away. 'But thanks for the offer.'

The butcher threw the scraggy carcass on to his stall and folded his arms, the gory blade of the cleaver resting against his cheek.

'Three weeks running we've had you toe rags coming here and causing trouble. This is a public market. Where decent men and women come to do business. Buying. Selling. Things that make the world go round. Having a smelly bunch of scallywags beating and stabbing each other in the middle of it all don't help me put food on my family's table.'

Samson looked ready for an argument. So Gregory stepped in, trying to smooth matters.

'Sir, sir. Nothing could be further from our thoughts. We're just Capulet's servants out hunting vittles for his banquet tonight.' He nodded at the goat. 'I'll ask the cook if she fancies some of yours. How about that, eh?'

The butcher didn't look convinced. All the same he stood aside and waved them through. 'Start trouble, you get trouble. That's a promise. If you want my meat best hurry. I'll be clean out of it in an hour. Business is good right now. Better stay that way.'

Gregory promised to tell the kitchen. Samson tipped his cap and winked.

On they walked beneath the columns. Tybalt, Capulet's nephew, had spotted them already. He was dressed to the nines today in a rich, red-chestnut jacket and matching britches, a round scarlet felt hat without a rim, a dagger on his left hip, a long, expensive rapier sheathed on the right. Most of the Capulets were fair, Juliet especially so. Tybalt had jet black hair, dark, twitching eyes and a surly, pock-marked face that rarely smiled. He never seemed interested in much except collecting monies due to the Capulet businesses, at knife point if need be. Mostly his uncle indulged him with fencing lessons, cash for clothes and all the latest weapons. In turn he was the family's soldier, an enforcer for anyone they dealt with. A handy if unpredictable fellow to have around.

The Montague servant Abraham was with another youth they recognised, Balthazar. Tybalt spotted him, saw his own lads too, nodded at Samson, a sign, unmistakable. Like the servant he was, Samson doffed his cap towards his master, marched towards the Montague pair then stopped and very theatrically bit his thumb.

Abraham was ready for it. One cheap dagger by his side. Same for his mate.

'Are you biting your thumb at us?' he asked.

Gregory shuffled up, folded his arms, leaned against a pillar grinning and watched.

'What?' asked Samson cockily.

Abraham laughed. 'Always the little one who has a mouth on him, isn't it? While his big friend stands back and watches. You heard. Are you biting your thumb at us?'

Samson did it again, grinned and nodded his head. People were starting to watch, the butcher of goats among them. Tybalt stayed half-hidden, beady eyes gleaming in the shadows. The red hat, tipped to one side the way a gentleman liked, made him look like a minor cardinal. There was another one from the monied classes around too. A Montague, Benvolio, cousin to their son Romeo. Not a bad fellow some said, training to be a doctor. He didn't wear the blue feather, didn't like fights. Nothing like Tybalt at all.

'Very observant of you to notice, friend,' Samson said. 'I do indeed bite my thumb. At you? I don't think so. But look.' Again he did it. 'I do bite it, though, certainly.'

Abraham and Balthazar didn't move.

'Best do what your sort are good at,' Gregory muttered and took a step forward. He was half a head taller than them, and broader too.

'And what's that?' Balthazar wondered.

The big youth laughed. 'Taking your scrawny arses out of here with your little tails between your little legs.'

Still they stayed where they were. Abraham said, 'My master Montague asked us to take a walk around the market to see how well our wine prospers against the inferior material sold by others. We didn't come here for a quarrel.'

Samson balled a fist. 'Your drink's not Garganega. It's that Trebbiano rubbish. Everyone knows that. We two are Capulets. Work for the big man in town. Boss of 'em all.'

Abraham came closer, reached out with a jabbing finger, poked at Samson, but didn't quite touch him. 'More than one big man in this town, friend. Our lord's as good as yours. Maybe better if you only knew it.'

Gregory cocked his head. 'Better?' He tapped Samson's shoulder. 'Did I hear right? Did he say *better*?'

'Aye,' Samson agreed. 'He did. So he's a liar, ain't he? Along with all the rest.'

The people around had pulled back. There was just Tybalt close, picking at his teeth with the point of his dagger. And Benvolio striding through the colonnades looking worried.

Gregory's determination to make the Capulet pair start the fight was waning. He wanted it anyway. So he stuck out his finger and jabbed Abraham in the chest.

'A skinny little flabby-faced liar. Like all the bloody Montagues and their ilk.'

'All right!' Abraham yelled. 'Let's have you.'

Crude knives out now, all four of them, they circled beneath the colonnades at the edge of the Piazza Erbe, grinning, fearful, ready.

* * *

Juliet wasn't the only one with her head in a book. In a thick and leafy grove of plane trees outside the city walls by the broad and energetic Adige, watched with puzzlement by ducks and cormorants and the odd passing barge, Romeo of the Montagues wandered idly along the path, stopping from time to time to curse his own predicament, then turning to his own octavo from Manutius to search for comfort there. In vain.

He was eighteen, a tall, thoughtful, handsome youth with straight dark hair cut in a sharp line just above the collar. At the end of the summer he would go to read law at the university in Bologna, or so his mother had determined. The Houses of Montague and Capulet were mirror images of one another, not that they would ever see matters this way. The Capulets derived their wealth from interests in the east and Venice. The Montagues originated from Milan and, though they had been in the Veneto for more than a century, continued to retain strong commercial links with relatives in Lombardy.

Each regretted the fact they possessed just a single child. That theirs was male proved of only passing comfort to the Montagues since Romeo, though masterly at fencing lessons, showed no interest in military matters or commerce. Left to his own devices, their son would prefer to seek a future in a diversion his mother, the dominant force in the family, deemed pointless, riddled with practitioners of dubious moral fibre and leading to poverty. The youth craved to be a writer. Whether a poet or teller of narrative tales, he couldn't quite work out. Not that it mattered, since the law – a profession which relied upon words, as his father had brightly tried to point out when the boy protested – was where his parents had decided fate would lead him. Very soon indeed.

To make matters worse, at the start of the summer he had decided that he was afflicted by a persistent and debilitating ailment and, upon inspection of the poetry books he owned, that it could only be diagnosed as love. The object of his passion was Rosaline, daughter of an ambitious horse merchant who lived beyond the city walls, in the newer quarters of the city across the elegant arched Roman bridge of the Ponte Pietra.

He'd first seen her at an outdoor song recital in the spring and was immediately captivated by her looks. She was tall with an enigmatic, understated smile and eyes of a colour he hadn't yet managed to determine since, on the occasions he'd tried to speak to her, he'd been too nervous to notice and she so embarrassed by his attentions she'd quickly rushed away. The first attempt occurred after he'd heard her sing as sweetly as a nightingale at a daytime concert in the grandly ruined surroundings of the arena, the imperial-era stadium that stood to the south of the city. Three times since – in church, at the market and, lastly, when they met by accident in the street – Romeo had tried to engage her in conversation, only to find himself tongue-tied and Rosaline either so bashful or bemused by his interest that she only waited a moment then vanished.

In all four encounters he'd only ever heard her utter a single word. *Scusami.*

Excuse me. And then she was gone.

That this was love he didn't doubt. All the symptoms he found described in verse were there. Never a night passed without his thinking of her, dreaming of her, seeing in his head the two of them together. Alone in the woods. Dancing. Laughing. And in his bed. That last happened a lot, not that he was willing to speak of it to anyone except, discreetly, in confession, though he wished with every fibre in his body there was some real secret in his breast – or better, hers – deserving of a priestly cleansing.

Books should have been a comfort. Verse more than anything. Poetry ran through Verona's veins. Catullus, the recorder of many kinds of love, had been born here. Petrarch, another chronicler of the heart, once lived in the city. When Dante was expelled from Florence under pain of death it was Verona's ruler Cangrande –the 'big dog' –

who gave him refuge. Yet every time and in every place Romeo looked for comfort, verse seemed to do nothing but jeer at his failings.

He opened the small bound copy of Catullus he'd brought with him and found, at random, another taunt.

'I hate and I love. Well may you ask me why. But I don't know. Only that it happens and I am tortured.'

He sat down on a fallen tree beneath the shade of an overhanging branch and placed the book on his knees. No fancy clothes for Romeo, no slashed sleeves and rich velvet. He wore plain dark blue britches, a linen shirt of saffron yellow for the season, and went about the world hatless because this seemed to him somehow poetic.

'I am tortured,' he whispered. 'Here. In a grove of plane trees. Close to the flowing river. Surrounded by the birds and animals of the forest who notice my agony no better than my so-called friends.'

There ought to be a limit to how much a man could feel sorry for himself. He believed he'd reached that several days before only to discover he was mistaken.

A thought occurred and it was briefly cheering.

'I'll go home and pen a poem. Like Catullus did for his Lesbia. Petrarch his Laura. Dante for Beatrice Portinari.'

Except Catullus and Petrarch and Dante seemed principally to write about rejection. They rarely got so much as a kiss. Romeo had been hoping for rather more than that, especially from the daughter of a horse trader, a man who would surely ache to place his offspring inside a grand Verona household.

A large stag beetle ambled past, black horns waving. It stopped and seemed to look at him and laugh. He raised his foot above the thing. The beetle kept on staring. Romeo placed his toes next to the creature and gently urged it along.

'Women can be cruel and horrible. Just like the world.'

There was a sound behind him, within the walls. A racket he knew. Angry voices. Shouts and alarums.

He picked up his book and trudged disconsolately back towards the city gate.

* * *

Escalus was a military man. By rights he should have been with the Venetian fleet in the Adriatic, waiting on the Turks. But four years before, in a clash near Cyprus, an arrow had taken his right eye and part of the cheek with it. A black patch and a small silver plate replaced them now. When he found himself restricted to *terra firma* his masters in Venice had given him Verona with a simple instruction: 'Keep the peace. With armies gathering on three sides of us, plague and financial uncertainty abroad, we have no time to deal with petty matters like riots and civil disturbance.'

He hated the place. It was easier fighting heathen warriors than maintaining order in a disputatious little city that seemed able to create an argument out of morning mist.

Most of the time he spent in his quarters in the Cangrande castle. That was where he felt at home. But the duties Venice had given him made his job as much that of city official as its marshal. So he was in the market tithes office at the foot of the Torre dei Lamberti checking that all due taxes were being paid when the sergeant walked in, saluted, took a deep breath and said, 'They're at it again, sir. Out in the market. Montagues and Capulets. Like cats and bloody dogs they are. Well, worse actually. I mean cats and dogs don't scrap like—'

Escalus adjusted his eye patch and wondered: perhaps it was best to let them fight it out this time. Then clean up the corpses later and count himself lucky there'd be fewer of the quarrelling clans to worry about when next they came to blows.

'What's it this time?'

'Someone biting their thumb, it seems.'

The trouble was… word of unrest got back to the Doge's palace faster than a horseman might ride sometimes. Venice had its spies everywhere. There were stone lion's mouths throughout the city, with invitations for citizens to post their anonymous accusations through them for the authorities to read. Most of those missives wound up on his desk, but not all, of that he felt sure. Nothing could be hidden from the Doge's palace. If he couldn't maintain order in a petty little spot like Verona the chances of him getting another command in the navy were gone for good.

'Biting their thumb?'

'A very rude thing to do if you ask me,' the sergeant replied.

'It's time these quarrelsome bumpkins learned their place. Fetch me the day watch. Arm them. Tell them to follow my every command.'

He got up and found the sword that had followed him through twenty-five years of service under five different doges wearing the horned bonnet known as the *corno ducale*, two Mocenigo, two Barbarigo and a Vendramin.

Escalus walked to the door of the tithe house and shielded his one good eye against the bright morning sun. He could see them, hear them. A fractious rabble, not yet a riot, behind the meat stalls. A bunch of youths – some servants – two others of nobler stock. Then four more figures came into view. Two well-dressed, middle-aged men scuttling along, followed by their women.

29

The sergeant walked up and stood beside him. From behind came the clatter of armour and the rattle of weapons against steel, the watch getting ready.

'That's all we need,' said the sergeant by his side. 'Capulet and Montague themselves.'

'At least they brought their wives to enjoy the show,' Escalus pointed out. 'And they shall see one. Get your men. Follow me.'

* * *

The rising heat made the piazza stink. Raw meat and rank cheese. Horse muck steaming from the cobbles. Benvolio walked into the centre of the circling servants, Montagues on one side, Capulets on the other. His sword was drawn, for warning, nothing more.

'Enough of this, lads!' he cried. 'No blood on Verona's piazza this day. Put away your knives. Go home. I'm sure there's work to do. Let's have some peace—'

'Peace!' It was Tybalt, out from the shadows, his long rapier drawn, his face keen and angry. 'If it's peace you want, why's your blade out? And these two scum of yours waving their kitchen knives around?'

The crowd were milling, muttering, getting angry and restless. The butcher started brandishing a club and yelling the kind of imprecations only country folk used.

Benvolio looked around him. Only two friendly Montague faces in the growing tumult, Abraham and Balthazar. Three Capulets, one of them Tybalt. Men perished quickly in circumstances like this.

'There's no need...' he started.

'I hate Montagues. As much as I hate peace,' Tybalt cried. 'Fight you, coward.'

With that he struck out, dashing his rapier through the air once, then straight towards Benvolio's breast.

All the fencing lessons came back then. Feint and parry. Riposte and remise. The two of them joined then halted, each holding back the other's blade with his.

'We are here to set an example,' Benvolio said. 'Not teach them how to riot.'

Spitting vile curses, Tybalt pushed him away. Benvolio stumbled on a tile made slippery by blood from the butcher's goat. Another move he'd learned returned. *Passato sotto*. He half-fell, stopped himself with one hand to the ground, waited on the attack. Tybalt, too angry to be wise, came on. Benvolio's blade rose, not towards his foe's stomach as it might but to his sword hand, finding the gap between loop guard and grip, nicking Tybalt's fingers, loosening his hold. There was a brief yell of anger and pain. Then the rapier flew to one side and clattered on the cobbles.

The commotion around them was rising. The brawl had begun.

Screaming obscenities, the butcher waded in, swinging a club first at Gregory then at Abraham, a handful of traders behind him, a little less keen.

'Let's have these buggers,' the man yelled. 'Stinking Capulets. Bloody Montagues. All the same. They think they own this place...'

Tybalt still stood there, one hand on hip, sucking at the cut to his fingers, not caring to find his weapon, staring at Benvolio, a look that said: another time. The servants bent under the blows of the butcher and the shopkeepers who'd joined him, brandishing knives and sticks, any makeshift weapon they could find.

'I tried...' Benvolio whispered, then heard a voice cry out.

'What noise is this? Give me my sword, Bianca. I will not have my servants beaten by this filth.'

31

Capulet was trying to push through the melee from the right, his wife struggling to hold him back.

'Don't be an old fool,' she pleaded. 'You haven't got a sword with you. At your age I shouldn't let you out of doors without a crutch.'

There was a furious howl to his left. A voice Benvolio recognised.

'Is that Capulet? Leave me, woman. Leave me I say. I must aid my own.'

It was Benvolio's uncle, held back by his wife, too, desperate to join the fray.

'I am a peaceful, law-abiding man,' Andrea Montague shouted, his patrician voice wavering amidst the din. 'But, by God, I swear I'll not take insults from any villainous Capulet.'

'No brawling, husband,' his wife told him. She was a touch taller and somewhat broader. Stronger too since Montague was a spindly, sickly man unfit for any kind of fight. 'Best not tangle with these thugs. We shall not...'

The words were lost. Benvolio tapped his cap to Tybalt and looked around him. Of late disorders seemed to happen almost daily in differing degrees. Some short and reluctant. A few long and brutal. This Monday morning affray lay somewhere in between, more a scuffle than a battle. Thankfully most of the market men stuck with clubs and mallets, keeping their blades well sheathed.

Then he found himself barged out of the way by a soldier in shiny metal armour. There was the sound of boots on old stone, and a hard Venetian voice, commanding, military, silenced them all.

Ah, fair Verona, Benvolio thought. *How we pass the time.*

Escalus pushed to the front. A soldier through and through, tall and ramrod rigid like a general. That black eyepatch and silver cheek guard were enough to silence even the most heated of those around him. Tybalt had quietly slipped back into the shadows, ready to slink out of the piazza altogether.

'Enough. *Enough*!' Escalus bellowed. 'Put down all weapons, clubs and all. I will not–'

'He started it, sir,' Samson piped up, jabbing an accusing finger at Abraham who now clutched his head, blood issuing from a slash in his scalp.

'I did not,' the Montague servant cried. 'He was biting his thumb. We merely wished to point out–'

'Quiet, you rabble,' Escalus ordered.

Capulet stepped forward. 'I was witness to this, my lord. These young men of mine did not set a foot wrong. They merely went about their business and were, as usual, subject to such slander and violence from the thugs of this accused house–'

'It's only slander if it's a lie!' Andrea Montague bawled. 'And, try as I might, I cannot think of any calumny of which a Capulet might be accused that does not bear some firm basis in the truth. They cheat and swindle, spread foul slander about their rivals and–'

Escalus's one eye twitched. 'I swear to God this flea-bitten town puts me in a murderous mood. One more word…'

The butcher was next to him, bloody club in hand, both scared and awed. 'I served with you, sir. In Cyprus. I was on the galleon when you suffered that terrible wound. It was a miracle. You didn't even whimper.'

The marshal squinted at him, trying to place the man. 'And now you're a butcher in Verona?'

'That I am. Trying to earn an honest living. Not easy when these two tribes of toffs cause havoc in the streets morning, noon and night. Three times we've had it in a month. And where's our business now?

I'm a citizen of the Republic. I swore to defend it. Time it did something to defend me–'

Escalus held up his hand. 'Time indeed. I've had my fill of rebellion. Of breaches of our precious peace. We've enemies all sides of us, plague not far away, God knows what other nightmares waiting in the wings.'

'Was them what started it, your worship,' Samson objected, then fell silent when the man's single eye fell upon him.

The quiet in the Piazza Erbe was broken only by the squawks of chickens cooped in cages and the distant wail of a crying infant.

'And for what?' the marshal's deep voice boomed. 'A stupid insult of the kind a child might utter. For nothing more than a petty jibe you turn this peaceful city into a place good men and women dare not walk.' He pointed at Capulet, then Montague. 'Hear me well. If any of you disturb our streets again, servant or lord I care not, you'll pay for it with your lives. Peasant, merchant or nobleman, the miscreants can go to torture then the gallows. Whatever your station I'll string you up by the neck myself and pull on your damned ankles while you writhe.'

He paused, looked round the crowd. With the eye patch and the silver cheek he resembled a glorious wounded eagle surveying its prey. 'Do I make myself clear?'

No answer. Then Escalus nodded at the sergeant.

'Capulet comes with me now. I'll deal with him in private. Tell Montague I'll interview him at three o'clock this afternoon. If he's late put the man in irons and let him fester in a dungeon for a while. This performance is at an end.'

With that he pushed through the mumbling crowd with a nod for the butcher, who saluted then gave a little bow. The soldiers took Luca

Capulet by the arms and dragged him in the direction of Cangrande's castle.

'We've having a banquet tonight, sire,' he said, pulling free and scurrying up to walk beside the marshal. 'Some very fancy recipes shipped in from Venice. Peacock. Have you ever tried peacock? All manner of delights. It would be the greatest honour if you...'

'I have better things to do. Besides...'

Word was in of a new case of plague in Soave. If that was confirmed it meant the disease was travelling west towards Verona. Escalus had issued orders: any suspected house was to be immediately quarantined, none allowed in, none allowed out, a red cross painted on the door. That command was to stay secret until it was required; he had no need of more unrest.

'As to the peacock it will be stuffed and reassembled according to a rare recipe from Constantinople,' Capulet waffled on.

'Sergeant!'

The soldier rushed up and said, 'Sir?'

'If that fool beside you utters one more word until I ask for it chuck him a dungeon and throw the bloody key in the river. Now...'

In the square, the storm abated as quickly as it had risen. Traders returned to their business. Benvolio went to the colonnade wall and closed his eyes. The sooner he could leave this place for more placid and learned streets the better.

He bought himself an apple. But before he could take a bite, someone called his name. That familiar, faint and wheezy voice: his uncle Montague. It seemed he wished to speak.

* * *

Benvolio's home was outside the city but he stayed with his aunt and uncle from time to time. Never long. Romeo, he liked, though he sometimes found his cousin a touch distracted. Francesca Montague was a sturdy woman, always well-dressed in the finest Venice could supply. Her husband stood an inch or two shorter, a thin and delicate man. Theirs was a happy marriage, principally because he deferred to her on most things. An afternoon in his study, with books and wine, was all Andrea Montague desired in his declining years.

But at that moment there was a spark of anger in his eye. 'What was all that about? I wasn't going to say it in front of Escalus but I'm rather with him on most points. We shouldn't pick fights with the Capulets unnecessarily. There are enough good reasons to do so without inventing them. And that young brute Tybalt...'

Benvolio knew his uncle was no fool. Luca Capulet's nephew had a bloody reputation in the city. 'As far as I can work out the Capulet servants started it. Yours responded. I did my best to part them. Then Tybalt turned up waving his sword in my face. I'm afraid I cut him slightly.'

Montague shook his grey head and said, 'Oh dear, oh dear, oh dear.'

'Escalus has dealt with it, Uncle. He's made his position plain. I doubt you'll have much trouble from the servants for a while–'

'He's going to deal with me, too, isn't he? It's not the servants I'm worried about. That young man of the Capulets has a wicked, vengeful nature.'

Francesca Montague barged in and prodded Benvolio with her finger. 'Never mind Escalus and that young Capulet thug. What about Romeo? Your cousin? Where is he?'

Benvolio had stayed with them the previous night. That morning he'd been woken by Romeo sneaking out of the house, and thought to follow him. Through the dawn light the young man trudged, beyond the city walls to a little wood that lay to the west of the river. He told them this.

'I tried to talk to him but he ran away. Romeo seemed so melancholy it made me feel the same. I'm sorry. I don't know why…'

'We're his parents. We've a right to know.' She looked around the busy marketplace. 'He goes out every morning. Then comes back and locks himself in his room. We've tried to talk to him. It's as if there's a worm eating at him from inside. What are we to do?'

It was the first time he'd ever heard Francesca Montague ask him a serious question.

'Perhaps the army,' her husband interjected. 'I fear for his sanity if he goes to Bologna on his own like this.'

Romeo was handy with a sword, Benvolio thought. One of the best he'd seen at fencing when he cared to show it. But there was more to being a soldier than weaponry. It required a certain state of mind. A detachment from interior, solitary thoughts. And that would surely be hard for the Montague's pensive and withdrawn son.

'There he is!' his mother cried. 'Across the square.'

She took Benvolio firmly by the elbow. 'You're his friend. His age. A close relative. You have a duty…'

'A duty?'

'To us, Benvolio. And to him. Find the cause of this melancholy.'

'And then a cure,' Montague added. 'Whatever it costs. Whatever it takes. He's our boy. We love him dearly.'

The tower bells chimed eleven.

'Well,' the old man added. 'We'll leave you to it. Best be off. I've an appointment with our fierce friend Escalus this afternoon. I need a nap before that.'

They turned. They left. Benvolio thought... *why me?*

* * *

He pushed through the crowd and caught up with Romeo at the edge of the piazza.

'Morning, cousin.'

Romeo's plain clothes were stained with grass and torn by brambles. He looked lost in a dream. 'It's still morning?'

'Just rang eleven. Didn't you hear?'

'The hours seem very long these days.'

'There was a little trouble with the Capulets again. Escalus is angry. For a change.'

Romeo waved a limp hand as if he couldn't care less.

'Why do you say the hours are long, cousin?' Benvolio wondered. 'They seem much the same to me.'

'Then yours aren't empty.'

'There's no reason yours should be either.'

They walked on down the lane, away from the bustle of the Piazza Erbe.

'Your mother and father are concerned about you.'

'They can't be that worried. They're sending me to Bologna next week whether I like it or not.' He groaned. 'To be a *lawyer*.'

'Lots of money in the law! Bologna's quite the place, I gather. The finest university in Europe. Lots of very clever people. And... um...

young ladies, too.' He stopped and looked at his cousin. 'Oh dear. I see it now. There's that look in your eyes. I am a student physician remember. So I must be observant.'

There was the faintest intimation of a laugh. 'Well, doctor. Your diagnosis?'

'You're in love.'

A wave of the hand again, more vigorous this time. 'Wrong. I'm out of it. Completely.'

'Of love?'

'Luck too. The lady's not interested.'

Benvolio ran his palm across his forehead and sighed. 'Oh, that's tragic! I have to say, though, I've seen the symptoms before. Love seems highly desirable from a distance. Then you get close up and find she's a rough and tyrannical mistress. Next thing you know you're out in the street with your britches round your ankles.'

'Very funny.'

'May I ask... who?'

'None of your business. And I could do without the sarcasm. A touch of sympathy–'

'I've tried sympathy in these circumstances,' Benvolio broke in. 'It just makes things worse. What you're suffering from is a kind of temporary insanity. We all know it.'

Romeo strode on. 'You do?'

'Yes. It comes. It goes. Who is she?'

'I said: none of your damned business. She's beautiful. And I gather reluctant to receive Cupid's arrow.'

Benvolio narrowed his eyes. 'I must tell you that in medical matters poetry has little efficacy. In fact it can make things worse. I may misconstrue your meaning and prescribe the wrong cure...'

'She's sworn to be a lifelong virgin, or so I gather. Doesn't matter how much money you've got. What you offer. Who you are—'

'They all say that. To begin with.'

'Rosaline means it…'

Benvolio's eyes lit up. 'Rosaline? The horse trader's daughter from over the river?'

'I didn't mean to—'

'Very fetching girl, I'll admit. She's sworn herself to chastity? You're sure?'

'So I'm told—'

'You haven't heard this from her own lips then?' Romeo didn't answer. 'Have you heard *anything* from her lips, cousin?'

'Waste of a beautiful woman. Ruined my life. I might as well be dead.'

Benvolio puffed out his cheeks and blew a raspberry. 'Rubbish. What you're suffering from isn't love, it's infatuation. The two are as alike and unalike as the plague and a simple summer chill. The cure's obvious. Stop thinking about her.'

'Ha! Some doctor you are. To do that I'd have to stop *thinking*.'

'She's not the only beautiful girl around—'

'Just *the* most beautiful.'

'If you cared to look—'

'Then all I'd see is how lovely she is in comparison to the rest. You don't understand.'

Benvolio put a hand out to stop him. 'But I do, Romeo. And I'll prove it.'

'By taking your finger out of my face first I trust.'

There was a touch of steel inside his cousin sometimes.

'I didn't mean to offend you. Keep your temper. What if I prove there's another, better than your seemingly chaste horseman's daughter—'

'*Seemingly* chaste? What do you mean? Do you doubt it?'

'No, no. Not at all. It's just—'

Romeo turned and grabbed him by the collar. 'This isn't a joke, Benvolio! I do not appreciate you treating it as one!'

The day was turning sultry. There was not the least sign of rain. It was as well the brief conflict in the piazza had taken place as early as it did. Hot weather sparked hot tempers. Somewhere Tybalt lurked, nursing that little wound to his fingers and a far greater one to his pride.

'I see it isn't,' Benvolio said, pulling himself from his cousin. 'Nevertheless infatuation, love, lust and passion... These are all ailments that may bring delight and torture in equal measure, and prove precious hard to separate from one another.'

'Rosaline's the only one for me.'

'That I very much doubt. Since you're fated to be a lawyer, I shall summon the evidence to demonstrate that fact beyond a shadow of a doubt.'

'And how do you propose to do that?'

'A very good question.' He took a deep breath and placed a finger against his cheek. 'An *excellent* one.'

Amused, Romeo leaned against the wall and gave his cousin a quizzical look.

'There!' Benvolio cried. 'A smile. First of the day.'

'*How?*'

'Let's talk about it along the way.'

* * *

The castle of Cangrande was a grim, imposing fortress on the banks of the Adige. From beneath its high battlements a well-defended red brick bridge with swallow-tail merlons ran across the river to allow for escape to the Tyrol and the north. Not that the fierce lord who'd built this stronghold a century and a half before ever found reason to flee. Now his successors, the Venetians, occupied its sprawling quarters, stationing troops and tax collectors in the barracks and offices, while maintaining a series of dark, damp dungeons for any the Republic had come to hate.

The worst offenders would be shipped off to the cells of the Doge's Palace or simply executed, by axe or noose, in the cobbled street outside. Two rotting heads on spikes had greeted Capulet at the main gate. He'd no desire to ask who or why. This was not a place any man of Verona wished to find himself, especially one who had intended to spend the morning planning an important banquet for a momentous occasion.

An hour he was made to wait in a dismal antechamber, listening to the groans and complaints of the prisoners in the dungeons below. Then Escalus summoned him into the guard room, bawled at him, then repeated in very florid terms his threat to execute any man, whatever his class, who broke the peace from now on.

After that, being a gentleman, the marshal shook his hand, declared he would make precisely the same remarks to Montague later that day and ordered him to leave forthwith.

Count Paris was waiting outside, brought there by the Capulet servant Pietro, a well-meaning if unintelligent lad the house had taken under pressure from the orphanage. They retired to a tavern by the river, watching the boats there. Traders mostly and a few traditional fishermen sending out sleek black cormorants to hunt the steady, swirling waters. When the birds came back with catches, a ring around their necks prevented them from swallowing their prey. After their work was done, they were allowed one of their own.

That, Capulet felt watching them, was the way of the world. There was an order to it. The masters guided, the minions obeyed and all received their just reward in the end. It was in much this fashion that the Venetian Republic – every government for all he knew – went about their business. To the Doge in his palace, the House of Capulet was simply one more dutiful boat upon the water, the men no more than glossy black cormorants going out to hunt for bounty, and keeping a little share of what they found.

Count Paris was an aristocrat from Florence and had fled when, two years before, the mad priest Savonarola replaced the traditional February carnival with what came to be known as the Bonfire of the Vanities, a frantic burning of everything deemed by the Dominican friar to be full of sin. Paris's family owned a flourishing bank and had been close to the hated Medici, both reasons for the ascetic friar to deem them immoral and fit for banishment and ruin. Paris had fled the city quickly, having taken care to move his money and businesses east into various parts of the Venetian Republic. Now, with Savonarola's ashes scattered on the Arno river, he was able to regain his old empire along with several grand homes in Florence, Verona and the countryside.

At twenty-six he was burly, strong, fit, with a bushy and carefully-manicured ginger beard through which flashed, a little too easily, a frequent and fleeting smile. A catch, Capulet thought, one that would tie the mercantile family of Capulet to old and noble blood going back centuries. If only his daughter could see it that way.

They drank white wine, Garganega naturally, and toyed with the almonds the tavern keeper had brought. The servant Pietro sat on the river bank whittling idly at a stick. Summer was fully upon the city, hot and humid. Capulet, a bulky, unfit man, was beyond walking far at the best of times. In weather like this he'd be glad to be home, lazing in a cool and shady room.

'Well,' he said, after recounting the morning's explosive events and Escalus's warnings, 'at least my foe's bound by the same terms and must, if he's sane, abide by them. To be honest with you I'm not greatly dismayed to be reined in a touch. Bad blood infects us all in the end. Montague and I are too damned old to be carrying on like angry youths forever looking for a fight. That nephew of mine, Tybalt, is no shirk when it comes to the sword but he's a violent young fool. At least they don't have one of their own like that to throw at us. From what I hear Montague's son's a pleasant enough lad. A bit bookish. Not fond of commerce. But then... how many of them are?'

Paris raised his cup and suggested a toast: that the young might learn the merit of trade. Their goblets met.

'You're both honourable houses,' the count said. 'Both merchants of similar size. And matching interests in many ways. It's a pity you've been at odds with one another so long. Imagine how great the two of your enterprises might be if, instead, you worked in tandem.'

Capulet harrumphed and indicated that there was a very long way to go before such a partnership might be countenanced.

'Consolidation. It's the future,' Paris insisted. 'A man can't conquer the world. Even Hadrian knew there were limits to empire. He couldn't keep hold of everything.'

'True. But his realm stretched from England to Asia, from Germany to Africa. Look at what we have in its place. Even Italy's divided head to toe by warring factions, every one of them good Catholics. Infidels on all sides. And now it appears there's yet another world for us to ransack, to the west across the Atlantic. Full of gold and opportunity… and it seems the Spaniards got there first. A long way from Venice, too. God knows I struggle to keep my toe in the market at the Rialto without worrying about lands no civilised man knew existed until that Genoese fellow Columbus sailed there. But the House of Capulet fares well enough, thank you. Business could always be better. It shall be.'

'With the right marriage,' the count said, and raised his cup again.

He was a persistent man. This was the third conversation they'd had on the subject in a month.

'As I said before, my daughter, while precocious in many ways, is still a child. Sixteen years old. Give her two more years and some of her adolescent fire may burn itself out.'

'Fire? I'm fond of fiery women.'

'I'd lay a large wager you wouldn't be so fond of a fiery wife. My daughter's wilful. Headstrong. Full of the ideas the young possess and cherish as their own as if the rest of us were never young ourselves. Bianca, her mother, was much the same. We had our quarrels. Our long and silent days.' He scratched his head, remembering that dark time. 'I dispatched her to Venice for a while when matters turned too difficult for either of us to tolerate. We lost our little boy. The company of nuns and, I gather, a sympathetic doctor, the lagoon air… or simply time and absence. They worked. Why, I neither know nor care. But then she returned and with her our contentment. Juliet was born to us and a livelier, healthier, noisier child you couldn't imagine.'

Another memory returned, one more bitter. 'That son we lost almost destroyed us. You see why I hesitate? Sixteen years old. Our only child, a delight to my wife mostly, and to me on those rare days we agree not argue.'

'Sixteen?' Paris laughed. 'There are girls out there married and with child before that.'

'True. And if you asked them… how many might wish they'd waited just a little longer?'

The humour died. 'I am twenty-six. My father's dead. I have no brother, not even a sister. I can trace my house back to the time of Augustus. I require heirs or it will die out with me. Children, as many as God may give us. Do not ask for patience. I may be stoic in business. Not in matters of family.'

'Nor I. Let me repeat. Juliet is our fondest possession. The one piece of me that will remain on this earth when I'm gone. I'd never say this to her face but the truth is this: I will not, cannot, gift her to you. She must be wooed, gently, from the depths of your heart to hers. My consent you'll have. But hers you'll need as well. Without it only storms would come and I am too old for yet more tempests. This nonsense with the Montagues is enough. Too much frankly. If you can wait—'

'I can't,' the count said plainly. 'If waiting's one of your conditions then say it and we'll part friends. It must be now. This month. This week. Tomorrow for all I care. Or never. She's of age and there is no impediment.'

He stopped then, aware that perhaps he'd overstepped the mark. The count placed his goblet on the table and made sure the servant wasn't listening.

'Make no mistake. I will love and honour your daughter. I've watched her from afar. Thought about her. Listened to all the delightful opinions men and women have of her here. I will make your Juliet the happiest and most pampered woman in all of Italy if only you'll grant me leave. No expense shall be spared. No property too grand. All I ask is her hand and that she grace my life with children.' His face clouded over briefly. 'I will still travel on... business, naturally. She will not find me tied to her day and night.'

Capulet knew exactly what that meant. He'd done a touch of womanising himself when he was younger. It was expected. But with the years he'd come to feel one love was enough, too much at times. The count, he imagined, would behave like most men of his station. A husband betrayed was a cuckold. A woman treated the same way was... a wife.

'I believe I've made my position clear, Paris. You have my blessing and I do not doubt you'll treat my daughter with all due respect. But first you must woo her. Convince her. Bring her to your side. If you can make my daughter love you then she'll be the one to demand a wedding. The very minute we can fix it. So much I can do for you... Nothing more.'

Paris threw his arms open wide. 'But... how?'

Capulet laughed and refilled their cups from the bottle. 'Through a little cunning. Tonight we'll have a banquet. A grand one. There'll be many guests, city folk mostly. Another on the list... a welcome noble from Florence.' He raised the cup. 'If you're free, of course.'

The count nodded. 'Name the time.'

'Eight. There'll be many pretty ladies. Young ones. Unattached. Great beauties, wonderful dancers among them.'

'Are you trying to tempt me elsewhere?'

'I wouldn't dream of it. I invite them only so you shall see my lovely Juliet is the fairest of all. But you can judge for yourself. Pietro?'

The servant didn't look up. His head was over the piece of wood in his fat and clumsy fingers.

'Pietro! What on earth are you doing with that knife? Take care you don't cut yourself.'

'A gentleman like the count must be fond of music,' the servant said. 'So I made him an instrument.' He grinned and looked a little bashful. 'Maybe he'd like to hear it.'

The boy got to his feet and ambled over. Then he put the sliver of wood in his mouth and blew. A single thin and reedy note filled the air. By the river two ducks rose.

'Them birds like it,' Pietro said with a broad grin. 'And you?'

Capulet clapped his shoulder. 'I think it's wonderful. Now…' He gave him a sheet of paper. 'Here is a task for you. Take this list of names. Go about the city. Find their houses and tell them Luca Capulet is arranging one of his famous banquets tonight. This may be short notice. But since all the food and drink are accounted for, some of it very special from Venice, too, they'll be clamouring at the door to get in.'

'I bet they will,' the servant said.

'Yes, yes. Find the people whose names are written here and tell them they're invited. Eight o'clock, prompt. We'll follow the Venetian convention so the young men should wear masks while the ladies go barefaced.' He got up to leave and so did Paris. 'Any questions?'

Pietro looked at the pair of them and blew upon his whistle.

'Very good, boy,' Capulet told him. 'Now go about your business. As we shall ours.'

The two men ambled off. The ducks returned. Cormorants dived and swam in the placid river. The boy sat down, scratched his head and stared at the scribbles on the paper in front of him.

'Find the blokes whose names he's written here? Easier said than done, mate.'

He blew his whistle again then went to the table and stole the last of the almonds scattered there. 'Can't read, Master. Never learned. If you'd ever asked you'd know.'

He held the paper up to the bright blue sky and stared at the scrawls of lines. However much he squinted none of it was any clearer.

'I need some help. A learned chap.'

Down the street a pair of young men were walking, deep in earnest conversation. One wore fine clothes, the other better than Pietro's own but stained with grass, brambles sticking to his britches.

'Or better even two.'

* * *

Benvolio said, 'Here's the point'

'Finally? The point? That didn't take long.'

'Sometimes you put out a blaze with water. But sometimes you put it out with fire. Bigger, brighter. Hotter. If you're giddy with agonising over Rosaline stop spinning round and round for heaven's sake. Find another girl. One who's not so...'

'Not so what? I keep thinking there's something you're not telling me.'

'As if. I only speak the truth. This is a temporary affliction of yours. Besides, a little perspective wouldn't go amiss. While you whine and wail there are people out there a lot worse off than you.' He stopped and pointed at the fool by the roadside, a servant in threadbare clothes blowing on a simple whistle. 'That poor soul for one.'

Pietro wandered up.

'Good day, fellow,' Romeo said. 'Nice whistle you've got there.'

'Made it myself. Little knife and a bit of wood. I'm good at whittling and whistling. Not a lot else. No use at reading at all. Are you any good with letters? You look the sort–'

'I can read my own fortune and it's full of damned misery.'

The servant grinned, a little baffled. 'I am a simple sort. It strikes

49

me you don't need to read proper for something like that.' He pulled a piece of paper out of his grubby britches. 'What I need to know is... can you make sense of all them words and squiggles? Might as well be a spider trailing its little legs through muck to me.'

'We're busy,' Benvolio told him. 'No time for games...'

The servant looked desperate. 'No game for me, sirs. My master's handed me this paper then hopped it. They're his orders to go fetch people for his ball this very night. Now I may know where most of the toffs in Verona live. But if you don't tell me which of them you want it's not a lot of use now, is it? Still...' He started to put the paper back in his pocket. 'If the two of you are similarly afflicted to poor Pietro here and cannot understand a word...'

Romeo groaned. 'Give it here.'

The hand was flowery, that of an elderly gentleman, he guessed. The note said, 'Signor Martino and his wife and daughters; Count Anselm and his beauteous sisters; the widow of Utruvio; Signor Placentio and his lovely nieces; Marshal Escalus and his nephew Mercutio; Cousin Arturo, his wife and daughters; my huntsman Di Capua and his fair daughter Rosaline; Signor Valentio and his wife; Lucio and the lively Helena.'

Benvolio, peering over, said, 'Helena's very lively indeed from what I hear. This is a fair assembly. All the fine families of Verona. Especially the younger ladies.'

'Where's this fair assembly to go?' Romeo wondered.

'Up,' Piero answered.

'Up...'

'Up to our place. Where else?'

'Which is...?'

'My master's.'

Benvolio slapped his forehead. 'Your master being?'

'A great and rich man called Capulet. Did I not mention this?'

'Perhaps you did...'

Pietro looked at them in anticipation. 'If you two gents were to point me in the right direction I'd happily let you in the back door. Lots of posh grub. Drink as well. I saw cook chasing a peacock round the garden before I came out. You ever eaten peacock?'

'Stringy,' Benvolio observed.

'Well, at least you got the chance to find out. The young men should wear masks. Like they do in Venice. All I want in return...'

He tapped the paper.

'We couldn't possibly,' Romeo said.

'Masks?' Benvolio wondered.

'Like they do in Venice,' Pietro told him. 'Apparently.'

'Let me read it,' Benvolio said, snatching the paper before Romeo could speak. 'We gladly accept.'

He went through all the names on the list. The youth seemed to know every palazzo and back alley in the city. All he required was the family. And then he had them pat.

'Eight o'clock,' Pietro said, stuffing the page back in his pocket. 'Come round the back and see me. I am in great debt to you, sirs.' He stared at them and for a second didn't seem slow at all. 'You're not Montagues, are you? 'Cos if that's the case I fear this invitation's not for you. In spite of all your kindness.'

'Good God... do we look like Montagues?' Benvolio asked with heat.

Pietro gulped. 'No. Not at all! Come take a cup of wine with us tonight. The place will be full of lovely ladies. Well above my standing sadly. But there you go...'

He blew on his whistle once more and was on his way.

Benvolio rubbed his hands with glee. 'There you were cursing your luck, eh?'

'Rosaline…' Romeo whispered.

'Horses hunt. And so do men. That father of hers is coming up in the world if Capulet's got him on his list. Mercutio's on it, too.'

The marshal's nephew had become a companion of theirs since he'd turned up from Venice, apparently under something of a cloud.

'But–' Romeo objected.

'But nothing. You heard. We'll stay hidden behind our masks. With Mercutio. The nephew of our beloved marshal. That means you've two friends in attendance. No one will know two foul Montagues have slipped into the place. Capulet's lining up every young noblewoman in Verona for this banquet. God knows why. You can eye up your Rosaline without fear or favour and not a soul will notice. When you see her next to them…'

'She'll still look beautiful.' His misery was back. His face forlorn. 'The loveliest under the sun. None can compare–'

'Because you never did! You'll see. I'd bet good money you'll reckon your swan a crow before the night's out.'

Romeo glared at him. 'A crow?'

'It was a turn of phrase. I'm not a poet. Just a man who tries to get by. You have got a mask, haven't you?'

'Don't we all?'

'To an extent,' Benvolio agreed. He looked at Romeo's torn, stained clothes. 'Now let's consider what you'll wear.'

* * *

They called her Nurse though it was fourteen years since she'd last taken the babe Juliet to her breast. Her real name was Donata Perotti, a fisherman's wife from Peschiera, a village on the shores of the vast inland lake of Garda fifteen miles to the west. Shortly after she fell pregnant her husband drowned trying to navigate a sudden summer storm. Their daughter died just three days old. The following week the woman was thrown out of her tithed house. Destitute, she'd found herself in Verona knowing what to look for: a rich family with a wife about to give birth. Most upper-class women viewed the idea of breastfeeding as abhorrent. If a wet nurse were available they'd hire her for a year or more after the child's birth, and hand over most of the motherly duties – cleaning, bathing, dealing with night-time yowls – to their temporary servant.

Capulet could be an ogre, but his wife was a kindly woman and didn't have the heart to make Donata Perotti destitute twice over. So, even though she could be loud and coarse and occasionally impudently rebellious, Nurse had stayed in the household, taking a small bedroom a few doors along from the extensive apartment over the garden where Juliet slept.

It was now four in the afternoon in the large study at the front of the palazzo.

'Nurse.'

Bianca Capulet's head was spinning from trying to manage all the arrangements of the coming banquet.

'Yef…' The woman's mouth was full of cold pork. Over the years she'd grown decidedly fat through scavenging the Capulet kitchen.

'Please don't eat in here. The furnishings cost a fortune. Where's my daughter?'

The servant woman swallowed down the last of the meat then chuckled.

'There's a question, eh? Where's Juliet? Where *is* that girl? I've been asking that day and night ever since she were tiny and still I don't have an answer. The young these days... Juliet! *Juliet!*'

The door opened and she walked in.

'There's no need to shout. I'm not deaf.'

'Your mother wants you.'

Juliet was still in her morning clothes. A simple linen shift. No jewellery. 'Well. Here I am–'

'This is a private conversation. Please...' Bianca Capulet shook her head as if this might clear it. There was so much to consider. Such a dainty and dangerous path to tread. The woman was making for the door, her big hips rolling as she walked.

'No, Nurse. I'm sorry. Stay here. I need a witness. Lord knows you've been here long enough. You're a party to these things too. My daughter's still a child...'

'Sixteen!' Nurse cried. 'Same number as her teeth. Top and bottom now all those baby ones have gone.' She opened her mouth, displaying mainly gums. 'Show your mother, love. I only got ten and a bit meself, all round. Rest fell out years ago. All the more reason we take good care of those little pearls of yours, don't we?'

Juliet stared at the two of them. 'You called me here to talk about my teeth?'

'Seventeen come Lammas Eve,' Nurse added. 'My little Lucia would have been about the same. Had she not died, of course, God rest her. Too good for this world. Too good for me if I'm honest.'

'Mother–'

'I were damned lucky your kind family took me in. Leaking milk everywhere I was and starving all the same.' She waddled over and patted Juliet on the head. 'You took care of that, didn't you, little one?

Couldn't get you off my tits for love or money. Had to put wormwood on 'em or I'd never have weaned you, greedy little monster–'

'Nurse!' Bianca Capulet pleaded.

'And if your bawling weren't enough we had that earthquake. You and the master were over in Mantua for business or something. I was determined this lass had had enough of me. Ye gods… the biting and the whimpering…'

'Please, Mother. Make her stop.'

'You fell on your back, girl, after that. You won't remember but I do. Lord and Lady out of the house. You tumbling on your little arse, all the kitchen lads laughing and looking, legs akimbo on the tiles. Bump on your head the size of a cock's testicle. That was a week, that was.'

'I'm going to scream in a minute,' Juliet announced.

Nurse was beaming, ear to ear. 'All the pain we go through and still you've got to laugh.' She patted the girl on the head again then rearranged her long blonde locks. 'You were the prettiest baby I've ever seen. I'll get a brush and do your hair. I just hope to see you married one day.'

Juliet retreated, hands on hips. 'Ah, right. I see what this is about now. You conspire–'

'Conspire?' Nurse asked, offended. 'What do you mean? I've changed you, fed you, cleaned up that bed of yours when you wet yourself in it. I've a right to hope to see your wedding–'

'Mother…'

'Both of you listen,' Bianca Capulet begged. 'Please.'

There was quiet for a moment. Then outside they heard someone running round the garden, a peacock squawking. A louder shriek from the bird, a victorious curse followed by silence.

'Marriage,' her mother said. 'Where do you stand on the matter now, Juliet?'

'Where I stood this morning. Indifferent beyond the point of outright apathy. I'm sure it's a great honour, but not one I dream of at the moment. Thank you all the same.'

Nurse guffawed. 'Oh, marriage is an honour. And what comes after too. You'll be dreaming of that before long at your age. I was. Couldn't wait—'

Her mother waved at the woman to be silent. For once it worked. 'You must think of it, love. There are girls younger than you in Verona already with child—'

'So?'

'I wasn't much older—'

'You lost a son! My father reminds of that fact day in and day out! Now he plans to marry me off...'

'Count Paris seeks you for his wife—'

'Paris!' Nurse did a little jump and clapped her white and flabby hands. 'That fine nobleman from Florence with all the money! Oh, there's a match from heaven, sweetheart. Such a fellow... He's like a god. Like one of them statues you see outside big buildings—'

'He's a man,' Juliet objected. 'Just a man. Also I saw he has a beard. *A beard!*'

Nurse chuckled, a low and knowing sound. 'Nothing wrong with a few whiskers. Get them rubbing up and down your back...'

'He's ten years my senior or more. With a beard. I do not know him. Any more than he knows me. I have other interests at the moment.'

'Such as what?' her mother wondered. 'All you do every day is read books and lounge around the garden.'

'I wish to see the world. Florence for a start. I told you. And I... I can teach Nurse to read.'

Nurse grimaced. 'I'm too old to learn new tricks like that. How many times do I have to say it?'

'You're a child,' her mother said. 'A girl. Even for a woman like me it's not as if we're... free to go wherever we wish.'

Persuasion was the only course. Bianca Capulet came and took her daughter's hand. 'Bear with me. Have patience. Paris will be at the banquet tonight. At least be civil. Observe him. He could take you to Florence.'

'And all I have to give him in return is my life?'

'He's a handsome man.'

'Very,' Nurse agreed. 'Classy as well. A right toff, much more so than your mother and father if you don't mind my saying, my lady. All that money...'

'Paris comes from an ancient and noble family. Your father's spoken with him. He's sincere and truly loves you. A bachelor's like a book without a cover. You're the final piece that makes his life complete. He knows that. He prays you'll realise it too.'

Nurse nodded. 'This house needs a baby's cry in it again. Not that I'll be feeding the little mite. Not with these dried-up–'

'Be honest with me, daughter. A quick, straight answer. Could you love him?'

'How can I know?'

'I'm not asking you to agree. Not yet. Just give the man a chance.'

Juliet sighed. Arguments seemed to fall from the sky sometimes, like rain. She wouldn't avoid them. But they weren't sought either. 'I'll try and like him. What more can I say?'

Even this small admission felt like victory.

'I never much liked my Pino,' Nurse observed. 'Not when I married him. Wasn't that keen afterwards to be honest. Argued all the time. But at least he was out on the lake all day. And nights, well…' That filthy laugh came again. 'Nights aren't for talking, are they?'

A knock on the door. Pietro was there holding out his piece of paper.

'I found them, my lady. Those people on the master's list. Told them all to come along tonight for it's a grand party you'll all be having. They moaned a bit about the short notice but free drink and food'll always get folk out in Verona, won't it?' He was beaming and then remembered something. 'Apart from Count Anselm. Him and his sisters are stuck at their country house apparently. Someone there's maybe got the plague. Servants reckon the place has got a red cross on it and soldiers won't let anyone come or go.'

'The plague. Where?' Juliet whispered.

The lad shrugged. 'This side of Vicenza I think.'

'That's a way from here,' her mother said. 'What state's the kitchen in?'

'Chaos. The cook's cursing the pot boys. The pot boys are cursing me. Everyone's calling Nurse all manner of names 'cos she keeps coming in and pinching grub.'

'I do not!'

'Well, that's what they say. But it'll all be ready, mistress. Eight o'clock. For you and your guests.'

Bianca Capulet smiled at her daughter. 'Nurse? Find the best dress you can. White in there somewhere as I said. Jewellery.'

'Bah,' Juliet muttered.

'That diadem we bought you.'

'I said, it hurts.'

'Love does hurt, dearie,' Nurse chipped in. 'But there's such a sweet and secret delight behind the pain. Let's get my girl even prettier and trap you the perfect husband. Happy days.' She winked. 'And then come happier nights.'

* * *

The three of them met at the promised place: the tombs outside the church of Santa Maria Antica. Romeo was dismayed to see Mercutio relieving himself beneath the columns when he and Benvolio turned up.

'Oh, for God's sake,' he complained. 'Do you have to piss on the royal tombs?'

Mercutio finished, laughing. He was a good eight years older. Both Romeo and Benvolio wondered what had happened in Venice to bring him to little Verona. And why he had no connections, no friends among men of his own age. All the same he was entertaining. Good company, if somewhat unpredictable.

'Royal? That lot haven't been royal here for donkey's years. This place belongs to Venice, to *my* lot, now.'

'If the soldiers see you…'

'Well, they haven't. And besides… what does it matter?'

The monuments were extraordinary creations, gothic and quite unlike anything else in the city. Raised stone coffins with ornate roofs, tucked by the side of the church the Scaligeri clan called their own. They were all buried here, the top ones named after dogs: Mastiff, Noble Dog. The fiercest of all, Cangrande, Big Dog, lay above the church portico, his stone sarcophagus bearing an imposing lifesize statue of him on horseback, laughing death in the face, a helmet shaped like a hound's head on the back of his armour.

But the family was history now. The lion of Venice had been standing triumphant over the Piazza Erbe since the Doge's men took control almost a century before, seizing Verona as one more prize for its empire.

Mercutio nodded at the stone warrior grinning like a fool on his armoured horse.

'Don't know what he's got to smile at. Death? His cousin poisoned him from what I heard. Bet he wasn't chuckling when that happened. You lot out here love your little potions, don't you? Back in Venice...' He made a fist, a pretend dagger in it. 'We just stab the blokes we hate.'

Romeo muttered something about respect. And caution.

'Caution?' Mercutio pointed a finger at the statue above the door. 'Cowardice, you mean. A dead man's statue ain't going to do anything, is it? And besides... if they don't want folk to take a leak here they should put a fence round it or something. Personally—'

There was a shout then. One of the city guards had spotted them.

'I stand corrected. Time to leg it, boys,' he announced and then set off running down the lane towards the river. A few minutes later all three of them stood breathless, laughing beneath the shadows of the Ponte Pietra.

'You'll be the death of us,' Romeo said, still panting.

'Death'll be the death of us. Nothing else. Let's have a look at your masks then. See if they pass muster.'

Beneath his arm Benvolio carried a sinister black *bauta* with a long, deep chin. Romeo had a plain white *volto*, a deathly face moulded to the skin.

Being from Venice Mercutio was familiar with the customs of masked balls.

'Your *bauta* is common,' he told Benvolio with a shake of his head.

'And as for that *volto*…' He laughed. 'A wonderful disguise. But how do you intend to eat or drink without lifting it and showing your face? At least the *bauta* lets you do that.' He wagged a finger at them. 'And remember. You two are on enemy territory here. The Prince of Cats will get his claws in you if he can. Don't give him opportunity.'

The Prince of Cats. Mercutio always called Tybalt that and gave a single reason. The Capulet youth was of such a black nature that, like the worst of felines, he couldn't wait to kill something, simply for the pleasure.

'So what are you?' Benvolio asked.

He grinned and showed them a shallow half-mask, barely covering his nose. 'Mercutio, of course. Nephew to our omnipotent city marshal. Unlike you two I want them to know who I am. That way there'll be no misunderstandings.'

They walked to a tavern three streets away from the Capulet mansion, and drank outside, stoking their courage with chilled wine. The season's lassitude had struck the city. Most of the moneyed classes were home trying to avoid the heat. The workers, too, if they had the chance.

'Will that servant really sneak us in?' Romeo wondered.

Benvolio felt sure of it. 'He seemed a decent enough lad. Not the brightest I'll admit.'

Mercutio was all smiles. 'They'll let me in. I can knock on the front door. I've got an invitation. But if you two are feeling a bit scared… no problem. I'll tell you all about the girls tomorrow. From what I've heard they'll be a lovely sight.'

'We have to go. For Romeo's sake. Rosaline's there.'

Benvolio knew from the glint his words raised in Mercutio's eyes this was a mistake.

'The horseman's girl from across the river. So what?'

'So...' The cat was out of the bag. Benvolio nodded at Romeo. 'Our friend has... feelings for her.'

Mercutio guffawed. 'Plenty of feeling been going on around that one. For quite a while. With quite a few I gather.'

Romeo glared at him. 'What?'

'Where've you been hiding? Randy Rosaline from the knacker's yard? Headed for a y-shaped coffin from what I heard. Not that I've been there myself, you understand. More's the pity. She's quite fetching in a dozy, doe-eyed kind of way.'

'You say—'

Benvolio came between them. 'He's making it up. You know what he's like. Everything's a joke. Rosaline's a fine and chaste young lady—'

Mercutio winked. 'Right. Chased upstairs and down. By half the lads in town.'

'Her reputation—' Romeo objected.

'What's a reputation, brother? Nothing more than what people say in the street. The things that go on behind closed doors, behind closed curtains, beneath the sheets... you don't know. And maybe I don't either. But I know this. Verona's not the pretty, godly place you lot pretend. Can't be, can it? It's just full of people. We all know what they're like.'

Romeo finished his drink and suggested they leave soon. 'We'll use the back door like the servant said. You take the front if you want.'

'Oh, surely you'll fly in there held aloft on a flock of white doves! All of them chirping... Rosaline! My darling Rosaline!'

'That's not funny,' Benvolio said.

Mercutio nodded and knocked back his wine. 'Wasn't meant to be.'

Romeo was walking off.

'Where are you going now? Is this party on or what?'

He went down to the river, to sit on the bank. The evening light was fading. A glorious sunset lay to the west. Early that morning he'd woken in the midst of a nightmare, a bloody one full of death and poison. That had driven him to those miserable hours in the grove of plane trees, as much as the constant nagging thoughts of Rosaline.

'Perhaps this isn't a good idea,' he said when the others joined him on the dry summer grass. 'The Capulets hate every last man who bears our name.'

Benvolio shuffled between him and the water, to get his attention. 'No one's going to recognise us, are they? You know she'll be there. Others, too. We agreed—'

'I had the oddest dream. Death. And violence. So close—'

'I had a dream too,' Mercutio cut in, cocky as usual. 'I dreamt that people who dream get it all arse about face. That everything they think they dream is the opposite of what they really dream. Because it's all a dream. You get me?'

Romeo gave him a cold stare. 'So a part of the dream should be true, then?'

'How do you mean?'

'If the dream's a lie, then anything the dreamer dreams must be a lie within a lie. Which by logic ought to be the truth.'

Mercutio shook with laughter. 'Oh. That's clever that is. I do believe you're right. I think...'

'I like you, Mercutio. In spite of yourself.'

'In spite of myself I like me, too. You know who you've been sleeping with?'

'I've never slept with anyone.'

'Oh yes, you have. We all have. Can't help it. Queen Mab.'

Mercutio drew up his legs and wrapped his arms around them, like a storyteller about to begin tale.

Benvolio sighed and asked, 'Queen Mab? Who on earth's Queen Mab?'

'She's the fairies' midwife.' He picked up a tiny stone. 'No bigger than this here pebble. A little team of dream horses drives her coach over men's noses while we lie asleep. Her wagon spokes are made of flies' legs, her roof from the wings of grasshoppers. Her dress is a spider's web and a cricket leg her whip. Her chariot's an... an empty hazelnut and here's the thing. Small as Queen Mab is she gallops through the world night by night. Through lovers' brains, after which, like our friend here, they dream of passion. She dances on courtiers' knees, and they dream of the perfect curtsey. Over lawyers' fingers, and they smile in their sleep thinking of the greatest fees. And the ladies.' He chuckled. 'She pirouettes across their lovely lips and smiles as they part to kiss their phantom lover, the perfect man to steal them from this dull, dull world.'

With that he threw the tiny pebble in the water.

'And then, if she smells the stink of the lady's breath, the angry Mab plagues those lips with blisters. After which she gallops inside a courtier's ear and he thinks to himself... aye, there's money to be had from some desperate fool in the morning. Here's a parson and she tickles his nose, so he says to himself... tomorrow I'll get a bit of cash from selling a fake indulgence to some gullible sinner. And look. Here's a soldier. She drives over his neck and all he can dream of is cutting foreign throats, of breaching castle walls and slaughtering every living thing that lurks behind. And then of rape and booze and booty. Aye. And she's the hag who tells young women, fresh to the marriage bed, how to lie on their backs and take it all. Never question the roaring brute above them. Because that's how things are and even Queen Mab can't change what beasts are men. Now can she?'

Romeo cried, 'Enough!'

'Enough,' Benvolio agreed.

'It is enough, friends. Mercutio is with you there. But it is the way of the world. More so than all these courtly romances they'd have us swoon over.'

Romeo picked up a clump of grass and started to pull at it, tearing dry shred from shred. 'I dreamt I died. That my miserable life came to an untimely end and nothing I could do might change it.'

'Queen Mab,' Mercutio said.

For once there was no quick and clever riposte. Romeo got up. They followed, brushing off the grass from their velvet britches and jackets. There would be girls. It was a time to look smart.

'Romeo,' Benvolio said, putting a hand to his arm. 'If you'd rather not–'

'No. Life's a journey and whosoever steers it knows the course. I'm nothing more than a passenger on this ship. What business is it of mine?'

The Marangona bell tolled eight.

'We're late already,' he said.

* * *

The poor ate spelt porridge and beans, tough wild chicory, and herbs scavenged from the hedgerows along with any offal they might find cheaply in the slaughterhouse. All of it devoured with greedy, greasy fingers off a single slice of hard dry bread.

The merchant and noble classes lived differently. Rich food, spices from the Orient, cheese from distant territories, exotic fruit, strange meat, all served on silver platters, consumed with dainty forks and precise, well-practised manners.

Capulet had returned from Venice with books, too. A pair of cookery volumes, one a hand-copied manuscript by Apicius dating from Imperial times, the second, Platina's more recent *On Honourable Pleasure and Health*, the first printed recipe book the new presses of Venice had produced. It was early evening in his palazzo. The reception hall on the *piano nobile* was now decorated with lilies and roses. A group of musicians was tuning up on a small stage in the corner as the guests began to assemble. The room was full of light and colour, the women in their finest silk, the young men behind masks, clutching at wine, aloof yet interested. The double doors that led towards the broad stone staircase and the garden were thrown wide open, allowing in the fresh night air and the dwindling calls of birds before the dark.

In the ground floor kitchen, dishes from both books Capulet had bought were being prepared by a busy round of servants, all flustered, not least because one of the master's own had marched into their midst, donned an apron and demanded to help.

'Am I doing this right?' Juliet demanded. She was up to her elbows in feathers, with blood stains all down the front of the apron. 'I've never plucked a chicken before. It's harder than I thought.'

'To be quite candid, Miss, no,' the cook said. 'Much as I appreciate the offer it would be far easier if you left us to the—'

There was a kerfuffle at the door and her mother marched in. 'I've been looking for you everywhere. What in the name of sweet Jesus are you doing here?'

Juliet put down the bird and rubbed her hands. Fluffy down flew everywhere. 'Learning how to prepare a chicken for the pot. Shouldn't every woman–?'

'No! That's why we have servants!'

The cook stopped working on the roasted peacock. 'I did point that out, Madam.'

'Then why did you let her do it?'

Cook was mistress of the kitchen. This was her territory. 'Because if the daughter of the master of the house comes in here demanding to shove her hand up a chicken's backside I hardly think a lowly soul like me's in a position to tell her she can't. Not least because I've spent most of the past hour trying to stuff a bloody peacock.'

'I'm almost finished,' Juliet complained, turning over the half-plucked corpse in her hands.

Her mother growled something then walked over and threw the chicken into a bin. 'That's the worst prepared bird I've ever seen.'

'It was my first.'

'Upstairs, girl! Nurse can run another bath. Then find you some clothes for the ball.'

'But…'

'Now!'

There was the briefest moment of mutiny, then she obeyed and the two them left the kitchen. Pots were stirred again. Cook huffed and puffed over the prize peacock. 'I don't know, Pietro. All that money they've got. It doesn't seem to make them any happier, does it?'

'Perhaps not,' the pot boy replied, 'but Mistress Juliet is always very kind to every one of us. I won't hear a word said against her.'

'That's true. As to that father of hers…'

'Kitchen's due its portion when all the toffs are finished, eh, Cook?'

Vast cauldrons of stock and stew murmured on the stoves. Over the blazing fire a line of mallards and partridges sat next to three suckling pigs slowly turning at the sooty hands of a young girl working the spit.

Cook didn't answer. She was too busy trying to stuff the roasted peacock back inside its feathers.

'And another thing,' Pietro declared. 'A couple of chaps I met who were kind to me in the street might turn up. When they knock on the back door they're all right–'

'Yes, yes,' Cook cried. She turned to him, a broad, triumphant smile on her face. The bird was whole again, neck upright, tail plumed, dead eyes replaced by raisins glazed in honey. All through the miracle of a forest of tiny wooden skewers. 'Take this fellow and all the rest that's done upstairs. Time we started feeding the ladies and the gentlemen. There's plenty more to come.'

Within half an hour the feast was set on great tables next to the musicians and the singers. It was to be the greatest banquet the palazzo had ever seen.

Boned roast goat's heads covered in white meat sauce and decorated with pomegranate seeds. Fried trout caught in Lake Garda by busy cormorants. Cucumbers with dill. Chicken pie with cherries. Tart with cheese and chard and saffron. And *pastissada de caval*, horsemeat stew slow cooked until it was near black, seasoned with laurel, nutmeg and cloves, a dish Verona had been eating for so long it seemed as much a part of the city as its old stone walls and the constant flow of the Adige.

* * *

Capulet left his wife to make the greetings as the guests arrived. Then, when sufficient had assembled, he entered arm-in-arm with Juliet, Tybalt in black jacket and britches, sulky at their heels. His nephew was unmasked, like Capulet, and the older men who thought themselves too ancient for such rituals. Tybalt, it seemed, disapproved of frivolity entirely. He was a miserable companion in the place.

Still, this was a social occasion. A speech. Capulet liked his speeches.

'Ladies! Gentlemen!' He held aloft his cup of Garganega white. 'Welcome to our palace. This is a glorious summer evening. A night for dance and merriment. And dance with you I shall…' He grinned. They all knew a laboured joke was coming. 'Provided that is you don't have corns. If you turn down my hand I'll know that's why.'

Someone tittered politely.

The young women had arranged themselves next to the food, as if they were another course. Fourteen girls, all in competing dresses, scoop-cut necklines everywhere, since it was the fashion to show a full pale breast. Silk from China, fine wool from England, Egyptian linen, Syrian damask. The colours matched those of the dead peacock: shining blue, radiant yellow, the fiercest scarlet. But each of them wore white, too – a teasing visible kirtle, a sash or a ribbon. That was the badge of maidenhood, the most precious gift a young woman had to bestow.

'Music! Music!' Capulet announced. 'My house is yours, friends. Take your delight of it, and ourselves.'

Then he turned and, *sotto voce*, said to the nearest servant, 'For God's sake get more candles in here. Didn't any of you buffoons realise night soon follows day? Open more windows. It's far too hot. Get those tables cleared the moment they leave the plates. Well? *Well, boy?*'

The lad rushed off to do as he was told.

'Go join your friends, Juliet.'

'I barely know those girls.'

69

'Then now's the time. Make small talk. It won't take long. Paris will be here soon.'

She breathed a deep sigh, said nothing and wandered off.

Capulet watched her walk slowly across the room. She was the most beautiful of them all. That he truly believed and not just because he was her father. Her dress was ruffed blue, the colour of the sky. In spite of all the pleading she wore nothing in her hair except a simple circlet. And as for white... only the sleeves of her chemise, visible from elbow to wrist beneath the silk gown.

Had there been time he'd have scolded her and told her she was an ungrateful child. A would-be husband deserved better and her wardrobe contained much fancier garb than this. But watching her now, unsmiling and silent next to her more garish, gabbling peers, Capulet realised he was wrong. Unadorned amidst such overdressed, glittering maidens, Juliet looked, despite her years, a woman, serene, secure, a cut above the rest. No, so many cuts he couldn't count them.

His cousin Arturo, a sickly man from across the river, limped over to join him, moaning about everything, the heat, the food, the state of the world.

'I'm past my dancing days, Luca,' he grumbled, falling into a chair. 'And so are you.'

'True,' Capulet agreed and took the seat by his side. 'I hope to God no woman takes up that stupid offer. It's too damned hot and I'm too ancient. Perhaps the remark about the corns will deter–'

'How long is it since we wore masks together?' Arturo wondered, gazing at the line of girls, all, except Juliet, chattering excitedly, eyes flashing towards the young men arriving through the mirrored double doors.

'How long is it since we looked at pretty fillies and felt a certain spring in the heel?'

His cousin chuckled. 'I think that's even more distant than the masks. Don't you?'

Lives had mid-points. Pivots upon which they turned. The cruellest aspect of them all was... a man never noticed. One moment he looked forward. Then came marriage, family and toil. And then, so soon it seemed, there was an instant when a sudden harsh epiphany would break upon him. The realisation that the time to look forward was past. Only a diminishing period remained in which to glance regretfully back.

This was why family mattered. In the act of passing life from one generation to the next there lay the smallest intimation of immortality. It was all an old man had.

'We danced last at Lucentio's wedding,' Luca Capulet said very gently, watching the young men begin to gather across the hall, masks roaming over the ladies, each of them wondering... which one of them might, if my luck holds, be mine?

'Ah. Your brother. That was thirty years ago!'

'No. Twenty-five. I remember it well. Six more years and he was dead. The only brother I had. Two years younger than me. Sick from dysentery in that stupid little war we had with Milan.'

A thought came to Arturo, half a memory. 'Whatever happened to that widow of his? I know you ended up with the boy Tybalt.' He took a long swig of his wine. 'Good vintage last year by the way. I congratulate you.'

Capulet could lie easily when he wished. 'I don't recall.'

'She came...' Arturo scratched his bald head. 'From Turin or somewhere.'

Lucentio's wife was a shy, simple woman. Not long after his death, with an awkward child in need of a father, she threw herself into the Adige. The cormorant fishermen retrieved her body two days later. It wasn't a pretty sight. The family kept the matter secret. She was as good as a foreigner. It wasn't difficult.

'Does it matter?'

There was a flurry of activity at the door. Paris appeared, no mask above his ginger beard. Perhaps he'd steal Juliet back to Florence where she'd be an unloved stranger, too.

'Considering this is your party, Cousin, you're looking bloody miserable,' Arturo told him. 'I know you're old but perhaps you'd best find yourself a mask. Be sorrowful to yourself alone.'

That was as good as a kick up the arse.

'No need,' Capulet announced getting to his feet. 'There's business to be done. Boy?' A servant raced up quickly. 'See to it that my cousin's cup is never empty. He's always been fond of wine, especially when it comes for free.'

* * *

Masked, to all the world anonymous they hoped, Romeo and Benvolio waited by the stable while Mercutio knocked on the kitchen door. A woman answered. She was holding a skinned rabbit, head up, dark eyes staring. One question only: are you Pietro's mates? A nod. Then, feeling a little like naughty children, they stole up the servant stairs and emerged by the doors to the great hall, struggling to stifle their giggles.

'This is fun,' Mercutio whispered, as they hovered by the door. 'If you two get away with it I reckon it'll be an escapade we'll be laughing about in our dotage. Excuse me, sir!'

He tapped the arm of a uniformed servant striding between the guests, a tray of drinks in his hands. 'My friends and I require wine. And an assurance there are no blackguard Montagues here. We are afflicted by the most delicate noses and could not bear the smell.'

The youth turned and looked at him askance. Behind his mask Benvolio took a deep breath. It was Samson from the market that morning, eyeing them up and down. 'If your noses are so sensitive I'd have thought you'd know the answer to that yourself.'

'Got a bit of a cold,' Mercutio said quickly.

'All three of you?'

'It's catching. A-tish-OO!'

Samson didn't smile for a second, just held out the drinks. Each took a cup. 'I doubt you'll find a Montague here. And if you did I doubt even more he'd make it home alive.' He nodded at the tables. 'Food's over there. Dance floor's free. Ladies are waiting for gentlemen to ask them. Fine ladies. *Nice* ladies. We want no trouble. But if we get it, friends, we'll deal with it. Like we did in the market this morning. You weren't there, were you?'

'Church,' Mercutio replied, singing a snatch of a hymn. 'Choir practice. Two baritones and a countertenor. Won't ask you to guess which is which.'

Samson stared at them for a long moment then moved on. Benvolio mentioned something about how Mercutio loved living dangerously.

'Is there any other way?' he replied. 'At least you feel... alive. Ah, ladies! Romeo. *Romeo*! Christ... look at that lot. Oh...' He wiped his brow with a theatrical sweep. 'I feel quite faint.'

Across the room the women were ranged in a line next to the musicians. Two or three were on the arms of gentlemen already. One was Rosaline, smiling more sweetly, more openly than Romeo had ever seen. The object of her affection was a tall long-haired youth who'd removed his mask and almost swept the floor with his arm as he invited her to dance.

Mercutio sighed as they watched the delicate, fawn-like girl step onto the floor. 'Rosaline looks as if she's gagging for it. You're not going to go all jealous on us, are you?'

'No. I'm not. Who's *that*?'

He wasn't listening. Mercutio's eyes had locked on a miserable creature trying to hide away from sight of everyone at the back of the line. She had mousy short hair, a sad, round face and an ill-fitting purple dress that might have been borrowed or even made at home.

'Personally,' he declared with a judicious nod, 'I prefer to go for plain girls. Gratitude's a more enduring emotion than love. A rather more honest one if you think about it, too. *Ciao, Ciao!*'

Without another word he was off. Benvolio saw one of the musicians take a break from his duties and announced he wished to talk to the man about the work they were playing. Romeo was suddenly on his own.

A different servant went past carrying food. Romeo stopped him and pointed to the girl across the room. The one with the long, unadorned blonde hair and the blue dress. A delightful face, young and innocent, yet knowing and intelligent. More than anything, he thought, she possessed an air of apartness. As if she didn't belong in this ornate and ridiculous evening any more than he.

'I need to know who that young lady is. Please.'

The servant uttered a pained groan then looked. 'I'm a hired hand for the night. Which one?'

'The beautiful one.'

The waiter laughed. 'They all look rather beautiful to me, mate.'

'The girl at the end whose... whose star shines brighter than the rest. Who looks like a dove out trooping with crows. Oh, for pity's sake... Isn't it obvious? It is to me.'

The waiter stared at him rather coldly. 'Must be love then. If we may cut the poetry for a moment... am I to take it you mean the blonde lass at the end in blue? White pearl necklace, hasn't spent hours faffing with her hair like all the rest of them? Very fetching but looks dead bored as if she might hop it any moment given half the chance?'

It was hard to see clearly through those tiny eyeholes. Romeo dragged off his mask. She seemed even lovelier. Then he remembered where he was and quickly put the thing back in place. 'Yes. Her.'

'Haven't got... a single clue.' He held out his silver tray. 'May I interest you in a sausage?'

'No.'

'Then you'll excuse me.'

She wasn't just bored. She'd spotted someone across the room. Perhaps the tall, older chap eyeing her as if interested. A man with a beard, ginger and full, clothes that spoke of money and influence. The girl was scuttling out behind the others with a sly and worried glance, heading for the open windows through which a soft and fragrant breeze was wafting.

The bearded fellow watched, unhappy, and didn't move. Romeo politely made his excuses as he worked his way through the crowd to follow her. Not noticing that, across the room, someone had spotted him the moment he'd removed the awkward, deathly white *volto*.

* * *

75

The flowing blue gown she'd chosen was as close as Juliet could manage to the one worn by the fictional Ursula in the paintings of Carpaccio. She'd thought of trying to recreate exactly the dress she had worn in her martyrdom but there was nothing similar in her wardrobe, nor a scarlet cape. Besides she hated black and her parents were, in any case, beyond such ironic gestures.

So she sat alone on a bench in the garden, beneath the apple trees, sipping at her cup of fresh pomegranate juice squeezed by one of the boys from the kitchen. It was her favourite and making it was a strenuous job she could manage quite adequately herself, though her father yelled if he saw her doing it.

He'd be mad she'd slunk out of the banquet without so much as a word. Her mother would be scouring the palazzo quarters trying to find her. The garden was almost dark now, barely lit by the few torches. The music, the food and the drink were the magnets for the evening. No one but a fool would wish to abandon all that frivolity for a solitary moment among the flowers and trees and vegetable beds that ran from the mansion to the wall by the Adige.

Then, to her displeasure, someone sat down on the bench by her side.

'I do not wish to speak, Count Paris. Another time...'

'Sorry. You mistake me.'

He had a nice voice. Calm, quiet. Perhaps a little tremulous.

'Oh. I thought you were someone else.'

'If you were expecting...'

'No, no. I wasn't. I just... wished for some quiet.'

'Me too,' he said. 'I hope you don't mind.'

She pointed towards the river wall. 'It's a big garden. Over there... can you see? There are apricot trees. The scent from them is delightful.

The same goes for some of the artichokes funnily enough. Though in truth they're just thistles. Apples. Oranges. Pears and cherries. I imagine we've more variety here than they ever had in Eden. I do hope that's not heresy. Why not go and take a look?'

'May I... sit with you instead?'

'If you must. At the very least take off your mask.'

Immediately he obeyed.

'I hate balls,' she muttered.

'Me too.'

'You're just saying that.'

'Well, I am. But I mean it.'

'Really?'

'Really. So many people in the world. Most of them quite decent, I imagine. But...'

When he wouldn't go on she asked, 'But what?'

'You only need one special person. *One*. That's all. You don't find them in a crowd, I suppose. I'm not exactly an expert.'

'You're a man. A least you get to choose.

He hesitated then said, 'Normally at a ball I'd... kiss your hand by way of welcome. May I–?'

'No. You may leave my hand alone. I don't even know your name.'

He was handsome though, not swarthy, not pock-marked, not... bearded. His eyes seemed soft and thoughtful and it occurred to her that perhaps he was quite sensitive. Not a manly characteristic but one she found quite fetching.

In turn, he felt lost for words on two counts. This close she was far more beautiful than she'd ever appeared at a distance next to the line of pretties arranged for all-comers at the dance. And he was in a quandary for what to say. A wrong word uttered. A stupid comment.

Momentous acts sometimes failed on something as quick and simple as the beat of a sparrow's wing.

'Romeo,' he managed finally. 'And you are?'

'Juliet, as it happens. I live here.'

He hesitated then asked, '*Here?*'

She turned and pointed at the palazzo. 'Here.'

'Ah,' he replied, and something crossed his face.

'What do you mean "ah"? You're not a Montague, are you? I heard they had a son of that name.' She laughed. 'No. Sorry. You can't be. They're all...' She pulled an ugly face. 'Piggy eyed with big fat tummies.'

'Who told you that?'

'I don't know. My father probably. He hates their guts. Every last one of them.'

He waited, silent. She looked at him again.

'Oh my goodness. You *are* a Montague. What on earth are you doing here? My cousin Tybalt will carve you into little pieces given half a chance. Even if someone else doesn't. We're deadly enemies. Didn't you know?'

'I'm no man's enemy.'

'Makes no difference to Tybalt. He'll kill you all the same. I first saw him pulling the wings off a butterfly when I was...' She made a sign with her delicate fingers: something tiny. 'This old. Why *are* you here?'

'I followed you.'

'Because...?'

'Because you looked like me. As if you didn't really fit.'

'I live here. I have to fit. I was born to it. Or so I'm told.'

'You're very beautiful.'

She sighed. 'God in a privy... if someone tells me that again...'

'Sorry. Well, I mean I'm not sorry. Because you are. Beautiful, that is. I meant...'

'You're not terribly good at this, are you?'

He laughed. 'No...'

'Do you always laugh when someone's rude to you?'

'No. I get mad sometimes.'

'Then... why laugh now?'

'Because you made me!'

She shook her head. 'By being rude?'

'By being... honest. I've been fooling myself I'm a poet. I'm a fraud really. Next week my parents send me off to Bologna. To become a lawyer. To spend my life in writs and torts and endless litigation. Nice work for frauds.'

'Say no.'

'I can't.'

'You're a man!'

He breathed a long, pained sigh. 'It makes no difference. They think they own us.'

'Then perhaps,' she said, 'they do. My father believes me to be his goods and chattels. I'm to be sold off to a man who wants me for his own. A *bearded* man. Vile and–'

'What would you rather do?'

'Ha!' Her laugh was bold and loud enough to scare a blackbird out of the apricot tree across the way. 'Anything. Everything. Do you know there's a new world to the west? The Spaniards found it. Full of gold and wonders none of us has ever seen.' She tapped his knee. He didn't seem to mind. 'A book I read said there are people there with heads situated beneath their arms.' Juliet placed a thoughtful finger against her full, pink lips. He watched, rapt, lost. 'Though I think it's best to accept that just because something's down on paper... it doesn't necessarily mean it's true.'

'I like it when you laugh.'

She found herself smiling. 'So do I.'

'I'd like to hear more of it. Tomorrow. The day after. The day after that...'

Her smile vanished. 'Why? Next week you're dispatched to Bologna, to become that driest of dry things. A lawyer. While I... am spoken for. By others, not myself. A captive. A tiny bird in a tiny cage my father and the rest have made for me.'

He shook his head. 'Not tiny. Never tiny. Not you.'

Juliet stared at the dry, hard ground. 'We're what they make of us. Never what we dream ourselves to be.'

'I don't believe that.'

'It doesn't matter. They do.' She lifted her head and looked at him. 'You're very odd, you know.'

'Sorry.'

'I didn't mean to be nasty. Perhaps I like odd.' She blinked. 'That's my hand you're holding.'

'Sorry,' he whispered again as his fingers crept away. 'I... I... It just... God, you're right. I'm terrible at this.'

'Lack of practice, I imagine.'

'You imagine right. Completely. Should I go?'

'Yes. I'm bored with pomegranate. Were you to fetch me half a glass of wine it's possible that, in addition to allowing you to hold my hand, I'll let you kiss me. Mark that word "possible" now. No promises.'

He was up in an instant. 'I'll get some drinks.'

'Romeo!'

Juliet was pointing at his face with a long, slender finger. 'The mask. You must wear the mask. Tybalt. Remember?'

'The mask. Got it.' He smiled. The dead white porcelain went back over his fetching features. She thought she heard her mother's voice calling from somewhere.

'Be quick,' she said then followed his every step as Romeo wandered through the twilight and the trees, past the roses, back into the palazzo.

* * *

Luca Capulet was halfway across the hall intent on mollifying a stony-faced Paris when his nephew Tybalt, no mask, no smile, took his elbow and dragged him into the shadows of a corridor.

'Have you seen my daughter?'

Tybalt tugged on the old man's emerald jerkin. 'No, but I've–'

'Take your damned hands off me! What's the matter with you? I throw a party that costs a king's ransom and all you can do is skulk around grim-faced like an angry mourner at a poor funeral.'

Capulet had been trying to help the youth ever since his younger brother had died and the mother killed herself. It was never easy. He was too argumentative and violent for the household, so most of his time was spent out on the estates, with unfortunate governesses and servants mandated to take care of him. School had come to an end after a succession of fights. The universities had all roundly rejected him, however much was offered by way of a bribe. He seemed happy – or at least as happy as he could ever be – acting as an enforcer for the business, harrying debtors, sometimes in ways the old man regretted when he heard of them.

Women seemed to hold little attraction, though there were worrying times when Capulet caught him casting a sly glance towards his daughter. Nothing had happened there, as far as he knew. Perhaps the military might work as a last resort, an admission of failure on Capulet's part. He doubted Tybalt would return alive from any engagement that entailed fighting. The youth was never able to let a quarrel go, nor were his skills with a sword as impressive as he liked to think.

'Someone has to look out for you,' Tybalt said, with a scowl. 'The rest of them are just drinking your free wine and downing your food. They're laughing behind your back–'

'For once in your life try to enjoy yourself. Look at those girls over there.' The pretty specimens were mostly taken but a few of the awkward ones remained. 'Why not try talking to them instead of storming round with a face like thunder?'

'This house's honour is my principal consideration. That and the health of our enterprise.'

'What's the point of money if you can't enjoy it? Ye gods. Sometimes I think you were born fifty years old.'

There was a bandage on Tybalt's right hand from the morning skirmish. No blood seeping through. No obvious hurt. The wound was more to his pride than his person. 'A Montague's here. Sidled in with his face behind a white mask. He thinks I didn't see him.'

Paris was watching them across the room. Capulet saw his wife dashing to and fro among the revellers. She looked frantic.

'And this, amidst all our jollity, is what makes you mad?'

His nephew glared at him. 'Uncle. This is a *Montague*. Our foe. He's come here to scorn us. To laugh in our faces.'

'Which one?'

'The son. Romeo. I'll fetch my rapier–'

Capulet took his arm and dragged him further down the corridor, behind the long drape that kept out winter draughts. 'Leave him alone. From what I've heard he's a decent-enough lad. Hasn't caused half the trouble you've brought me–'

'He insults us. In your palazzo–'

'Yes. *My* palazzo! I won't have violence against him here, beneath my roof. What would people think? The shame of it–'

'I cannot tolerate him!'

Capulet pushed the youth hard against the wall and pinned him there with an elbow.

'You will do what I say. Am I master here, or you? You cannot tolerate him? By Christ, you try my temper. Start a mutiny among my guests, will you? Be gone. I've heard enough.'

Tybalt's face creased in an ugly, coarse snarl. 'He disrespects us.'

'Respect? How much do you show me? None. Nothing but contempt. For all I've done. The years, the money I've spent...'

The curtain shifted. His wife was there. 'What is this, husband?'

'A frank discussion, somewhat overdue. Have you found her?'

She shook her head. 'I've been all over the place. Count Paris seems a patient man but even saints have limits.'

'Keep looking,' he ordered. Then, when the curtain parted for her to leave, he bawled at a passing servant, 'More lights, Pietro! More food! Get those musicians playing louder!'

The drape fell. Tybalt had that insolent, arrogant look Capulet hated. 'The young. The bloody young. You think you know it all.'

'I know a Montague when I see one.'

Capulet let go and nodded down the passageway, out to the back. 'You're an impudent little cur. What love I owed your father's long expended.'

'And my mother? What love did you owe her?'

A good question, well-aimed. It hurt. 'That foul temper of yours will come back to haunt you, nephew. Mend your ways. Or one day those ways will decide to come and mend you.'

Tybalt laughed then, a rare, unpleasant sound. 'I don't know what that means. But since it pleases you I'll leave. Be happy. As to that Romeo bastard—'

'Forget him! You heard Escalus this morning. The next time there's mischief in these streets there are hangings on the way.'

'I bid you goodnight,' he said with a short bow.

'Get you to the warehouse and stay there. Don't show your miserable face here until I ask for it. Which may be never.'

Tybalt hesitated, taken aback by that. 'Very well. I hope this Montague enjoys himself. His little jape may seem sweet to him now. Tomorrow—'

'Oh, for pity's sake... just go. You ruin my mood.'

What was that look on him then? Hatred? Scorn? Or simply a cold sense of disappointment? The slim black figure vanished down the corridor. Capulet followed his every step.

'Even the child of my brother fails me now,' he whispered. 'As I fail him.'

* * *

Romeo returned with wine as she'd asked. Juliet peered into the goblet and pulled a face. The moon had cleared a narrow bank of cloud. The garden felt like a little twilight world of its own. Just the two of them, the trees, the night.

'You said you only wanted half a glass. So that's what I brought.'

'A woman doesn't always say precisely what she wants. She expects a man to appreciate that.'

Again, he felt lost and hopeless. And he wouldn't wish himself anywhere else on earth. 'Sorry.'

'You apologise too much.'

'Sorr—'

She raised an eyebrow. He took her hand again. They talked idly, randomly, of home and study, of art and history. He told her of Catullus and Petrarch and Dante and how much he'd come to love them.

'Poetry,' she said and nothing more.

'What's wrong with poetry?'

'Well.' She withdrew her hands and placed her fingers together. 'The thing that connects them all is loss as much as love, isn't it? I'm not allowed to read Catullus. Mother says he's unsuitable. But didn't he spend his life pining for someone?'

'The sun may set and rise, while we contrariwise, sleep after our short light, one… everlasting night.'

Juliet nodded. 'Very good. Petrarch had this thing for his… Laura, if I recall…'

'The breeze that moves her blonde and curly hair is softly stirred by her in turn—'

'Fine, fine. And Dante… er, Beatrice…'

'Beatrice Portinari. Most glorious lady of my mind…'

'Point taken!' she cried. 'Thank you.'

'I'm sorr—'

'No.' She clapped her hand across his mouth. 'Poetry's all well and good. But don't you see?'

Juliet removed her fingers but stayed close to him. He could hear her breathing, feel it fall like a warm and gentle zephyr upon his cheek.

'See what?'

'They lost. Catullus his Lesbia. Petrarch his Laura. And as for Dante... if I remember rightly he only ever met the woman twice. She was quite horrible to him then upped and died.'

For the first time since he'd entered Capulet's palazzo he thought about Rosaline, who now seemed a shadow, little more than a vague and vapid illusion.

'I am aware of this,' he whispered, watching her take a sip of wine. 'You drink your wine so beautifully.'

'Do I really? So, what were they truly in love with? Not a woman. Just the idea of her. The scent. The illusion. The convenient way her picture fitted a gap in their imagination. *Here I am miserable,* they whine. And why? *Because I'm rejected.*' She snorted and it was a delicious sound. 'That may be all well and good for a purveyor of verse but it's a pretty poor recipe for life.'

'I think I'll pass on poetry for a while.'

She appeared lost in herself.

'That's how he sees me,' Juliet murmured.

'Who?'

'Paris. This count... this *bearded* count I'm supposed to marry. I'm just a thing he wishes to own. A possession. He probably feels much the same way towards his favourite horse.'

'Refuse him then.'

'Fine words. Easier said than done.'

He let go of her fingers. 'Words are all I have. I hold your hand and I'm not worthy of it. Let alone a kiss.'

She snorted. 'Pah! What tosh!'

'Tosh?'

'Who are you to say you're not worthy? Just because you think I belong to another?'

'No. You belong to no one but yourself. You're too good. Too perfect...'

Her laugh then was a throaty, tempting chuckle. 'You do not know me.'

'Juliet of the House of Capulet.'

'My Montague enemy. If I'm to be thrown into the cell of matrimony with that man I'll be damned if I go there before I kiss another.' Tongue-tied, he hesitated. 'That was an invitation, Romeo.'

He moved closer, lips pursed. This was something unfamiliar to both of them. Neither knew who should take the lead and who the passive part. Very slowly they closed on one another. A brief meeting. Two sighs, two faint whispers, hands to heads. And then, embarrassed, they both retreated.

She laughed. He did the same.

'You're very... proper.'

'Proper?' he asked.

'I mean. That was how I imagine a kiss reads in a book. Or a poem.'

'So...' He pulled at his hair. 'How should I kiss you?'

'As if it was the first kiss we've ever shared. And the last. Before that bearded ogre steals me away.'

'I won't let him.'

'We've barely met...'

'I've been waiting for you all my life. In my dreams...'

'This isn't a dream. Far from it.'

'Then... I will save you.'

'How?' she whispered, wide-eyed, suddenly pleading.

'Um…'

That was all. She blew out her cheeks and frowned. Then held up her empty goblet. 'Fetch a little more wine, please. I'll think about it while you're gone.'

Romeo leapt to his feet.

'Mask!' she cried.

He fumbled the *volto* back in place.

She sat, hands on her lap, staring into the darkness. The garden was not hers alone. Moths and mosquitoes buzzed everywhere. Mice and rats and rabbits scuttled all around. Then there was a hoot and a sudden flap of heavy, powerful wings. An owl launched itself, a ghostly grey shape flying through the trees, falling to the bare earth by the wall. It seized a mouse there, took the thing to a corner. The night was briefly rent by the tiny beast's screams as the bird's sharp beak set about its work.

'Poor thing,' she said. 'You should have run.'

* * *

Finally Capulet reached Count Paris and offered to refill his glass. The man was less put out than he expected. Perhaps more magnanimous than the occasion merited.

'I didn't come here for drink,' he said simply.

'No. Well, I'm afraid she's… indisposed. You know young girls. Hot flushes. Hot tempers. Sheepish with strangers…'

Paris lost his smile. 'So tell me. Is she fierily shy? Or shyly fiery? Which is it now?'

Capulet helped himself to some passing wine. Under pressure Paris agreed to do the same.

'None of this is easy,' said Capulet. 'It never has been with her. It's a brave task. For any man—'

'My ancestors fought at the side of Caesars. I like brave tasks.'

'Just as well. I hope you don't mind my mentioning this. But… the beard.'

The count stroked his perfect whiskers. 'What about it?'

'The thing is… as you may have noticed looking round this room… in Verona the current fashion is for a man to be clean-shaven.' He laughed a little nervously. 'Fashion. What does it matter in the end? But the young do pay inordinate amounts of attention to what they deem fetching. Or not. Would you consider perhaps shaving it—?'

'My father had a beard. His father before him.'

Capulet took a sip of wine. It was a very good year, as Arturo had mentioned. 'My father had one too. I didn't feel a lesser son for failing to follow in his lead.'

The count stared at him and asked, 'Do you know Florence well?'

Capulet had been there twice of late, trying to drum up business after the fall of Savonarola. He was of the opinion the place fared best with the Medici at its helm. The so-called Democratic Republic that was now in charge seemed to embrace all the inner bickering of old with none of the firm grip the bankers brought.

The last time he was there, six weeks before, he'd learned Montague and his son were in the city, too, chasing the same prospects. He'd travelled alone and come back with nothing. Word was they suffered much the same indignity. The Florentines liked to choose the people they worked with and make them grateful. The count, he judged, was cut from that same cloth.

'Well enough,' was all he said.

Paris embarked upon a story about a painter Capulet dimly

recalled. A man named Botticelli who'd been one of the favourite artists of the last two Medici princes before the house fell. For them he'd produced bright and colourful canvases: the birth of Venus, rising naked from the ocean in a giant scallop shell; the goddess with a sated Mars, satyrs blowing trumpets in his ear to rouse him; *Primavera*, an allegory of Spring, a series of enchanting mythological figures gathered in a mystical wood.

'Art is largely a mystery to me,' Capulet noted.

'It's not art I'm talking about,' Paris retorted briskly.

The woman Botticelli portrayed in many of his canvases, the count said, was Simonetta Vespucci, acclaimed as the greatest beauty in Florence in her time. Wife to a lord, mistress to at least one Medici, she was equally adored by the companionless Botticelli. When she died at twenty-two he was heartbroken. Years later, after Savonarola came to power and demanded bonfires of all the citizens' vanities, the artist burned many of his own canvases of her in the Piazza della Signoria at the lunatic priest's behest.

'You're sure?'

'I watched. I know, too, that this is what happens when a man becomes solitary. When his life belongs to him and him alone. That way lies the road to misery and destitution. Botticelli followed it himself. He's now a ruined man, pleading for pennies for canvases when once he worked for princes, begging more than anything for one thing alone: that when he dies he'll be buried in a hole at Simonetta Vespucci's feet. In her church in Ognissanti.'

Capulet looked thoughtful. 'We'll get you married. I will speak with my daughter–'

'I tell you this because of the beard. A few months ago when I was in the city I took such pity on the man I paid him a pittance for a portrait of myself.' He stroked his whiskers. 'As I am today. As I shall be all my days. Can you imagine?'

'Imagine what?'

'We are married. That picture stands in pride of place in my hall. And all the men and women who see it ask… who is that fellow? That *bearded* man. It can't be Paris since he's clean-shaven. So… who?'

It occurred to Capulet that a portrait from a pauper was a small obstacle to stand in the way of a wedding. But that was not the true impediment here. It was the man's self-importance. Juliet's duty was to bend her ways to him. There was no other solution.

'I take your point, Paris. It was ably and gently made.'

The count finished his drink and placed the cup on the silver tray of a passing servant. 'You're her father. Tomorrow we decide matters. I will treat her well though, if I'm honest, your station in society is somewhat lower than my own. If she will not marry me I'll find another, a true aristocrat this time, not a merchant's daughter. I'll love her just the same.'

'Tomorrow…'

'Or never. Goodnight.'

* * *

Romeo came back with another glass and a revelation. Mask on, he'd edged close to Juliet's father and heard him speaking to the bearded count.

'About me?' she asked.

'No. It seemed to be about Florence. And painting.'

'My father hates painting!' She took her wine, leaned back and looked at the moon. The evening had moved so quickly. Romeo's brief absence had given her room for thought. 'That's why he wouldn't take me to Florence the last time he went. There's a place called the Brancacci Chapel. It has a pair of frescoes: Adam and Eve before the Fall and then after when they are expelled from Paradise into the world we know. I said I wanted to see them.'

Juliet looked around the garden. The noise indoors was diminishing. Soon the banquet would be over. She'd have to return to the palazzo and meet her parents' wrath.

'Why?' he asked.

Because of what she'd read. So much of life seemed to be about obedience. Do what your father says. Follow the words of the priest. When you transgress confess to your sins, always. Prostrate yourself. Do penance. Apologise. Whatever you do... never ask the obvious, heretical questions.

Where would we be without sin? Without that choice what point would life have at all? How can there be light without dark? And what if some sweetness lies in wait there? Why invent temptation if no one can ever touch it?

Her books said those frescoes hinted at these nagging, awkward conundrums. A perfect couple in Paradise on one side, naked, ignorant of themselves and their physical existence. On the left the fallen pair, stricken with grief for tasting the fruit of the tree of knowledge, cursed with God's punishment. Miserable but enlightened, entering a world – a *new* world – as full of delight as it was of danger. And ultimately... the sentence the Almighty had delivered upon them. Death.

She looked straight at Romeo and asked, 'Which is best? To exist forever in ignorance? Or to choose a life that's brief but... full and real? Where you can feel the blood pulse through your veins? Can love someone with all your heart and never mind the consequences?'

'Here's to full and real and loving,' he said and raised his cup. 'Always. I'd rather live a single day in your sweet presence than countless lifetimes without it–'

'That's very poetic. Yet you kiss so very properly. As if I'm your aunt or something.'

His head went down. She patted his soft brown hair.

'Whatever you do, don't say sorry! And please don't pout.'

She got to her feet and reached into the branches above her. These apple trees were old. They had been there when she was little and surely would prosper long after she was gone. An ancient variety, the gardener said. Pink-striped fruit, sweet and crisp. This summer had begun early and stayed hot. They were ripe already. She picked the plumpest, a firm and perfect specimen.

'What–?' he began.

Her finger rose to his lips to shush him. 'Stand up, please.'

Juliet sank her teeth into the fruit: a forceful, decisive bite. Mouth full, she stood on tiptoes to kiss him, forcing the flesh and the juice into Romeo's mouth with her lips and tongue. Her mind went somewhere it had never been before, and so did his. A wild place full of nameless joy and a promise that no other soul alive could see. She dropped the apple, which rolled across the grass and she laughed, pulling back just a little from his tight arms and roaming fingers.

'That is my breast your fingers close upon,' she whispered in his ear.

'It's your heart I seek.'

Don't stop, she thought. *Don't stop. Don't...*

In this sudden, frantic passion her foot caught on his ankle and she tripped, holding on to him so close, so tightly that he fell, too. Both of them rolled on to the warm lush grass of the Capulet garden beneath the watching moon. On the lawn he kissed her again and this was so much better. His inquisitive fingers found a line of buttons behind her back, worked through, beneath the chemise, touched soft skin, the gentle curve and hollow of her spine. Then further...

'No, no.' She pulled away, stood up, smoothed down the dress as best she could. Leaves and blades of grass fell from her. 'Too far, too fast.'

He struggled to his feet.

'The moon is full,' she said. 'And we are mad.'

'God keep us that way.'

'I am to wed, Romeo. A stranger. No one can save me.'

He fell to his knees. 'You will marry me.'

She blinked once, then twice. Then, without thinking, burst into laughter so loud she had to put a hand to her mouth to quieten herself.

'You will marry me,' he repeated.

Stifling her giggles she sat down on the bench believing this the sweetest, strangest night she'd ever spent.

'But how?'

'You *will*...' he began again.

'I heard you the first time. For a would-be poet your use of language is quite shameful.'

'What–?'

'The order of one's words matters. Listen to me now. The way it should be spoken.' She composed herself then stared him straight in the eye. 'Will you marry me? *Will* you marry me?'

'Yes.'

'Yes what?'

'I'll marry you! That's done then...' He took her hands again.

Shaking, laughing, she pushed him back to the grass. He lay there. Juliet, not knowing how this came into her head, lifted her dress to her knees and straddled him, like a victor over a vanquished enemy.

Their eyes were silver with the moonlight. Their fingers roamed, playing fondly with skin, with hair, with lips, with teeth.

'I would marry you...' she whispered. 'If it were possible. Honestly. You could carry me away on a white charger like Saint George rescuing a damsel in distress.'

'I wouldn't wish to remain a saint long after if that's all right with you.'

His hands were beneath the silk, on her bare ankles, gently rising.

She giggled. A dog barked somewhere. Then there were rapid footsteps and a coarse voice broke the night.

'Bloody hell fire! What in the name of our dear sweet Lord is this I see before me?'

Romeo's hands shot out from underneath her dress. Juliet scrambled to her knees, turned and saw a large round form silhouetted against the starry sky.

'A... a... game. That's it, Nurse. A game.'

The woman let loose a deep and scurrilous chortle. 'Aye. And I've heard all the many names that game possesses.' She reached down and patted Juliet's head. 'Best you get inside now. Your mother's looking for you and given the racket you two have been making it can't be long before she finds her way out here.'

The girl swore quietly then pushed herself to her feet. Romeo rolled to one side and did the same.

'I know you,' Nurse said. 'You're Montague's lad. Are you soft in the head? That young monster Tybalt will have your guts for garters just for sticking your nose through the door. Let alone trying to tup the master's daughter in his garden.'

'It was a game!' Juliet cried. Then, more quietly, 'Just... that.'

The woman guffawed. 'And there's a gentleman in there thought himself betrothed to you tonight. I've seen some tricks of yours over the years but this one surely takes the biscuit. Look, lad...' She grabbed Romeo's arm and pointed into the trees. 'There's a side door over there. By the vegetable patch. That fool gardener never remembers to lock it. So you pop out the back. I'll sneak my little girl inside without her father spotting. If I can.'

He didn't move.

'You're either daft or rash or both,' she added. 'Which it is I care not. But for your own sake and that of the miss here be off with you.'

With that Juliet rushed forward and kissed him quickly on the lips. He held her until the woman made more squawking noises, then bowed awkwardly and started for the trees. Nurse watched and as he passed slapped him hard on the backside with the flat of her hand.

Juliet put her hand to her mouth, giggling.

'Goodnight, my love,' he said. 'I will not fail you. And lady...'

'Goodnight!' Nurse bellowed.

'My love...' Juliet added with a wave of her fingers.

One backward glance and then he was gone.

'Nice bottom on him. I'll say that for your young man.'

'You were too familiar, Nurse.'

'Too *familiar*? Really? Me? How far did that game of yours go? If you don't me asking.'

'Not far enough,' she said, without a second thought.

A big broad grin broke on Nurse's face. 'Patience, my little duck. One way or another I doubt you've got to long to wait.' She clapped her fat hands. 'So. Shall we try to get you in the house and safely up to bed? With no more skirmishes along the way?'

* * *

A little while later Romeo found his friends in the street outside the palazzo. Then, full of wine, Mercutio led them to the old Roman arena, a sprawling pile not far from his own quarters in the Cangrande castle. Romeo had never liked the ancient stadium. They told too many tales about it. Of how the pagans had ushered Christians and beasts out of cages to their slaughter in front of cheering crowds. Then, later, Christians led pagans and yet more animals for just the same.

During the day it remained a stage for performance, for concerts, gymnastics and the occasional showy execution. When darkness fell the ancient stones became the lair of whores and cut-throats. Somewhere sane men avoided.

Benvolio had passed the evening listening to the singers and players, chatting to them when they were free. A fresh way of notating music was being developed in Venice. With it, and the rise of the printing press, came the prospect that new kinds of song and instrumental works would spread throughout Italy and beyond.

'It's all terribly exciting,' he declared, seated on a stone bench by the arena's edge, after giving them a brief explanation of what he'd heard from the Capulets' hired band.

'I can hardly contain myself,' Mercutio declared. 'Where would I be without that knowledge?' His speech was distinctly slurred. 'Oh, I know. With my lovely Anna.' He clutched his arms about his chest, as if in an embrace. 'Oh, sweet Anna! Darling of my dreams! Kiss me, kiss me now.'

Then he stopped and elbowed Romeo. 'You can imagine that with your lovely Rosaline, can't you? She of the y-shaped coffin–'

'Oh, do be quiet! That's all done with.'

'Found another then? I thought I saw you eyeing someone else? Me? I'm a one girl man. Well, not even that if I'm honest.' He spat on the grimy cobbles. 'I did my best with plain little Anna. But frankly...'

'Asking her if she wanted to go outside for a tumble probably wasn't the cleverest idea,' Benvolio suggested.

'I thought you were talking to them musicians, genius. It's rude to eavesdrop.'

'You were bellowing so loud it was hard not to.'

''Cos of your flaming music! Yes! And besides... what I actually invited the young lady to join me for was a *fumble*. Not a tumble. *Fumble*. I am a gentleman, believe it or not. I'd never suggest such a thing to a girl first time out. Wouldn't be proper. Second time's different–'

'Tumble,' Benvolio insisted. 'It was tumble.'

'Be that as it may... the point is...' He scratched his head and looked round. 'I forget. Where are we? How did we get here? There's ladies of the night hang round these stones. And worse.'

Romeo sighed. 'We followed you.'

'Well, who's the fool then?' He winked. 'Got that lover's look in your eye, you have. Queen Mab's been whispering in your ear, hasn't she? I can tell. Queen Mab. Queen Mab...'

Benvolio grabbed Mercutio by the arm. 'I'm taking this one home. It's bedtime for you, friend.'

'Ah, to bed. To sleep. To dream. Look at this one's face. I swear he's blushing in the moonlight. Who is it now, Romeo? Not one of Capulet's relatives, I hope, or you'll have that grim bugger Tybalt jabbing his rapier up your bum.' He flapped at Benvolio. 'Hands off, will you?'

Benvolio kicked him in the pants and got a laugh and a curse in return. Then he looked at Romeo. 'You'll be all right? This one's coming with me whether he likes it or not.'

'Not...' Mercutio complained.

Benvolio grabbed him by the scruff of the neck. 'Don't hang around here on your own, Romeo, please. We got out of Capulet's place alive. Two miracles don't happen the same night.'

He walked with them a little of the way, Mercutio still babbling on and on about Queen Mab. Then, at the line of houses on the city side of the arena, they headed towards the Cangrande castle. The Montague palazzo was much like the Capulets': another small fortress, this time set against the river to the west. Ten minutes on foot, no more.

'Take care,' Benvolio cried.

'And don't you listen to Queen Mab,' Mercutio added. 'That little lady'll just get you into even more trouble.'

Even more?

Romeo laughed in spite of himself. The night had been so... strange. He'd no need of a tiny fairy in his ear making promises, for good or bad.

He wondered at their friendship sometimes. It was real and affectionate. Escalus's nephew could be funny, sincere, kind. And irritatingly outspoken, often voicing thoughts Romeo shared but kept unsaid. It was as if Mercutio, though older than the rest of them, had never felt a single hurt in his life. Or that he'd built a shell around himself to make sure he never suffered pain. Instead he'd blunder through the day wondering where cruel Queen Mab might take him. There was something to be said for that safe form of cowardice. It made for temporary torments, fleeting passions swiftly abandoned.

The sky was clear and full of stars, the moon so bright it made every brick and stone, wall and parapet, swallow-tail merlon and high fancy tower as clear and real as could be. She was no dream. Juliet was the one he'd longed for all his life and never known till now. He was not going home at all.

Soon he was by the river. The low and elegant shape of the Roman bridge stood to his left, its ancient lines shining in the moonlight. The long wall by its side belonged to the Capulets. Behind lay the lawn where they'd kissed and she had straddled him. Triumphant. Willing. His to save. She'd wanted that even if she didn't say as much out loud. And his to love.

The gate, the nurse said, was left open by the idle gardener night after night. On subtle tiptoes he stole along the river bank. Creatures moved around him, ducks and cormorants, rats and voles.

He heard voices then. One so sweet and full of promise he strained to hear her every angry word.

* * *

An explanation. That was what her father wanted. Though he was too angry to demand it in person, so instead Juliet was forced to wait the best part of an hour to face her mother after she'd dealt with the kitchen and the staff. Nurse looked on, silent, amused, conspiratorial.

'I felt giddy,' Juliet said, when finally Bianca Capulet arrived.

They were by the open garden windows in the empty banqueting hall, the servants clearing away the remains of the food, the dirty plates and glasses, and sweeping litter from the stone floor.

'Giddy?'

'Yes. I needed some fresh air. So I went and sat in the garden. You could have found me if you'd looked.' She smiled, as sweetly as she could. It was hard to stop thinking about Romeo and how far matters might have travelled had Nurse not interrupted them. 'I'm feeling better now. A *lot* better you'll be pleased to hear.'

'Oh, Juliet.'

She'd had seen that pained look too often. The one that said: *I know your games. I've witnessed them so many times. Please don't try to fool me with these lies again.*

'I'm sorry. It was thoughtless of me. How did your party go?'

'*Our* party. It was for your benefit. Did you eat a thing? Talk to a single soul?'

Juliet's eyes caught Nurse's then. The woman coughed into her fist but stayed quiet.

'I'm sorry I didn't feel well. I'm sorry father's upset with me again. It was best Count Paris didn't see me like that, anyway, wasn't it? He wouldn't want to marry a sickly girl. I imagine. If–'

Her mother's hand stretched out, soft fingers held her bare arm. She thought of the way Romeo had touched her. It was with just this same tentative reluctance. Love – and her mother did love her, she never doubted that – came with a reticence that seemed to border on fear. Perhaps that was part of the adventure. The secret stab of excitement that came as one stepped away from the safe and familiar and entered the shadows where all manner of unseen, unknown things might lurk.

'You can't run away from this, you know. All young women head for the altar. Either as a bride or a nun and we know the latter's not for you.'

'Very true,' Nurse agreed. 'On both counts, Madam.'

'Perhaps Paris isn't for me either. Have you considered that?'

She remembered when her mother's hair was fair, almost as blonde as hers. Of late it had started to thin and turn grey. There were lines on her cheeks, crow's feet around her eyes that had never been there before. Age or strain or both. It hurt Juliet to think that perhaps some of those marks were caused by her.

'I'll tell your father you didn't feel well and thought it best the count didn't see you that way. That tomorrow you'll feel better. You can meet him here in the morning.'

'Tomorrow I could be dead,' she snapped, and wondered immediately what odd impulse had made her form those words.

Her mother looked ready to weep. Or scream. 'Please, child. Not again. Don't say those things. Even in jest.'

'In *jest*?'

'I mean–'

'I'm tired. Good night. I hope I didn't ruin your evening. Truly.'

With that Juliet set off for the stairs.

The two women watched. The back of her blue dress was stained with the green of the garden grass, her hair was dishevelled, brown leaves falling from it as she climbed the broad stone steps to her rooms.

Her mother stared, wide-eyed.

'She fell over when I went to fetch her,' Nurse said quickly. 'Clumsy little thing sometimes. Bright ones often are.'

Bianca Capulet said not a word.

'But you're her mother. I suppose you know that.'

'If there's something going on…'

'You'd be the first to hear, my lady.'

'Be sure of that, Nurse. Better me than my husband.'

'Aye,' the woman said. 'I know.'

* * *

In jest.

She didn't joke about the grave. How could you? And how could her mother be so surprised that anyone born in Verona didn't feel its cold, dark presence on every street, in the churches, the government halls, the countless piazzas?

Death was a stalker in the shadows, ever-present, always watching. A year before, as a treat supposedly, they'd gone to San Zeno, a vast church outside the walls, so tall it hurt to look at the wooden ceiling that sat like an upturned boat high above the congregation. Her father disliked the place. Showy, he said, and always asking for money.

But this was May the twenty-first, the anniversary of the translation of Saint Zeno's remains to the basilica that bore his name. Most of Verona would be there. Perhaps afterwards they'd talk business.

Juliet had visited the place rarely and with good reason. It was beautiful but it also stank of death. The man was Verona's first bishop, laid in the grave, martyred some thought, a millennium before. He was an African and a statue near the high altar depicted him with a round black face, a friendly smile upon it. In his right hand sat a fishing rod, a silver dace dangling from the line. He enjoyed throwing his hook and line into the Adige the stories said, just as a good bishop liked to fish for men.

In the crypt below, lit by smoky yellow candles, lay Zeno's body encased in a glass coffin. He wore a smart red robe, too clean to be a thousand years old. A gold mitre sat on his head. A silver mask covered a skull that had crept into her imagination and haunted her for weeks after. Above the crypt, out in the nave, Zeno stood before them in wood, almost lifelike, smiling with his fishing rod. In the chamber beneath the stones he was nothing more than bare bones and leathery dried flesh, all clothed in the grand scarlet gown of a bishop because this strange spectacle was something the church deemed 'holy'.

That shocking contrast seemed to escape most everyone else in the congregation. It was all Juliet could think of. So instead she looked at the altar, at the paintings of saints and martyrs, a crucifixion, raising her head as the hymns and chants and sermons seemed to continue forever. Above those still and serious figures, high in the vaulted ceiling, someone had painted a perfect blue night sky dotted with golden stars. That was pretty. That was a place she'd like to be.

After the interminable service was over they'd filed out, her father desperately trying to talk to some men whose business he sought.

Inwardly she felt furious at being dragged to this grim, slow spectacle. As they headed to the piazza outside the basilica she asked again the question she'd thrown at him the very first time he'd taken her to San Zeno. A gigantic rose window stood in the upper façade of the church above the square. The locals called it the Wheel of Fortune because around the room were carved six figures, some in joy, some in agony, supposedly depicting the brief and shifting nature of earthly life as it turned, sending half of them up to heaven, the others down to hell.

'Father,' she said, interrupting him as he tried to converse with a banker keen to find new customers for his loans. 'The window...'

'I'm talking–'

'I've asked you this before and you never answered. Why does God let one man rise and another fall like that? If the world's so random and merciless what's the point of anything? I don't follow. It doesn't make sense.'

Any more than keeping old bones rotting in a crypt, wrapped up in gold and silver and red linen for all to see.

'I've told you before. I'm not a priest. Ask one of them.'

Later, in Sant'Anastasia, at another pointless confession, she had asked again and got no good answer. Just the same platitudes she received when she asked why a kind, just God demanded death as recompense for the gift of life he'd given in the first place.

Because that's how things are. It wasn't an answer at all.

She got out of her evening clothes and hung them up tidily, knowing the quarrel that would ensue if she threw them on the floor. Then she found a shift, plain, long and cool. The night was too hot for anything else. She didn't feel like sleeping. The evening had been too odd, too alluring, to contemplate that.

Barefoot, she went to the windows, threw them open and walked on to the balcony.

'Oh, Romeo,' she sighed. 'Why do you have to bear that name? Montague, I mean. Romeo's quite...'

Quite a part of me somehow.

She was talking to herself.

'A sign of madness.'

Or love. Which was, perhaps, the same.

There was a long couch on the balcony. Comfortable. Sometimes she slept on it, a lemon-oil candle by her side to keep away the mosquitoes. Outdoors the world was real and the endless sky seemed to smile on her, just like the blue ceiling in San Zeno which was so much more fetching than that cruel rose window with its flailing figures caught between life and death. She lit the sweet-smelling candle and placed it on the tiled floor beside the couch, then found two pillows and tucked herself beneath a single sheet. The stars were so brilliant they might have been pin pricks in a great black velvet sheet set against the dazzling eternity of heaven.

He was here somewhere, in Verona, thinking of her, too. She knew that.

'Sweet dreams,' she whispered happily. 'For now and all time forward.'

* * *

Romeo waited until the heated conversation inside the palazzo walls died down. Two voices he could place: Juliet and the woman servant who'd disturbed them in the garden. The third, soft and older, could only be her mother.

When he heard the hall windows close with a slam he pushed at the rickety side gate he'd used earlier and once again found himself in the garden of the Capulets. There he sat down by the wall, yawned, stretched out his arms, exhausted. His eyes seemed to close themselves. And straight away he found himself dreaming.

Juliet. Juliet.

Her lovely face filled his imagination, her bright, bold voice whispered in his head. He saw them striding hand-in-hand beside the flowing Adige in August. Walking through deep snow in the lower Tyrol as winter came. Peace there was in this place, everywhere. Between them. Between their respective houses, too. With this adoring devotion came a broader harmony that had been lost to so many for years.

All through love. Real love. Not the affected infatuation Rosaline had offered him. This was flesh and blood, a fond and physical passion that bound the two of them together like shipmates set upon the journey known as life.

Together.

Another welcome, arousing image came then. They were naked as the pair in Eden, fresh with ardour, rolling on the grass. Arms wrapped around each other, entering a private, secret place...

A sound. A bell. The Torre dei Lamberti. The real world pleading for his return.

'Damn,' he muttered, rolling to one side as he woke against the wall. It was all sleep's cruel trickery.

He had registered only the last peal so he'd no idea how late it was. Only that hours might have passed. The night was cooler, the moon lower in the sky. Rashly he'd stolen into her garden and simply slumbered. An opportunity lost.

Cursing, he got to his feet.

'Ow!'

Thinking only of her, he'd stumbled straight into a patch of brambles at the base of the riverside wall. Sharp thorns. Thick head.

Through the blackberries he stumbled, the thorns ripping at his velvet britches though he barely felt them. Her balcony lay ahead, the stone carvings on the front outlined by the moonlight. Candles burned, dim and smoky yellow on the wall. Then he saw her slim shape standing by the edge, nothing but a white night gown about her person, above it that face, that hair. The sight of her stirred his heart. He tripped and felt another stab of spines.

'*Ow!*'

Artichokes. He'd never liked them.

She leaned over the balcony, one hand on the thick trunk of the ancient vine that ran twisting up from the ground.

'Who's that? Who's there? You woke me. Thank you very much.'

Timid, too reluctant to show himself, it was the best he could do to whisper, so low she'd never hear, 'Oh God, Juliet. Let us live together. Let us love. And damn the opinions of old men. They're not worth a penny.'

Her voice grew more strident, yet not loud. 'If it's a burglar I'm warning you. Best make yourself scarce. We have guards here. And dogs. Both fierce.' She hesitated then. 'I am saying this softly, however, by way of warning. And in case... in case you're not a burglar. Just someone who happens to be passing. Or...'

He scrambled nearer and still didn't dare show his face. The sky betrayed the faintest rosy hint of morning. 'Dawn breaks and Juliet is the sun. Farewell moon. Goodbye stars. She shines too bright...'

'Whoever you happen to be. Thief. Villain...'

'I'd be both and steal your heart, my love. If only you knew. If only I dared.'

She waved a dismissive hand out towards the garden. 'That's it. I'm off to bed now. Shortly.'

'To bed.' He didn't want to think of this. 'And here I am. Tramping through her garden. Watching like a craven coward...'

Just then Juliet leaned over the edge of her balcony and peered into the trees below. The moon outlined her face against the pale palazzo stone. 'Romeo. If it's you messing about down there kindly show yourself. I feel a proper clown stood out here in my nightshift.'

All the words he knew deserted him. Not so her.

'Damn it. Why am I talking to thin air? What stupid turn of fate made you a Montague in the first place? Tell your father to get lost. I'll do the same to mine. Marry me and I'll happily cease to be a Capulet. I mean–'

'Marry?' he whispered, voice trembling with excitement. 'We said we'd marry.'

He was about to step out and reveal himself when she threw

something – a glass, he thought – straight off the balcony. It whizzed past his head and shattered on the path. Cross words followed.

'It's names that make enemies here though none of us got to choose the one we're born with. Eight letters of the alphabet are my foe. Not you. Never you. And what's Montague? A word. Not a... a hand or a foot. What's a name in any case? You could call a rose a beetroot and still it would smell as sweet.'

He edged against the palazzo wall and there she was, elbows on the balcony edge, head in hands, staring at the growing dawn.

'So there's the answer, my Montague. I'll dispatch my name. You throw away yours. Then take me. All of me. I'm yours. If only...'

He lurched out into the open, stumbling through the rose bed and cried, 'I hear you, sweetest!'

Juliet gazed down at him, half-surprised, half-embarrassed. 'Less noise, please. Do you want the world to know?'

He came and stood where she could see him clearly, arms wide open as if to catch her. 'I'll shout my love from every tower in Verona if you'll give me leave. There's an endless night to be slept for both of us. Before it comes give me a thousand kisses, then a hundred, then a thousand more, and a second hundred, and then... and then–'

'Is that poetry again?'

'Catullus. He was born here.'

'I know!' She paused and put a finger to her lips. 'He's filthy, isn't he? That's why Mother wouldn't let me have the book.'

'Only in parts.'

'What parts?'

'It doesn't matter! I take you at your word, my darling. Give me your heart and baptise me how you want. Romeo's a dead man. Rechristen me as you wish...'

'They'll set the dogs on you in a minute. Or worse my cousin Tybalt. Do you want to rouse them all?'

'No. Just you.'

Juliet laughed. 'You've managed that. In any case... what is this? Hanging around my garden, listening to my private thoughts.'

He went and stood by the vine, then put a hand to the gnarled trunk, wondering if it would hold him. 'Well they weren't *that* private, were they? Otherwise I wouldn't have heard. If the name of Romeo upsets you, fairest, change it. You from whom the radiant sun does shine like–'

'How did you get here?'

'On love's light wings I scaled those walls. No stone, no fortress keeps out a passion like mine. Not your family–'

She leaned over the edge and squinted down the garden. 'So the gate's still open. I hope those wings work when Tybalt catches you. Otherwise there'll be murder.'

He bowed graciously, and swept the air with his right arm. 'I'm more afraid of a single cold glint in your eye than twenty of their swords. Just look on me a little tenderly, please. That's sufficient armour–'

'This poetry of yours could get tedious.'

'It's done with. When we're married.' She didn't laugh, didn't budge, just looked at him. 'As we agreed. Later this very day.'

Then he took hold of the vine and climbed up, hand over hand, feet struggling for grip upon its flaking trunk. The balcony was high. And more distant than it looked. He flapped an arm out towards her. It was a long drop down. With an amused sigh, she reached out, grabbed him, helped him over. Romeo set foot in the palazzo of the Capulets for the second time that evening. The two of them stood there for a moment in each other's arms. He kissed her. A natural kiss, full of love and passion and heat. So much she retreated and said, quite shyly, 'That was more convincing. Anyone would think you've been practising.'

'Only in my dreams.'

She raised her fingers and stroked his cheek. 'Tonight was nice. I'm flattered, honestly. But how can you really love me?'

'Count the ways. I—'

'No. Don't bother. I knew you'd say that. Boys do. Men do. And swear their love then see another pretty face. Or ankle. After which they're gone...'

'Never...'

'They say that too. Half the gods in heaven are laughing at lovers' broken promises. Be honest with me. Here I am, half-dressed, half inclined to... believe you.' She looked up at him, an earnest, searching expression on her face. 'Am I being too forward? That's not good, I know. If you like I could be a bit more remote. Distant...'

'No, no really. This is perfect. Honestly.'

'I agree I've got a sharp and unguarded tongue sometimes. But if I say yes I'll mean it. Much more than all those girls who'll lead you a merry dance. It'll be yes for ever and ever. World without end. Well, as long as these little lives of ours may last. And, by the way...'

'Yes?'

'I'm only speaking candidly like this because you had the temerity to eavesdrop on a lady's secret thoughts whispered from her balcony.'

That seemed a little unfair.

'It was quite loud for a whisper. In fact I thought you might be hoping it was me and—'

'A whisper.'

He recalled the sharp voices he'd heard earlier, her mother and the woman servant.

'A whisper it was. I swear with all I have, by the blessed moon that's now fading over these orange blossoms...'

'Oh, don't swear on the moon. Please. Anything but the moon.'

'Why?'

She folded her arms and frowned. 'Well... it's such an inconstant thing. Waxing and waning like that. Driving people mad. Are we both lunatics then? Terrible idea.'

'What precious thing do you want me to swear by then?'

'Swear on your own good name. If you're honest, as you say, that's good enough surely. You can be precious to me. I can be precious to you. Why would we need more than that?'

'With my heart then...'

Juliet looked back into the room. He followed the line of her gaze. There was a bed there, large, four-poster, the sheets untouched. The sight of it made his heart leap.

Then she said, 'Thinking about it, let's not do this swearing thing right now. It's late. Or early. Romeo. I love to see you. Honestly. But... it's as if we're trapped in something that moves too quickly. Like an hourglass where the sand doesn't trickle as it should. Just runs and runs.'

He took her in his arms again. 'Let it.'

'But sands run out. And lives with them.'

The bed. The sheets. The thought of her... 'I am so full of passion for you. Without a touch, another kiss, they may as well run out right now. If–'

She reached up. Her lips touched his. Her hands found his back. While his worked beneath the delicate nightgown and touched the soft warm skin there. It was as if a wasp had stung her. She retreated, eyes down.

'Too soon for that.'

'One more poem,' he promised. 'Just one.'

This rhyme had followed him ever since he'd slipped from her in the garden below.

'Just one,' she agreed.

He waited a moment and thought to himself: *if all my life depends upon these few words then say them well and truthfully.*

'My mistress' eyes are nothing like the sun

Coral is far more red than her lips' red.

I have seen roses damask'd, red and white,

But no such roses see I in her cheeks–'

She tapped his arm and stopped him. 'Red coral wards off the evil eye, Nurse says. Not that she ever tells me what the evil eye truly is. Do you–?'

'And in some perfumes is there more delight

Than in the breath that from my mistress reeks.'

Another tap. 'Are you saying my breath smells?'

'No! Only of you? May I finish?'

'If there are no more insults.'

'There were none before…' He coughed and fought to concentrate. On this final passage depended everything.

'I love to hear her speak, yet well I know

That music has a far more pleasing sound;

I grant I never saw a goddess go;

My mistress, when she walks, treads on the ground:

And yet, by heaven, I think my love as rare

As any she belied with false compare.'

She waited to make sure he'd finished.

His hand rose to her face. He took a strand of her hair in his fingers, looked at it, at her, in wonder. 'I think my love as rare—'

'Did you make that up yourself?'

Trying to sound serious, he explained, 'There's a theory no art is original. That there are only seven different stories in the world, with countless variations. The skill lies in creative improvisation, not a false sense of novelty.'

She smiled. 'Well, I won't ask who it was then. Still... it's the sentiment that matters. Will you please stop staring at my bed?'

He couldn't stop himself. The neat white sheets, gauze drapes around them to keep out the night insects. And an odd painting: a grinning young girl, a little like Juliet, holding up a childish charcoal sketch of a woman, all stick arms and stick legs. A gift from her father she said when she saw he'd noticed. Painted from life when she was eleven and trying to draw herself. The hair was wrong, the face a mistake, the eyes too big. But she kept it on her wall all the same, to please him since, in his own way, her father tried so hard to do the same for her.

'May I come in? It's getting a little cold out—'

'No.'

'But—'

'No! How can you even think such a thing?'

'How can I not?'

Her fond fingers brushed his face. Then came a kiss that lingered. For a brief and tantalising moment her fingers played upon his chest. 'If we are wed, Romeo. When—'

'Today!'

She didn't laugh. 'How?'

'Secretly. By a friar I know. A good man who will always do God's work.'

'I can't...'

'We meet. We say our vows. No Count Paris for you. No Bologna for me. Just us. Our lives together.'

'And after? Our parents... What will they say?'

He shrugged. 'Either they embrace us. Or they hate us. So long as we have each other... does it matter?'

'Then perhaps we live in a palazzo? Or become beggars in the street?'

'If I'm with you I'm happy. That's all I know.' By the balustrade he went down on bended knee. 'The humblest beggar you will ever meet implores you, Juliet. Marry me. This very day. Then we tell the world and dare it to damn our love.'

She took his head and clutched it to her. The birds were waking in the trees. The edge of the golden sun had begun to rise over the riverside wall. There was a brave new world beyond it. And freedom, or at least the promise of it.

'Tomorrow seems so soon. We only met—'

'You've doubts?'

Her hands reached round his neck. 'No.'

'Either we do this now. Or they'll find out and tear us apart. You know that.' He got to his feet. 'This morning. Nine or ten.'

'I can't get out of the house so soon. They'll stop me. Later. The afternoon. Is it... is it possible?'

'I'll make it so. Or die trying.'

A door crashed somewhere inside the palazzo, so loud it made them jump. Then a loud, coarse woman's voice cried, 'Juliet? Is that you awake? At this hour? Lord knows it's hard enough to get you out of bed for breakfast...'

Another bang. She was approaching.

'Ten o'clock. Send a messenger you trust to the Piazza Erbe,' he said. 'I'll make arrangements...'

There was the clatter of big feet and the door to her bedroom opened. She took his head in her hands and kissed him one last time quickly, desperately.

'Go, Romeo. Go now! I shall see you soon. When we are wed.'

He climbed over the balcony, no hesitation, no clumsiness, then scrambled down the old vine so quickly the leaves and tiny, half-formed fruit followed him like confetti.

When we are wed.

The words went round and round her head. And his.

* * *

Nurse burst in, anxious, bustling through the book-strewn room. Juliet was still on the balcony, smiling at nothing but the glorious dawn.

'You're awake, girl.'

'So it seems.'

'I heard something.'

Juliet pulled her nightshift about her. It was cold and she'd never noticed. 'A cat.'

Nurse narrowed her eyes. 'One that talks? Not Tybalt? I heard they call him Prince of Cats. Always sneaking round the place, claws out. Was it?'

Juliet's eyes grew round and angry. 'He's my cousin!'

'Happens all the time with country folk. Closer than that too. You are an innocent.'

'No, I'm not. More to the point... he's Tybalt. Please.' She shuddered. 'The very thought...'

Nurse went to the edge of the balcony and looked over. She was staring straight at the bench and the patch of grass where they'd lain. Their shapes were still there, just visible in the morning dew. 'Well, little one. If you don't want to confide in me—'

'Don't call me that. I'm sixteen. Nearly seventeen. If my father had his way I'd be married before the week is out.'

'Oh, Juliet.' She came and took the girl by the shoulders. 'Don't grieve so, lass. A woman doesn't come into this world with many choices. You got more than most.'

'Not the one I crave.'

Nurse held, hugged her. Like a daughter. The child she'd lost.

'Can you keep a secret?' Juliet whispered in her ear.

'How many have I kept in the past?'

'This is the biggest. The most I'll ever ask of you.'

She crossed her fat arms and laughed. 'I'm your servant, Juliet of the Capulets.' A nod back at the quarters behind them. 'Not theirs.'

Ten of the morning. The Piazza Erbe.

Her messenger was found.

Part Two: A Paradise for Fools

Friar Laurence was a slight and smiling Franciscan brother who seemed, to most of his adoring flock, younger than his forty-six years. This was all the more remarkable since those same guileless looks had saved his life in circumstances that would have aged, if not destroyed, most men. He'd grown up in the southern coastal city of Otranto with his younger brother Nico and their widower father, a cheerful merchant who sold fabrics in the market. Then, one hot July morning, an Ottoman fleet bearing eighteen thousand troops landed on the beach.

The fighting that followed was swift and merciless. By nightfall the entire population had fled behind the walls of Otranto's castle. A siege ensued. Most soldiers slunk off for safety in the night. Fifteen days after the Ottoman forces arrived they stormed a garrison defended by priests, civilians, women and any youngster able to bear a weapon. The elders of the church were slaughtered as they prayed. Healthy women and children of working age were sent for slavery. The rest the Turks murdered with as much imagination as they could muster.

The last eight hundred and thirteen men alive were told they would be spared if, at the point of a sword, they converted to Islam. When every man refused they were led to the Hill of Minerva and beheaded one by one. Laurence was sixteen at the time and intent on joining his father among the martyrs. His brother Nico, though two years younger, was always the stronger and pleaded with a Turkish soldier to spare their lives, lying about his brother's age. Laurence could say nothing since Nico had punched him into submission and at that moment he was so dizzy he could not speak.

And so they survived, to be shipped in chains to Constantinople, once the heart of the Byzantine Empire, later Venetian, now capital of a Muslim state determined to strike hard at every point the compass offered. There, fortune found them once again. The brothers were bought by Paulus, a kindly and wealthy physician, born Christian in Athens, and converted to the religion of the Turks which he followed rigorously for purposes of survival much more than belief.

There was a necessary distance between the two brothers from that point on. Laurence never lost a nagging sense of guilt that he'd cheated martyrdom. Nico, influenced by the pragmatic Paulus, berated his sibling for his misery, saying life was life, and death would come soon enough without the need for any man to hasten its arrival.

Amidst these fraternal squabbles the physician taught them what he knew about herbs and poultices, infusions and tinctures that might stave off fever, colic and, with a little luck, the plague. His mansion was a few doors away from Hagia Sofia, the great church built by the Emperor Justinian almost a thousand years before, now turned into a mosque. One bright June morning, fifteen years before, the boys found Paulus in the hall, money in hand, papers for travel, a sad but friendly farewell on his lips.

'Your service is done,' Paulus told them. 'What feeble wisdom I have the two of you now possess. Go.'

'Why?' Nico asked.

'Because I'm enough of a physician to understand I'm dying. When I'm gone they'll sell you to whosoever offers the highest price, regardless of their nature. I doubt the dead have consciences. Even so I'd rather not find out.'

'Go where?' Laurence wondered.

Paulus tapped the travel papers. There was a map, drawn in his own spidery hand, along with some instructions.

'Home, of course. To Italy. Tell them when you get there that good and bad exist in every man. Muslim, Christian, Jew and heathen. Until we recognise that truth and act upon it we shall never, any of us, live in peace.'

He had them gather their things then showed them outside. There, in the bustling Constantinople street, he patted the two of them on the head, Laurence first, then Nico, not that he showed either special favour.

'Make the sick well. Heal anger and division most of all. Because these vile ruptures among us drive men apart and lead them to whatever devil they choose or chooses them. That is the most difficult sort of medicine. Leave the easy kind to the many quacks you'll find upon the way.'

The addresses were for two apothecaries Paulus had dealt with, one in Verona, the second twenty-five miles south outside the Venetian Republic in the independent city state of Mantua. Neither of them knew this part of Italy but still they went. Nico to Mantua and a sickly bachelor who maintained a market stall in what was once a round church supposedly based on the Holy Sepulchre in Jerusalem. And Laurence, to disobey his master's orders once and once only, when, on reaching Verona, he walked straight to the Monastery of San Francesco al Corso and took Franciscan orders.

Though perhaps, he often thought, Paulus had pointed him in this direction from the very first, since his parting note included a quotation of Saint Francis from his 'Canticle of the Sun'.

Be praised, my Lord, through our sister Mother Earth who feeds us and rules us and produces diverse fruits with coloured flowers and herbs.

As the summer morning broke over Verona, Laurence was remembering those words as he worked his little patch of paradise, the garden. The monastery was a complex of dark cells with a small, frugally-decorated church and, towards the river, a green and verdant plot so large it might have been a modest farm. Vegetables took up the lesser part; the few kale, cabbages, leeks and onions the poverty-loving brothers of San Francesco al Corso required. Mostly the rich dark earth grew medicinal herbs for the monastery's patients: followers of the Franciscan churches, Dominicans, Jews, heretics. Laurence, who was chief apothecary in all but name, never asked and never cared since sickness knew no creed.

When he heard a familiar cough behind him the friar was on his knees removing seedlings from a patch of motherwort, a fertile herb he used for depression and ailments of the heart, and a species that liked to stray beyond its own allotted bed.

'Romeo,' he said, and plucked out the last of the errant seedlings. 'I'd know those nervous footsteps anywhere. Good morning, boy. You're looking tired. But well. Kneel down and help me.'

The Montague boy was always willing. Perhaps one day he'd make a gardener, too.

'With what?'

'Tending the herb garden,' the friar said and placed his wicker basket by the tidy bed. 'I need to refill our stock. There may be plague on the way.' With a pair of crude scissors he snipped a few leaves, held them to the light, sniffed them, nodded, and placed the slender green blades in his pannier. 'Understand this. Some herbs are medicine. Some poison. And a good few a little of both depending on the dose. This...' he plucked a few stems from something that looked like hairy mint. '...is horehound. It can cure a sore throat. Perhaps save a man's life from the poison they know in Rome called *cantarella*.'

'The sort the Borgias use?'

'Shush,' the friar urged him. 'Don't waste your time on gossip, son. This pretty blue flower is called monkshood which may dispel the most severe or fevers. Or, in excess, put a man in the grave within the hour.'

Romeo's fingers shrank back from the blooms. Laurence pulled a leather glove onto his right hand. 'Keep calm. It's the root that does the work and I'd never let an apprentice deal with that. The Romans called this potent wonder aconitum and said it grew where the three-headed monster Cerberus drooled poison as he fought Hercules.' He lifted the smallest specimen and cut a length of tap root with a knife. 'But it's just a plant. The earth is both nature's mother and her tomb. Nothing's so evil that it doesn't give back a little good. And nothing so good it may not perform a little evil in return.'

'Friar...'

'Virtue may turn to vice. And vice to virtue. One way or another we choose.'

Laurence tucked the monkshood root inside a goatskin pouch and placed it in his basket. 'You look the same, Romeo. And you look different. Lovelorn but... happy. Excited even. I haven't noticed that in a while.'

A shy smile was all he got. No words. The friar groaned. He was the one person to whom Romeo had confessed his infatuation for the horse trader's daughter from across the river.

'Rosaline. Don't tell me she gave in at last.' He removed the glove and wagged a finger. 'I hope there's no sin here. If it's forgiveness you're looking for—'

'No,' said Romeo. 'Something much... greater.'

The friar waited and, when he realised it was pointless, got to his feet. 'I see this is not a conversation for these open fields. Let's go to my cell. Darkness and seclusion.' He lifted the wicker basket. 'And we'll put these little leaves to bed.'

* * *

The Capulets took breakfast together in the palazzo dining room at eight. Juliet was still in her nightshift, a gown thrown over it. Her parents were dressed and beyond complaining.

Luca Capulet ate mountain ham and cheese as usual, washed down with milk. Her mother much the same. Juliet picked at some fruit from the garden, drinking a goblet of pomegranate juice squeezed by one of the kitchen boys. She did it better, she thought. More flavour, less bitter pith. *When we are wed.* Then she'll make her own.

'Count Paris...' her mother began.

'Why are we at war with the Montagues, father? I know the consequences. How we can't talk to them. How our servants brawl in the street and Tybalt looks to stick his stupid dagger in any of them he can find. But I'm unaware of the causes. Why?'

Life, Capulet said. Business. Both were much the same.

Paris was due in the house in an hour. Her mother wanted her bathed, dressed, hair tidy, manner polite and sweet.

'Is it true you and Andrea Montague were friends when you were little? Best friends?'

He stared at her across the table, a piece of ham on the fork before his mouth. 'Who told you that?'

'I don't remember. They seemed to think it common knowledge.'

Her mother intervened as usual. 'It's rare for childhood friends to last. People change.'

Juliet waved a chunk of apple at her. 'I understand that. But it's not that they're no longer friends. They're bitter enemies. We all are as a result. I do think I ought to know why—'

'Business!' he cried. 'I told you.'

She looked at her mother as if to say: *is that it?*

Capulet stopped eating and pushed back his chair. His daughter thought he was about to storm out of the room. But he didn't.

'You're a girl,' he said.

'A woman surely. If I'm to be married.'

'A woman then. You've no need to worry about business. A man does. Montague and I inherited these trades. He got the Trebbiano grape. We have the Garganega.'

'Lots more besides that, Father. Even a girl understands we sell all kinds of things.'

'It began with the grape! The argument, that is.'

Nearly two decades ago, he said. The Capulets had a contract agreed in principle with an aristocratic house in Venice. 'My *friend* stole his way into the deal, offered several sweeteners and seized the sale before there was a signature on the contract.'

'Not an amicable act,' Juliet agreed. 'Why did he do it?'

He didn't speak. Finally her mother answered, 'It was when his wife was pregnant with that boy of theirs. Montague said they needed the money.'

'And we'd just lost a son!' Capulet roared. 'How could he even think of it?'

His wife reached over and took his hand. 'He didn't think, Luca. Or perhaps... knowing of our bereavement, he wanted to make sure his wife received the best care possible...' She looked at Juliet, a sad smile on her lined face. 'I wasn't well after we lost your brother. I went to Venice myself for a while. There was a doctor there who helped. Some nuns.'

'My own friend cheated me,' Capulet muttered in a low, hurt voice.

'They were mad and desperate times, husband. None of us knew what tomorrow would bring. Riches or disaster. Or just another day.'

This conversation pained him. He pushed away the plate and announced he'd lost his appetite.

'If the boot had been on the other foot, Father... would you have done the same to him? If your family really needed it?'

'We didn't.'

'I know. All the same. To lose a childhood friend and replace it with a feud. To hope their house will one day lie in ruins–'

'Oh, for the love of Mary!' Capulet bawled. 'Why talk business with women? What's the point? You fail to understand the smallest detail.'

Juliet met his stare and didn't waver. 'Explain it to me then and let me try.'

'I've no wish to ruin the Montagues. Why would I? They're our foes in business, much the same size, much the same in competence. If they vanished someone else would take their place. Perhaps a more capable man. A bigger house. With more money and friends further afield. A man always has enemies. Better they're weak than strong. I'd never dream of trying to force Montague out of business. Why? When I've no male heir to run my own house? Only... only...'

His voice faded to nothing.

'Only me.' She finished the sentence for him.

They sat in silence. No one moved.

'So that's the role Count Paris will perform. Not so much my husband as your proxy son. I marry him because it's good for business.'

He raised his voice. 'This coming century belongs to merchants. Not kings. Not popes. Not emperors. To the likes of us. But only if we remember our duty—'

'Duty…'

'Yes, duty! I do not wish the fruits of all my long, hard labour to perish with me. Is that so hard to understand?'

She glanced at her mother and said, 'We could, between the two of us—'

Bianca Capulet laughed out loud. 'Don't be ridiculous. Even if we had the knowledge, no merchant, no trader, no great family will entertain commerce with a woman.'

'Tybalt then—'

'Tybalt's a vicious young fool,' her father snapped. 'I wouldn't trust him with the stables.'

Capulet pulled his jacket about him. 'Paris is a man of standing with a name far nobler than ours. You should be flattered he even considers a commoner for a bride. The man will make you a loving husband and see you're both well cared for after I'm gone. That is that. How else is my mind to be at rest?'

She took her time finishing the last piece of apple and then the pomegranate juice. They watched her, both of them, expecting an impudent response. It was hard not to deliver it, too. There were so many that flitted through her head. Most, she realised, were childish, and the time for childish things was past.

'Do you think you could be friends with the Montagues again?' she asked, heart beating so quickly she wanted to put her hand there, where Romeo's fingers had wandered the night before, and try to still it. 'If an unexpected turn of events might heal that rift? End that pain? If–'

'No. I can't imagine such a thing would ever happen. Or why.'

'But if something unexpected came about… A kind of gift say…'

'Then I'd tear the thing to shreds in the face of the fool who offered it.' He got to his feet and glanced at her. 'I know everything I do is wrong. That if I say something's up you'll say it's down. If I turn left you'll tell me we should have gone right. That this is the very definition of wrong… whatever it is I do.'

She raised her index finger to object. 'That's not entirely fair.'

'But it is. And I understand that is how it goes with stripling girls. There are devils in your blood and it's fathers who must feel their pitchforks.'

Bianca Capulet's eyes were firmly on the tablecloth.

'The choices I make are for this family. For your future. I try to look beyond the present and the near and see what may happen when I'm cold in the grave. That's what a man must do, out of love and devotion and duty. I never expect your gratitude, daughter. But, by God, I do not deserve your disobedience or – worse – your contempt.'

With that he walked out, shaking.

She toyed with the remains of the apple but there was nothing left except core and pips. Her mother sat quietly weeping by her side.

'Let me clear the table,' Juliet said as she began to pick up the plates.

'We've servants for that. Just get dressed. Something pretty for once. Please.'

'Very well, Mother. I will.'

* * *

Laurence's cell was in the eastern section of the complex, by the lane that led to the city cemetery along the river. He'd chosen this location deliberately. The skills Paulus had taught the two of them in distant Constantinople provided temporary alleviations. As their Greek master always said, quoting one of his forebears… no man can cure death. But with luck and application they might put off the dreadful day a while. The nearness of the graveyard was a constant reminder of that duty.

Romeo knew the monastery well. His family had supported the Franciscans here for years. They were cheerier than some of the other orders and cared little for money or the trappings of the material world. The friar's room was large and shady since the single-shuttered windows gave out on to the cloisters around which the other brothers' cells were arranged. Laurence's work gave him twice the space of his fellows. A large preparation table stood at the heart of the chamber, a place where herbs were dried and boiled and stored in jars of oil. A rack of larger bottles, all carrying Latin names, was nailed to the plain brick wall. Next to it stood a smaller sideboard with stacks of vials in different colours, blue, red, green, orange and purple.

Pretty things. Romeo wandered over and played with them. A handful were black, with a skull on the front.

'Rats,' the friar said when he noticed what Romeo was holding. 'There's a thought abroad that perhaps the pestilence is carried somehow through them. In their fur or filth, I imagine. So, in concert with my brother in Mantua, we've developed a concoction that may be sprinkled on grain to kill the creatures. Quickly. In a day or so.'

Romeo picked up a bottle and shook it. The thing was empty. 'They say there's plague in Vicenza. Any day it could be here.'

'They do. But we make that for order only. There are some people who'd gladly use it on folks they regard as rats with two legs. I take great care with everything I dispense. The black bottles most of all. Now…' He placed the wicker basket on the nearest table and sat down. 'Your problem.'

Families high and low in Verona knew Laurence, liked him and were aware of his odd and tragic background, too. There was no fooling him, no point in beating about the bush.

'I've been feasting with my enemy. And come back sorely wounded.'

Laurence raised a narrow eyebrow.

'With love,' Romeo added. 'And in return I've wounded in a self-same fashion the most fetching woman alive. We ache for one another. You can cure us.'

The friar leaned back on his hard wooden stool until he found the cool brick wall. He studied the young man in front of him and spoke the truth: no physician or apothecary could cure the sick unless an ailment was well and truly stated.

'My heart's set on Juliet, Capulet's daughter. And her heart's set on me. The two of us are agreed. We wish to marry.'

'Holy Saint Francis! Where? How?'

'Where and how don't matter. Only when. Today.'

The lightest imprecation fell from Laurence's lips.

'If it's for the reasons I suspect—'

'It isn't. The girl's a virtuous maid. She would not… We would not countenance any other way.'

'Then why the haste?'

'Why the wait? We *know*. And besides, her father would like to marry her off to some Florentine count, a man she's never met. And my parents will send me off to Bologna within the week. It can't wait. We are meant for each other. I never felt God's will more strongly. Nor Juliet. What else is there to say?'

The friar picked at his habit, toying at a spare thread. The garment looked ancient, as if it were passed down from another. 'Well, this *is* a turn-up for the book, I must say. It was only a few days ago you were in here whining about how much you adored the girl Rosaline. Now it's another. A Capulet too. You're young, Romeo, and a young man sees love with his eyes, not his heart–'

'You told me off for dreaming about Rosaline often enough.'

Laurence nodded. 'I scolded you for doting on her. That's not love. I didn't tell you to bury one infatuation and replace it with another.'

'No, no.'

Romeo pulled up a stool and sat next to him. The brothers at San Francesco mingled with the world. They didn't hide from it like recluses. Still they took vows of chastity and the Franciscans usually kept to them. A few were married men before. But not Laurence.

'Believe me, please. The advice you gave was true. Rosaline was a childish fantasy. Juliet is not and we both know it. Let me bring her here this afternoon. Talk to us. If you don't see the love we share then…'

'All this haste, Romeo.'

'It's not of our making. If we don't marry now she's lost to a man she despises and I'm stuck alone in Bologna, drowning in dusty books. Let me bring her here this afternoon. If after you've seen us, you don't believe me then…' He picked up a sprig of greenery from the basket. 'Reject us like two weeds among your herbs.'

'You do seem very determined. I've not noticed that in you before. Is she of age?'

'Sixteen. And I'm two years older.'

'I know how old you are. I've tended you since you were a child.'

The law on marriage was simple. It was a contract between man and woman. There was no need of ceremony. Not even the presence of a churchman. At sixteen any couple might declare themselves betrothed with nothing more than marks on a piece of paper. Laurence told him this.

'You don't need me. If you're so intent on—'

'But we do. We wish to become one in the sight of God. Till death us do part. And when the Lord has blessed us then...' He hesitated, sniffed at the plant, put it back in the pannier. 'Then, this evening, together, we inform our parents. Capulet and Montague. We tell them of our love and pray this enmity that's divided them, and Verona, for so long must end.'

In the shady cell Laurence felt cold. An old Greek's words were in his head, spoken in the clear and kindly voice he'd last heard fifteen years before.

Make the sick well. Heal anger and division most of all. Because these vile ruptures among us drive men apart and lead them to whatever devil they choose or chooses them.

'You think that's possible?'

'*Omnia vincit amor*. Love conquers all.' Romeo laughed at himself. 'Virgil. I must stop quoting verse. It peeves her. A bit.'

Friar Laurence felt himself back in Constantinople at that moment, trembling at the thought the world might be not be black and white at all, but a difficult shade of grey. 'Poetry's your every other word. You'd let it go for this girl of the Capulets?'

Romeo took the older man's hands and peered deep into his genial grey eyes. 'I will do whatever it takes. Anything at all. I love her. With that love we will bring our two families together so that they may witness our devotion. When they do... they'll know. They'll bury this ridiculous vendetta. We will all be one.'

The friar looked at his basket. The leaves and stalks and roots there cured maladies. Sometimes. To heal not just a single life but two noble families, kept apart by a cruel, unnecessary hatred for so long? That was a remedy worth a lifetime's work. One no man could possibly refuse. Paulus would have reached for it without a second thought.

'Fetch your young lady here. I will talk to both of you. If all is as you say I'll marry you myself, with all the fond blessings this humble servant of the Lord may offer.'

Romeo cried out with joy and hugged him.

'We haven't done it yet,' the friar pointed out as he fought to shrug off the quick, excited embrace.

'We will, though. When you see us you'll witness the truth for yourself. Soon...?'

'Today for sure. But wisely and slowly we take this. For they that run too fast and never think...'

'What?'

They fall, Laurence thought. So heavily at times. Like another two in a garden long ago. 'Never mind. I'll see you here, in my cell. Come straight to this place directly. The witnesses...'

'It has to be just you. If they knew, her parents, mine... I hate to think.'

'This is very untoward.'

Outside there was the toll of a bell, a mournful hymn, the sound of someone sobbing. Romeo shivered.

'There's a funeral in the cemetery beyond the cloisters,' Laurence explained. 'A young beggar we took in from the street. She was past help sadly.'

'I'm sorry.'

Laurence shook his head. 'That's kind. But you never knew her.'

'And she's gone.'

The friar sighed. 'Death tugs at your ear. "Live now," he says. "For I am coming."'

Romeo sat speechless. Laurence laughed then winked at him. 'You're not the only one who knows a little Virgil. Let's hope we may bring some happiness into this world to set against the misery of going out of it. Off with you now. You've work to do. A labour of the heart, and that's both the lightest and the heaviest there is. So... *shoo!*'

* * *

Usually Juliet dressed quickly and decisively, putting comfort over fashion, practicality above anything her mother demanded. This morning she didn't know what to choose. Something ugly and unflattering to deter the count intent on wooing her? Or, if Nurse came back with a rapid summons from Romeo, a dress fit for a wedding?

In the end she compromised: no hat, no fancy *finestrella* sleeves as most of the girls had worn the previous evening, slashed shoulder to elbow, undershirt pulled through them. No circlet, only a single necklace of pearls about her slender white throat. The dress she chose was cream linen, wasp-waisted with a modest square neckline. Too old for her. The garb of a spinster wasting away her years. But also of a mature woman assured of herself. That was how she wished to feel, hiding her anxiety about the day ahead.

Just before ten she watched Nurse leave the palazzo by the back gate. A good few minutes after the hour bell had sounded – punctuality was always to be avoided – she came downstairs and found Count Paris with her mother waiting in the hall. He was dressed to the nines in an ornate fashion she thought more suited to Venice or Rome than small Verona. When she entered he bowed, then made flattering comments about her appearance without, it seemed to Juliet, much looking at her at all. There were introductions, then they were left alone. She smiled and said nothing.

The beard was combed and shaped and primped, a creature in itself, a small ginger pet that had come to nestle on his chin and fallen fast asleep. It emitted a perfumed scent and was hard not to stare at, wondering when the beast might move. Or what his real face would look like underneath.

He was in the middle of an interminable pronouncement of honeyed flattery when she said, 'I'd like to walk in the garden if you don't mind.'

Another bow, a flourish of his velvet cap. The hat was dark green with a gold band around the edge and – this had to be deliberate – a pheasant feather dyed scarlet, the colour of the Capulets, stuck in the brim. It clashed with the fabric but she imagined he didn't notice. Or perhaps wouldn't care. How things looked was unimportant. What mattered was the function they performed.

They walked outside and she couldn't stop thinking about the night before. That first meeting in the garden, the laughter, the teasing. The kisses and how they'd rolled together on the grass. Then the way Romeo had climbed up the old vine and she'd helped him on to the balcony above. She looked up at it. The stone figures carved on the front, Bacchus chasing a succession of nymphs, seemed to bathe in the glorious gold of the morning sun. If only they could relive the night before. Nurse might sleep a little longer. And this time, when he asked to come into her room, she'd lead him willingly to her bed.

'Your window?' Paris said. 'Your balcony? I have balconies galore in all my properties. You shall choose the ones you prefer.'

'Thank you. Most kind.'

'And they will call you Countess.'

'Names,' she whispered. 'People do make a fuss about them, don't they?'

She couldn't take her eyes off the leering, drunken figure of Bacchus, grasping the shoulder of one of the young women he sought. This was an image used repeatedly in paintings of the old gods. A lecherous man of middle age seeking the flesh, willing or not, of any young woman he desired.

'It seems to me it was never much fun to be a nymph back then. All you did was lounge around naked waiting for an old sot full of wine to come and take you. After that you die. Or get turned into a tree which must be much the same.'

'Lady... I'm sorry?'

'No.' This was important. *Think*. 'I'm the one who should be sorry. I prattle on. It's one of my many faults. You wouldn't believe how many I possess. Too numerous to count. Just ask my father.'

To her great embarrassment he went down on one knee, right next to the bench where she'd sat with Romeo. There Count Paris fumbled in his fancy jerkin, took out a small cloth pouch and removed from it a ring. Eyes averted, firmly on the ground, he said very bashfully, 'Please. Please take this.'

Men were odd with women, she decided. Either too forward or too shy. This one much the last. She took it anyway. The band was gold, scratched and old, the colour of the dying sun. There were words inside. She dimly remembered something the foreigners liked. A poesy ring, inscribed with a loving message.

Juliet squinted trying to make out the letters scrawled in faint writing, very worn through being close to someone's finger she guessed. It was English, a language she could just about manage.

'I have obtained whom God ordained,' she read out loud. '*Obtained*?'

'It was my mother's. She came from London. Apparently it's a popular rhyme there.'

'Popular with wives? *Obtained*?'

He was staring up at her with pleading eyes. 'I took that from her finger when she died.' It was all Juliet could do not to drop it. 'My father was murdered when I was an infant. My mother raised me and was the most glorious, holy woman in the world. I said I'd keep her ring until I found another worthy to wear it.'

'She raised you alone? And ran your house's trade in Florence?'

The question appeared to baffle him. 'Of course not. That was my stepfather's job, naturally. My mother was busy with the household–'

'And have you?'

He looked lost. 'Have I what?'

'Found another worthy to wear it?'

He had the appearance of a sad puppy begging for a favourite toy. 'I believe so. Finally.'

She was trying to keep her temper but this was hard. Juliet folded her arms and gazed down at him. 'So there were others?'

'I am twenty-six. True love is elusive–'

'You mean they said no?'

The puppy seemed about to cry.

She sat on the stone bench and slapped the space beside her. 'Kindly get off your knees, stop looking at me that way and sit here. I'm a practical woman, not a little girl.'

'I see this,' he said and joined her. 'Let me spell out the business issues then.'

She listened as he recounted an inventory of his properties, in Florence, Verona and beyond. Then a detailed list of all his commercial interests. After that his farms, the land they covered, the crops they grew. His family – an ageing stepfather, mind gone, and a few cousins who seemed of no importance. Then the bloodline of the Paris dynasty, which appeared to include distant kinship with a couple of popes, one emperor and a warlord who'd killed a lot of Goths. Finally his religious leanings – a good Catholic, more fond of the Church than he was of the present pope – and his membership of any number of Florentine guilds of which she'd never heard.

'You will gain a husband of substance who loves you. Who will do anything to make you happy. The ring I offered. Do me the honour of wearing it and I shall adore you all my living days.'

Juliet leaned back on the seat, closed her eyes and murmured, 'Oh sweet Jesus...'

'Your father is agreed–'

'Then why ask me? Why bother?'

'Because I wish you to be happy. The woman I–'

'Count Paris. You do not know me. Any more than I know you. I'm flattered by your attentions but truly... How in these circumstances may you profess your love? For a stranger?'

There was an expression on his face she found a touch obtuse. As if this idea had never occurred to him.

'Most wives barely know their husbands when they're married. The bond is built after, surely. It comes with children.' He looked her up and down in a way she didn't enjoy. 'A son's important. A daughter an additional blessing if one should come along. Your hips are slim but not so much I think to cause a difficulty in birth—'

'My hips! You wish to marry me for my *hips*?'

The fond smile fell. There was a cold glint in his eye she hadn't seen before. 'You said you were of a practical bent. I thought you'd appreciate that in another. Without a family a nobleman of my standing is a creature of no importance. Just dust to come and nothing left behind after two thousand years of glory.'

She stood up and glanced around the garden. A place she adored. She couldn't wait to leave it. 'I am grateful for your time and interest,' she said, holding out the gold ring he'd taken from his dead mother. 'But my finger's too small and this too large. It'll never fit, sir.'

He took the thing, no smile on his face. 'It will, my girl. I'll make it.'

Then, without a backward glance, he was gone, marching up the stone steps into the palazzo. Those last words of his had an implicit meaning, a threat she couldn't miss for all the world.

A while she stayed there, thinking of what Nurse might be up to in the Piazza Erbe. Wondering how she and Romeo might break free from this present peril. Paris was right in one respect: most brides never knew their husbands. Never had any say about the man with whom they were supposed to spend the rest of their lives. That was the way of things, as her mother would insist. But the way of things was there to be questioned. This was fourteen hundred and ninety-nine.

'No one owns me but myself,' Juliet whispered in the garden.

Not even Romeo, she thought. *We are equal or this isn't love at all.*

The storm had to be weathered. Finally she dragged herself back inside. Her father was grim-faced at the dining table, a cup of wine before him. He rarely drank this early. Paris was gone. Her mother bustled in and took her into the hall.

'Have you seen Tybalt?'

'No. Why?'

'He's been storming round the city making threats all morning. Your father's worried he may do something rash. They had a terrible row.'

'I am not my cousin's keeper.'

'Not even keeper of yourself! You promised me you'd be at least polite to Count Paris.'

'I was. Did he say otherwise?'

Her mother glanced towards the table where Luca Capulet sat staring at his wine. 'He didn't say anything at all. Your father's going to talk to him again this afternoon. Love, love...'

Juliet barely heard her. There was a picture in her head. The stone front of her golden balcony, the figures there coming alive. Bacchus, leaping, grasping, thrusting his way towards the naked nymph below him.

'Daughter. There will be a wedding. Believe me.'

'Truly... I do,' Juliet said then placed a brief and tender kiss upon her mother's cheek.

* * *

The threat of pestilence was now public. Soldiers had begun hammering posters to the arcade walls of the Piazza Erbe, warning of restrictions ordered that day by Escalus on behalf of his Venetian masters. Reports of plague cases had now spread beyond Vicenza and Soave. There was a suspected death in Mozzecane to the south on the way to Mantua. Everyone knew what that meant. Verona was built like a fortress, with the miniature castles of families like the Capulets and Montagues inside. It was easy for Escalus and his forces to seal the city completely, allowing people to arrive and leave only through a single route, the bridge that ran from the side of Cangrande's castle across the Adige to open land north of the river.

From midday all other bridges would be closed and no one allowed in or out without written proof they had prior business or the approval of the authorities.

A burly infantryman was nailing one of the notices to a pillar by the Arco della Costa. A dingy, curving whale's rib, or some would have it the bone of a monster, hung beneath the arch and had for as long as any could remember. The locals said it would stay there until a man who'd never told a lie walked beneath.

Mercutio nudged Benvolio, looked up at the whale's rib and said, 'I'll never touch another drop of drink again. Oh look! It hasn't moved an inch.'

Benvolio laughed. 'As if you've never told a lie before. How is the head?'

Mercutio had a hangover and wanted the world to know. 'It's the kind that makes you pray for death. Anything for relief.'

Stay there, Benvolio told him, then went into the apothecary shop by the arch and returned with their trademark remedy, a green potion: iron and seaweed and herbs in a leather cup.

'Is that supposed to make me feel better?' Mercutio grumbled.

'No. Worse. So next time you get invited into a grandee's palazzo you behave with a little more decorum and try to stay half sober.'

It was a night though. They both agreed on that. Mercutio had arrived back at his quarters in the castle so late the soldiers hadn't wanted to let him in.

'Mind you,' he added. 'I wasn't the only chap out on the tiles. If there's anyone who needs reminding about his decorum it's Romeo. Where the hell is he? Went round his place first thing to see if he was all right. Seems he got home dead late, left right early. His mother's not best pleased. You know what I think?'

'I soon will,' Benvolio answered with a sigh.

'I reckon he was sniffing round that Rosaline after all. She's tormenting him. Driving the poor soul mad. That's the truth of it.'

The soldier left to put up another poster along the arcade. Mercutio read the order out loud, then groaned. 'Brilliant. That means we're stuck in this dump until some pompous civil servant in Venice decides otherwise. Shame. I was thinking of taking a break. Getting bad-tempered around here. There'll be blood on the cobbles if they keep people cooped up too long.'

Benvolio had been up early too, asking questions, seeking answers. There was an awkward, unpredictable air about the city he didn't like. As to the travel ban... he doubted that would last. Mozzecane had suffered an outbreak of infection two weeks before. No one had died. The illness seemed to have disappeared of its own will. The fatality that caused the authorities concern was probably, he thought, simply a re-emergence of that more benign ailment, perhaps affecting someone who was already frail.

'I've worse news. Old man Capulet's kicked out his nephew Tybalt. There was some kind of argument at the banquet last night. The little thug's roaming Verona saying he's going to take it out on Romeo for stepping through their door in the first place. He wants a fight. A duel. He left a note demanding it at Romeo's place this morning.'

'What?'

Benvolio pulled a letter out of his trousers. 'I managed to get hold of the thing before his parents saw.'

Mercutio groaned, wiped his sweating forehead, threw the cup to the ground and leaned against the stone buttress.

'What is it?' Benvolio wondered.

'What is it? Tybalt? Are you serious? Romeo's dead already. Even if that buxom whore Rosaline hasn't taken his life the Prince of Cats will do it for him. Ye gods…'

'They can't fight,' Benvolio said. 'It won't happen. Your uncle Escalus forbids it.'

'Sod that. You can't turn down a duel. Where's the honour? And Tybalt…'

'What of him?'

'If he looks like he's running away that's when you watch out. I've seen that evil bastard fight. He's short on skill but fast and dirty, as wicked as any fellow alive. I tell you. Romeo's a dead man. Unless he wants to take the coward's option and flee.'

Benvolio tapped a finger on the poster.

'Oh.' Mercutio slapped his cheek and winced. 'Forgot. In that case he'd best pick his shroud 'cos sure as anything he'll be wearing it before the day is out.' He stuck a finger in his ear and twirled it. 'Shame really. All that stupid poetry apart, I rather like him. And—'

Quiet, Benvolio ordered. There Romeo was, striding through the market as if looking for someone. He seemed bright and cheery. Nothing like the miserable, lovelorn creature of the day before. Benvolio waved. Romeo waved back then, as if this was a second thought, came over and shook their hands.

'Enjoy the party?' Mercutio wondered.

Romeo thought for a moment and said, 'Very much. Didn't we go through that last night?'

'Last night I was three sheets to the wind in case you didn't notice. Way things are going I'm planning to be in much the same state shortly. What with the news–'

'The plague,' Benvolio interrupted.

'And plenty else besides. I heard you didn't go home last night, Romeo. Went to bounce the mattress with Rosaline, did you? In the circumstances I hope so.'

Benvolio waved him into silence, and succeeded for once.

'No,' Romeo said. 'I didn't. I'd rather not–'

Mercutio wasn't even listening. He was looking back into the market where a large woman was pushing through the crowd towards them.

'Oh my God! Will you look at the face on that? She's coming over here by the look of it.' He nudged Romeo with his elbow. 'This isn't your new true love, is it, mate? I've got to say… the sight of her's doing my hangover no good whatsoever.'

The nurse saw him, then nodded and marched across. For the market she'd picked a long dress that looked as if it had been made out of coarse dyed sacking, with a white mob cap to cover her straggly grey hair.

'Stand in the shade, Missus,' Mercutio said the moment she turned up. 'Do the sun and the rest of us a favour. Perhaps we can find a bag for that head of yours.'

She turned a brief acerbic smile on him. Then said to Romeo, 'I like your friend, young Montague. He's funny, isn't he? May we have a quiet word?'

'A quiet word!' Mercutio cried. 'She's touting for custom. Ask if she's got a little sister, by little I mean a quarter her size. And don't pay much either 'cos you're following in the footsteps of an entire army. I'd put money on it.'

The woman marched up, grabbed his collar and shoved him hard against the wall. 'I've eaten up little minnows like you whole, sonny, then spat 'em out bones and all. Now bugger off out of here the pair of you. I've business with your better.'

'You're hurting my throat, Madam. Moreover we have news to impart to our dear friend Romeo.'

'Tell him later. Let's have a good old pinch at these instead.'

Her right hand fell clutching at his britches. A high-pitched scream followed, one that attracted some curious looks from the stalls beyond the arch.

'Cheerio, little fellow,' Nurse said, then let go with a final squeeze.

Mercutio yelped and took the hint. Benvolio touched his cap and followed him into the crowd.

'Nice company you keep, lover boy.'

'They're better for the knowing.'

'Well, I suspect I'm going to be denied that pleasure.' She folded her flabby arms and took a good look at him. 'So my young lady plans to dump a count, a nobleman with great holdings and a fine position, all for the likes of you?'

'It's her choice. I will make her happy.'

The woman didn't look convinced. 'If you're leading her up the garden path you'll have me to answer to. What I threatened for your friend I'll do to you for real. Then hand 'em back pickled. Juliet's my sweet girl. I've nursed her since she was tiny. Brightest, most beautiful young thing I've ever known and–'

'Lady, lady.'

She looked at him askance. 'I'm a servant. Don't lady me.'

'If Juliet sent you she loves you, too. You know her. Do you think she'd ask this lightly? That she's a foolish girl who'd send you here on a whim?'

'No.' She frowned. 'That lass is as bright as any creature alive.'

'Then if you can't trust me... trust her.' He took her leathery hand. 'We're meant for one another. All shall be well. Today we'll be married. Tonight, the houses of Capulet and Montague will be as one.'

She glanced around the market. 'My little girl thinks you have a good heart. As if that's all a man needs in this life.' There was the tramp of heavy feet, the clank of metal. A group of soldiers, chain metal jackets, swords by their sides, marched through the stalls pushing to one side everyone in their way. 'This town's in a funny mood. Weather's too hot. People too damned grouchy. Days like this that sun beats down on you forever and folk forget their manners. Rain, that's what we need. Only idiots are minded to riot or turn murderous when they're wet.' She leaned forward and bent towards his ear. 'You two must take care.'

'I will. As you've taken care of her since she was an infant.'

If this woman went back to the palazzo and reported ill of him to Luca Capulet there'd be no wedding, no future for either of them. Only a bleak loneliness for him, and chains for her.

'Speak of this to no one, I beg you. Tell Juliet to leave the house for confession this afternoon at two. I'll meet her at San Francesco al Corso. There we'll both confess... our love for one another. The friar will marry us. Tonight we'll be man and wife. Here...' He reached into his pocket and held out some coins. 'Take this for your pains.'

She scowled at him and didn't move a finger. 'Money? You think

I'm doing this for cash? Keep it! Truly. Not a penny. It's for my lovely girl's sake I come here.'

'This is nothing less than you deserve. You risk your master's displeasure.'

'I'm Luca Capulet's property. I risk that every day, with every breath I take.'

There was a brief sly shadow in her face. Then she seized the coins. 'You're right though. I am owed. I'll make sure she's there. This afternoon at San Francesco. You do your duty. I'll do mine.'

At last. A few hours and it would be done.

'Commend me to your mistress.'

'As if you need that. Count Paris... I'm warning you. He's a big important man. Maybe not as fetching as you but a lot more powerful. Bent on having her and he's the kind of fellow who likes getting what he wants. Juliet's father's with him, too.'

'Your point?'

The woman laughed at him. 'The young. You just don't see things, do you? I told Juliet straight before I came here. Paris is a better bet than you and always will be. Secure, rich, got houses here and there. That's what a wife needs. Love's a fine thing but it don't put bread on your table or fine dresses in your wardrobe.'

'I'll do that.'

The coins went into the pocket of her copious skirt. 'You'd better. What I'm saying is... take this lass of mine today or you've lost her. And maybe that'll be for the best. Let God decide. He usually does.'

The troop of infantrymen came back, feet stamping, swords slapping against chain mail. Some of the market men were yelling at them for interrupting their trade. Romeo thought about what she'd said: rain would be welcome. The day was too hot and feverish. A thunderstorm might be on the way, one brief cataclysm and then relief.

The woman turned to go. He reached out and stopped her.

'Madam. I beg you. Don't betray us.'

There was a sudden vicious look in her beady eyes.

'Don't betray yourself, lad,' she snapped back. 'That seems more likely to me.'

'I didn't mean to—'

'Farewell then. I'll commend you to my lady as you asked.'

She waddled off, pushing people out of the way as easily as the burly infantrymen.

On the far side of the Piazza Erbe he saw a hand waving. Benvolio and Mercutio were there, by a stall that sold bread and meat and beer.

The Torre dei Lamberti chimed noon. Two hours to waste. He couldn't face going home, trying to avoid the inquisitive questions there. His father was an easy-going man in most things, provided they didn't involve the Capulets. His mother never would let go.

So he wandered out into the piazza and felt the sudden harsh heat of the sun fall upon him like a furnace newly opened.

* * *

'Love,' Mercutio said, munching on a rib of pork as Romeo turned up. 'I do know what it is. The beastly thing explains my present plight.'

Benvolio knew he was supposed to ask. 'Your present plight being?'

'Stuck between heaven and hell wondering which way Queen Mab's going to drag me.'

Tell us then, Romeo said, and Mercutio did. Of a Venetian girl called Filomena Mocenigo who lived in a palace on the Grand Canal.

He was a student of navigation, destined for the Republic's merchant fleet, spending hours among the charts in the nautical college next door in Dorsoduro. The pair of them flirted then fell in love. A chaste romance soon turned into a secret, passionate affair conducted behind the closed curtains of gondola cabins and in the gardens of any mansion or convent they could enter of an evening.

'She had these sparkling eyes that never left you. Long dark hair. A face like an angel. Voice, too, sweet and high. The most perfect princess. I'll never see a lovelier pair of tits in my life.'

With a miserable grunt he threw the pork bone into the gutter. A few puffs of black cloud had appeared in the July sky.

Benvolio knew he wanted the obvious question: what happened?

With a laugh Mercutio looked at the two of them. 'Provincial boys. You haven't a clue. Think this little vendetta between Capulets and Montagues is something? In Venice we do things proper. Wasn't that long ago we chopped off the head of the Doge himself, on the stairs of his palace, just for getting up the snouts of the wrong folk in town. Hanged ten of his pals out in Saint Mark's Square, britches down around their ankles–'

'What happened?' Romeo repeated, feeling the minutes pass like hours.

'Answer's there in the name. Mocenigo. Venice has got the Golden Book. If you're noble enough to be in it – and the Mocenigo lot surely are – you've won a ticket for everything. Government. Money. Trade. And you marry within your own circle, don't you? If you didn't you'd have all that nasty common blood circulating round your precious veins. My lot used to be fishermen until they signed up to lose life and limb for the Doge's navy. Our sort aren't supposed to dally with the aristocracy. I was lucky to get off with a whipping.'

Romeo had to ask. 'What happened to Filomena?'

'They locked her in a nunnery in Murano. Couldn't marry the girl any more, could they? Spoiled goods. A common lad had been there. Didn't matter that most of the eligible gents who'd likely be her husband had mistresses all the way from the Rialto to the Arsenale. And weren't above stopping off at the whorehouses in San Barnaba when they felt like it.' He raised his cup of beer. 'That's when I first met Queen Mab, you see. Just when you think you've got somewhere. When you've fooled yourself life's about to become one big bed of roses. Then that little fairy waits her moment, comes out like an earwig in a bowl of cherries and chuckles... more fool you.'

He raised his cup to them. 'Cheers! Here's to the plague. At least the pox is honest. Oh, I meant to ask, Romeo. Talking of flowers... what sort do you want?'

'Flowers?'

'For your coffin. You do know, don't you? I thought that fat old boot had come to bring the news.'

Benvolio stepped in and told him: Tybalt had been going about town making threats. He'd left a letter for Romeo at the Montague palazzo, a formal demand for a duel.

'I managed to retrieve it from that servant of yours, Balthazar, this morning. Before your parents saw it. He seems a good lad.'

'He is,' Romeo murmured.

'Sorry to say it, old chap, but my money's on Tybalt.' Mercutio took another swig of beer. 'God, I feel dreadful. This bloody hangover's getting worse—'

'Leave the ale alone then,' Benvolio told him.

He grinned and raised the cup. 'Beer's the cause and beer's the cure. You could rush off and get a fencing master to top you up with a few quick lessons. Maybe give you half a chance. But he's a foul and dirty bugger I'm telling you. Doesn't play by any rules from what I've seen.'

'I'm not fighting him!'

Mercutio stared at him, speechless.

'There are good reasons.'

'You mean you're fearful? If it's that come out and say it. Don't beat about the bush.'

'There are good reasons! I can't...' He wanted out of here. Some peace. Time to think. 'I can't say more.'

Mercutio came up and prodded his chest. His breath stank of ale and meat. 'You don't need to. A man has challenged you to combat. Honour demands you meet him. Either that or crawl off into a corner somewhere and don't bother me again. I'm not in the habit of hanging around with cowards.'

Benvolio intervened. He looked angry for once. 'We were there, too. If Tybalt's got a beef it's as much with us as him.'

'It's Romeo he's picked. You've got to face him. Or you might as well piss off out of Verona the moment they lift the locks on those damned gates. That's it.' He threw up his arms. 'I'm done with this nonsense. Another ale I reckon and maybe a spot more grub...'

He lurched off towards the bar. Romeo closed his eyes.

'Ignore him,' Benvolio advised.

'Mercutio? Or Tybalt?'

'Both.' Benvolio looked at the sky. 'This will blow over. Just like the weather. It's nothing. Go home. Keep out of sight. Escalus will deal with Tybalt if he keeps roaring round town looking for a fight like this.'

Good advice, Romeo thought, and shook his cousin's hand.

He walked away from the piazza and the crowds, down to the

arena. The quacks were out in force around the colonnades, selling the usual plague remedies to the gullible: holy relics, tin crucifixes touted as silver, bunches of herbs to hang around the neck on a piece of string. And potions in bottles, some like those he'd seen in Laurence's cell that morning, a few in strange shapes supposed to pass a little magic to their contents.

He bought two bunches of rosemary and lavender, prettily tied together on a slender plait of straw. A dumb woman was making them, advertising her lack of a tongue. A sign next to her said this was not punishment for a crime but the work of a cruel and faithless husband. Romeo didn't believe the herbs she sold would work for a moment. Or even her story. But she was poor and he had money. That was all he needed to know.

After this he walked down to the stretch of river that adjoined San Francesco al Corso and found shade beneath a scrappy elder bush, not far from the cemetery. He could see the modest monastery portico from where he sat, a lone friar tending the flowers there. The Adige was quiet, no barges, no cormorant fishermen now, just squabbling ducks and the occasional rise of a trout. Perhaps the soldiers of Escalus placed orders upon the water too. A brave man might enter Verona – or escape it – by swimming across the river. But it was broad and swift-moving, with weirs that had taken lives in the past. Like this, the city was a castle under an invisible siege, barred to everyone without. A prison for those within. There was no way he and Juliet could escape their furious parents by this or any other route. Once wed they would have to face them and take the consequences.

A different bell from another campanile tolled somewhere, higher in tone than that of the Torre dei Lamberti.

One hour, the minutes trudging past. All around him time moved the way it wanted, in the steady flow of the river, the scorching sun edging across the brilliant sky. He saw now that the patch of countryside opposite was the grove of plane trees where, the morning before, he'd wandered in misery, thinking only of Rosaline. In a single day his life had changed, from false love to true, from the dreamily disconsolate state of youth to the awkward, half-knowing condition of adulthood. Before, he'd been dejected over stupid, selfish cares. Now he was worried – frightened if he were honest – for another, one more dear to him than any he'd ever known.

Which was better? Which worse? It seemed an idle question. Time had made it so. Queen Mab, who'd so brutally robbed Mercutio of his happiness, had decided that. In her fairy grasp lay joy and passion, but death and misery, too.

As for Tybalt... He decided he'd think nothing of him at all. This was a time for love and reconciliation, not violence on Verona's streets.

He pulled out the two straw necklaces with their bunches of herbs. It was ridiculous to believe a few dried leaves would save a single soul. They were an act of charity, an offering for an auspicious future, the kind men made to the old gods once upon a time.

A prayer, he thought. Friar Laurence would have one. Something quiet and beautiful and appropriate. Perhaps there was a poem, too. But Romeo could think of neither. So he walked to the river bank and launched both plague necklaces into the bright air, watching the busy water take them, rolling and turning till they vanished downstream.

* * *

Juliet waited until the house was quiet then tiptoed down the stairs, Nurse trying hard to do the same three steps behind. By the side door they crept out into the yard only to walk straight into her mother talking to one of the stable hands.

Her dress was the same as that morning. Just a simple felt hat and a bible in her hands were new.

'Where are you going?'

'To confession. I fear I've caused you all pain.'

Bianca Capulet sighed and shook her head. 'That's very thoughtful, love. But really… this isn't a problem for priests. A friendly word with your father–'

'That will come. I promise. And soon.'

Her mother's eyes fell on the large woman standing in the shadows. 'Two of you for confession then?'

'Been a long time, my lady. Big old chest I've got here and there's plenty it wants rid of.'

Everything hung in the balance. One word, a simple 'No' and then what? Could she stride out anyway in defiance? And what hope would there be of reconciliation after that?'

'Go on then,' her mother said, with a nod towards the gate. 'It's time for laughter in this house not angry voices.'

Juliet grinned and thanked her. Then they walked south to the ruined Roman gate of the Porta Leoni, a relic from another age, now attached to the blind brick side of a recent house like a mask set upon a dead face.

'I was getting a bit worried there,' Nurse said, as they marched along.

'God is with us,' Juliet replied happily.

'I truly hope so, little one. Do you love this Romeo?'

'Of course! What a question.'

'Hardly know him, do you? But I guess he'll get you out of the clutches of Count Paris.'

This was too close. 'I don't know what you mean. We've lots in common.'

'He seems a nice lad. Good looking. This whole escapade's a mad thing. Mind, what's the point of life if it's boring? That man above didn't put us on this earth to twiddle our thumbs. He needs something to gawp and laugh at, too. Did I ever tell you about my uncle Felix and his goats?'

Juliet smiled, said nothing, crossed the street and walked into the drab and ill-lit alley that bore the lion's name. They'd hardly taken ten steps when, in the gloom, they bumped straight into three youths dressed in black, sneers on their pinched faces, legs out, shoulders too, making sure they blocked the way.

'Well, if it isn't my dearest cousin,' Tybalt hissed and put a gloved hand straight to Juliet's throat. 'How goes it in the palazzo of the Capulets? I am barred from there, it seems. Your father no longer favours his dead brother's son.'

'Get your hands off my lady, you little villain!' Nurse yelled as the other two held her back.

Juliet knew that pair. Foul-mouthed, troublesome thugs from the tenebrous grim arcades called Sottoriva behind Sant'Anastasia. Petruchio and Lorenzo.

She looked Tybalt boldly in the face. 'You will leave us both alone. You and your cronies. Or, by God, my father's wrath will be upon you even further.'

'You've a pretty look about you. Soft skin too. The rest isn't bad. I know...' He grinned, coming closer. 'I spy on you when you bathe. There's nothing I haven't seen.'

'When… my… father hears…'

'Then I'll say you made it up. You're a born liar, cousin. Everyone knows.' Tybalt laughed and let his grip grow loose around her neck. 'Besides… the old fool's kicked me out anyway. What else can he do?' The hand came back, suddenly tighter, pushing her so hard against the dank brick wall her breath caught. 'You stuck-up little bitch. He's only in this foul mood because you won't marry that bastard Paris and open wide your legs–'

She slapped him then, hard and fast across the cheek. His hand left her throat, went to his belt. A dagger sat there, and something else, small and thin, like a giant, gleaming pin, a stiletto half-hidden beside the long rapier that lay against his thigh.

Juliet laughed at the sight. 'Three blades you require, then. You must be truly lacking in other quarters.'

The weapons stayed where they were. His face came up, teeth bared, eyes white. 'I just need one to take a life. Especially a little thing like yours.'

'Tybalt,' Nurse yelled. 'Get you and your mates out of here before I scream the houses down and bring all the guards Escalus has about your stupid ears.'

She didn't wait but began to bawl. The loudest scream Juliet had ever heard.

'Murder, murder! Assistance, citizens, for there be villains out to kill us. Fetch Escalus and his men. Murder. *Murder…*'

Windows opened down the alley, curious faces peered round the sunny corner at the end. Petruchio took fright first. Between the woman's cries he said, 'Escalus promised he'd hang anyone who broke the peace. I'm not getting strung up for this old bag and a scraggy girl we haven't got our hands on.'

With that he took swiftly to his heels.

Around the corner bright shapes came, the sun gleaming on their armour. Soldiers. Lorenzo went next, scampering in the opposite direction. Tybalt stayed, looked Juliet in the eye.

'I'm taking someone's life before this day's out. Come what may. I'll do your father a favour and put one of his vile enemies in the grave. The way I should've done last night if he'd had the sense to let me. Then I'll be back in his good books, you watch. And when I'm in the house again perhaps you and me should have another little private talk. While you bathe, lady...'

His hand rose swiftly, found her breast, tweaked the nipple hard between thumb and forefinger. She would have cried with pain but refused to give him comfort.

'Yer bloody louts!' a soldier cried, dashing towards them. 'What game is this?'

'A deadly one,' Tybalt whispered then, catlike, slid away into the shadows.

Late as ever the guards arrived, breathless and panting in their heavy armour. The day seemed hotter, closer, the air stale and full of threat.

'Villains the lot of them,' Nurse said, adding a few choice peasant words, too. 'Nice of you to turn up though, gentlemen. Eventually. You lot ever caught anything except a bloody cold?'

Juliet got her breath back, thinking quickly. This was no time for petty complaints or arguments with soldiers.

'You know them little snakes?' the sergeant asked.

'Not me,' Nurse said.

Juliet shook her head. 'I wish I did, sir. Then I'd give you their names. But sadly...'

He didn't look too disappointed. 'Pretty girls like you shouldn't walk down narrow and shady lanes like this, love. This city's up for trouble at the moment. What with this boiling hot weather and all the rest. Stay out where folk can see you.' He nodded at Nurse. 'Even with your pet dragon in tow these streets aren't safe right now.'

The big woman grinned and made a mock salute. Even so, the soldiers saw them to the open road at the foot of the lane, and then to the footpath by the river bank.

'That Tybalt's an evil little sod,' Nurse said when they left. 'Are you all right, love?'

'I couldn't be better.'

There he was, just a hundred yards ahead, waving his cap. She raised her arms. Romeo ran along the river bank, grinning, shouting. Then reached her, breathless. Trying to find the words.

'I always thought my little girl would have the biggest, fanciest wedding,' Nurse said, watching the two of them. 'Portraits by a famous painter. Presents. Lots of people. All the best food and drink from everywhere.'

'Don't want it,' Juliet whispered. Romeo took the hint and kissed her. 'Any of it.'

'No,' he agreed. 'We've everything we need. More than that.'

By the banks of the Adige they embraced. Hand-in-hand, the large old woman waddling behind singing a risqué wedding song from Garda, Juliet and her Romeo walked into the monastery of San Francesco al Corso and headed for Friar Laurence's shady cell.

* * *

They asked Nurse to stay outside.

'This is for us alone,' Juliet said. 'In case something… goes wrong. Best you weren't a witness.'

'I'm not frightened!'

'I know. But all the same…'

'I wish you two lovers all the best. You know that.'

Juliet hugged her. Then they went into the dark cell. It was cool and welcoming, like a cave almost, a true sanctuary from the world beyond. There was a bible on the table along with a contract for the two of them written in Laurence's careful, cultured hand.

He bade them sit and poured three cups of water fresh from the monastery spring. It was so cold it tasted of winter: a time of ice and snow when Verona cosseted itself in warm wool and waited for the flowers to bloom again. Then Laurence sat back in his chair and gazed at them.

Romeo shrugged and said, 'You told me you'd have questions.'

'I do.'

'Then what?'

'Just the obvious. You're asking for the blessing of the Church. Of God himself. Yet where's the proof of love?'

'The proof of love!' Juliet cried. 'Where's the proof of God then? I mean really–'

'Laurence,' Romeo interrupted quickly. 'We're certain in our own minds. What do you want?'

'Tell me why you love one another.'

Juliet sighed again. 'Why? There's a why to this?'

'I have to ask…'

'We…' Romeo was struggling. 'We understand.'

Juliet linked her arm through Romeo's. 'Very well. Why? He makes me laugh. He makes me feel I have a friend at last. And when I tease him—'

'Which happens quite a lot actually,' he interjected.

She grinned. 'He doesn't get cross at all.'

'Because I deserve it mostly. And it's said with such sweet humour.'

'All the same...' Laurence said. 'No witnesses. No loving parents. Even if I do as you ask any lawyer could unravel the thing in an hour. You understand what I mean?'

'No,' Romeo admitted.

Juliet squeezed his arm. 'He means it's not a proper wedding. If our parents take against us—'

Laurence nodded. 'They could dismiss it. As easily as they might tear up any contract written in haste.'

'Then,' said Romeo, 'we'll convince them. And marry again, the way they want, with all that pomp and finery. In Sant'Anastasia. Saint Peter's itself, if they like.'

'And if they hate us,' Juliet added, 'we'll take ourselves from their presence and live as best we can.'

'As paupers? You're the offspring of rich merchants. Do you have any idea what that means?'

Romeo held her hand. 'If we're together we're never poor.'

'Never,' she agreed. 'Can you not see, Friar?'

'I see... two young people who are deeply fond of one another. But marriage is for life...'

'For life is how we want it,' Romeo insisted.

'No other way,' she said. 'Here we are. Risking the anger, the rejection of both our families. Knowing that tonight we may be embraced by them or back in this quiet and generous place begging for charity. Is that not enough?'

'Perhaps,' Laurence said in his gentle cleric's voice. 'I've married many couples in my time. Sudden passions may seem sweet at first. One thing I've learned. The love that lasts is the love that's slow and moderate. It's the gentle touch of a close and tender bond. The fire and fury of quick passion burn like a forest blaze caught in the fierce wind. A quiet consolation on the other hand—'

Juliet picked up the contract. 'Then let us speak these vows. Marry us and have done with it. Afterwards I'll return to my family, Romeo to his. Tonight we'll meet and tell them all. Show them what we have together. Then take the consequences whatever they may be.'

'And if I refuse?'

'You won't,' Romeo cut in. 'You're a kind man. If we walk out of here unwed our futures will be shaped by others. You told me you were a slave once. You wouldn't wish that on another.'

The friar clapped his hands. 'You are a persuasive pair. And I am in the mood to be a romantic fool. I hope the Lord smiles on all three of us. The ring?'

Romeo squirmed. 'We have no ring.'

'No friends? No witnesses? No ring? Just a weary old friar and his bible. I tell you both again. If your parents should take against this match they'll annul it in an instant.'

'So you told us,' she said, impatiently.

'Then all that's left is for you to accept these vows.'

He picked up a piece of parchment, old script upon it, the page well-thumbed from use. In the cool cell, his hand trembling a little, Laurence read. 'Will you, Romeo of the House of Montague, have this woman to be your wedded wife, to live together after God's ordinance in the holy estate of matrimony? Will you love her, comfort her, honour and keep her, in sickness and in health; and forsaking all others, keep you only unto her, so long as you both shall live?'

Her fingers clasped his, Romeo beamed at Juliet and said, 'With every breath in my body, with everything I own. Yes. Yes. A thousand times yes. A thousand thousand–'

Laurence looked over the top of the page. 'One suffices. This is a wedding not a poetry reading.'

'Here, here,' Juliet agreed.

'Juliet of the House of Capulet. Will you have this man to be your wedded husband, to live together after God's ordinance in the holy estate of matrimony? Will you obey and serve him–'

Her fingers unwound from Romeo's and she tapped the paper. 'I don't wish to appear pedantic. But unless I'm mistaken I didn't hear anything in Romeo's vow about obedience. Or servitude.'

Laurence stared at her. 'It says "obey" and "serve".'

She sucked a quick breath through her teeth and squinted at him. 'Same thing really, isn't it?'

'They're just words. Very old words.'

'Words that weren't in the other vow. I was only wondering… perhaps it's a mistake or something…'

Laurence showed her the paper and its two different versions, one for the groom, the other for the bride.

Romeo held up a hopeful finger. 'I'm happy to obey. And serve. Joyfully, with all my heart. We can go back to my vow and put obedience and servitude in there.'

'No, no!' Laurence cried. 'It's a ritual. A ceremony. The words don't matter. It's how you feel. For pity's sake all you need do is sign the piece of paper and you're married. You two surely need no vows at all.'

Juliet went to the table, took up the quill, dipped it in the inkwell, found the place at the bottom of page and scribbled her name there. Then she came back, grinning from ear to ear, and took Romeo's hand again. 'Dearest husband. I will love, honour, and keep you in sickness and in health; and, forsaking all others, keep only unto you, so long as we both shall live. And thinking about it I'd rather I died before you because the idea of a world alone is too much really—'

'No, no, love! Me surely. I go first for I couldn't bear to be without—'

'At the risk of repeating myself,' Laurence snapped, 'this is a *wedding*. Or supposed to be. May we leave all discussion of funeral plans for another occasion?'

'I think we're finished now, aren't we?' Juliet asked.

'Almost, thank goodness.'

Laurence gestured at the table. Romeo scribbled his name on the contract.

'You may kiss now, the two of you. Tenderly and not too eager, please. This is a holy place after all.'

They didn't seem to hear. Or, if they did, took no notice. Laurence sighed and went to his case of bottles. The one he wanted was near the top, a small dark vessel sealed with a cork. He found it, blew off the dust, retrieved a box of sweet biscuits bought that morning then scrabbled among his tools for a corkscrew little used of late. When he returned they were hand-in-hand, damp-eyed and delirious.

'Man and wife,' he declared. 'Now that's done, let's drink a well-earned toast.'

It was the oldest, most precious vintage he had. Vin santo, holy wine from Tuscany, made from a harvest dried on hurdles set above the ground then fermented slowly and stored. Ten years old this was. Sweet as honey and much the same colour.

'The grape's Malvasia,' he pointed out. 'Not Garganega or Trebbiano. So I sit in the middle of your two warring houses and pray with this ceremony those pointless battles may be over.'

He poured three glasses, then raised his own.

'*Salute*, my young lovers. May you both live long and happy lives beneath the gaze of God.' It was a year or two since he'd had strong drink. The vin santo nearly made him cough but it tasted wonderful. 'And thank you for the oddest and most congenial wedding I've conducted in many a long year.'

Juliet came and kissed him on the cheek.

'Wipe away the traces of your tears, child,' the friar said. 'This is a time to be happy. And pass your joy on to our bleak world.'

'We will, Father. We promise.'

'Ah, we all make promises. It's what others do that breaks them.'

The two embraced once more and asked a few simple questions. Who kept the contract? What else, if anything did they need to do?

Love one another, he said. It seemed such a straightforward notion. Yet the truth of it was as broad and complex as humanity itself and, at times, just as difficult to explain.

They left then. Romeo would see her safely to the street near the Capulet palazzo. After that he would return to his own home and plan for the momentous evening.

Friar Laurence watched them go, waving as they walked towards the portico gate, wondering what he'd done. Men and women were more unpredictable than the herbs he tended daily. They were still swift to bloom and flourish, and quick to wither, even to die for no good reason. This wedding of theirs had happened with the best of intentions. That, at least, was a start, and a start was all a humble friar could offer.

Across the perfect blue horizon, against the bare peaks of the lower Alps, a band of black clouds was growing. Another line from Virgil came to him as he watched the couple stride across the monastery's short, well-tended lawn.

Latet anguis in herba.

In the grass there lurks a snake.

They're always there, he told himself, watching the two young figures go arm-in-arm through the gate, only to unwind themselves once the street was near.

Serpents.

Hiding. Waiting. A man might stamp them out. If only he could see them.

* * *

Benvolio stayed with Mercutio, worried that his friend was heading for more trouble. He kept drinking, moaning, getting more and more ill-tempered by the minute. Verona matched his mood. The soldiers were everywhere, harrying people going about their ordinary business, telling them to go home and stay inside. Picking on the hawkers who'd crawled out of the woodwork, selling plague cures in place of the trinkets and fake relics they usually traded.

All the while the afternoon got hotter, more humid, heavier, until it felt as if the angry sky, leaden now with thunder clouds, bore down on them with every step. Finally they stopped, not far from the Porta Leoni where Juliet had met her furious cousin earlier. Mercutio sipped wine from the flask on his hip.

'Enough drink. Let me take you home,' Benvolio begged. 'These streets are too hot to be outside. There are Capulets abroad looking for a fight. On days like this the blood of the mildest man starts to stir. Even—'

Mercutio laughed. 'Even you? The mild and gentle Benvolio. We've both had our share of brawls. You're no saint. Not a one among us is.'

It was true. But that was a while back. Life, it seemed to Benvolio, came in stages. Young and innocent child. Angry, baffled, bewildered adolescent. Then the quiet, perhaps cowardly acquiescence that came with age. Men called it maturity. It wasn't that really. Just the dull acceptance of one's fate.

'I've seen you lose your rag, Benvolio. Don't make out you're any different from the rest of us. Just because you're off to university, all ready to become a lawyer. What do your lot call it? When you get a deed to something?'

'The fee simple, you mean.'

'That's it. What's the fee simple worth for your life? Or mine? Any of us stuck in this crappy town waiting on the plague? Or Tybalt with his sharp blade? In the end we're all just fodder for worms. Dust in a coffin going rotten.'

Benvolio shrugged his shoulders and wondered whether it was worth pointing out that Romeo was the one heading for a lawyer's trade. It was medicine for him. But he decided it wasn't worth it. Pretty soon he'd abandon Mercutio to these grim dark lanes. There seemed little purpose in trying to save one so determined not to save himself.

'Fee simple?' Mercutio muttered, chucking his cup of beer in the gutter. 'Only simple thing around here's you, mate. And me. We're bloody mugs and—'

There was a distant rumble of baritone thunder from the lowering sky. A few drops of rain dotted the worn cobbles around them. Across the street, emerging from the Via Leoncino, came three dark figures, scarlet feathers in their caps: Tybalt, Petruchio and Lorenzo.

Mercutio rubbed his hands with glee. 'Finally this day changes for the better. Here they come. The ugliest buggers the Capulet tribe have got to offer.'

Tybalt and his fellow thugs still hadn't seen them.

'Let's just leave it,' Benvolio said. 'They haven't spotted us. Turn round. I'll walk with you back to the castle.'

Mercutio grinned. For a moment it seemed as if this quiet retreat might happen. But like everything else it was a trick. He dodged Benvolio's arm, walked out into the light, put his fingers in his mouth, let out a loud and piercing whistle and waved. Tybalt and his peers stopped straight away and looked across the lane.

Out of the corner of his eye Benvolio caught sight of Romeo walking down the broader street from the direction of the Capulet mansion, straight towards them, smiling, as if in a daydream.

'Leave this to me,' Tybalt told his cronies, then marched jauntily across, hands in britches, grinning.

'Look what the stinking cats have dragged in,' Mercutio yelled as he approached. 'Their smelly little monarch, stinking of piss like all his creatures.'

Tybalt winked and tipped his cap. 'Good afternoon, sir. A word with one of you.'

A tap on the blade that sat upon his hip and Mercutio said, 'A word? Is that all I get from a Capulet? I'd hoped you'd pluck up the courage for a strike at the very least.'

The smirk on Tybalt's face vanished. 'I'll happily provide that if you want it, friend. You consort with that Montague villain, Romeo?'

'Consort?' Mercutio laughed out loud and slapped his sides. 'God the words you stuck-up little-town prats use. *Consort?* What are we, mate? Minstrels? Is that a lute sitting on my hip then? You want to see me play it?'

Benvolio stepped between them, one arm out to each. 'This is a public place. Soldiers all around us. You know what Escalus said. He'd hang...'

Mercutio pushed him out of the way. 'I'll hang myself rather than turn my back on this piece of shit. Don't need my uncle to do it for me.'

'Then remove yourselves to a private place and reason this out there. Mercutio. Tybalt. Take your dispute elsewhere. Go now. Here all eyes are on us and... and...'

Romeo had reached them, still smiling, puzzled by the scene. Tybalt lost interest in Mercutio immediately.

'Good day.' He beamed and tipped his hat again. 'If it isn't my man–'

'He's not your man,' Mercutio roared. 'I am, scumbag. Talk to me.'

But Tybalt didn't. 'Greetings, Montague. The affection I bear for you means I can think of no better term than this. You're a low villain. A coward. A thief who sneaks into the homes of better men to steal their food and wine and–'

Romeo's good mood vanished. He looked around him. Tybalt's little gang watching from the alley, a few curious spectators gathering, knowing what was on the way.

Calmly he said, 'The affection I bear for you is real, Tybalt, and puts aside all your adolescent insults. I'm no villain. No coward. No thief. All this I excuse. You do not know me. Perhaps tonight you shall–'

Tybalt moved back, drawing his rapier. 'Tonight? No, thief. Now.

You will not run. All the injuries you've done me. My uncle. Draw
your weapon and let's have done with this.'

'With what? I have never injured you.'

'I'm a stranger in my own household. Rejected by my family.'

Romeo shook his head. 'That I'm sorry to hear. But it was not at
my bidding. Believe me... the name Capulet is as precious to me as
it is to you. Perhaps more so.' He turned and waved the youth away.
'I bid you good afternoon, Tybalt. Tonight we should talk more of
this and make our peace.'

Two steps he'd taken before Mercutio moved, blade out, the
bright length of it sweeping the steamy air. 'If you won't have this
worthless rat, I will. Up Tybalt! Stand firm. I'll fight you if he's too
yellow.'

He was swaying. Half-drunk. Tybalt looked at him, head to toe,
amused. 'You're sure of that. Or is it the drink I hear?'

Mercutio's rapier cut a lazy circle in front of his face. A duel was a
duel. There were rules. No man started until the other agreed. 'The
Prince of Cats! I'll start with the first of your nine lives and deal with
the rest right after.'

'Up then!' Tybalt cried.

A clash of blades. Their hands met, faces taut with rage, teeth bared.

'Scared now, aren't you?' Mercutio bawled, spit flying with his
words.

Tybalt pushed him back. The rapiers rose. Romeo walked between
them from one side. Benvolio from the other. Tybalt's meeker
companions stayed back as the crowd gathered to watch the growing
brawl.

'This is done,' Romeo shouted. 'Put up your swords. Mercutio. Do
as I ask.'

'Both of you,' Benvolio urged.

Tybalt pushed past. The long slim blades met again.

'Stop this!' Romeo yelled. He wound his arms round Mercutio, back to Tybalt, daring him to strike a spineless blow. 'For shame. Heed your uncle's words, friend. He said no fighting in these streets on pain of death.'

'What pain is there in death?' Mercutio cried, tight in Romeo's arms. 'With that crowing scoundrel marching round this place like he owns it? Ah–?'

There was a clap of thunder, close. Then more spots of rain. In the confusion Romeo felt a sudden push, saw a glimpse of something slender and sharp, like a pin grown large and deadly.

'And now we go,' Tybalt cried, pulling back quickly. When Romeo turned the three of them were dashing, almost running, north towards the fish market and Sant'Anastasia.

Another peal of thunder, closer now, and fat spots of warm, slow rain.

Benvolio was looking round, worried. The soldiers would surely hear of this. Whether it was enough to bring down the wrath of Escalus...

'A spot,' Mercutio muttered, holding out his fingers. 'I feel a spot.'

Romeo took his hands away from his chest then looked at his own outstretched palms. The rain was on them, mixed with blood.

The pin. The long and deadly pin.

It all came clear at that moment. While Romeo gripped his friend trying to keep him from the duel, Tybalt had stolen round with his long stiletto, taken a sly stab at the gap between jerkin and britches, hard into his side.

'I am hurt,' Mercutio whispered, then stumbled to the wall, head up to the darkening sky, eyes wide open, shocked. 'I am hurt. I am hurt and Tybalt walks scot free.'

The two of them came close and looked. There was a stain starting on his tunic around the waist.

'Oh,' he groaned and slid down the wall to the damp cobbles, clutching at his waist. 'Fetch me a servant, villains. Fetch me–'

Romeo knelt down and looked for the wound. 'I can't see anything. How bad–?'

'Christ! It's just a scratch, mate!' Mercutio cried. 'What do you think? A plague on both your bloody houses. Capulet and Montague. I had him, Romeo. Why come between us? He got his little damned stiletto out and... *Oh!*'

His head fell to one side. The storm burst. A downpour fell upon them like a sudden rush from heaven.

'Fetch me a good coffin and a quick hearse,' Mercutio said, so softly they could barely hear over the thunder. 'For I am–'

His mouth fell open. His fingers dropped from his waist. A torrent of blood, as fast and free as the rain, gushed on to the black stones. As black, as dead as Mercutio's eyes.

'This is my fault,' Romeo whispered. Benvolio's hand came to rest on his sodden shoulder.

'It isn't. It's Tybalt's. He did this. Leave him to Escalus and–'

Romeo got up and felt for the sword on his belt. 'This is my fault. Mercutio was protecting the honour I refused to defend. And now he's dead.'

Benvolio stood before him. The sky was dimming so rapidly it looked as if night was descending on the city, with rolls of thunder coming thick and fast. 'I will hold you back as you did Mercutio.'

'With the same result? No. Love has done this to me–'

'What?'

'Love has made me weak and like a woman. Softened what courage I had.'

He pushed Benvolio out of the way and withdrew his blade. So many fencing lessons he'd had, forced on him by his father. Still, he could fight. Could find a cold fury in him too, when needed.

'This day's black deed shapes what's to come. Tybalt may start the misery but I shall end it.'

'Romeo!'

'Keep clear from me, friend. What happens now lies on my account alone.'

Blade out he edged his way through the crowd. Close to the route Tybalt must have taken he grabbed a youth nearby and held him by the throat, rapier next to his cheek.

'Where did he go? Tell me or I swear I'll—'

'Two of them ran off to the bridge!' The kid had bright and frightened eyes. 'Don't hurt me. I didn't do anything.'

'*Tybalt?*'

'I heard him say he was off to hide in Sottoriva down among the whores. Plenty of shady places for his kind there.'

The sky boomed. The clouds overhead seemed solid black, so close it felt as if they might fall and swamp the streets themselves.

Rapier in hand, Romeo set up a steady pace and headed north.

* * *

Sottoriva.

'Below the shore' the name meant. It was a dark arcade of tenements that ran beneath the Adige bank from the fish market to the walls of Sant'Anastasia. Whores and vagabonds and a few impoverished pedlars populated these grim and rotting buildings festering like a hidden sore set apart from Verona's grander quarters.

By this time rain ran everywhere, writhing deep rivulets both sides of the cobbles, a filthy grey torrent of muck and mud and worse. Figures dodged beneath the low colonnades, hiding from the weather and much else besides.

Romeo raced through the torrent like a madman. The rain had plastered his hair to his skull, his clothes to his body. Both sides of Sottoriva he worked, bellowing Tybalt's name. Eyes glinted fearfully back at him from the shadows of the mean arcades where the flood waters of the storm bucketed from door to door.

There was a low, yellow light in the darkness to the left, in the colonnade on the city side. It was a shrine. A small statue of the Virgin sat inside a miniature portico of the kind the Romans might have built. Fresh flowers, even in this grim place, were set by the grille. Wild ones, he saw, as he got closer. No man or woman here could afford to buy better.

Candles burned by the image, though, and someone had paid for them. The dim light they cast began to stir something in him. The promise that even in the darkest, most inhospitable of moments there might be the faintest prospect of grace.

Then a voice came out of the shadows one door along and he was back in the day again, the red fire burning, hating.

'Run away, Montague,' Tybalt called, a hazy shape by the smoke-stained pillars. 'You did it once already. Follow your nature, coward. Be gone from here or meet your fate.'

The water here was thick and deep. It swilled around his ankles as cold as the tomb and stinking of humanity. As his eyes adjusted he saw they were near the end of the colonnades. The brown brick wall of Sant'Anastasia stood out in the open at the end. Not far away was the piazza before the church. An open space, back in the city proper.

'My friend's dead, Tybalt. Your cowardly blade took his life. One subtle stab while I held him from your grip.'

A laugh. 'You helped me. I give you thanks for that. But death only if you come on.'

Then he stepped out of a doorway ahead. Soaked to the skin like Romeo, blade out, ready to fight. The Virgin watched with blind stone eyes.

'Now,' Tybalt yelled and was at him, rapier flashing, left hand behind his back, a classic stance. Romeo parried, thrust at him in return. These lessons had been drummed into him by a master from Padua. Hour after hour they'd spent practising by the grey river, in the hot mornings of August, the freezing afternoons of January.

The words of the man came back to him.

Fight through instinct. Only dead men think.

So he didn't. He feinted, parried, let Tybalt expend his sudden fury and energy as they tramped through the ankle-deep water like two lone hateful soldiers stranded at low tide.

Four times Tybalt came at him. Four times Romeo fended him off.

The swordmaster's advice was easier said than followed. Romeo couldn't help it, couldn't thrust from his memory that beautiful moment in Laurence's cell. Their clasped fingers, their love shared.

Tybalt retreated and scuttled round the corner, stopping on the gleaming rain-soaked cobblestones outside the façade of Sant'Anastasia. There were people close by. Witnesses. Soldiers not far away in all probability.

'Every word I said back there is true,' Romeo told him, as he caught up. Tybalt gasped for breath, trying to summon the energy to make one more lunging assault. 'I have good reason to love you, friend. And you good reason to show affection to me.'

'No Capulet loves a Montague.'

The storm was moving slowly on. Bold beams of sunlight had begun to peek through gaps in the black clouds.

'But they do, Tybalt. *She* does.'

'She?'

Romeo edged closer, his rapier lowered a touch. 'Your cousin Juliet. We married this afternoon. Tonight we tell her parents and mine. This bloody vendetta is over.'

Tybalt laughed. 'For a dead man you have a strange sense of humour.'

Romeo held out his empty left hand. A peaceful gesture. 'This is no joke. Juliet's my bride. I'm her husband. Our two houses must come together and heal all these years of needless wounds.'

A quiet moment. From the corner of his eye Romeo saw Benvolio enter the side of the piazza.

'My cousin?' Tybalt asked. 'She's her father's daughter. Neither of them gives a damn about me.'

There was another battle here, inside Romeo's head. Between the red rage over Mercutio's murder and the warm love he felt for Juliet. The rational part of him knew that one defeated the other. But a man wasn't always rational. Or else he wasn't a man.

'Come with me now. To Escalus. We'll tell him what happened. I'll be honest and say Mercutio insulted you. Attacked you. That you in defence of yourself...' An image of that sharp and deadly needle rose in his head. He fought to stifle it. 'That you, in the same heat, responded. Mercutio was his nephew. You'll need all the help you can get.'

'I will,' Tybalt agreed with a nod. 'This is kind of you, my new-found cousin. A generous offer indeed.'

He threw the rapier to the ground and extended his right hand. 'I take this bargain, Montague. It's well made.'

Romeo dropped his blade then. On the damp piazza of Sant'Anastasia their two hands met.

Tybalt was an inch or so shorter. He had a smile on him. One that was hard to interpret. His handshake was firm and gripped Romeo's so tightly it was hard for him to move his fingers.

The words of the dead fencing master came back to him.

Not every opponent's a gentleman. Watch where the other hand goes. And look for treachery.

'So you married her?'

Another roll of thunder, distant this time. The storm would soon pass.

'I did.'

'In that case, tell me. What's it like? That soft, sweet place between her legs?'

A long moment. Another fading growl from the sky.

'Romeo!' Benvolio cried out from the arcade. 'His—'

Tybalt's left hand flew out from behind his back and there the blade was, sharp as a pin, dark with Mercutio's blood. He dragged Romeo towards him, aimed the point straight at his midriff.

Then hesitated. Smiling. Puzzled. Pained.

Staggering back, he dropped the slender weapon and bent to look at his belly. Romeo's dagger was stuck there, hard in up to the haft.

The red rage and the left hand won. Perhaps they always did. Romeo kicked Tybalt's feet from under him. Laughing, crying, Tybalt twisted as he fell, landed hard on the knife, bellowing with angry pain. The soldiers were running at them, yelling, Benvolio too. Another figure stood close by. One he recognised. The big woman. Juliet's nurse, watching, hand to mouth, tears streaming down her flabby cheeks.

Romeo dragged the dagger out, heard only a low, pained groan in return, saw trembling fingers clutch fearfully at the bloody wound and then go still. He raised his hands and waited for them to seize him.

There was no pleasure in this moment, no sense of victory. Only a harsh refrain he knew would come to haunt him for all the black days that remained.

An hour ago I was a loving husband. Now I'm a foul murderer.

Strong arms gripped him. A boot to the shins brought him hard to the ground, head bowed, face over the slain Tybalt whose dead black eyes stared up at the clearing sky.

* * *

Juliet was on her balcony struggling to think, to plan, to have anything in her head but joy tempered by trepidation. Wondering what words the two of them might use to turn shock to surprise and then delight when they told their parents that evening. The Montagues had a milder reputation. It was her father she feared the most. The anger and disappointment he'd feel at losing the marriage – of his daughter and, more important, his house – to the aristocratic Paris. And the discovery that he'd been usurped by the son of his greatest enemy.

How?

Be honest, she thought. Tell the truth. Show them the love that brought her and Romeo together. Then wait and hope and pray.

After that Romeo would be in her arms. Perhaps in her bed if they hadn't been thrown out of the palazzo. That would be the sweetest moment of all. A time of discovery and revelation, the two of them like butterflies emerging from their silken shells.

Her quiet reverie was broken by shrieks and screams. The door behind burst open. Nurse stumbled in, grey hair a mess, her heavy face grim with anger, wet with tears.

'Oh God, he's dead, love. We are undone. Alack the day! He's gone, he's killed, he's dead.'

The coldest shiver ran down Juliet's back. 'What…?'

Through the open door she could hear other noises rising up the stone staircase. Wails and cries of grief and fury.

'Your Romeo. Who would have thought it?'

Keep calm, she thought. Understand this. For every step forward now will carry danger.

She raced to the woman and tried to catch her darting eyes. 'Please, Nurse. Don't torment me now. Romeo's dead?'

'In the piazza before Sant'Anastasia.' She crossed herself quickly, twice. 'I saw the wound, I saw it with my own two eyes. Stabbed straight through his breast. A piteous corpse, a bloody piteous corpse. Pale as ashes, all bedaubed in gore… Oh, God.' She tore off her grubby cap and threw it on the floor. 'I may not forget this easily.'

'Dead…?'

'I saw it.'

Juliet's voice turned soft and weak. 'Then so am I. We shall share the same coffin…'

'Your Romeo was the murderer, girl! That vicious lad of yours. To think I went along with all this nonsense… Lord knows what the master will do…'

'Then...?'

There was a look in the woman's face she didn't recognise. All these years together. So much trust at times, some open, some private. Now it was as if she didn't know her.

'He's murdered Tybalt. I came straight on him standing over the poor little bugger's body. A mouthy little villain your cousin I'll grant, but still your flesh and blood.'

'Killed Tybalt? Why? There must have been a reason!'

Her old face turned ugly and dismissive. 'A reason? *A reason?* The young in this city never let up brawling. Rogues the lot of them, stabbing another to death on God's ground. There's no trust in any of them. No faith, no honesty in men. These sorrows make me old. Shame on that dog, Romeo...'

'He surely had some cause!'

'You'd defend the bastard who murdered your cousin?'

As calmly as she could Juliet said, 'If Romeo killed Tybalt then surely it's because my cousin wished to do the same to him. Perhaps he knew. About us. You saw what he was like. Only this afternoon he had his hands round my throat...'

The commotion downstairs had ended. Then she heard her father's furious voice and the front doors slammed.

'Where is he now?' Juliet asked.

'Where murderers belong. In the marshal's dungeons. Your parents have been summoned to meet Escalus. The Montagues, too.'

'What... what will happen?'

'Either they hang him or banish him. Whichever, he's gone from here. You'll never see your Romeo again, that's for sure.'

Fast thoughts. Deep desires.

'I'll not die a maid. I will not.'

'Your father knows nothing of the nonsense you two got up to today. Best for both of us it stays that way. Look to Count Paris…

'That man shall never touch me… Please. If Romeo lives get word to him.'

Nurse shook her head. 'Why, love? What's the point?'

'I brought him to this. If he can somehow come here…'

'How's that possible? He's in a cell. Maybe headed for the gallows.'

Juliet was desperate. Clutching at straws. 'You said he might be banished. If that's so then find him. He knows the way to this room. If there's a chance…'

The woman stepped back. Her tears had stopped. 'Think of yourself. Your own future. You wish to break your heart twice over?'

'Once will do,' she said firmly. 'A single night. He's owed that and so am I. Let tomorrow bring whatever it will. You're good at these ways of the world. Find him. If there's a means he can come to me secretly then… let him try.'

'Juliet–'

She kissed the woman's flabby cheek and wondered at the response. 'I must see him.'

'If Master should discover me playing such games I'm out on my ear, aren't I? One more beggar woman out in the street. And who's going to throw the likes of me a penny?'

The purpose of this reprimand was obvious. Juliet went to her table, found what money she had, then opened her box of jewellery.

'Bring him here and this is yours. Everything I have. Take it.'

The woman could scarcely keep her eyes off the jewels and the coins. 'That is a kindness…'

Juliet snapped the lid firmly shut. 'When he's here…'

'If he's not hanging by the neck I'll do my best. But I tell you, girl.

You keep this quiet. If by some miracle he does reach your bed this night, that's it. Tomorrow your father will have other plans for you. For pity's sake don't mention that nonsense you got me into this afternoon. He'll have me in jail for treachery. And you... Heaven knows...'

Her heart was in her mouth. 'Will you do it?'

'Well.' Nurse couldn't take her eyes of the jewellery box. 'I'll try.'

* * *

Escalus had taken Cangrande's war room as his office, the grandest chamber in the castle by the river. From the long window he could see the bridge across the Adige, now, with the plague restrictions, Verona's only entrance and exit point. Around three walls ran a high frieze with Cangrande's coat of arms: two crowned mastiffs climbing a ladder. Beneath was a pattern of brightly-coloured geometric motifs and a painted curtain on the dado. A violent fresco of fantastical animals engaged in bloody battle occupied all of the fourth wall.

On the shiny walnut table in front of him sat a long sword, old and dusty, the fabric fraying on the handle, rust staining the guard. Luca Capulet looked at it. They said it was Cangrande's own weapon, buried with him in the stone tomb set beneath his equestrian statue over the door of Santa Maria Antica, that Escalus had watched his men lift the lid of the sarcophagus then reached inside and wrestled the weapon from the dead lord's fingers.

The weapon filled the room with a subtle smell of dust and the dead. This was a very different place from the guard house in which Escalus had delivered his warning the day before. That old blade before them made a statement: *You are mine now. To do with as I wish.*

He sat with his wife on one side, the Montagues on the other. They looked older, Luca Capulet thought. He would have laughed in other circumstances. Of course, they did. It was many a long year since the four of them had occupied the same room. Time had dealt its blows, yet the enmity between them had never wavered.

Romeo was in custody in the cells downstairs. Tybalt's body had been handed over to the church, along with the corpse of Mercutio. Because of the plague restrictions both would be buried in the morning. No open coffins, no lengthy mourning ceremonies were allowed. Escalus was firm on that, as he was on many things.

Benvolio, the only witness the marshal wanted, sat on a chair between them, fidgeting all the while.

With his one good eye Escalus stared at him across the table. 'Care to tell me what you told the soldiers? Who began this bloody fray?'

'Tybalt, sir…'

'An unreliable witness!' Capulet cried. 'This lad's a Montague. How may we believe a single word he says?'

Benvolio glowered at him. 'I am an honest man. Whatever name I bear. Listen to my testimony and you'll see I spare no one any blame.'

'Well said,' Escalus told him. 'Then speak.'

'Tybalt began the fight after Mercutio's stupid bating. The two were of equal blame. Romeo tried to part them. Tybalt…' He groaned, remembering. 'He had a hidden stiletto and stabbed Mercutio with it slyly while Romeo held him back. After that…' he looked at Andrea and Francesca Montague, 'your son was rightly angry. I tried to stop him. But he was so fast and furious, so far through the crowds I couldn't. What happened then… you must ask Romeo.'

'He won't speak,' Escalus said.

Benvolio shook his head. 'Why not? I saw it all. Tybalt tricked him. He dropped his sword, made as if they were friends, and found his stiletto, just as he did with your nephew. Romeo stabbed him to save his own life. It was clear—'

'Liar!' Capulet roared. 'This is the only witness? A partial one.'

'I tell no lies. I was there…'

'Go, Benvolio,' Escalus ordered. 'I have no further need of you.'

When he'd left Capulet cried, 'Hang the blackguard. Or cut off his vile head. That's what you promised, Marshal. So do it.'

'And you'd have demanded Tybalt's neck if matters were the other way round?' Montague asked. 'Tell me, Luca. Does your wrath lean one way only?'

For an answer he got nothing more than a low and ugly curse. Francesca Montague took out a handkerchief and dabbed at her damp eyes. Bianca Capulet watched from across the room then said, 'Two deaths are enough, surely. A little compassion and understanding—'

Escalus shuffled his eye patch and turned that steely look of his on each man in turn. 'Capulet and Montague. Your two houses bring nothing but violence to this city. Perhaps I should hang the pair of you instead.'

'Perhaps,' Montague agreed. 'If I may take my son's place in the noose I'll do it. And pay any fine you choose to levy. He's young. A poet in his head. Not a warrior. Nor a murderer.' He looked at the couple opposite. 'We must bring this pointless vendetta to an end.'

'You should have thought that through when you started it!' Capulet bellowed.

'Thought of what?' his own wife asked, by his side. 'That we might lose a nephew? Them a son? And Escalus here a relative of his own?'

'A foolish distant one,' the marshal said. 'Mercutio brought trouble on himself in Venice. The young are never happy. They see the rising of the sun as treachery and its setting as a slight. Yet he is dead. And so is Tybalt, slain by Romeo. One has paid the price. The other...?'

'Take me,' Montague begged. 'Take all I own, sir. But let my dear misguided son live.'

The day was dying beyond the window. No horses moved upon the bridge. Verona was locked behind its own walls. A place secure, as tight in the marshal's grip as he could make it.

'The law allows for self-defence,' Escalus announced. 'I cannot hang a man who acts to save his own life.' He turned his one good eye on the Montagues. 'Especially when he has parents who may contribute generously to the army's coffers.'

Andrea Montague sighed. His wife wept. Luca Capulet swore bitterly beneath his breath.

The marshal reached for his pen and some parchment.

'Nor need I tolerate him in this city. A poet, you say? Then I'll give him Dante's sentence. I banish him on pain of death. If he sets foot inside the territory of our dear Republic after tomorrow he shall suffer summary execution. No trial. No pleading. No chance of mercy.'

'Thank you,' Francesca Capulet whispered.

'I haven't finished. You will pay a fine of one month's revenue of your business. In gold and coin to my treasury this very night. Romeo will spend his last hours here in the company of the friars of San Francesco al Corso. Your church, I believe.'

'You send a foul murderer to a monastery?' Capulet cried. 'If–'

Escalus turned on him. 'Silence. Or, by God, you'll be the next to feel my wrath!'

'Again these bastards cheat me...'

The marshal chose to ignore that. 'Pray your son learns some lessons from the holy men there. Once you pay the fine I will issue orders for the gate.'

'May we see him?' his mother asked.

'Not here in Verona. Find him wherever the youth fetches up. He'll have until nine in the morning to present himself and take a horse hence. Where I care not. Only that he's gone. If he tarries a minute too long then...'

He reached across the desk, grasped Cangrande's dusty sword and banged the pommel hard on the table like a judge delivering sentence.

'I am done. And so are you.' His one eye roamed over the men. 'I cannot heal this rift between your houses. Only you can do that. A handshake today would be a start. Will you oblige me?'

'Aye, Marshal,' Andrea Montague murmured, misty-eyed. 'That I will.'

He stood up, hand trembling as he held it out.

'Over my slain nephew's body,' Capulet grumbled. 'You call this justice?'

'I called it,' Escalus growled. 'And I am marshal here. So justice it must be.'

'Then we're robbed once more! Come, woman!' he roared and dragged his wife with him from the room.

* * *

The soldiers who took Romeo from the castle to San Francesco al Corso told him nothing. At the monastery they handed an order from Escalus to an anxious Friar Laurence and waited as he read it.

The sergeant nodded at Romeo when the brother was finished.

'This criminal's in your care tonight. No visitors. Not his family even. If he hops it my orders are to kill him on the instant.' A bitter sneer then. 'Murdering little villain. If it had been up to me I'd have his head off and stuck it on a spike over the bridge right now.'

Laurence nodded then pointed out that it wasn't up to the sergeant at all.

'We'll leave him to God and you then,' the soldier said curtly. He winked at Romeo. 'Oh please, lad. Do us all a favour and leg it from this holy place. All the trouble we're dealing with right now. Plague and wars and God knows what else. And what do you do? Start a street fight and stick some stupid Capulet kid in the guts.'

'Capulet? Laurence asked.

'Tybalt,' the sergeant said. 'The merchant's nephew. Escalus lost his own blood in all this savagery, too.'

Laurence crossed himself. 'Come, Romeo. Inside.'

The sergeant fetched Romeo a kick along the way then patted his sword. 'If I catch you anywhere but on your way out of town tomorrow morning I'll take great pleasure in splitting you in two with this good blade. Then drink a long toast to a happier world right after.'

'I believe you've made your point,' the friar told him. 'Several times over. Now if you will...?'

He shuffled off cursing into the dark.

'What news?' Romeo asked, watching him read the marshal's letter once more. 'What does Escalus want to do with me?'

'A gentler judgement than you might have had. He'll let you live, but banished. Like Dante. You must never return home again. On pain of immediate death.'

'This cannot be...'

He showed him the order. The family was to suffer a heavy fine. Romeo would be confined to the monastery until morning then expected to present himself before the castle bridge before nine. There his family would provide a horse and he'd be told to take himself from the territory of the Republic before midday.

'Be patient, son. This earth of ours is broad and wide and you've not seen a portion of it.'

'Patient? There's no world outside this city. Only purgatory, torture and hell. Banishment's a worse punishment than death. If Escalus had any mercy he'd hang me now. He's just cutting off my head off with a golden axe and smiling at the stroke that murders me. How dare…?'

'Sit down, you ungrateful child!' the friar ordered.

The sound of his anger, something he'd never heard in all the long years he'd known the man, silenced Romeo. He did as he was told. Laurence fetched two cups of wine. Not as good as the rare vintage with which they'd celebrated the wedding that afternoon. But suitable enough for a wake, he said.

'You killed a man and for that our law demands your life. Escalus has put that to one side and turned the black word "death" to "banishment". This is mercy if only you could see it.'

'If I'd not slain Tybalt he'd have killed me.'

Yet, Laurence pointed out, Romeo never told them that. They both knew why. Too many questions in the heat of the moment and a greater secret might have emerged.

'So what am I to do?'

Laurence went to his desk and scrawled out a brief letter. Romeo watched. It appeared to be in Greek, a language unknown to him.

'This,' the friar said, 'is for my brother Nico in Mantua. Outside the Republic, but a few hours' ride away. He's an apothecary there. A good man, if a touch disputatious. We are…' He sighed. 'Very different. But of the same mind in some things. He will give you a bed for the night. An introduction to the court there. Take it…'

Romeo didn't move.

'Your opportunities are limited,' Laurence pleaded. 'The alternative is to wander this dangerous land alone and find your own place in it. Or a new grave somewhere. *Take it*!'

He did and asked, 'What else?'

'What else? Be quiet. Be good. Be sensible. Prove to the court of Mantua you're the decent lad we all know. Then, in a week, a month or two, we'll petition Escalus once more. I'll tell him you acted to defend yourself. That you deserve a second chance. A pardon. Permission to return here and become the worthy citizen you were before.'

Romeo said nothing.

'Balthazar – the valet who comes with you for confession sometimes – he's to arrange your horse for the morning. The boy lives outside the city but works within the walls. Does he have a warrant to cross the bridge when Escalus closes the gates to the rest of us?'

'I believe so.'

'He's a trustworthy soul?'

'Yes, but–'

'Then he can be our conduit to you in Mantua. Juliet's and mine. When there's news he'll bring it. For God's sake, Romeo... speak!'

'Friar. Her father will try to marry her to this count... Paris. Is that... possible?'

Laurence went to his desk and retrieved the contract they'd signed that afternoon. No witnesses save him. A legal paper but...

'I told you all this. Both of you. I'm a humble friar. This is just ink on parchment. You haven't even spent a night with your bride. All Luca Capulet need do is set a lawyer upon the matter and–'

'How long?'

The friar shrugged. 'Go to Mantua. Impress the court there. Have them send good reports of you to Escalus. With a little luck and effort on your part we can have you back here, married in the sight of all, soon enough…'

There was a rap at the door. Laurence told Romeo to retreat to the dark corner. Perhaps the Capulets were organising retribution of their own. But it was Nurse there complaining about the long walk through dark and unwelcoming streets.

'Romeo, sir?' she said, short of breath from the hurried effort. 'My mistress sends me…'

He came out of the shadows. 'Juliet? How is she?'

The woman took off her mob cap and looked around. 'Confused. As are we all. A little frightened. And full of tears.'

'She thinks me a murderer.'

'And why do you reckon that is? She thinks you her husband, too. What others say makes no difference it seems.'

'Then tell her–'

'Oh no!' the woman cried. 'That's for you, lad. You must come to her. This is her wedding night. Whatever you've done. Whatever comes next. You know the way, my mistress says. To her bedroom. To her heart. Then find it by midnight or else–'

The friar came and stood between them. 'This is too dangerous, Romeo. You heard the guards. Stay here. Be safe. Leave for Mantua in the morning. I'll send word as we've agreed.'

'Safe? What's safe to me? I cannot–'

The woman tapped Laurence's shoulder. 'He may walk with me, Friar. If anyone asks I'll say he's my idiot son. Nice to look at but soft in the head.' She nodded at him. 'Not that far from the truth if I'm honest. As to the morning, lad… that's up to you.'

Romeo looked at the friar. 'One night. Then our marriage is surely real.'

'Not to her father. That can never happen now. I was a fool to listen to you in the first place.'

'Brother Laurence. I *must* go.'

There was no dissuading him. Laurence saw that. Romeo downed his wine and made to leave.

'The letter,' Laurence said, holding out the parchment. 'For my brother, Nico, remember? He has a stall in the market in the old Rotonda of San Lorenzo. Find him there. Give him this. Take Balthazar into your confidence in the morning. With God's help all will turn out well.'

Romeo took the message then held out his hand. 'You've been kinder to me than ever I deserved.'

'But kindness sometimes kills,' the friar said and they shook. 'Be patient. Remember what I said? They that run too fast and never think...'

There was a grim and pessimistic tone to his voice at that moment. An uncharacteristic one.

'I recall you never finished the sentence.'

'Then I'll do it now. They fall.'

* * *

Luca Capulet got back to the palazzo still furious at Escalus, the Montagues, the world. The place was in disorder. The servants were weeping for Tybalt, out of duty not love. Juliet had locked herself in her room. She was badly shaken by her cousin's murder, or so her mother thought. Nurse was nowhere to be seen. This infuriated

Capulet too: it was that woman's job to see to their daughter when she was in one of her moods. Words would be had on that front before long.

But first he drank. Not Garganega wine this time but the spirit the farmers made from pomace, the leaves and stems and seeds left behind after the pressing of the grapes, fermented then distilled into a strong, clear, fiery spirit. Capulet had an arrangement with a group of farmers in Bassano, sixty miles away in the foothills of the lower Alps behind Vicenza. They made this spirit there and called it grappa. It was cheap and strong, and coarser men loved it. Capulet, too, at times like this. Bassano was quiet and bucolic, nothing like Verona with its schemes and feuds and pompous military masters. He'd taken a lover there once, a decade before, a beautiful, accommodating courtesan with a house overlooking the river Brenta. The grappa was to blame, or so he told himself. Perhaps it was time to go back and find out.

Not now. This was a moment to drown himself in drink and let the fire of that rough liquor stoke the blaze inside.

Tybalt was dead, murdered by a Montague. The lad he'd never loved. That had been impossible ever since the snarling, vicious creature had come into his household. Still, he was a Capulet, his dead brother's son. Child of a troubled woman who'd resisted all efforts to implant her into the family.

He thought of their last argument, the night before. 'If I'd been firmer from the outset...' Luca Capulet told himself. 'If I'd been the stern father I should have been to the boy, instead of listening to my wife and tolerating his tempers and his demands...'

Households were like small armies. They ran on hierarchies and rules, on orders to be followed without question. Men understood that implicitly. It was women who brought weakness into the equation, pleading for a compassion that only led to disobedience, for a lazy indulgence that brought mutiny and shame.

'Learn your lesson,' he muttered and took a gulp of the harsh spirit. It burst in his mouth, pain and pleasure in one. 'Only a fool makes the same mistake twice.'

There was another rebel in this household, even closer to his blood. He loved the child, for all their rows and the loss that came from heading a family without a son and heir. That was why he indulged her capricious nature, the resolute disobedience, the casual contempt she showed him on occasion.

What was it Escalus had said?

The young are never happy. They see the rising of the sun as treachery and its setting as a slight.

They were the only true words the miserable old bastard had uttered. Banging Cangrande's sword on the table like that. Capulet swore beneath his breath. His wife had vanished. The servants had left him alone with a flagon of drink, a cup and all his burning anger.

'They must be broken,' he declared, smelling the grappa fumes rising from his throat. 'They shall be too.'

He walked down into the kitchen. Pietro was the only one there, stuffing his face as usual.

'Take my food out of your mouth, boy,' Capulet ordered and watched him sputter on some cold goose. 'What word is there from Count Paris?'

'Nothing. Not since he left the house this morning.'

Then he picked up the wing in front of him and gnawed on it again.

Insolence. It was everywhere.

Capulet didn't strike his servants often. Perhaps not enough. He marched over, slapped the boy hard around the head. The meat skittered across the kitchen as Pietro uttered a surprised and high-pitched yelp.

'Sorry, sir,' the boy pleaded. 'And may I say... I am sorry for your loss also.'

'My loss? My *loss*? Insolent brat. I should take my whip to you. What does a creature like you care for this household? We're just coins in your pocket and a scarlet feather in your cap. Don't try and fool me otherwise.'

Capulet went to where they kept the drink and gazed at the rows of bottles and flasks. 'Go to Paris,' he said, without bothering to look at the boy cowering behind him. 'Tell him I wish his presence here tonight. To raise a toast to our joint venture.'

Pietro whined something that sounded like a question. Capulet grabbed a flask and turned to stare at him. 'What?'

'Is that all I'm supposed to tell him? I mean... it's late. There's bad feeling out there on them streets. If I may give him better cause...'

'Tell him that should he come to see me this night the prize he desires is his for the taking. No further arguments. No more equivocation. He may have it for himself two days hence. Tomorrow we observe a wake. After that a wedding.'

Pietro gulped.

'A wedding?'

'That's what I said. Same food. Same drink. Same... guests for all I care. *Go!*'

The boy ran out then, scampering into the warm, dark night.

* * *

193

Half an hour later, close to the Capulet palazzo, as he scuttled along the Porta Leoni next to the nurse, Romeo saw Paris and the servant Pietro heading in the same direction. He sank into the doorway of a butchers, cap down on his head. Nurse waited a few houses along. The count seemed too preoccupied to notice anything. He went into the palazzo courtyard, followed by the servant.

Without another word, Nurse vanished inside. Romeo skirted the side wall until he found the gate into the garden. It was open. Half-running, he was through. The ground was fresh from the storm but the old grapevine beside her balcony had mostly escaped the downpour. Heart ready to burst, he climbed it slowly, carefully, in the light of the moon and stars. By the time he got there, Juliet was waiting for him, forewarned by the nurse.

The room was tidy, no books on the floor, no clothes, nothing but the gleaming tiles. She stood by the bed in a simple shift. Arms open, he entered her room for the first time.

'Love...'

Juliet, eyes blazing, walked straight up and slapped him forcefully on the cheek.

'Why?' was all she asked. '*Why?*'

Outside an owl hooted. There was a far-off peal of bells. Midnight in the city. The last he might ever know. Romeo told her what had happened.

'I tried,' he pleaded. 'I'd hoped to calm him. Appease him. Perhaps one day make him a friend—'

'Tybalt? He had none.' She sat on the bed. 'There was a black thing deep inside him. I think my father tried to rid him of it. I didn't. I never had the... patience.'

'Perhaps there is that in all of us.'

'If so, all the more reason to resist it!'

'He would have killed me. I had no choice.'

'Oh Romeo…' She took his hand and lightly kissed his cheek. 'There are always choices. We just pick the wrong ones.' She sat and patted the sheets beside her. 'Sit with me. This predicament is mine as much as yours. When must you leave?'

'First thing,' he said. By midday he'd be in Mantua, seeking out Laurence's brother. He told her of the plan for his servant Balthazar to be in secret contact with her and pass on any news between them.

Juliet shook her head. 'We need no messenger. I'll come with you. We can leave this place together. They won't divide us.'

'You can't.'

'Why not?'

Gently he swept a strand of blonde hair from her eyes. Tears were forming in them like tiny glittering jewels. 'Without papers no one can quit this city.'

'Then we admit the truth! We married in secret and they all must make the best of it!'

'Do that and we won't be married at all. They'll find a lawyer and annul it. Laurence said so and he's right. It will be as if it had never happened.'

'And then they foist me on Paris.'

'While I'm still banished they mustn't know. Not yet. I murdered your cousin. I'm a villain. If they find out our secret, we'll always be apart.'

'When I can I'll leave. I'll find you.'

While waiting in the cell, he'd run through every option in his head. To flee. To beg. To lie. Or simply admit the truth that they were married in secret and their families would have to make the best of it. At the end of every imaginary road lay disaster. 'No. You'd be hunted as soon as they realise you're gone.'

'Let them look. This is my doing as much as yours.'

'All you brought was love.'

'With good reason, Romeo! I can ride. I can run...'

He held her slender shoulders and peered into her glistening eyes. 'I will not make a fugitive of you. Besides they'd find us. No one hides from Venice. I'd be hanged as a felon and you brought back to Verona in shame.'

'Then...'

He waited. 'Then what?'

The tears were close, and her face full of bitter anger.

When she didn't go on he said, 'We must listen to Friar Laurence. Of all the men I know he's the wisest and most decent. He says I must leave and you must stay. So we abide a while. His brother will make approaches to the Mantuan court the moment I arrive. They will appeal for clemency. When Escalus finds it in him to pardon me I can return. I will fly here...'

In a low and bitter tone she whispered, 'On love's wings?'

Words from the night before when the world seemed full of poetry. A flowery, pointless expression he saw, though said with devotion.

'Whatever means are fastest. They will not keep me from you.'

His hand crept round her waist. The kiss was longer, bolder. 'This man they want you to marry—'

'Count Paris,' she hissed. 'I will deal with him.'

'You will. You'll make him wait.'

'And wait. And wait. And wait. Till Judgement Day if I must.'

'You are my love. My only love...'

Gingerly, his pulse beginning to race, he edged back the shoulder of her robe, saw the pale skin there.

She pulled his head close, ran her lips through his hair, found his ear and whispered in it, 'You stink. Bear with me.'

Juliet tiptoed to the door and asked Nurse to bring hot water for the tub.

'Thought you might need that,' the woman whispered, handing over some jugs. 'Got it already. Watch out. There's talk going on downstairs. Make too much noise in all your pleasures and they'll surely hear.'

'Let them. Perhaps that would be an end to it.'

Nurse looked scared. 'No. Just a terrible beginning.'

Romeo took the jugs and went coyly to the tub behind her black lacquer screen. Juliet removed her night clothes and stretched naked on the sheets. When he returned he smelled of lemon and pomegranates, the essences she used herself. He had his long shirt on and stared in wonder at her pale bare shape upon the bed.

One candle stood by the bedpost while moonlight streamed through the open windows. As he reached to extinguish the flame she stopped him.

'No. I want to see. I practised a verse for you,' Juliet whispered, reaching for a pot of something by the bed. 'And brought a gift with it. Your shirt, Romeo.'

He removed it and asked, 'A verse? Right now?'

'No other time. It's from the bible. Here...' Juliet put two fingers into the jar she'd stolen from the kitchen. They came back covered in a treacly pat of sweetness which she smeared above his lips then thrust inside his mouth, feeling tongue and teeth and warm damp flesh, spreading the stickiness everywhere.

In his ear her hot breath whispered, 'I am come into my garden, my spouse: I have gathered my myrrh with my spice; I have eaten my honeycomb with my honey; I have drunk my wine with milk.'

Her mouth, open, willing, closed on his. Tongues met. Fingers wrestled. Honey between them. Then, 'I sleep, but my heart wakes: it is the voice of my beloved that knocks, saying, Open to me, my sister, my love, my dove, my undefiled: for my head is filled with dew, and my locks with the drops of the night.'

With a tentative stealth he began to move above her. She pushed him back then softly straddled him the way she had in the garden. So close now, so near to that first magical meeting.

'My beloved put in his hand by the hole of the door, and my warm quarters were moved for him. And... ah...'

The Song of Solomon fled her throat and retreated to her feverish mind. Still living there, beneath the rush and heat.

I rose up to open to my beloved; and my hands dropped with myrrh, and my fingers with sweet smelling myrrh, upon the handles of the lock.

Then the words returned so briefly she had to cry them.

'And I opened to my beloved...'

Beneath the candlelight and the silver moonbeams, watched by the eager eyes of the painted child on the canvas behind the rattling, squeaking bed, they turned and wrestled, moans high and low, slow and quick, filling the airy perfumed room.

Time stopped. As did the world, nothing in it but Juliet and her Romeo, lost in a solitary paradise of passion. Blind to the bargain being struck a floor below.

* * *

Count Paris sat in the downstairs study, a glass of grappa in his hand, taking two sips from it only. Bianca Capulet was there, too, at her own insistence, drinking nothing. Her husband made up for their abstention. Angry, determined, he was a man cheated, by Escalus, by Montague. By everything around him.

'You have my condolences,' Paris said with a nod. 'This Romeo who slew your nephew–'

'A rogue. A thief. Like all the Montagues.'

'We do not know that, husband,' Bianca Capulet told him. 'Tybalt was scarcely an angel himself. What happened–'

'You heard the sergeant's report! The villain dragged him on to the piazza of Sant'Anastasia and stabbed him through the gut.'

Paris stayed silent. Capulet eyed him and asked, 'You know this Montague boy?'

'He was with his father in Florence a while ago. Seeking business. I met them briefly.' He placed the cup on the table. 'The old man seemed unremarkable. The boy quite pleasant...'

Capulet waved his goblet in the air with such force the drink spilled on him. 'A man is judged by his actions. Not his appearance. They wanted your money?'

'They sought it. I turned them down. It was my belief...' His eyes glittered as they crept to the stone stairs. 'My desire that we should have commerce of our own. In trade. In matters of the heart.'

Bianca Capulet stared at the shiny tiles and the spilled liquor upon them and kept quiet.

'Will Juliet be joining us?' the count wondered. 'Since you summoned me I assumed–'

'She's very upset by today's events,' her mother said, before her husband could answer. 'Tybalt was her cousin. They were not... close. Still... the way he died.'

He nodded. 'I understand. These times of woe afford no space for love, I fear. I should leave you in your grief. Tomorrow I return to Florence. This city has proved barren for me. I will not come back soon.'

'Hear me out, Paris!' Capulet demanded. 'Were it not for you I'd have been in bed hours ago, thinking of a funeral.'

Paris demurred. 'This is surely not the time...'

'There's none better! Tybalt's gone. We all die some time. I must think of this house's future. My daughter–'

'I tried to talk to her this morning as you asked. My words fell on deaf ears. I'm not an accomplished lover. I cannot woo with poetry or honeyed words. If a woman doesn't want me for what I am then...' He looked at her mother. 'You told me you'd persuade her.'

Capulet waved his cup about. 'We lacked the time! This miserable, bloody day...'

'Then I thank you for your efforts and must bring this fruitless adventure to an end.'

He was on his feet. Capulet dashed to stop him.

'Listen to me. My nephew's untimely death has taught me well. A father is master of his family or nothing. With Tybalt I was lax and acquiescent. With Juliet, too.'

The count waited, interested. 'And now?'

'A daughter will obey her father. In all matters. As it should be.'

'She's not our property, Luca!' Bianca Capulet cried. 'The child has a mind of her own.'

'Aye,' he snapped. 'And don't I hear it day in, day out? Sixteen years I've listened to that constant yapping. From this moment on that girl will be ruled in all respects by me. Paris here's as good as a son as far as I'm concerned. He loves her. He'll have her. We'll join our separate houses and make them one. By God, this week I'll do it too... What... what?' The drink had befuddled him. 'What day is this? I forget now...'

'Tuesday,' Bianca said with a long, pained sigh.

'Right. I knew that. Tomorrow, we bury Tybalt. On Thursday Paris marries Juliet.'

His wife came and stood by him, outraged. 'One day after our nephew's funeral. The whole city will talk of our disrespect for the dead.'

'Let them talk! You think I care what those scum think?' He took the count's arm. 'This good man shall get the girl he loves. And she *will* marry him, by God. Go tell her. She's got a husband. No arguments. No more fights. I'll drag her to the altar myself if need be.'

Paris laughed. 'That would not be seemly.'

Capulet calmed himself. 'You're right. Won't happen either. Children buck against you when you give them opportunity. Remove the choice and they know their place. I'll inform the girl. This marriage is made. Not in heaven. But by me.' A chuckle then. 'The household god.'

He raised his cup. Paris found his. Bianca Capulet watched them toast, then drink. Her husband's cold eyes found hers. 'Go, Bianca. Wake the child. Make it clear. She's got a husband. In two short days she'll be a wife.'

'To Thursday,' Paris said and raised his drink again. There was a lecherous look on the count's face Bianca didn't like at all. 'To the marriage bed. And children. A grandson for you soon after.'

Happy, he left not many minutes later. Capulet sank back into his chair. His mood was mixed. Elation, exhaustion. Perhaps a little shame.

'Fetch more spirit. Then do as I say. Wake the child. Get it over and done with.'

She retrieved the half-full cup from his shaking fingers. 'No to both, husband. You've drunk enough. Juliet can hear her fate in the morning.'

He turned his glazed eyes on her. 'You think I'm wrong?'

'I think... with a little time... we might bring her round.'

'There is no time. You heard the man. He marries her now or leaves for good.'

'I've never known you bow to ultimatums before.'

'Paris is a man of substance and breeding. This is different.'

'Yes! It is! Juliet's an unusual child. She's not a pretty bird you can trap inside a cage.'

He was on her then, face red, spitting out his words. 'But I have! And Paris will keep her there. Comfy and loved for the rest of her leisurely life. Not a care in the world. No need to earn a penny. No hard decisions to make. Heaven for her. Idleness and luxury. What else does a woman want?'

Then he snatched back the cup and drained it, coughing and choking on the strong and fiery drink.

She left him, and decided to go Juliet's room in any case. Tomorrow would be difficult. Perhaps it would be best to broach the subject when her daughter was too tired to argue.

Along the passageway that led to her quarters she found the nurse dozing on a chair some way from the bedroom door, a collection of empty water jugs by her chair.

'Madam,' Nurse said as she approached. 'What is it?'

'I think I ought to talk to her. Matters are coming to a head. Why are you here? Not in your room?'

'The girl's terribly upset with all this news. She wanted a bath and I fear suffers a nightmare. Leave her be, I beg you. Tomorrow's soon enough, surely. I'll wait here in case I'm needed.'

She thought she heard a noise. Juliet tossing in her sleep perhaps, wracked in a sweaty nightmare.

'It is hot in here. This day was like a long bad dream.'

'In the morning, my lady. She'll be more accommodating then.'

'Please God. You know her better than I in some ways. She must rise first thing. I have to speak with her before her father does.'

The nurse nodded and gave her a gap-toothed smile. 'A wise decision as always.'

'Goodnight,' Bianca Capulet said and went back to her quarters, there to await her husband's heavy drunken form. And sleep perhaps. Ahead of the fateful day to come.

* * *

The bout was over. Damp, exhausted, they lay in each other's arms listening to the night noises: birds and insects, a dog's bark, the occasional drunken shout in a far-off street. Once she shivered, hearing faint voices down the long corridor that led back towards her parents' quarters. Then came Nurse's firm tones and nothing more.

The candle had fluttered throughout their quick passion. She put a hand to his cheek, admired his face in the waxy light and said, 'I thought that might have lasted longer.'

'But...' Romeo blinked at her.

Quickly she added, 'No, no, love. Don't take that wrong. It was an observation not a criticism. We must learn to be frank with one another. No lies, no secrets...'

His face was shiny with sweat. There was a wry smile on it. 'I thought it would take longer, too. There's candour for you. I'm sorry—'

She rushed to put her fingers against his lips. The honey was still there, dry and sticky. 'Don't say it. There's no need. We're like the first couple on that wall in Florence. You the new Adam. Me a second Eve. Innocents fallen straight out of the garden.' She hitched herself up on one elbow to look at him. 'I imagine they needed a little practice, too.'

'Lots,' he said, and touched the tip of her nose. 'Daily. Morning, afternoon and night. Until we tire of it. Or become so proficient we can stay in bed forever.'

He yawned then picked up the thin sheet and drew it over them. She didn't know why. Their easy nakedness seemed as natural as the way they'd found one another on the bed.

'I will come for you, my Juliet. Soon. As soon as I can.'

'And if you don't... I'll come for you.'

With that he took her fingers in his and peered at her intently. It was a curious sensation. Her father had looked at her this way sometimes, mostly when she was younger and more malleable. It was an expression that was both caring and, she thought, proprietorial ...patronising.

'We must be patient, wife. They that run too fast and never think... shall fall.'

She waited a while, becoming aware again of the world beyond the window, a place of promise and plague, wonder and misery. Then quietly she said, 'You must run fast to outspeed death. Sometimes, in my mind's eye, that's the way I see you. Icy and pale, stiff in a stone tomb...' The unwelcome image came to her again. 'Me the same, somewhere by your side. It's a silly waking dream, I know. My mother told me she had them. Perhaps it's a little demon in our German blood.'

The quietest sound of slumber left his lips. She looked and saw his eyes were closed. Romeo slept and she couldn't bear to rouse him. Softly, she slipped out of bed, found her nightgown then sat on the open balcony, looking at the stars. She thought of the new world they must be shining on at that moment. And a new century soon. One that would surely belong to them.

The Song of Solomon came back to her. The closing line in that fragment she'd whispered to him in her passion.

Alone on the hard chair, next to the grape vine he'd climbed twice and would descend a final time with the coming dawn, she repeated those missing words, though every syllable filled her with dread.

'But my beloved had withdrawn himself, and was gone: my soul failed when he spoke: I sought him, but I could not find him; I called him, but he gave me no answer.'

Juliet looked back at the bed and the man sleeping there.

Out in the garden something scurried, rustling through the dry leaves. A cat. A rat. A serpent. The world was full of unseen things. Some harmless. Some as deadly as could be.

Along the corridor, across the many halls, she heard her father bellow a wordless roar of anger.

Juliet wiped an unwanted tear from her eye then returned to her bedroom, closing the windows behind her. He didn't wake when she stole beneath the sheet beside him.

'This must not be our last night, love,' she said in the quietest whisper. 'But when again…?'

A door slammed somewhere. Her mother's angry voice echoed that of her father's. Sometimes he hit her. Never when Juliet was around. That would have been… unseemly.

Unmanly, too.

She pulled a second pillow into her arms and held it like a child. Then, in time, she slept.

Part Three: Such Sweet Sorrow

When he opened his eyes, Juliet was upright next to him in her nightshift, wide awake, hands around her knees. Rose-pink dawn had begun to break, bringing with it the lyrical song of a bird.

'Don't stir,' she said, putting a hand to his chest as if to stop him moving. 'Listen to the nightingale. She lives in the pomegranate bush. I know her voice.'

He struggled up anyway and leaned against the cushioned bedhead. 'The light...'

'It's not dawn. Just a comet or a meteor or something. Perhaps the day will never come.'

The bird sang again.

'That's the lark, love. Morning's herald. And that's the rising sun. But call them what you want.' His right hand found the fabric on her shoulder and gently moved it aside. Romeo's lips brushed the skin there. 'The marshal's men can kill me now. I'd die content. Better a happy corpse than...' he stared at the windows, 'than leave Verona. And you.'

She pulled the gown around her and withdrew a little. 'Don't say that. This isn't a game for children.'

'I know.' He touched her again. 'How are you then, sweet Juliet?

If it's not day let's talk a while. Or if you like... resume our practice...'

She got up, walked across the room, opened the long windows then stepped out on to the balcony. 'You must be gone from here. Everything's amiss. Even the lark sings out of tune.'

He came to stand behind her, arms around her shoulders, lips on her neck. She pushed him back.

'No, no. I'm sorry. I should never...'

'Never what?'

'Get dressed. There'll be soldiers all over the city soon. I've no wish to see you hanging from a noose.'

One more brief kiss and he whispered, 'The greater the light, the darker our woes. Be patient, sweet Juliet. We will see each other soon. As soon as I can make–'

From inside the palazzo came three crashes so loud the racket made them jump. Romeo raced for his clothes. Juliet walked to the bedroom door and opened it a crack. The nurse had her head to one side against the wall.

'Time to be moving,' she whispered. 'Your mother's up and about and your father will be too once his head's cleared. If they catch him here–'

'Tell her I sleep.'

She shook her head. 'That won't work. She wants to see you. There's a funeral coming. And other things on her mind.'

'Then say I'm ill.'

The woman groaned. 'You can't put this off, love. Chuck that boy out of your bed.'

'That boy's my husband.'

Nurse laughed. 'And how many people witnessed that? You two

and a priest who's away with the fairies half the time. One night of pleasure don't make a marriage. If it did half the world would be wed twice over.'

Juliet closed the door and bolted it. Romeo was pulling on his boots. He checked his money, found his hat. No blue feather. Just a plain black velvet cap, the kind any traveller might wear.

The door rattled. Someone was trying to open it. There were two loud raps and then her mother declared firmly, 'Juliet? Will you kindly let me in? We need to talk.'

'Go,' she said quietly and they embraced one last time. She followed him out to the balcony and watched as he climbed down the old vine. At the side gate Romeo turned and waved.

'Poor thing,' she whispered and didn't think to gesture back. 'You should have run.'

The bangs on the door were getting frantic. She dragged her gown more closely around her and went to open it.

Nurse was through first, bustling towards the bed. 'Such a tormented night that lass has had. I will change this bedding for sure.'

The sheets.

She glanced at them. Their love, their sweat, their passion now seemed reduced to nothing more than twisted cotton. Nurse scooped up all the bedclothes in her hefty arms and scuttled out of the room.

Her mother was sniffing suspiciously.

'Even virgins sweat,' Juliet told her. 'I'm sorry. I've opened the windows. It was a hot night. I dreamt. I tossed and turned.' A smile. Time to change the subject. 'And father? He seemed... loud when I last heard him. How is he?'

'He has a thick head and a vile temper as a consequence. Best stay clear of him for a while. Black.'

'What?'

'Black. Tybalt's funeral's this morning. You must wear black. You have something?'

She shrugged. 'Just the dress you bought me the last time we buried someone. Nurse will have to let it out. I'm... bigger. Older now.'

'True,' Bianca Capulet muttered. 'Be ready by nine. We must talk. You know of what–'

'I can guess.'

'And your dress–'

'Black. You said. Black it shall be.'

She waited. Her mother stared at her, aware something was different here.

'Let's try and make this day peaceful, daughter. With a modicum of respect. I know you didn't like Tybalt–'

'Did you?'

'He didn't deserve to die like a base thug in the street. At the hands of that vicious son of the Montagues.'

'You know the circumstances? Tybalt had arguments aplenty. He killed someone himself last year. No one banished him for that. If only they had.'

Her mother looked around the room again. 'The books from Venice...'

'You asked me to tidy them. So I did.' She began to close the door. 'And now I'd like a little time to...' She put a finger to her cheek. 'Mourn. Yes. That's it.'

In a moment she was alone.

No tears. Just anger. A sense of relief, too. She'd come so close to telling her mother everything, to spitting the truth out loud, straight in her disbelieving face. Lies seemed to spin around her everywhere.

But then… as Laurence said, their brief marriage would be unwound in an instant, annulled by the fury of her father.

Face to the door, determined not to cry, she whispered to the polished wood, 'If I must bear false witness, by God, I'll do it. Even to them. And do it well. I'll plot and scheme and…'

There was the lightest of knocks on the other side. She stopped and opened it a crack.

Nurse was there placing two jugs of hot water on the tiles. 'You have a bath, love. Busy day ahead.'

'Busier than they can know.'

Nurse stared back and for the first time Juliet wondered about her. Whose side she took. Her own, most likely.

'Be wise, girl. Think of yourself. Your mother will want to see you very soon.'

'I heard.'

Nurse didn't move. 'Those things you kindly promised me yesterday. For fetching him here. I hate to ask…'

Juliet opened the door and beckoned to her dressing table. 'Help yourself.'

'Not now. No rush, eh?' She put a finger in the water and tested the temperature, a gesture she must have made a thousand times over the years. 'There's plenty of time to come.'

* * *

Cap low, Romeo flitted through the waking city. No one looked. No one stopped him. Within a few minutes he was by the guardhouse on Cangrande's swallow-tail bridge presenting his papers to the same surly sergeant who'd seized him on the piazza of Sant'Anastasia the day before.

Balthazar was waiting with more money and a horse, its saddle bags packed with clothes. He was a year younger than Romeo, the son of a baker who lived across the Ponte Pietra, close by the ancient amphitheatre that stood against the hill outside the walls of the city.

The sergeant barely looked at the servant's warrant to enter the city for work. But he went through Romeo's exit papers line by line. The two of them excused themselves and went to check the horse. Young, fit, the animal seemed ready for the three-hour ride south. Romeo thanked Balthazar for the money and the mount.

'Not me you should thank. It's your parents. They're heartbroken they can't see you off themselves. One day soon in Mantua they say…'

'Aye,' Romeo said. 'One day.' They were far enough from the guards not to be overheard. 'May I trust you, Balthazar? In a matter so… private I'd trust no other man. Not my father even.'

He was a short, fair-haired youth. Decent, quiet, faithful. 'Sir! I am your servant and have been since I was a boy. Have I given you reason to think me a double-dealing sort? I–'

'No, never. Take no offence. But what I must confide in you–'

'Whatever it is, your secrets rest safe with me. If I'd seen that rogue Tybalt yesterday I'd have stuck the Capulet rogue myself and saved you all this trouble.'

Romeo laughed. 'Then you'd surely be dead. It's only my name that's kept my neck out of the noose.' He looked at the grey river, empty now, not a single boat, scarcely a bird even. 'My name…'

Balthazar coughed to get his attention. 'A servant's a servant. You tell me what you want.'

He did then and watched as the lad's eyes grew wide with shock.

'You wish me to convey messages between you and the Capulets? The *Capulets*? Who got you into all this trouble in the first place?'

'Just to the daughter. Juliet of that house. And this… trouble is of my own making. No one else's. I should have walked away and I didn't. You live the other side of the bridge. You've a warrant to come and go. This plague ban needn't stop you.'

'Maybe not. But the Capulets are our enemies.'

Romeo leaned on the red-brick wall, wondering how long it took for hate to die. This young man had no reason to loathe the Capulets. Any more than Tybalt had good cause to hate him. At some point this bitter rancour had to fade. How many would suffer along the way?

'You mustn't think like that. Old rivalries soon will be forgotten if—'

'Oi!' the sergeant bellowed. 'Montague! Get your bony arse over here.'

Quickly Balthazar said, 'I may not understand any of this but you're my master. I'll bring anything the lady tells me straight to you in Mantua. That's a promise. No, no.' Romeo was offering him coins. 'I do it out of loyal duty. I'm paid for that already.'

Romeo thanked him swiftly and returned to the guards. They were grinning, looking him up and down. The sergeant waved the paper from Escalus in his hand. 'It says here that should we find you anywhere in the territory of the great Republic of Venice from midday on we must, without delay, take your life.'

'I understand that.'

One of the soldiers tapped the paper. 'Don't say how though, do it? Leaves that small detail to us. So what do you reckon, mate? Any preferences?'

They liked a joke, he guessed. A little fun before he was on his way.

'I do not intend to give you reason or opportunity, sirs. But should the occasion arise... I imagine you have your methods.'

The second soldier butted in. Another face familiar from the piazza of Sant'Anastasia the day before.

'I saw what this vicious young bugger did yesterday. Stuck one of his own kind, another toff, straight through the belly. I know we tend to hang 'em. But that's much too good for the likes of him.'

The sergeant nodded gravely.

The first guard agreed as well. 'And as for an axe... I mean that's quick and painless they reckon, so long as you do it proper and the fellow don't move his head.'

That wasn't right either, the sergeant declared. Though being professionals they wouldn't make it a mess of it at all.

'We could chuck him in the Adige,' one of them suggested. 'In a sack. With a rock. Like we do with cats.'

'I take water from that river,' the sergeant cried. 'Are you trying to poison me?'

They scratched their heads for a while, enjoying their game. Romeo folded his arms and waited. He had no choice.

Finally the sergeant's eyes lit up. He jabbed a finger in the air with a joyful cry. After that he went into the guardhouse and came back with a length of black wire attached to a lump of wood.

'Oh, genius.' The first soldier had happy tears in his eyes. 'When did we last garrotte anyone? I can barely remember.'

'Vicenza,' his mate said. 'Two years ago. That bloke from Naples who stabbed one of our lads over a card game. Poor sod's eyes almost popped out. Tongue went kind of black. Lots of gagging and croaking, too.' He scratched his long and florid nose. 'I'm not sure we did it right at all.'

The sergeant walked round and round, staring at Romeo's neck.

'You know what I think, lads. We need some practice. This one here...' He opened up the wire loop and slipped it over Romeo's head. From the bridge, by the horse, Balthazar watched in horror. 'Just the right size.' The metal noose tightened against Romeo's throat, enough so he could barely breathe. 'We need to find ourselves a stool and a piece of timber for his back.'

Balthazar raced over and pushed his way between them. 'My master's got papers that say he's clear to leave here. If you lot don't allow him over that bridge, by God, I'll go to Escalus myself and tell him what you're up to. Right now!'

The sergeant laughed and loosed the wire round Romeo's throat, then unlooped it and dangled the thing in his hand. 'Only checking to see it fits. Don't think us choosy. Either of you will do. Way things are going right now... who's going to spot one more corpse among many?'

Balthazar jabbed a finger in his face. 'I'm warning you.'

The bell in the Torre dei Lamberti started to toll.

'One...' the sergeant said gleefully. 'These papers say you've got to be out of the Republic by midday. Out of Verona by nine.' Another bell. 'And that was two.'

Romeo ran to the mare, ready by the wall, Balthazar fast behind him. The threat of pestilence had done its work. There was no one crossing Cangrande's bridge. He could gallop the animal all the way over the river. Verona ended at the far side.

He jumped onto the saddle. Balthazar slapped the animal's haunches and the beast leapt forward.

The horse's hooves set up a rat-a-tat across the stones. Over the racket Romeo could just make out the ninth bell as he reached the river bank, with it the distant braying laughter of the guards.

Don't turn round, he told himself. She was there somewhere. To look back was to invite peril into their lives again. He'd done enough of that already.

Ten minutes on, in the flat fields going south, following the dusty track through vines of Garganega on one side and Trebbiano on the other, he found himself peeking over his shoulder anyway, against his better instincts.

Verona's barbed rooftops, that line of miniature castles he'd grown up with, rose on the horizon against the grandiose backdrop of the mountains. From this distance they looked like a glorious crown of thorns.

He slowed. The horse protested. The beast wanted to run. So he let it, racing hard, the summer wind in his face, the repetitive sound of its beating hooves filling his ears, dulling his thoughts. When he next looked back the crown of thorns was gone. He was in the flatlands, the plain that ran all the way out of the Veneto south to Mantua.

By a shallow stream that fed a field of wilting artichokes he passed a hamlet of rough country cottages, spurring on the beast since some soldiers were milling round. There was a red cross on the nearest house which seemed to interest them far more than a single passing horseman.

Plague, Romeo thought. It was closer to Verona than ever.

* * *

Juliet stood with her mother and father in the cemetery, her head swimming with memories of the illicit wedding in the monastery of San Francesco a little way along the path. No clouds now, no wind. Just the unforgiving sun. On this airless day, surrounded by the greying monuments, stone angels casting long shadows, grieving cherubs, she felt as if she could smell the dead mouldering in the earth beneath them.

A pale wooden coffin was all she saw of Tybalt. On the far side of the graveyard Escalus, in black to match his eyepatch, silver guard shining on his cheek, had just seen his nephew Mercutio placed into the ground. The servants said the lad should have been shipped back to his family in Venice. But the marshal had forbidden it. The restrictions on movement applied to the dead as much as the living. Only the unwanted like Romeo escaped the net, for the simple reason they knew he could never come back.

Father Cesare, the dour Dominican priest from Sant'Anastasia who weekly heard her feeble confessions, saw to the ceremony. All the old words. Ashes to ashes. Dust to dust.

Juliet stared at the coffin and thought for a moment she could see through the plain timber lid, Romeo inside, pale and stiff and ready for the earth.

Oh God, I have an ill-divining soul. It imagines death everywhere.

'Daughter?'

She didn't take her eyes off the grave. 'Mother?'

'I thought you said something.'

'Only a prayer for Tybalt. To wish him on his way.'

She wondered what she'd say to Father Cesare the coming Sunday when he invited her into his wooden box.

I married in secret, my father's enemy. Then I slept with him. If only I could be in his arms now instead of this stuffy upright coffin, listening to the judgemental words of a priest who knows nothing of who I am and what moves me...

Then it was time to go. Funerals were short, mourners for a surly thug like Tybalt few.

'We need to speak,' her father said.

'May I walk alone? Along the river? To compose my thoughts. These last few days–'

'No.' He took her arm firmly. 'We will talk now.'

He was unshaven, his eyes pink and rheumy. The night had been long for him too, she guessed. Filled with drink and anger, not love and new discoveries.

The little crowd around the grave was dispersing. She was soon left alone with her parents and the priest. Father Cesare doffed his cap and, seeing he wasn't wanted, walked back towards the chapel. The sextons were busy shovelling dense brown earth into the grave. It was impossible for her to connect that plain and simple box vanishing into the ground with the sneering, teasing creature Tybalt. That unhappy bundle of fierce emotions had surely vanished on the cobbles of Sant'Anastasia the day before. All that was buried here was the shell, a carcass of meat and bones soon to turn to dust.

'Do you love me, Father?'

'Of course I do. It's why I act this way.'

'Let me walk a little while then. I won't vanish. Or run away.' She looked at Escalus who was now talking to the priest by the chapel door. 'I couldn't even if I wanted, could I?'

'No.' It was her mother who spoke though the tone might have been her father's. 'And don't ask such presumptuous questions. Of course we love you.'

Her father's hand gripped her arm more firmly. 'It's why we know what's best.'

What's best?

If only she could flee. If only she could tell them. But while she had the courage she understood too well the consequences.

'As you wish,' she said and went in silence back to the palazzo and her fate.

* * *

Romeo was out of the Veneto within two hours. Another and he found himself approaching Mantua, a city new to him, though its wily political character was known throughout the north.

Isabella d'Este, wife of Francesco Gonzaga the second, the current marquess, ruled mostly as regent. Francesco was a notorious mercenary leader, once in the pay of the Venetians, now more dependent on the Borgias in Rome where he spent most of his time. This way Mantua clung to its status as an independent state, one so small it was always in need of powerful friends.

As Romeo rode in from the plains he realised it could scarcely be more different from the place he'd left. Four artificial lakes surrounded the city, wide defensive moats created from the river Mincio that flowed from the snowy heights of the Alps. A tall castellated wall ran the length of the northern border. After that, four bridges crossed the lakes, expanses of water so large they appeared to support a small fishing fleet as well as trading craft headed for a harbour visible in the distance.

He was stopped by a guard when he reached the first gate and gave the response Laurence had suggested. He was a student wishing to talk to the apothecary Nico on behalf of his brother, a Franciscan friar in Verona. The man asked for papers. All he had was the letter Laurence had given him and that was written in Greek.

The soldier grumbled at that, talked to his sergeant, came back and waved him through.

'That fellow from Otranto's the only apothecary hereabouts who isn't a bloody quack. Since it's Nico and you seem a harmless sort you're in.'

'Thank you.'

'One thing, mind. I heard all them fools in Verona were worried about the plague,' the man said opening the gates.

'There are reports of it. I passed a house along the way. The red cross—'

'Spots. That's what those folk had or so we heard. You don't get spots with plague, lad. Boils. Spewing. Lots of nasty stuff. Not spots.'

'I'm sorry—'

'When you get back to Verona you tell them that. We don't need their scaremongering driving people down here. Ask your friend the apothecary. He understands all there is to know about pestilence. We haven't got it. And nor, I think, have you. Now on your way.'

The bridge over the lake was low and pretty, with no crenellations, no threatening militia. The city he found on the other side was delightful, most of the houses around the centre painted with frescoes on their exteriors, all classical scenes, bright and jovial. The sight cheered him until he found the square he wanted, only to see that was called the Piazza Erbe too. An unwanted reminder of home, of Juliet, and with it an ache of longing.

The directions Laurence had given him led to a small round building, much like a classical Roman temple. It had once been a church. Now, in a city full of grander places of worship, the Rotonda of San Lorenzo had turned into a marketplace, with food counters in what was once the circular nave, more obscure services on the floor above.

Up the stairs he found three apothecary stalls set side-by-side. One run by an African, the second the property of a Jewish man with long locks and traditional garments. The last was occupied by a smiling fellow of forty or so, built like a soldier, wearing red wool britches and a leather jerkin. He had Laurence's eyes, intelligent and searching, but there was a worldly air about him the friar lacked.

Romeo introduced himself and gave him the letter. Nico bade him sit down next to a row of jars and bottles much like those he'd seen in the cell in Verona and began to read.

'The apothecary business interests you?' Nico asked when he'd finished.

'Not much. All these things you have here... your brother has them, too.'

The man shrugged as if to say: why not? 'You've read this letter?'

'No,' Romeo said. It was Greek. A language beyond him.

Nico folded the thing up and put it in his pocket. 'Never mind. Welcome to Mantua. I gather you'd rather be here for as brief a time as possible.'

'I must return. I have a wife.'

'And a death sentence hanging over you. For murdering a man.'

True, he agreed and left it at that.

'Odd thing for a poet to do.'

'I'm not a poet. I'm not anything.'

'We're all something. Virgil came from Mantua, you know. We can visit his cottage if you like. Perhaps that might spark a bit of cheer in you–'

'I have to return home. As soon as I possibly can. Your brother said you might be able to introduce me to the court here. If they support my case...'

The apothecary got up and started closing his shutters. 'Right then. No time like the present.'

Outside on the gallery, after he'd boarded up his little shop, he said goodbye to the Jew in Hebrew and then what Romeo assumed to be the same to the African in a language beyond comprehension.

Downstairs Nico picked up a bag of almonds and chewed a few. 'Nice fellows my competitors,' he said, nodding back at the floor above. 'Charlatans both. One would sell you a dead lizard and tell you it cures sores. The other a piece of firewood that was supposed to be a splinter off the True Cross. Which won't do anything at all.'

Romeo took the almonds he was offered. 'And do your cures work?'

Nico smiled, then winked. 'Only if you believe in them. Let's go to the palace and see if I can talk you in there.' He brushed at Romeo's jacket. 'You're filthy from the road. Do something about it, lad. You're about to step into the presence of royalty and they don't much appreciate scruffs.'

* * *

Back in the palazzo Luca Capulet demanded water straight away, gulped at it messily then glanced sideways at his wife.

'You tell her. If there's any need for me I'll be in my study. Making plans.'

'For what, Father?' Juliet asked. 'I'm here. You can speak to me directly.'

He glanced at her sideways. 'You can't spend the day in mourning clothes. Change them.'

'Perhaps I feel they fit my mood.'

He sighed, picked up his glass and wandered off.

Her mother winced as he left. 'Your father's still a little delicate. Let me find something nice for you, love. Please…'

Upstairs they went. Juliet chose a light dress, a simple shade of brown. She wasn't having anything picked for her. The room was tidy and spotless. Nurse had been everywhere. Fresh sheets. Fresh linen by the tub. Flowers in a vase, roses and lilies from the garden. The balcony windows were open. The day was stifling and silent save for the buzz of insects. Perhaps the birds couldn't summon the energy to sing.

'Happiness...' her mother said, pacing the room while Juliet changed. 'That's what we need. Tybalt is buried. We must live.'

'I'm sorry for my cousin. But you know what he was like.'

'Yes. And hasn't he paid for it? Your father was rambling last night about sending a rogue to deal with the Montague boy. The guards on the bridge said he was heading off towards Mantua.'

Her heart thudded. 'Deal with him?'

'He had it in his head he could have the villain murdered. Poison. Stabbed in some dark alley as he deserves. Put him in the earth and we'd gain the revenge Escalus won't give us. There's not a servant here who'd do it, of course. Even that little bully Samson–'

'I will.'

Her mother stopped. 'You'd what?'

'I'll go and... follow him. Do whatever you ask. Just give me the opportunity.'

Bianca Capulet laughed. 'That is kind. And brave. But you're a girl–'

'I won't be satisfied with this Romeo until I see him...' Her mind was racing ahead of itself.

'See him?'

'See him dead, I mean. You've no need of servants. Give me the chance–'

'No, no, child.' Her mother closed her eyes for a moment, as if in

223

pain. 'Vengeance is a matter for men, not us. They have a hunger for it and never see the consequences. It was the drink talking. Your father's not a murderer. It wouldn't be proper.'

'None of this is "proper", is it?' Juliet asked a little too harshly.

'Tybalt's dead. The Montague boy's as good as. We'll never see his face in Verona again. Unless it's in a noose. That's enough for me.' Bianca Capulet smiled. 'Now. Let's try and think of joyful things instead.'

'Joyful...?' It came out as a whisper.

'Your father's a prudent, thoughtful man. I know it doesn't always seem that way. But he bears burdens we never witness. A happy day he's arranged for you.'

There was a tremor in her voice then. Juliet heard it and wondered. 'What day is that?'

'Your wedding. It's arranged. The service. The flowers. A choir. Count Paris makes his preparations, too.'

'I told you. I'm not ready. Give me a little time...'

Her mother looked her in the eye. 'This procrastination on your part must end. The deal's been struck. Your father and Paris decided last night. You'll be wed tomorrow. In the morning. Father Cesare will marry you in Sant'Anastasia where you were baptised.' With tenderness she touched her daughter's long blonde hair. 'I'll bring in women to make you the loveliest bride this city's seen in years. Whatever it costs—'

'This is too soon! You haven't asked me. Paris... I don't know this man. And when we spoke it was... awkward.'

A laugh again, bitterness beneath it. 'It's always awkward at the start. How do you think it was for any of us? The time for argument's over. You know—'

'Don't tell me what I know!'

Juliet's voice rose to echo round the room. Angry tears began to fill her eyes. The painting on the wall, the little girl with her stick drawing in charcoal seemed to mock her. As if the grinning figure there said, 'You understood it was coming all along. And simply used Romeo to fool yourself otherwise.'

'I know I do not want this. I will not marry yet and that is that.'

'It is arranged!'

'Then un-arrange it! Or send me to this Montague in Mantua. If I don't kill him I'll marry him instead. You hate him, too. Perhaps that would be a greater punishment for both of us—'

'Be quiet, girl. Speak moderately and with a modicum of sense.'

'Sense? You'd marry me to a stranger? Against my will? Tomorrow? And you dare preach to me of sense?'

There'd never been blows between them. There wouldn't be now. But she did push her mother out of the room, with all the force it took to move her struggling, protesting frame. Juliet bolted the door with a slam, weeping, crying, cursing with all the words she'd never used out loud before.

After a little while a hesitant voice came through the polished wood.

'Daughter?'

She didn't speak. The tears were running freely. She wiped them away with her arm.

'Juliet... in an hour I'll come back for you. We will discuss this with your father. Calm yourself. Think of your family. Of your duty to us. As we think of ours to you.'

'I think of Mantua and nothing else! Send me there!'

After a long pause her mother said with firmness, 'Tybalt's death has distressed you more than I imagined. More than you realise yourself. Young girls may become hysterical—'

'Hysterical?'

'It's a fact. I will arrange for a physician. He can find a potion that will soothe your nerves.'

Her response came unbidden, as if some instinct seized on any slight opportunity. 'The only medical man I'll talk to is Friar Laurence from San Francesco. At least he's kind—'

She could hear her mother's laboured breathing. Then Bianca Capulet said, 'The Franciscan? If that's what you want. He'll have a drug to put you right. But first you must speak with your father. One hour. I'll knock on your door.'

One hour.

'The time will fly,' she murmured.

On Cupid's wings. And there's the joke.

* * *

The monumental quarters of Verona were cramped and jumbled, constructed piecemeal over the centuries with little thought for design or planning. Mantua seemed grander and more organised by comparison, as if the little town wished to be a miniature Venice or Rome. The apothecary gave him some necessary background before they reached the complex of palaces and fortifications that formed the regal household. This, Nico said, was a state with great aspirations and a sense of independence. It paid well to heed both. That way lay swift elevation and, with luck, for Romeo, a letter recommending Escalus show mercy to a son of Verona who'd come to repent the hot-headed fury he'd displayed on a single summer day.

'Ingratiate yourself, lad,' the apothecary advised. 'Flatter her. Tell her what she wants. If you're lucky she'll take you on her staff for a pittance. Doesn't matter. One day you'll get those papers and then you'll be on your way home.'

'How long?' Romeo asked.

Nico smiled and didn't answer.

Finally they reached their destination, the castle of San Giorgio, a turreted fortress overlooking one of the lakes and near the harbour. The walls were of soft golden stone, more appealing than the red brick of Cangrande's castle by the Adige. Inside, the building seemed more palace than stronghold. Nine paintings greeted them in the reception hall, gigantic, imposing canvases documenting the triumphs of Caesar. They were as grand and colourful as anything Romeo had seen in Florence. The work, Nico said, of Mantegna, Mantua's favourite artist, now resident on a fantastic salary at the court so that he was never tempted to roam.

It was as well Mantegna's magnificent depictions of an imperial triumph were there to welcome them. There was precious else to look at as they waited more than an hour in a sweltering corridor while servants and clerks and others whose purpose Romeo could only guess at came and went. The court of the absent Francesco Gonzaga the Second seemed a busy place, buzzing like a hive in which serious young men in dark suits carried documents and pens about as casually as the young of Verona sported daggers.

Then a face appeared at the door and said he was summoned. The apothecary nodded at him. 'You're on your own now. Be polite. Be sharp. Be lucky. I'll see you outside when you're done.'

The man who called his name was black. Not with the swarthy colour of the men of the south, of Sicily and the like, that he'd seen at home. This man was black as coal, with round and serious features and a shiny silk costume of scarlet and silver stripes designed to show off his muscular frame.

227

Romeo followed him down a corridor of portraits – men mostly, Gonzagas he assumed – then they entered the private office of Isabella d'Este, Marchesa of Mantua.

She sat on a kind of raised throne next to a long, wide window that looked out over the placid lake. Her attire was even more extraordinary than that of her servant. The dress was of green velvet set with gold and gems. The arms were billowing, the low neckline covered modestly with fine gauze. It was hard to take his eyes off the most unusual aspect of her gown: the openings over her breasts through which a pair of timid brown nipples were peeking.

'You're staring at something.'

'No, no, your Highness. I'm not. I promise.'

Instead he gazed up at the towering bookcases next to the throne. A small brown and white monkey was perched on top. When it saw him the creature scampered down, chattering, stole a pear from a fruit bowl on the table, then curled up on a cushioned bed by the fireplace and started to eat very noisily.

'You're from Verona,' Isabella d'Este said, as if nothing odd had happened.

'I am.'

'Banished for murdering a man.'

'The villain killed a friend of mine, in a cowardly cruel fashion. I was… full of anger. He threatened me. The red heat came. Now I'm banished and full of regret and shame. For which I truly curse myself.'

She was looking at the paintings. All portraits of herself. 'Your personal feelings are of no consequence. It is for the state to deliver justice. Not the individual. Though…' A thought occurred to her. 'I am the state. And I am an individual. So perhaps I'm being pompous.'

She had dark eyes, small and keen, and seemed far more alert than he felt after a night in Juliet's bed and the ride across the plain.

'No, my lady. You are right.'

'I usually am.'

She asked him about Escalus and which way his troops were pointing: north, south, or west? It seemed an odd question to throw at him. Mantua surely had a web of spies throughout Italy. They would know more of military matters than he could ever glean from gossip round the Piazza Erbe.

'I think they mostly look within, your Grace. Verona's a fractious city. There are families that loathe one another far more than they hate a distant foe. Perhaps plague's around the corner, too. Escalus wishes to keep the public order and awaits his turn to fight the Turks if they come.'

'A sound observation,' she declared. 'A sound policy on the marshal's part. And what do they say of my husband out on your streets?'

Romeo was puzzled by that one. 'I've never heard ill spoken of him. He was a friend of Venice. He's now a friend of Rome. In all honesty what gossip we have in Verona tends to local matters. If–'

'My husband's in the Vatican, bedding that poisonous and poisoning harlot Lucrezia Borgia. My sister-in-law for God's sake. The bitch. They say her father's lain with her along with all the rest. You heard that, did you?'

There were so many stories running round about Alexander the Sixth, the man once called Rodrigo Borgia: that he ravished his own children and the infants of others; tales of sorcery and the summoning of demons inside the holy chambers of Saint Peter's; even that a pact with seven devils sent by Satan had secured him the papacy in the first place. More plausible accounts ranged, too, of how anything from a cardinal's hat in Rome to a bishopric in distant England might be bought with an adequate gift of gold, a promise of soldiery or simply an offer of soft and supple flesh.

'No, Madam. I'm not one for tittle-tattle. I've been distracted of late.'

Her response was long in coming.

'I see you're lovelorn,' Isabella d'Este said eventually. 'You wear the symptoms about your person. They're as obvious as the weals and blisters of a man about to die of pox.'

He felt older. As if a single day had aged him years. 'I have personal matters to attend to. My business. None so weighty they should trouble a great lady such as you.'

'The heart,' she sighed. 'They say it breaks. Does it? Can one die of love? Or only the physical consequences of it? The jealous rages. The self-inflicted pain. The violence that stems from abandonment or simply being spurned.'

'I'm a student of poetry, not a man of medicine.'

'And verse gives you no lessons?'

No good ones. That he'd learned from Juliet. All the men of letters he'd adored were enthralled by love's rejection, not its fond acceptance.

'I believe poetry exists to ask us questions. Not furnish answers. In this respect perhaps it wonders... if a man cannot love another, how can he love himself? And if a man cannot love himself then what lies in his future but rage and hate?'

And death, he nearly said.

'It's not just men. That whore in Rome...'

She pointed to a drawing on the wall. A portrait, side-on, a clever tactic since it disguised the plumpness of Isabella d'Este's face. 'They claim Lucrezia's the most beautiful woman in Italy. Why? Because her devil of a father is Pope and they daren't say otherwise. Yet how many paintings of her have you seen? And by whom?'

None, he admitted. But Verona belonged to Venice and it was unlikely pictures of a Roman pontiff's offspring would be welcomed there.

'And how many portraits do you see of me? They're everywhere. I mix with artists, with intellectuals. They're my equal and I theirs. That drawing is by my great friend Leonardo, here a few weeks ago on his way to Venice. Da Vinci is the spirit of our age. A man who dares and stops at nothing. A genius who draws as well as he paints and sculpts. And looks inside these bodies of ours. You should see his deft anatomies.' She held out her arm and flexed her chubby fingers. 'He detects the way we work. How God made us. How we follow in his image. This new world before us belongs to men like my Leonardo. And women like me.'

It was a conversation that would have sparked some interest in Juliet. The very thought depressed him.

'If you die in my service, Montague, I'll hand him your corpse. He can carve you open and see if that heart of yours is truly broken.'

'It isn't, Madam. Not yet. Not quite. I am in your service?'

She made the kind of disappointed noise his mother affected when she found him exasperating. The monkey squeaked once, angrily, then threw the pear core into the fireplace.

'You do speak Greek?'

It occurred to him that Mantua must be a curious place. It was the second time he'd faced that question in a matter of hours.

'Not a word. My father said there was no point in filling a child's head with a dead language that had no place in commerce.'

'Commerce!' she cried. 'You think there's nothing to this world but commerce?'

'My father's choice–'

'Your father's wrong. And you're the one who'll pay for it. I have no room in my household for any who cannot speak the language of Homer. Save for the Africans who are innocent savages too unworldly for academic matters. Oh, and the jester. The last one was a rogue we sent to the scaffold.' A thought amused her. 'That position comes with a fine house outside the castle and free costumes. But the fool's hat is made for the short and hideous. While you have the foolish words you are far too tall and fetching to behold.'

She pulled a tiny white handkerchief from her sleeve and waved it at him. '*Adieu*. Find your place in the world. It may be in Mantua but not my service. If you kill a man in my city I'll hang you without a hearing. Then summon Leonardo to fetch his scalpel and look for whatever black and ugly thing lurks beneath your ribs. *Adieu*.' She waved more frantically. '*Adieu*.'

'Madam, *adieu*,' he said and left the room.

* * *

The windows were open in Luca Capulet's study, the heat relentless. He sat in his grand leather chair waving a peacock fan to no great effect, sipping water mixed with wine.

An hour his wife had waited, then she'd persuaded Juliet out of her room. The girl now occupied a stool in front of him, like a felon before a judge, her mother as an advocate by her side. The nurse had argued her way into the conversation, promising Bianca Capulet her support. She stood at the door, leaning on the frame, fat arms folded, face flushed and sweating.

Juliet listened to her father dictate the list of proceedings for the following day. The time she would be visited by women to prepare her. The hour she'd leave the house. How Father Cesare would begin the wedding ceremony in Sant'Anastasia.

'Tomorrow will be a long and complicated day. It's important you follow my directions.'

She waited for him to finish before she said, 'There will be no wedding.'

Capulet closed his eyes and muttered something. When he opened them he tried a forced smile. 'I'm aware this is unusual. That your tears for your cousin Tybalt are not yet dry—'

'Send me to Mantua. I'll dry them on the man who murdered him.'

He scoffed at that and told her not to be ridiculous. Then set a sour eye on his wife. 'I give you a life of ease and luxury. All I ask in return is that you instil some small sense of obedience in this child...'

'I have tried, Luca!' Bianca Capulet cried. 'God above, I've tried.'

Juliet agreed. 'She has. The answer's still no.'

Her mother gave her a savage look. 'Sweet Jesus. There are moments I wish you were in that coffin we put in the ground this morning. Not that vile cousin of yours—'

'Thank you.'

'At least he made a show of fidelity towards this family!'

'Indeed, mother. And killed men for it. A greater devotion I can scarcely imagine.'

'Stop this,' Capulet ordered. 'Both of you.'

'The girl is beyond us, Luca. Admit it.'

'I admit no such thing. Juliet. Let me make sure you understand this. I have arranged a match with Count Paris. A rich and honest nobleman from an aristocratic line that goes back centuries. He adores you and will provide for you and love you all his days. Are you not grateful? Aren't you in the least proud to be the object of such a man's devotion? Or that tomorrow you may call yourself a countess?'

She laughed. 'Oh, I'm grateful you think so much of me. Call me a countess if you like. But I will still be the same. As to pride... *Paris is a stranger!*'

He swigged back some of his drink. 'This ingratitude I can do without. You'll marry him tomorrow. If I have to drag you there tied to a bloody cart.'

'All I ask is a little time. If you'll listen to me–'

His face turned red. He banged the cup hard on the desk. 'I've listened enough! Long and hard. Get out of my sight and prepare yourself. Or else leave this house forever, you disobedient wretch.'

Juliet rose. 'A few months. Weeks even–'

'Do as I demand or take yourself off to a nunnery or a whorehouse... I don't care which so long as I never see your impudent face again.'

Tears were starting in her eyes. 'If only–'

'Enough! I've spoken.'

'Husband,' Bianca Capulet cut in.

'I should have beaten some civility and respect into this child when she was an infant, and spared us all this pain.' He shook his fist at Juliet. 'You think it's too late now?'

'I do,' she answered. 'But if it gives you satisfaction to try...'

'Out! Out! Not another word. Before I fetch my whip.'

'You are too cruel,' Nurse cried.

'Ha! Lady Wisdom speaks, does she? This little bitch was in your hands all these years. You think you did a good job, woman?'

'Do not call her such dreadful names, sir! Juliet's a decent, steadfast girl. I'd stake my life on it. A brighter child I never–'

He flourished his fist again, face a brilliant red, temper lost entirely. 'Be quiet, you wittering fool. Save your bleating for your peasant peers. By God, you make me mad, the lot of you. Day and night, every hour the Lord gives, I've worked to make a wedding for her. Now I find the child a gentleman of the noblest parentage, this whining little marionette of mine says…'

His voice turned loud and cruel. He put his hands to his cheeks to mock her. 'I cannot wed, Father, since I do not love this man you've found. And further more I'm young. And would rather sit in my room and sew and read *and like every wastrel woman alive do nothing of moment all the long hours the day provides.*'

Capulet struggled to his feet and approached her, his fists clenched so tightly she could see the whites of his knuckles. 'If you won't wed tomorrow then find yourself a gutter to live in. You won't stay in this house, eating my food and drinking my drink. Go and hang, beg, starve, die in the street for all I care. And when they put your corpse in a pauper's grave I won't acknowledge you there either. Nothing of mine – not all this money and finery I've slaved to bring you – will do you good henceforth. Think on it, daughter. Marry or be damned. You choose. This is the last time we speak of it, I swear. Now…'

He swept the table, glass, papers, books and all, sending them flying to the tiled floor. 'Two children the Lord blessed me with and took the wrong one early.' Wild-eyed he raised his fist to the ceiling. 'What did I do that you should rob me of a loyal, obedient son?'

The three women stood in silent shock. There'd been storms aplenty in the palazzo. But none so fierce.

'To hell with this. And wives. And daughters,' he roared, then stormed from the room, slamming the door behind him.

Juliet turned to her mother, voice fragile for once, mind in turmoil.

'Is there no pity anywhere in your hearts? In you at least, Mother? Can't you see how I hurt?'

'Juliet–'

'A month's delay. A week even. Why the hurry?'

'Because Paris will not wait! He's as exasperated by your dithering as the rest of us.'

'One day's notice I am to be married? This is dithering? Do not abandon me. I beg you. Father attacks us both in this...'

'With some reason! I'm an obedient wife and should have given him a daughter much the same.'

'He hits you! I hear it!'

'Never you, though. And look at us now. Your father's right. This decision is yours. You dare ask me to choose between my husband and my daughter? We are women. We obey...'

'Then make room for me next to Tybalt in the tomb. My bridal bed can be in that grim monument–'

'Oh, child,' Nurse begged. 'Don't say such things lest the spirits hear...'

Bianca waved at her to be quiet. 'These histrionics must cease! Do your duty, Juliet!' Then came a sudden and unexpected vehemence to her voice. 'Or do you think you're different from the rest of us? Better than every wife and daughter who went before? All of whom have made these sacrifices.'

'So because you suffered I must too?' For a moment she thought that might earn her a slap. But no. 'All I wish... is to marry the man I love.'

'Then learn to love him! After you're wed. You're not the first and you won't be the last. Nurse! Take this child to her Franciscan friar. Tell him to find a drug that brings the girl back to her senses. Otherwise...'

She started to pick up the things her husband had swept to the tiled floor.

'Otherwise?' Juliet asked in tears.

The look she got was little short of hatred. 'Otherwise? A wife, a nun, a maid, a beggar, a whore... You've made it clear. Your life belongs to you alone. You choose. I care no longer.'

* * *

Gone Juliet was, in short order. Together with the nurse she walked out of the palazzo, head bowed, down to the river, to sit on the bank beneath the shade of a hazel tree watching the wildfowl on the busy water. Laurence's cloisters were a few minutes away. She'd no wish to disobey her parents' demand when it came to visiting him. Though she did not share the intention they so fervently wished upon her.

The nurse stayed silent all the way. When they were seated Juliet turned to her. 'Donata. Talk to me.'

'Oh, lord.' The woman folded her arms. 'If I'm being called by my name it must be serious.'

'Donata. Donata Perotti. You've looked after me since I was a baby. I suckled at your breast.' She sighed at that. 'As you so often remind me.'

'Funny, isn't it? I get closer to you than your own mother in some ways. But I'm still a servant. I don't have a name really. Don't worry, Juliet. I'm happy like this. I know my place. We all should. Hard to get through the day if you don't.'

There was a message there, and not a subtle one.

'How can I prevent this? I have a husband. You know. Comfort me. Counsel me.'

A pair of ducks swam past, the mallard chasing the hen, squawking, struggling to climb on the bird's back. Still the nurse stayed silent.

'Please talk to me. I've heard your voice every day of my life. The world doesn't feel right without it.'

The nurse took a deep breath. Juliet knew from the look in her eyes what was coming. 'You want the truth? Really?'

'Of course.'

'Here it is then. Your Romeo's banished, and nothing in the world's going to bring him back. If he tries, he's dead. If he doesn't, he's gone. To another. He's a fine-looking lad. His eye will wander before long...'

'No, never. We swore–'

'They all swear, darling! Until they get what they want. Then they find another to swear to.'

'Not Romeo... You don't understand. I led him into this.'

Her old hands tightened on Juliet's young fingers. 'He didn't do anything he didn't want to. Your Romeo's just a man. Not a saint or a god. I think it best you marry this count. Your father's right. He's a lovely gentleman. As far as prospects go, Romeo's nothing next to a chap with a dynasty like that. Paris is an eagle, girl, and that young fancy lad of yours a handsome, skittish sparrow, flown off for good. A few months down the road you'll remember last night fondly and realise it was never going to be anything but that. One sweet moment of love with a boy you'll never see again. Paris is here, he's willing, he's rich and he'll make you happy. This... husband. Well... you've got no witnesses, nothing but a piece of paper your father would rip to shreds in an instant if he found it. No one but me knows he's even been in your bed, and a servant's no use in court. As far as this city's concerned, you're not married at all. Romeo's dead...'

'But he isn't.'

'As good as. You live here. He's God knows where. Neither of you any use to the other. Nor ever will be.'

The mallard was on the hen, savagely biting her brown neck as she squawked in pain. The cock bird's tail was pumping hard. Then it was done. The two parted, the male flying off across the river in search of other company.

'I know it's not what you want to hear. But you asked for the truth and you got it.'

I am alone, Juliet thought. *And always was. Just too dim to notice.*

'Well?' Nurse asked. 'Want to shout at me? Go ahead. I don't mind.'

Juliet kissed her on the cheek. 'I asked. You answered. Go home now—'

'I will see you to the friar.'

'No. Tell my mother I'll go there as she demands. I will ask him for a... potion to cure these ills. And confession, too. For all my impudence and disrespect.'

The nurse stared at her. 'You changed your mind? You're saying you'll marry Paris now? Tomorrow?'

'Tell them what I said. I'll talk to them when I return. Help yourself to whatever you want from my jewellery box. I promised that. Best not let my mother see you.'

'No, I won't.' She clapped her hands just as she had when she was singing the ribald wedding song the day before. 'Oh, love! I knew you'd see sense in the end. We all of us fight battles. But not losing ones. Young Romeo's just that. He always will be. Tomorrow you get a proper wedding. Rich man. Lots of prospects. I wonder if he'll be needing a woman servant for that new household of yours...'

'I'll ask him.'

'So kind. So kind…'

Juliet stood up and smoothed down her pale dress. Paris had passed them without noticing they were there. He seemed to be headed for the monastery, too. Perhaps her mother sent him, planning they should meet. All around her the ones she loved were making preparations. She felt as if she were nothing more than a cog in the mechanism of a relentless machine, turning to the will of others.

'I will see the friar. Leave me now.'

'Happy days! Then… happy nights…'

Nurse waddled happily back towards the city.

'Faithless,' Juliet whispered. 'After all these years. I never knew you were so faithless.'

Paris came into view again, striding beneath the monastery portico with a jaunty, expectant step.

Juliet waited a while watching the ducks on the river. Then she walked through Laurence's neat garden of herbs, on to the cloisters and the modest covered arcades, head down, aware of the cemetery at her back.

* * *

Out in the street Romeo looked around at Mantua's grand square, the imposing castle, the ducal palace next to it surrounded by scaffolding, builders climbing over the walls like busy spiders. So much ornamentation and ostentatious wealth. Scarcely an inch of plaster on the regal buildings had gone unadorned. There was a house opposite as Isabella said. Small doors, small windows and a tricorn hat painted by the front window. Doubtless the unfortunate jester's, though what might lead a clown to the scaffold he couldn't guess. Nor could he take his mind off Juliet and Verona. Whatever Escalus had threatened, he would return and steal her from behind the cruel walls of the red-brick prison that separated them.

Nico the apothecary came out of the shadows of the colonnades by the castle. 'Well? How'd it go?'

'Badly. There were these odd servants. And a monkey.'

'So…?'

'And her nipples were poking out of her dress! I think she's slightly mad.'

'Here in Mantua we prefer to think of our lady as eccentric.' They set off for the Piazza Erbe. 'You need to understand. This isn't Verona. What you saw was business as usual in the Castle San Giorgio. Isabella's regent and rules the way she wants. She designs those dresses herself, you know. Lots of posh women copy her. None of our business. We have but one job in life. Give the toffs what they want, take their money, then go safely home. It's important to fit in with the gentry and try not to giggle.' He grabbed Romeo's elbow. 'You didn't, did you? Giggle?'

'No. Nor did I get a job. You need to speak Greek apparently.'

Nico blew out his rosy cheeks. 'Ah. The old Greek excuse. She hasn't used that one in a while.'

'Pardon?'

'No one ever gets anything out of Isabella d'Este at first asking. Third time lucky is the best you can hope for. Especially if you turn up here the day after murdering someone. She's being cunning as usual. We'll get there. What do you want to eat?'

Nothing much, he said, and recounted the awkward conversation about her husband and Lucrezia Borgia.

Nico tutted. 'God, it must be bad if she's mentioning it to

strangers. We're dead lucky it's Isabella ruling the roost here, not him. If it weren't for that good woman the flag of Venice or Milan would be flying over this place not our own. That husband of hers is a wrong 'un. Good at war, terrible at everything else. Including choosing bedfellows. The Pope's daughter is the least of his problems. I had one of his household round not long ago asking if I had a cure for the pox. Wanted it for an *acquaintance*. Right. If he's been hanging round Roman brothels her lord's going to pick up something so nasty no man alive can cure it. Isabella won't want him. Nor will the Borgia woman either. Bad end coming there.' He shook his head, as if this were a personal matter. 'He'll be saying his prayers before long and begging for deliverance. Fat lot of good that'll do him.'

'What? Prayer?'

'Yes, prayer. I don't care what mad fantasies my brother's been serving you up in Verona but don't expect any from me. I've seen what that Lord of his puts up with and I don't like it. Call this a Christian land? When half the warlords who pray to the same God can't wait to chop each other to pieces? Thousands of willing idiots happy to go along with that, too?'

They were soon back in the piazza. The place was so much smaller than Verona, but perhaps richer. And those painted houses... he couldn't decide whether they looked fetching or ridiculous.

Nico stopped and looked about him. The old rotonda church where he kept his stall was busy with trade: cloth and food, wine and religious trinkets for the faithful.

'That place is built on a temple for the old gods, you know. Jupiter and whoever they were. So many of them and they were always at it, fighting and loving and taking sides. Just like us. Now we have this new one. Just him. Maybe that won't last either. And we'll have the Turks along tomorrow telling us… things are different, folks. You worship this one now. Don't argue.'

Romeo liked this unusual, disputatious man. 'But you would. You always do. Your brother told me.'

Nico stared at him. 'Up to a point. If there's a foreigner waving his sword around telling me what fairy story to believe you think I'd bicker with him? Do I look daft to you?'

'No, but—'

'No, but nothing. Muslim, Jew, Zoroastrian, all those funny religions they have out east. Whatever they are… I don't care. The answer's the same. If the world belongs to them just tell me where to kneel and show me the prayers I'm supposed to say. You know what they used to teach us back when we were little kids in Otranto? Some old fool called Tertullian. "The blood of the martyrs is the seed of the church." What a load of cobblers. I've seen more martyrs' blood than most men and, let me tell you, the only thing that grows out of it is women wailing, misery and yet more violence. When a dead man comes back from the grave and tells me I'm wrong I'll change my mind. Till that happens I'll keep this life I've got, thank you. It's the only one I know.'

He clapped his hands. Embarrassed by that outburst, Romeo thought.

'Well. Here endeth the lesson. You do want some grub, lad. Everyone has to eat. We'll try the Lady Isabella again on Friday. Say nice things about that horrible monkey of hers next time. That usually helps.'

* * *

243

Paris sat in the cool of Laurence's cell, looking at the jars and vials, impatient to be away.

'Tomorrow?' the friar asked when the count had told him the news. 'You wish to wed the Capulet girl *tomorrow*? This is impossible. They only buried her cousin this morning.'

'All the more reason to get on with it. Her mother said she'd be here. Why is she late? Tardiness is a sign of sloth. One I refuse to tolerate.'

That, Laurence suggested, was an opinion best left until after a wedding ceremony. 'I know nothing of a visit from the girl. The haste of all this concerns me—'

'It needn't,' the count snapped. 'Capulet wants it and so do I. The ceremony will be for the Dominicans to hold, not you. I'll deck the city with flowers. Verona won't have seen a wedding like this in years.'

Somewhere close a plainchant began. Laurence felt lost. The monastery was a place for quiet and worship. Not scheming and deceit. He'd seen enough of that already. 'From my experience the happiest marriages often have the most modest of beginnings.'

Paris sneered. 'And what would a celibate friar know of that? You *are* one of those who stays true to his vows, I presume?'

Laurence rarely formed quick opinions of a man. The count was to be an exception. 'I do my best. Do you know Juliet's feelings? Have you asked her?'

The question seemed to surprise him. 'We have met and spoken. I walked her in their garden. The time's agreed. The priests are booked. Her father's about to spend a small fortune on a banquet and I shall do the same, twice over. What else is there to know?'

'I counsel you to… pause a little. A few weeks. Months even. She's an intelligent girl, a touch headstrong, perhaps. You need to coax her to your side.'

'Nonsense. Capulet says she weeps immoderately for her cousin. What use is it to talk to her of love in that case? Venus doesn't smile in a house of misery. That will come later. When we are married.' He smirked. 'She is a beauty, a prize. Tomorrow night I'll wipe away those tears with a passion the likes of which will leave her breathless. Panting. Sixteen! I'll teach her things—'

Laurence's eyes flitted to the door. Juliet had entered in silence and stood there, listening.

'You'll teach me what?'

Paris laughed, amused by her presence, not embarrassed in the least. He got up and took her hand, bowing effusively. 'The ways of love. As a husband should. We're happily met, my lady, my wife.'

She withdrew her hand. 'Not yet.'

He beamed and said, 'Tomorrow.'

'So I'm told.'

They sat down and he shuffled his seat close to her. 'Your mother said you came to make confession to the friar.'

She nodded.

'To confess you love me, Juliet.' He winked. 'I know.'

'I come to confess my love, sir. Yes. In that you're right.'

'See!' He grinned defiantly at Laurence. 'She adores me. I told you. Tomorrow morning we will seal that love before God.' Another wink, lascivious this time. 'And in the evening, beneath the sheets, with one another.'

'Your hand is on my leg, Count,' Juliet told him in a venomous tone. 'This seems forward. The goods have not yet been paid for.'

He removed his fingers, sliding them down her thigh. 'But they shall be, sweetest. In ways you'll never forget–'

Juliet edged away from him. 'Friar. If it would suit you more I will return a little later. I can wait in the garden.'

Laurence looked at Count Paris and didn't smile. 'I have time for you now, child. Later doesn't suit.' He nodded at the door. 'This is private. You must leave us.'

Paris got up, happy, slapping his thighs. 'God forbid I should come between my beloved and her little monk. Talk to her, Friar. Prepare her well. Don't give away any of our manly secrets, mind.' He put a finger to the side of his nose. 'That's if you know any. Quick…' He bent down and in a flash placed a wet and clumsy kiss upon her cheek. 'There's a taste of it, girl. Your father can rouse you in the morning. I'll rouse you tomorrow night, that's for sure.'

They stared at him in silence until he strode out of the cool and shady cell.

Laurence went to the door, bolted it, returned and shook his head. The plainchant ended. The room was as quiet as the grave until she spoke.

'I will not marry that man. I would rather take my life–'

'Do not say that!'

'Then what?'

'He's adamant your father's agreed. The time is set. Tomorrow. And nothing will prevent it.'

'If I could show him the vows we signed–'

'I warned you! Against your father it would be difficult enough. Wave that piece of parchment at a man of influence like Paris and he'll laugh in your face as he throws it on the fire. And where's your so-called husband?'

'So-called? You married us!'

True, he thought. That was a rash act. A foolish effort to bring two warring houses together. Now, they were more apart than ever.

'I can see no way out of this. None whatsoever...'

Then words failed him. Out of her dress she'd retrieved a small and slender dagger. Juliet raised the weapon, delicate fingers round its shank. The point glittered in the late afternoon sun streaming through the cell window.

'God joined my heart to Romeo's and you our hands. Before I'm sold off like a slave to another I swear by everything I know I will use this sharp blade to end things.'

'There is no greater sin,' he whispered.

She laughed. 'Not forcing a woman to marry against her will?'

'No suicide has hope of redemption—'

'You think I care?'

He looked around him at the little room. She did, too, seeing the bottles and the vials and jars.

'My mother said you could give me a potion. Some medicine to make me *better*.'

He reached across the table, took her hands and gazed into her eyes. 'It's the world that's sick. Not you. I lack a garden big enough to find a cure for that. If only...'

He went quiet, thinking.

'If only what?'

'You'd take your life?'

'I will. Tonight.'

Laurence got up and found a blue glass vial. Then an empty black one, a skull on the side. 'If you're brave enough to face death then...' He closed his eyes and whispered, 'Oh, God, forgive me. Do I make this dreadful condition worse?'

'I will kill myself.'

He showed her the little blue bottle. 'This is a simple herbal tonic. You may tell your mother I gave it you. Then throw it away.' He shrugged. 'It's largely useless anyway. But *this*...'

He uncorked the black vial and turned it upside down.

'Is empty,' she said.

'As always. It's made for poison. To kill the rats and plague with it, or so we hope. I distil the doses to order. It's too dangerous and too volatile to keep any other way.'

She took the bottle from him. 'Your poison's kinder than the knife?'

'I don't know. I've never found a rat to ask. But that's not what I'll give you. Watch. Listen. Carefully.'

Half an hour it took, crushing, mixing, boiling, burning. The little cell filled with strange aromas, some floral, some foul. At the end, he had a few spoonfuls of a dark and viscous liquid which he poured carefully into the bottle with the skull.

'Go home. Be pleasant. Say you'll marry Paris in the morning. Tonight sleep alone. No one in your chamber, no one near. Then...' He held up the vial. 'When you hear the midnight Marangona strike, drink this down.'

She took the bottle. 'After which I die.'

'So it will seem.'

Juliet cocked her head to one side, waiting.

'This is a powerful narcotic. You'll look dead to any but a physician. Your breathing turned so shallow it will scarcely be perceptible. The same for your pulse.'

She shook the bottle and gazed at it.

'The roses in your lips and cheeks will fade to the colour of pale ashes. Your eyes fall shut. Your skin turn cold.'

'But I'll be alive? They will know.'

Laurence picked up the blue bottle. 'Not if no one deals with you but me. Tomorrow morning I'll visit your home. There I'll tell your parents I gave you this simple tonic. And you…' He picked up the black vial. 'Stole this while my back was turned. After which we'll find you. I will judge you dead. For them. Tomorrow evening, twenty-four hours or so after you take this draft, you'll wake. Refreshed, the Ottomans always said. As if the drug renewed you.'

'Where?'

He pushed back his chair. 'The crypt of the cemetery chapel. A private place.'

'A charnel house?'

'The dead need somewhere to lie before they go into the ground.'

She thought for a moment. 'What else?'

'I'll send one of the brothers to Mantua. Romeo can take the friar's cloak and papers, and return in his place. For midnight tomorrow.' Laurence grimaced, thinking. 'There he can find you in the dead house. You can flee.'

There was no expression on her face at all. '*Then* what will my parents think?'

He shrugged. 'That you were stolen. Or miraculously revived and ran. That's the best I can offer, Juliet. I'm a humble churchman. Lies and scheming are not for me.'

'You seem quite good at them.'

He bit his tongue and said, 'Wherever you go—'

'Venice. Rome—'

'Wherever you go you must write to your mother and father when you can. Tell them you're alive. Tell them about Romeo.' He sighed. 'Send them to me for confirmation if you like. The consequences—'

'This is my battle, Friar. Not yours. But I will write.'

'Then perhaps one day you'll be reunited. Parents and children. Capulets and Montagues.'

'Perhaps. You must show me this place where I wake from the dead.'

'Why?'

'Because I want to see it. I wish to be prepared.'

Laurence found a torch and lit it from the candle. 'Very well. Come.'

* * *

The cemetery was a short walk along the river. The chapel stood at the end of a path bordered by a high wall and cedars, with an iron gate at the road which was locked after dark to keep out robbers. It was a low building with a crucifix over the stone porch. He asked her to wait and went inside. After a moment he came out and said the place was empty. No priests. No corpses.

They walked through the small chapel. Then she followed him down damp, worn limestone steps into a chamber beneath the earth. A line of tracery windows allowed some light to shine on three worn marble tables in the centre. A pair of plain wooden coffins stood beside them, for paupers, Laurence said. It was a quiet, bare place with a smell to it she didn't want to think about. Water was trickling somewhere close.

'As I said, the drug should last a day. But nothing's perfect. All I can guarantee is that sometime in the night you'll wake up. If Romeo's not there for you...'

'Then in my shroud I'll wait.'

'I'll tell him to bring clothes. And money. And to think of where you'll go. Let's stand outside, child. Enjoy the day while we can.'

They did that and couldn't think of anything else to say. When the sun began to dip towards the western horizon she turned to him and asked for the vials.

'I will swallow this gladly,' she insisted when she took them. 'I will live. When I wake Romeo will be there. So the two of us can flee this place and find... somewhere...'

He was nodding, a little too anxiously. She embraced him and kissed his cheek.

'I'm sorry for the distress I've caused you, Friar. I hope to bring it to an end. But I will not live a slave.'

'As I did.' Laurence pointed towards the monastery and his garden. 'Everything I know... I learned in the servitude of a kind and honest master of a faith we're told to hate.'

'Yet, if you had had the choice?' she asked. 'If you came to a crossroads and one way led to slavery, the other to freedom...'

'God made my choices for me. Through the agency of my dear brother.'

She tapped her head and said, 'I make my own.'

Laurence frowned. 'We all like to think that, don't we?' He led her back to the lane that ran to the city. 'Go, Juliet. Be strong and certain in your resolve.'

'How will you reach him?'

There was a young friar in the monastery, Laurence said. A quiet, reliable lad. He could take some medicine, and papers that said it was destined for physicians treating plague in the south. The guards wouldn't argue over that.

'John can carry a letter for your love. I'll tell him where to meet you tomorrow night. After that...' He couldn't finish the sentence for a moment. From the look on her face Juliet didn't need it. 'After that you're in the hands of God.'

'Then,' she said gently, 'in him... in *Him* we trust.

Laurence watched her go. John, he found in the presbytery. He told the lad very little except that he had to deliver some goods to an address in Mantua, and messages with them. Then he wrote two letters, one for Romeo, a second in Greek for his brother, sealed them and told the young friar they were private, for the eyes of their recipients only. After that he scribbled a document from the monastery bearing its seal, asking for all to give free passage to a young friar carrying potions for the sick. There was only one mule available, a slow and elderly creature. It would have to do.

As the day began to die he watched John lead the sluggish beast towards the Cangrande castle and the bridge.

The lad couldn't reach Mantua before dark. He'd have to stay somewhere and finish his journey the following day. If Romeo returned by horseback he could be in Verona by evening when Juliet would be waking. In his head Laurence had added up the hours and minutes, the miles as well. This was all possible. It had to be. Lives hung on it.

'Mine among them,' the friar whispered looking at his garden.

Unwanted grass and nettles were rising beneath the careful rows of balsam, mint and rosemary. They came from nowhere, overnight. In a blink of an eye sometimes it seemed.

He found his hoe and bent to work. The days ahead were like the weeds. They both would come regardless.

* * *

The apothecary had one spare room. In that small space, on a single cot, Romeo curled up exhausted as the afternoon came to a close.

Nico had decided not to return to work. Instead he occupied himself by playing with chemicals and herbs, alembics and a rickety contraption of distilling equipment. Sounds came periodically through the door — curses, cries of joy, the occasional puff of a chemical explosion.

Was this the new world they'd talked of? A lonely place of strangers? Of rulers who lived with monkeys and houses that bore paintings on their exteriors, like tattoos on a primitive?

Two days before he'd been nothing more than a spurned, spoiled child, heart set obsessively on an impossible love for Rosaline, a girl whose face he could now barely remember. Then they'd sneaked into Capulet's banquet. From that moment on, from the second he saw Juliet's face, his life had been seized by a relentless passion that brooked no analysis, no attempt at reason.

He recalled what he'd told Isabella d'Este when she tested him about poetry.

If a man cannot love another, how can he love himself? And if a man cannot love himself then what lies in his future but rage and hate?

'And death,' he murmured now.

How much of love was the noble sacrifice that verse portrayed? How much a selfish, obsessional need to possess another? He'd felt jilted. Juliet was faced with a forced marriage to a man she didn't know. Had they, as a result, raced headlong into something they could not understand? And, through their rashness, he was now a murderer, banished from her and all of the Venetian Republic. For all that he'd told Juliet, he *was* a murderer. Cold-hearted and deliberate. Every second of the encounter that began in Sottoriva remained with him, each blow and cry and parry. He could have shrunk from them all and left Tybalt to the watch. Instead, he'd let the red rage win. Romeo knew what had fired it too. The last words her vile cousin had uttered.

Tell me. What's it like? That soft sweet place between her legs?

'It's heaven,' he whispered to himself. 'Like the rest of her. The touch of her. The sound. The scent.'

He'd become a man possessed, who craved to possess in return. This was a dangerous breed of madness that seemed without cure outside oblivion.

Perhaps that would be the kindest thing for them both. Perhaps he should steal out of the apothecary's warm and hospitable home, secrete himself down a shadowy nook in Mantua's ornate streets, open his veins with a dagger and wait for the endless dark to fall. He could picture it in his head now just as easily as he could remember the feeling of his blade piercing Tybalt's chest as it took his life.

His reverie was shattered by a louder cry of victory in the room beyond, followed by an outburst in a strange tongue. Greek, perhaps. Laurence had written his missive to his brother in that language Romeo couldn't read. It was no accident. He wondered what it said.

The door opened. Nico was there, a look of pure joy on his rugged sunburnt face. 'Hallelujah, my new friend! Give praise to whatever god it is you worship. For truly this is a momentous day.' He had two metal cups in his hands, a scarlet liquid swilling over the top. 'Here.'

Nico held out a goblet. Romeo took it. The metal was warm, as was the liquid within.

'I have no need of medicine. Or a drug.'

The apothecary scowled. 'Medicine? I do that stuff for work, lad. You don't think I spend my leisure hours on it as well?'

'Then?'

'Booze. Liquor. Gut-rot. That's what this is. Well, not gut-rot, I hope. A distillation I have invented myself. Good grape spirit bought from a merchant in Modena. Afterwards infused with myrtle orange and pomegranate... cumin, coriander.' He scratched his head. 'The rest I forget. I've written it down though. Somewhere. And besides...' He wagged a finger at Romeo. 'I know you Verona businessmen. You'd steal it if you could...'

'I would not!'

'Well, some of you might.'

'The colour?'

It was bright red and quite clear, the smell sweet yet bitter too.

'The colour's a secret. Are you going to have a sip or just stare at it?'

Nico tried his, more than a sip. Romeo did the same. And coughed. Then coughed a little more.

'Is it too strong?' the apothecary wondered. 'Too coarse? Too sweet? Too evocative of the orchard? Come. Give opinions. That's why you get it for free. If I'd perfected the bloody thing you'd be paying for it.'

A little too strong, Romeo thought. A little too sweet. But...

He thought of Juliet's garden. The fragrance of the oranges and pomegranates. And Laurence's, too. There was fruit in the concoction, but the flavour was as much of the monastery as the Capulet palazzo. An apothecary's drink, herbal, spicy like medicine and with a bite.

'I think you should sell it,' Romeo declared.

'I agree. I'm bored with potions. One more cup for you and then it's bed. You look as if you haven't slept in days. And tomorrow... who knows? I'll find my way into the castle and see if the lady Isabella is in a more accommodating mood. The monkey!'

'The monkey?' Romeo asked.

'Remember. Kind words about the monkey. They never go amiss. Now...'

Another draft of sweet red liquid. That tasted better somehow.

'This may give you strange and vivid dreams,' Nico warned as he handed it over. 'It's the valerian. But…' He finished his cup and looked ready for another. 'It's a just a dream. That's all. Like us I guess.' He waved his cup around the tiny room. 'One big dream we call the world. And the best we can do is make sure it's not a nightmare.'

'I'll drink to that.'

Two old pewter cups met in the hot and stuffy room.

'It'll all be fine, Romeo,' the apothecary promised. 'You sleep now. With any luck your little love will come and pay a visit. Then tomorrow we'll go about getting her back in your arms for real. *Salute*!'

'*Salute*,' Romeo replied.

* * *

Luca Capulet was issuing orders to the servants when Juliet returned to the palazzo. She hovered by the door to his study, eavesdropping. Gregory, the only one who could write, was making notes, Pietro by his side. Nurse stood by the window, listening to the master's orders.

'Invite all the guests we had on Monday,' Capulet ordered. 'Then I'll give you a fresh list and double their numbers. Find me twenty of the best cooks. I have one daughter only and this shall be a memorable moment. For me… if not for her.'

'We won't have any bad chefs,' Pietro said. 'I'll make them lick their fingers.'

Capulet stared at him and asked, 'What good's that?'

The lad looked at his mate for support. 'Well… I mean… that's how you tell a bad cook, isn't it? If he won't lick his own fingers you know there's something up.'

'Just go and do it, will you?' They vanished down the stairs to the kitchen, muttering. Capulet glanced at the nurse. 'Why am I surrounded by idiots?'

'Do you have further need of me, sir?'

'Did my daughter go to see Friar Laurence?'

'She did. On her own. I thought it best.'

'Is there any chance he might have instilled some sense into her head? Instead of all that peevish nonsense...'

Juliet walked in, came straight up to her father, kissed him once on the bristly cheek, then knelt before him.

'No more games, my headstrong child,' he whispered. 'Where've you been?'

'You know, father. To the holy brother. He urged me to beg your pardon.' She pulled the blue vial from the pocket of her dress. 'Friar Laurence bade me drink this to bring me to my senses.'

'Sound fellow,' Capulet declared.

Juliet took his hand and looked up into his eyes. 'Forgive me, I beseech you. From this point on I'm ruled by you. Then Count Paris in your stead.'

The nurse looked shocked, Capulet amazed.

'This is true? Not another ruse?'

'Every word, sir.'

He clapped his hands and cried, 'Mother! *Wife*! Fetch her!'

The nurse found her in the laundry, issuing orders. A joyful Bianca Capulet came and listened to Juliet make her promises again.

'Paris must be told, husband.'

'He knows already. I met him at Laurence's.' Juliet glanced at her. 'I'm glad you sent him there. Truly. I'm sorry for all the trouble I've caused. It's time to put an end to it.'

Capulet cried with joy and reached for the cup of wine on his desk. 'A toast! A toast! To matrimony! And dutiful children! This is blissful news indeed! Tomorrow we'll do it. God bless this friar. We're in his debt.'

She still knelt before him, head bowed. Capulet remembered all the harsh words he'd used that morning.

'Stand up, child.' She did and awkwardly he hugged her. 'I am... sorry for this brief storm that came between us. I said things I never meant. You're my precious, much-loved daughter. I could no more hurt you than I could harm your mother. Or myself.'

'I know,' she replied.

Then she kissed him one more time on the cheek. Her mother embraced her. The nurse babbled something none of them heard.

'I need to think of clothes and jewellery. Then sleep. The last night in my little room before I become a bride.'

'Aye,' her father said. 'All things change tomorrow. Go with her! Both of you. That's women's territory. Clothes and gems. Nothing a man need be near.'

She didn't move. There was something in his eye. A tear, she thought. Of relief. Of joy. Perhaps of a sorrow that his child would soon be his no more.

'Thank you,' Juliet said and left him with a smile.

The friars' vials, one black, one blue, were in the pocket of her skirt. She'd hide them in a drawer somewhere while Nurse and her mother weren't looking. Then choose a dress and jewellery for a wedding that could never be.

* * *

Night was sweeping over Verona. By the swallow-tail bridge the guards who'd bullied and threatened Romeo had spent the best part of an hour checking the papers Friar John had brought from Laurence, throwing a variety of pointless questions in his direction.

'Brave young chap,' the sergeant said. 'Ferrying medicine out there when you know plague's about. Not worried you might catch it, then? Wake up spewing, your face squirting pus like custard, all ready to die?'

'I trust in God,' John told him.

The three soldiers laughed and slapped one another about the arms.

'Don't we all?' one asked. 'But does he trust in us?'

The second put a fat finger into his ruddy nose as if this helped him think. 'If the Lord doesn't, I doubt it's from any lack of care on his part. I mean he must be a very busy chap what with all the nonsense going on. People finding them new lands across the sea for one thing. Millions of new souls to worry about…'

'He's God, you idiot,' the sergeant cried. 'He can't be any busier now than what he was before. That's what God means. All-knowing. All-powerful. Nothing surprises him. How can it? If he invented it all? Ask this lad here if you don't believe me!'

They stared at John. He pointed to the saddle bags on his mule. 'It's getting late, sirs. I have some way to travel and only this old beast with me.'

The first guard swore and spat in the gutter. 'I reckon God's just bored. And we get to do all this running around living and dying to keep the fellow amused.'

'Blasphemy!' the sergeant bellowed. 'I could have you strung up for that.'

'My point exactly!' the soldier replied.

The second one nodded at the mule and suggested it was time John got moving. 'Don't know why you're hanging round here chewing the fat with us, lad. You're a bold one setting foot across that bridge right now. Either that or daft as a brush.'

The sergeant squinted at the young friar and gave him back his papers. 'My money's on the second. You take your quack medicine out there and give people a little hope. They'll still be dead in the morning. You with them. And if you're not, don't think you can come back here infecting us with your dirty diseases. Man of the cloth who's poorly looks much like one of us in the same condition.'

'Thank you, sirs.' John packed the papers alongside the supply of medicine in his bags. 'I am grateful for the richness of your advice.'

'Getting dark too,' the first soldier added. 'Can't believe you wasted all this time gassing to us. You should have been on the road hours ago. There's cut-throats and villains out there who'd have them bags off you in a flash.'

'Some of them like pretty young boys as well,' the second said. 'Especially in a cassock.'

John gave them a wry salute then led the grumbling beast through the gatehouse and onto the red-brick bridge. He'd travel as quickly on foot as on its back. The creature was old and frail. There was no need to add to the burden it carried already.

* * *

A full moon hung in a deep blue velvet sky. The night was heavy with a heat so humid the air seemed to swim before her, thick with insects and a fearful anticipation. A white dress lay on the bed, ready for the seamstresses who'd add gold braid to it in the morning. There was a circlet too and they'd talked of flowers and perfumes. The ritual of marriage had begun.

Then, laughing, her mother and the nurse looked around the room, ready to go. One last fond kiss came from each.

'Such a pretty dress,' Nurse said. 'Such a beautiful bride she'll make.'

'She will,' her mother agreed. 'Tomorrow will be a long and happy day.'

'I hope so,' Juliet added, feeling as if she were a character in a painting. Like Carpaccio's Ursula, an object, there to be admired and observed.

'You wait and see.' She stroked her daughter's cheek. 'Don't fret. This habit of yours... of worrying about everything. There's no need, my sweet. The stars shine down on you and Paris. Look at them.'

Hand-in-hand they walked to the window, brushed aside the curtains and gazed at the night sky. It was alive with all the constellations, some of which Juliet could name thanks to those books she'd brought from Venice. She wondered if she would ever return to the pleasure of turning those pages, finding new surprises among them, something to make her wiser and more ready for the world.

'Every shining star smiles down upon you, Juliet. Two will have your names for sure. Aligned in perfect symmetry across the heavens. Now you're past your doubts, all bodes well. And shall be.'

All she could think of was to whisper, 'Yes, Mother.'

Then they were gone.

She had put the two vials in a drawer where they kept the oils for the tub. The blue one she discarded. The black she took in her hands. When she removed the cork stopper the smell struck her: strong, full of flowers and something exotic. She turned the bottle and watched the viscous black liquid crawl towards the neck. It would be so easy to pour it away, to pretend it never existed. To meet Paris tomorrow and let fate take her wherever it led.

Perhaps the friar was wrong in any case. She'd wake as normal, put on the dress, go to Sant'Anastasia, led to the altar like an animal for sacrifice.

Or it might kill her. A thought, then. What if Laurence had given her poison after all, afraid that to let her live would reveal his subterfuge in marrying her to Romeo in the first place? Men lied; men arranged matters to suit their own desires.

'Not Laurence,' she whispered. 'He's a good soul. I'm sure of it.'

But what if she woke early in that dreadful charnel house? Would Tybalt's ghost rise to haunt her, the way he had in life? Or seek Romeo for taking his life upon a rapier's point?

The black bottle felt slippery in her sweating grip. Then, as if possessed of a life of its own, it tumbled from her clumsy fingers and fell on the tiled floor. The dark liquid escaped the narrow neck and rolled onto the terracotta like syrupy blood.

Fate, she thought. It loathed prevarication. Here was the decision before her. To take or to leave.

'Wait on me, Tybalt,' she murmured, getting down on her knees. 'Here, to you I drink. And Romeo, too.'

She bent over and carefully licked every drop she could straight from the warm brown tiles. The tincture had a vile, sweet taste. When she was done she picked up the spent bottle, filled it with water from the jar, swilled that round and swallowed it too.

Slowly, carefully, still in her day clothes, she found her way to the bed. One night before they'd lain here together, sweating and turning, finding such joy in one another, two becoming one. The face on the wall, the curious, smiling girl, eyes too big, hair the wrong colour, amused by her charcoal stick figure, had followed every sigh and wrestling moment.

If only that painted face possessed a mind, a memory. The ability to see and learn.

From somewhere came a low sound, a buzz like a hungry mosquito with the most bass of voices. Its source was inside, not out. She knew that in an instant.

Her eyes grew heavy. She stared at the girl on the wall.

'Watch me now,' she murmured as her vision began to change, narrowing like a tunnel dwindling to nothing. 'Watch...'

The buzz became a roar and then the blackness took her.

* * *

Twelve miles south of the city, Friar John's mule stumbled into a pothole in the shadows and shrieked with pain. From then on the beast began to whine and limp. John had a little money. Enough to borrow a horse perhaps if an innkeeper or farmer felt like taking pity on a man of the cloth. But it was late. Bright as the night was beneath the shining moon, this was no time to be abroad. There was an inn ahead, a miserable place he'd stopped at once before only to be shocked by the rough behaviour of the customers and the foul language of the landlord.

Twenty minutes on lay another, a more genteel place with a tavern girl who'd smiled prettily at him once. A decent meal, some female company, a beer or two. A straw bed.

It was not a hard decision. So John and his grumbling mule pressed on, step by steady step. Soon the place appeared. There were men further ahead on the road. Soldiers or villains perhaps. He didn't want to find out. He urged the animal into the yard, got water for it in the stable, then went to the inn door and found it open.

The downstairs hall was empty.

'Hello?' he cried and heard his voice echo round the dark corners ahead.

By the stairs there was a single sputtering oil lamp. Feeling baffled and a little scared, Friar John began to walk around the place, not calling out any more. Just looking.

The kitchen was empty too though there was food on the table. Half a roast chicken, some bread, a bowl of cold spelt porridge. He pulled a leg off the bird and munched on it as he wandered. From the windows he could see the stable and it struck him now that the only animal there was his own. John opened the back door and called out once more. Hens clucked somewhere and perhaps a pig stirred. Nothing else.

Choices.

He'd gone on when he might have stayed elsewhere. Too late now for regrets. Though perhaps he could persuade the mule to retrace its tracks and lumber back down the road to the other inn. At least there might be people there.

His feet were about to cross the threshold at the back when he heard it. The faintest, most pathetic of cries. A child, perhaps. Or a woman so feeble she sounded like one.

The noise came from upstairs. It was just a voice. No one moved.

John was twenty-one, an orphan from a village on the way to Vicenza. The Franciscans had taken him in when he'd been found wandering the streets destitute and starving. Everything he had he owed to them. God, too, he imagined. Or so they always said.

And he was a friar. Not a monk made for a solitary existence of private worship and introspection. A Franciscan was there for the world at large, to help when others shirked the task.

'I will, too,' the young man said, recalling all the teaching he'd received from Laurence and his brothers.

With that he lobbed the remains of the chicken leg into the yard and set off up the steps. Whoever was there heard him coming. The voice turned louder and more shrill. For no good reason at all John retrieved a rag from his pocket and put it over his nose. There was a smell ahead. Of sweat and something else.

The first two rooms were empty. The door to the third was open. The air at this end of the building was close and far too hot. The lamp ahead of him trembled in his outstretched hand. John went in.

'Water,' croaked a shape, huddled on a cot by the window. 'For pity's sake, my dear lord. Water. I beg you.'

He remembered the pretty barmaid from the time he'd stopped here. This was her, he felt sure from the country voice. But shadows hid her from him. He asked where the others in the tavern had gone.

'Please. I beg you… Drink. My throat is parched and I can barely speak.'

He had a flask on his hip. Water mixed with a little wine for the journey. John came close, lamp in hand. He thought he heard horses outside, and voices. Perhaps the men had gone out hunting rabbits. There'd be a feast then, good fresh meat charred from the fire.

'Your master's returned,' he said, pulling out the flask. 'No need to worry now. They'll…'

Her hand came out and grasped his wrist. An iron grip, her skin damp, cold as the grave. The girl's face rose before him. It was the one he remembered. At least he thought so. But her cheeks and brow were sweaty and dirty and as he got closer he saw they were covered in spots, some small, some large, some bloody where she'd scratched at them.

'He ran away. I beg you. Do not leave me...'

John fought to get her fingers from his skin. It was hard. She scratched him, screeched at him, started to wail and cry.

Already he was retreating, legs shaking as he took the stairs two at a time, the oil lamp shaking in his hand, sending its waxy light all around the dark corners of the inn.

* * *

They slept. They dreamt. The shining moon stood over the world, beneath it so many different reveries.

In Mantua, Romeo had a fitful slumber as the valerian took hold of his imagination and raised from it such visions of the night before. Juliet's body slick with sweat, the sweetness of her mouth, the softness of her skin. His racing, feverish mind recalled the smell of her, the way she tautened beneath his touch, the wild sighs she whispered in his ears. Then came a swift, cathartic release. And a buzzing sound in his ear. Like an insect. But it wasn't and he knew it. The tiny whirring creature was Queen Mab.

For Luca Capulet the night was dull and heavy, made so by drink and fatigue. In bed at his side his wife kept waking, her head full of visions of the day ahead and vague frets that, like flies too, hovered round, so persistent she couldn't ignore them, yet so intangible there was nothing there to name, to swat, to see.

The nurse, Donata Perotti, found herself back near Garda, gazing at the silver lake and the boats fishing there, fetching home pike and trout, shad and chub, eel and perch. A face came to her: young and smiling. Her sister Chiara, half-forgotten after the bleak patch that followed the death of Donata's husband and child. But alive. She knew that from travellers who reached Verona. One day they'd meet again. Perhaps soon.

Friar Laurence had a nightmare, one that woke him screaming from a shallow, writhing slumber. The dead had come into his small dark cell, fragrant with his herbs and potions. Juliet, Romeo, Tybalt among them. They were looking into his face, one word upon their lips... *why?*

Because you demanded it, the dreaming Laurence answered. *While I was too weak and meddling to refuse.*

Twenty-five miles south his brother Nico was wreathed in pleasant drink-fired memories of Constantinople. From the Seraglio Point he could see the shining waters of the Golden Horn teeming with vessels large and small. In his garden their cheerful master, Paulus, was serving them a meal – meat from a charcoal brazier, fresh fruit and goat's milk – all the while lecturing them on which herb to use for flavour and which to bring good health.

In her bedroom above the Capulet garden, captive to an opiate stupor, Juliet went deeper and further than the rest. She dreamt she'd returned one last time to the basilica of San Zeno. Not to the crypt where the embalmed corpse of the African lay stately in his robes. That had always frightened her. Instead she stood in the piazza outside, staring up at the great rose window, the Wheel of Fortune. The six figures around the circumference were in front of her, alive, breathing, crying, screaming, those on the right falling miserably from grace, the ones on the left rising in their stead. The blind goddess of luck would spin the wheel around and fate with it. In this sharp vision she saw something she'd always missed before: that the ascent of one party depended upon the fall of another. Men went up because others tumbled down. All at the whim of the blind creature who loved to play this game, not caring who prospered and who faded, who lived and who died.

In this languid state she stayed before San Zeno, eyes locked on the stone wheel. As if moved by a gigantic invisible hand the marble circle began groaning and straining at its setting in the portico, twisting the living figures trapped in its façade, sending them screaming one way, then another, back and forth in endless torment.

Stop, the dream Juliet cried, her ears full of their shrieks and the grinding of the stone wheel that trapped them. *For pity's sake...*

The basilica was still. Perhaps the goddess listened. Half of the figures lay again in agony, the other in joy.

Move, the dream girl whispered.

And so, with a pained howl, the great circle did, sharing round the suffering and the anguish among all.

* * *

Friar John reached the back door, gasping, frightened, trying to think. There were no other animals at this tavern. Only his own lame mule. It was late. There'd be villains about. The trek back to Verona was perilous. But there was plague here, and that was surely the greatest danger of all.

He stumbled out into the yard, tripped over something, found he was falling forward, straight towards the dry mud ground.

Then a hand came out to stop him.

'That were clumsy,' a muffled voice told him.

'Thank you, sir...' he began. And stopped, his heart thudding in his chest.

There were four creatures there, clear in the moonlight, all clad in billowing black cloaks. They sported the long beak-like masks of the men they called the Plague Doctors, and resembled nothing more than gigantic pale crows, sniffing at the posies of herbs they carried with them.

'You know what to do,' the tallest of them said.

The nearest peeled off, a bucket in one hand, a brush in the other. He went to the tavern door and slapped a large cross upon it. Red, John guessed, not that he could tell clearly in the moonlight.

'You...' the lead one said, pushing John back inside. 'How many left in there?'

'One. I was a visitor. Looking for shelter. I just stepped through the door for a look. I've touched no one. There's just a girl there.'

'Aye,' the man said. 'A sick girl. We talked to her man some way back.'

All hope seemed to be deserting him.

'And?' John asked.

'And now he's locked in a plague house too. Just like you're going to be.'

His hand came out. A heavy leather gauntlet ran all the way to his elbow. The man grabbed the hood of his habit and dragged him back.

'I'm a friar,' John pleaded. 'In the saddle bag of my mule there's medicine. At least let me keep that.'

The white-beaked mask seemed to hesitate.

'Take what you want. Be quick about it.'

He dashed and got the bag. They watched him retreat into the house. Upstairs she was still bleating for water. He'd go and see her now. There was no choice. That had been made for him. As for his task, the apothecary in distant Mantua... the letter John carried from Laurence was useless. Even if he could get out of the plague house the mule could scarcely travel, and all the other horses had been taken.

The tall Plague Doctor came to close the door. 'We're shuttering this up with planks now, lad. Don't so much as think as trying to get out. Or it won't be the plague that kills you.'

'How long for?'

The beaked head of the tall one turned and stared at him with black, blind eyes. 'You're a sight more amenable than most we've had to deal with. I'll say that for you.'

'*How long?*'

'There's a physician doing the rounds tomorrow. If you're the same we'll leave you a while. If you're worse we're not coming near.'

'And if we're better?'

He laughed. 'Then God's kinder to his own than he is to the rest of us.'

John stood in the kitchen, listening to the hammers and nails clatter against the door and windows. First the back and then the front. They were boarding up the place, leaving the two of them to die. He wondered how many days men like this waited. What told them it was finally safe to enter the plague house and take out the corpses.

'I die of thirst!' cried a faint and angry voice above him.

There was a pump in the corner by a sink. The inn had its own spring. He raised some water, smelled it, tasted it. As sweet as any he'd known.

That feeble cry came down the stairs again. 'I know you're there. I can hear you. For the love of Jesus... bring me something to drink.'

Friar John threw the saddle bag over his shoulder, filled a jug of water and climbed the stairs.

Part Four: Violent Delights, Violent Ends

Thursday. Another humid July morning. The garden of the Capulets was alive with butterflies fluttering through a busy army of servants setting up trestle tables, building gazebos in the orchard, arches of roses and honeysuckle to make a winding path through the greenery. Luca Capulet had decreed this would be the best wedding Verona had known in years. He wouldn't count the cost or stomach anything less than luxury.

In the kitchen, pheasants, peacocks and quails were being stripped and prepared for the ovens. An entire table was given over to three pastry cooks making tarts of dates and quince and figs. Chickens roasted next to lambs. During the night two hogs were put on spits by the garden gate, local boys brought in to turn them constantly for long hours to come. Now the aroma of pork and herbs and garlic drifted through the borders and the fruit trees, mingling with the scent of flowers and spices from the palazzo.

The musicians of the previous Monday were back, in greater number and with a small choir. As cooks worked, as Bianca Capulet bustled from table to table issuing orders about decorations and seating, as her husband watched with quiet pleasure from the bower seat beneath the pomegranate tree, viols were tuned, voices tested.

Over them all the bell of the Torre dei Lamberti chimed nine. Capulet looked up at his daughter's balcony window. The curtains were closed. No sign of life there. He remembered the time Juliet demanded a little apartment of her own inside the palazzo. She couldn't have been more than nine or ten. Always an independent child. Stubborn and wilful. Much like him if he were honest.

He asked one of the servants to bring him a cup of iced water with the slightest touch of Garganega in it. Later he'd move on to wine alone. And then, after the marriage, when all the guests had gone wearily home, he'd sit alone in his study with a bottle of fine brandy. Satisfied with a job well done, finally.

An independent mind was to be admired in principle. But in practice...

The boy came back with a pewter goblet full to the brim. Capulet sipped at it. More wine there than he'd wanted but it would do. His wife came and sat next to him on the wooden bench, tapped the cup and gave him a warning glance.

Gently he said, 'I know, I know, dear. Fret not. There's barely a grape in it.'

'No arguments this day!'

'The storms of recent times are over. I shall return to being the peaceable husband you desire. And then...' He closed his eyes and beamed with pleasure. 'This palace will be for the two of us. As it was when we married.'

She sighed, smiling. 'Thank God for that. I wouldn't have been without her for all the world. But it's time the girl grew up.'

'We're all slaves to one thing or another, aren't we?'

His wife frowned and said she didn't follow.

'I mean... a man's a slave to his wife and children. And his business, too. Women to their husbands. All of us to God. The young think they're above it all. That this world of ours will change just because a few numbers alter with the century. The Borgia Pope dies and goes to hell at last and by some miracle a holy man's elected in his place. Or...' He laughed. 'And this amuses me the most... A foreign adventurer crosses the ocean then, like a pirate, finds a far-off land of savages to plunder. And behold! Everything we know... every last fact and certainty we've lived with for as long as any man remembers... we throw them out. Dead wisdom. Spent and useless. Because the world's turned upside down. The young know everything and the old are nothing more than dribbling fools. Ha!'

'Things do change. We bend with them or we break.'

He winked and raised his cup to her lips. She took a draft and winced at the strength of it.

'I want you sober. And in good temper. All day long.'

'What about the night?'

'The night... we'll see. Our little girl will be gone to this fresh life of hers by then.'

He kissed her cheek and whispered a few lascivious words in her ear. She glanced at the balcony. 'It's past nine, Luca. She should be up. Paris will be here before long. There's much to do. Women for her hair and dress. All manner of preparation.'

He raised his cup again. 'Well, here's a toast: let the men steer well clear of ladies' boudoirs!' Another wink. 'Until it's bedtime and our services are needed.' She laughed and he realised he hadn't heard that sweet sound in a while. 'Send that mouthy woman of hers to wake her, love. We won't be needing her around the place after today.'

'I'll put her in the kitchen–'

'Put her in the street for all I care. I've only taken her impertinence for Juliet's sake. When she's gone…'

Raised voices disturbed them from the hall behind. Capulet turned and squinted. His eyesight was no longer good. 'Who's that making a racket on a day like this? Who dares?'

There was a figure in a grey habit, arguing with two of the servants.

'I think it's the Franciscan. Friar Laurence,' she said, getting to her feet. 'He seems… perturbed.'

* * *

Nurse was in her room, getting bored and restless, when she heard the chimes of the Torre dei Lamberti and thought to herself: enough's enough. The girl was never good at rising. But staying in bed on her wedding morning was too much to take. Donata Perotti couldn't wait to dress her, comb her long blonde hair, find the right jewels, coax her slim frame into the wedding dress and with it a calm and amenable mood. There was a lover to be forgotten amidst all the rush. That thought had hung over her all night even as she dreamt of Garda, her sister and fresh fish simmering in a pot above the coals.

Determined, she got up and hammered on Juliet's door. There was no answer. It wasn't the first time. Gingerly, she walked into the room saying, in a loud voice she'd been using ever since the girl was barely off her breast, 'Mistress! Mistress! Oh, what is this, little Juliet? I swear you're a slug-a-bed again, snoring beneath your sheets on such a day as this.'

The windows were closed, the curtains, too. The room had a stuffy, close air about it. She glanced at the shape hidden beneath the bedclothes, never stirring. Juliet was always an awkward one. No reason to think today would be any different.

'Why, love, I say. Sweet girl! A bride you'll be and soon!'

She swept aside the curtains and threw open the windows. The fresh air of the garden greeted her and then the rich aroma of roasting hog.

Looking at the bright horizon and the gulls circling over the river she said, 'And not a word from you, lass? Not a peek from beneath your pillow?'

Juliet hadn't moved an inch, just stayed locked in that awkward shape the young loved, knees drawn up, arms tucked in, face side on, half hidden. Not the slightest sign of stirring.

'Just as well you get your sleep. That young man Paris won't be giving you much rest tonight. Oh, God, give me patience.' Her voice rose. 'Juliet. *Juliet*. You want me to send up that count and let him take you in this bed of yours?'

On the wall the painting of Juliet, young and bright-eyed with the charcoal drawing, stared at them.

'Lord, he'd give you a good fright if you let him. How you sleep!' She went to the bed, rocked the frame then drew back the sheets. 'Still in yesterday's clothes, child?' the nurse said, quietly now. 'What game is this? What–?' Her heart began to beat too quickly. She bent down and shook Juliet as gently as she could. 'I must wake you, girl.'

She gripped her shoulder harder. 'I must–'

Under the pressure of the nurse's strong arm, Juliet moved. Her mouth fell open. No sound from her throat. No blink of an eye. Just a couple of drops of dark liquid leaking from her blackened lips onto the bleached white linen sheet.

'Oh girl…' the woman whispered. 'My beautiful, darling girl.'

Reaching out, she touched her arm. Cold skin. Cold and clammy. A small black bottle rolled out from under the delicate fingers of the girl's left hand, fell to the tiles and shattered there with a quick, sharp crack.

* * *

The noises from the house were getting louder. Capulet threw his cup to the grass and doddered up the steps. There the cause of the argument became clear. An anxious Friar Laurence was asking to see Juliet. Paris, as her suitor, was demanding to know why. The two servant boys, Samson and Gregory, were not of a mind to let anyone do anything until someone else turned up and told them to.

The friar saw Capulet approach and asked, 'May we speak privately?'

Laurence had an odd and shifty air about him.

'Say what you have to say in front of all of us. Then leave my home. This is a happy day and a hectic one. I do not appreciate disturbances. The marriage of my daughter and the count here–'

'There may be no marriage!' Laurence cried. Out of the deep pockets of his habit he pulled a small black bottle, a skull upon its side. The sight of it silenced them all. 'Your daughter came to me last night. She said you sent her for a tonic to cheer her mood.'

'We thought it best,' her mother said.

'I gave her such a remedy. Good advice, too.' He nodded at Paris. 'And to her groom. Or so I thought.'

As did we, Capulet muttered, remembering her sudden cheerful mood when she returned, and how she'd knelt before him.

Laurence brandished the black bottle. 'This morning I found one of these was missing. My back was turned a while. I had to fetch her the tonic. I fear…'

'Fear what?' her mother whispered.

'I fear she stole a vial of poison. It pains me sore to wonder why. I must see her...'

The scream that broke their wrangling was loud and so full of agony it chilled them even in the relentless morning heat. The Franciscan pushed Paris to one side and soon was flying up the marble steps, his grey habit flapping round him like a cloak.

A door opened somewhere. Through it the shrieking came, powerful enough to hurt the ears.

Capulet had lived with that voice since a month after Juliet's birth: the nurse, not that she'd ever sounded like this.

One line only she yelled, over and over.

'*Oh lady, lady, lady. Not dead. Say not dead...*'

* * *

In the boarded-up inn fifteen miles south of Verona fortune's wheel had turned. The tavern girl now sat in the kitchen wearing a grubby grey shift, wolfing down spelt porridge Friar John had made, swigging at wine and water.

During the night, after he'd calmed her and given her something to drink, he'd taken a closer look at her spotty face. Then he'd gone to his saddle bag and found, among the medicines, a thick milky lotion Laurence had made from camomile, bees wax, rosewater, almond essence and beef lard. He'd persuaded the girl to dab it on her spots with a little fluff of cotton. The itching had ceased soon after and when he'd washed her a little, ignoring her squawks, he'd found more candles and a mirror in another room, brought them back and told her to look.

'Plague,' she'd whispered.

'It's not plague.'

John had been orphaned when he was six. The years when he lived with his solitary father were still in his memory. Their village was a tight little community sharing everything, including common sicknesses when they arrived.

'It's varicella. Chickenpox. You've never had it? Not when you were tiny?'

She hadn't answered, just kept dabbing at her spots and, after a while, when he'd persisted in his questions, gone straight to sleep.

Now, in the kitchen, he asked again. She looked at him, a spoonful of porridge halfway to her open mouth, squinted with two bleary eyes, and said, 'What?'

'Most children get it. When I was small and it came to our village they made us all sit in the same house to catch the sickness once and get it out of the way.'

'You're sure it's not the plague?'

'I'm certain.'

The spoon went in and, through a half-full mouth, she said, 'You think I'll live then?'

The story she'd told him as he'd cleaned her up, getting better by the minute, was depressing. Her man, the landlord, had taken one look at her face and panicked, grabbing all their money and the one horse they owned.

'Those spots won't kill you. What are you going to do now? Without him?'

The spoon went down. He felt as if he'd uttered the most idiotic question she'd ever heard.

'Wait for him to come back, of course? What else am I supposed to do?'

She was the pretty girl he remembered. It was clear now even in the meagre morning light that made its way through the boarded-up windows.

'He abandoned you.'

'He thought I had the plague. If it had been the other way round I'd have hopped it, too. Not bloody daft, are we?'

John got up and started banging on the boards they'd hammered round the windows.

'Anyhow,' she went on. 'You were ready to leg it as soon as you saw me. What's the difference?'

The planks were hammered in. But with a little effort he thought he might shift them. There wasn't a sound from outside. Not even a whinny from the mule.

'The difference is... I didn't know you.'

'No. The difference is... you're a man of the church. Supposed to look after us all. On behalf of God, your master. That's your job, isn't it?'

He got a chair and jabbed the leg against the loosest plank. It came free. When he pushed again he saw a chink of bright daylight and through it an empty yard.

'Among others,' he agreed, thinking of the mule and the long journey to Mantua. He was more than halfway there he reckoned.

'You...' Her voice was loud and coarse. 'Are meant to take care of us, body and soul.'

'We are. I'm sorry. Do you have any tools? Hammers? Mallets?'

She was scraping out the last of the porridge. 'Maybe. But you can't have 'em.'

'Why not?'

'Because!'

All the warm feelings he'd held towards this girl in his memory were fast fading.

'Because of what?'

'Because there's red crosses all over this house and that means plague! If we break out of here and start wandering round they'll kill us anyway. Then chuck our carcasses in a lime pit. Don't they teach you nothing in that monastery of yours, Mister Monk?'

'Friar,' he murmured.

'Same difference.'

'It isn't.'

'It is to me.'

But she was right. No one went beyond the red cross. You were dead the moment you passed it. All they could do was wait, for her faithless lover or the physician the Plague Doctor had spoken of the night before.

The errand to Mantua seemed lost. He went to the bag and retrieved the two sealed letters Laurence had given him, one for the apothecary named Nico, the second for the murderer Romeo. There seemed no reason not to open them now.

The brother's letter was in impenetrable Greek. The second had given him pause from the outset. Friar John didn't understand why he was carrying a missive to a banished felon who was lucky to escape Verona with his life. It had occurred to him during the night that perhaps these letters were the true purpose of his mission, not carrying potions from one apothecary in Verona to another twenty-five miles away.

So he broke the seal on Romeo's letter and read it, telling himself the pressures of these changed circumstances breached any promises he'd made.

The girl made more food, frying fat bacon, cooking a couple of eggs alongside. Not that she offered him any.

After a while she said, 'That's not very nice language for a man of the cloth. Swearing oaths like you're a common sailor. I must say I'm shocked. Even my man don't use words like what you're muttering under your breath.' She jabbed a fork into an egg on the hob and sent bright yellow yolk splatting everywhere. 'I'm shocked. Honestly.'

The friars of San Francesco had given him many things. A home. Food. Friendship. Direction. Most of all, though, they'd given him faith and trust, in himself and others.

'Shocked I am.'

'So you said.'

'How long do you think it'll be before someone comes?'

Now, reading the lies and deceit implicit in Laurence's letter to the murderer Romeo, he felt cheated and used. If Laurence's scheme had gone to plan, the Montague villain would have returned to Verona in his own cloak, using *his* papers. A murderer in a habit, while John lingered with Laurence's brother awaiting instructions.

He wouldn't be going to Mantua to deliver it, even if someone arrived to remove the red crosses and the boards within the hour.

'I said…' the girl went on.

'I heard you. I don't know.' He walked to the stove and pushed both letters, Nico's and Romeo's, into the fire beneath the pan. Then broke a couple of eggs into the lard for himself. 'In truth… I don't know anything at all.'

* * *

This was sleep but not sleep. Life yet not quite life. She couldn't lift a finger or even raise an eyebrow. But something of this old familiar room and the people bustling, weeping, shrieking around her came to Juliet in this thick and swimming slumber.

Then her inward eye blinked and opened and she found herself back outside San Zeno on the scorching piazza cobbles, wearing the white dress her mother had picked for the wedding. A mahogany coffin was entering by the bronze doors beneath the turning rose window and the Wheel of Fortune. The whole basilica seemed to squeal and screech as it shifted to an unseen mechanism.

'Not my coffin,' she said as she watched the shiny wooden box vanish into the dark belly of the church, towards the red-robed corpse of the saint deep in the crypt.

'No.' It was her father, grey-faced before her. Long velvet jacket the deathly colour of his skin, white britches, black leather riding boots, a whip in his right hand. He cracked the crop on his heavy thigh. 'Mine, child. You put me there.'

'Not true...' she whispered and found herself crouching on the hard cobbles, white dress getting grubby from the dust blown around by the baking day.

'All this...' His roar was as loud as the universe, his face bigger than the façade of San Zeno going slowly round and round, good to bad and back again, behind him. 'All this is your doing. The bitter fruit of your vile and disobedient soul.'

A low repetitive chant filled her mouth, her head. 'I am me and only me. I am me and...'

The whip came out and switched her face, just as it had once when she'd gone riding with him out in the countryside and tried to race off when he'd told her to stay.

There was no pain. This was a dream.

'Leave the child,' her mother cried. Bianca Capulet stood beside her husband, his face wreathed in anger, hers wracked with pain. 'We did this. Not her. Never.'

Luca Capulet brushed her aside, swatting her with the crop. 'She stole that potion and thrust a dagger in my heart. Then lied to me about her acquiescence. Killed herself beneath my roof—'

'It wasn't like that, Father.' Her voice had the calm and patient tone she knew annoyed him. 'I am me and only me. I am me and…'

'This selfish child,' he snapped and again the switch flew at her. 'Death is my son-in-law now. Death my heir. Death it was she wedded. By God I should have whipped that child, time and time and time and…'

She squeezed her dream eyes shut against the flying scourge. His angry tones faded, only to be replaced by a different voice, musical and clear, like that of an angel calling out her name.

When she looked up a young woman was where her parents had stood. She had long fair hair, a gold circlet round it, a blue dress that seemed to hang on the skeletal frame beneath. Her face was bloodless and too perfect, as if from a painting or a fresco in a church. It took a moment to place this vision.

'Child. Look at me.'

Ursula, Carpaccio's martyr from Venice stood before her.

'You are not real,' the dream Juliet whispered.

The apparition had eyes like deep pools of inky glass. Like the liquid Laurence had given her.

'Besides…' This was so obvious she failed to understand why it hadn't occurred to her till now. 'We all die. So each of us is a martyr in that sense.'

'Look at yourself then.'

The dream saint held up her hand. In it was a mirror, circular and shiny, gold round the rim, just like the one in her room. Behind her the stones of San Zeno moved again, more quickly. Their moans were loud enough to be an earthquake or the tremors of a volcano, like Vesuvius exploding in a book of old stories a young girl had read, in another world, a different life.

Juliet gazed into the convex mirror and saw herself reflected there, still as a corpse, just like the mythical Ursula in Carpaccio's painting of her dream, though this was her bedroom in the palazzo of the Capulets, her sheets, her window, her balcony. Her lifeless body, head on a hard white pillow, eyes tight shut. Instead of the painting of her younger self, a small rose window hung against the wall, San Zeno's in miniature, marble circle moving round and round, tiny figures set in its circumference, writhing from pain to joy with each rotation.

No shining angel in armour at the foot of her bed either. There was Romeo, clothes bloodied, dagger in hand. Too fearful to come near her sleeping form.

'My love...'

Ursula's black eyes bore down on her. The deathly saint snapped her fingers. He was gone and Juliet's dream cry of loss and agony went with him. The familiar door opened. A line of sad-eyed nuns entered, all in black. They came to her, undressed her, washed her body, took out a shroud and wrapped it round her thin cold form. Then, when she was decent, Laurence returned, men with him carrying a pale wood coffin.

'Do not let me see this...'

'How can you not?' It was her father's voice again. 'You brought it on yourself. On us.'

'I am me and only me. I am me and...'

He shouted something then and in that bellicose, wordless yell there was such anger, grief and hatred she felt dream tears start in dead dream eyes.

When she looked again he was gone. Just the mirror now, as big as the room, the world itself. In the glass her shrouded body lay in the hands of quiet, serious friars lifting her into the coffin, Laurence watching, his eyes boring into hers.

'No lid, Friar,' she pleaded but they fetched it anyway and stood there, grim faces all, ready to put the final piece in place. 'No nails. For pity's sake... no nails.'

In a loud, firm voice Laurence said, 'No nails.'

As if he'd heard, and she'd no idea whether that was dream or real. Or somewhere in between.

Still they lifted her, then gently let her down. The light vanished. She heard them grunt, felt the coffin move upon their shoulders and, through the dark and the timber, she heard the low, sad sound of her mother weeping.

Yet, she thought. *I live. For now.*

* * *

Balthazar had been in the service of the Montagues since his father placed him there when he was ten years old. He'd grown up with Romeo, as much a friend as a servant in all those years. On occasion they'd fish together on the Adige. Sometimes ride in the low mountains. There was nothing the baker's boy wouldn't do for Andrea Montague's son. That morning he'd left his house at eight, crossed through the sentry post on the Roman bridge, got a nod from the guards who knew him, then stationed himself close to the Capulet estate to wait for orders.

The daughter would send a message, Romeo said. How or when Balthazar had no idea. So he got himself an apple and mooched around the street near the palazzo gate. He'd taken care to remove the blue feather from his cap and silently prayed that the Capulet thug who'd bitten his thumb at him in the Piazza Erbe the previous Monday wouldn't show his face. At least Tybalt, the vilest one of all, was dead.

The busy traffic – butchers, flower sellers, carts with fruit and vegetables – going to and from the palace seemed to suggest something was afoot. Daring to get nearer he approached a fishmonger who was pushing a cart bearing baskets full of wriggling Garda eels.

'What is all this business, sir? Such commotion I have never seen in my friend Capulets' place.'

The man scowled at him. He was a surly sort, stinking of fish and with an undercurrent of hard spirit on his breath. 'A scruff like you knows this lot of toffs?'

'I've friends in service. Looks like there might be a wedding on the way. That right?'

The fishmonger laughed unpleasantly. 'Or maybe a funeral. Not much fond of either. Both end up with misery.'

'But–'

'Look, lad. I came here like everyone else from the market. We heard there was a sudden marriage coming up. Next thing I see is a Franciscan friar and a bunch of nuns marching in there looking like the world was coming to an end. '

'What happened?'

'Oh lord. Do I know? Do I care. You want some eels?'

'Sorry…'

'This bloody town.'

With that he pushed his cart down the lane. Balthazar went back to lurking in the shadows. More people turned up, some nuns with them. It felt odd loitering round the Capulet place. Guilty almost, as if he were a nosy spectator who'd come across an accident. Or a hanging.

The tower bell was striking noon when finally something happened. A cortege came out, a coffin on it. No doubting that. He knew, too, there was only one question to ask.

Balthazar set up a jog trying to keep up with the men pushing the bier along the cobbled street, down to the cemetery death house he reckoned. The obvious destination.

'Where does this sad party go, friend? Who do they lament?' he asked one of the people at the back.

A face turned and stared at him malevolently. He caught his breath. It was the fat lad from the previous Monday, the one who'd been making noises about sticking someone. There was no scarlet feather in his black cap. Tears were streaming down his cheeks.

'Who wants to know?'

The boy was either too stupid to recognise him, or too distraught.

'A friend of mine who was dear to poor Tybalt. It seems the Capulets get naught but misery. Unless I'm mistaken. I'd rather grim news came straight from my lips than find its way through rank gossip off the street.'

'Juliet,' Gregory muttered. 'That lovely daughter of theirs. Pretty as a flower and sweet with every one of us. Lord knows I cannot believe that precious young thing is gone. Truly. The mistress weeps,

287

the master rages and swears all around the palazzo. Our house feels cursed. Perhaps it is.'

They were getting close to the Porta Leoni. The coffin was bouncing up and down on the wooden bier, rocked by the rough cobbles. He squinted at Balthazar. A hint of recognition in his piggy eyes.

'This friend of yours?'

'Someone who loved her,' Balthazar whispered. 'Or so I think.'

He doffed his cap and walked briskly back to the Ponte Pietra, passed the familiar guards there with a nod. His father's horse was behind the bakery, well-watered and ready for the road. Then he saddled up and set off for the lane by the river that led south, outside the city walls, straight to the road to Mantua.

From the old amphitheatre he heard a familiar angry, puzzled voice behind him. Balthazar didn't need to look. It was his father calling for the horse.

'I need him, Dad. Busy,' he murmured. 'Sorry.'

Mantua was a place he'd never been. Three hours ride there he guessed. Three hours back. Grim news to take his master.

'Giddy up,' he said, and lightly spurred his steed.

* * *

The physician came to the inn sometime in the early afternoon, his white, beaked mask slung over his shoulder as if it wasn't needed. Friar John spoke to him through a gap he'd made in the planking. It wasn't a long conversation. The man was from Vicenza and had been making the rounds of all the properties the soldiers had closed and daubed with scarlet crosses. There was a plague here of a kind, he said. An infectious one, too. But the diseases it carried were panic and ignorance, not pestilence and death.

'Chickenpox,' John said through the gap in the window. There were soldiers behind the physician, no masks now, shuffling on their big feet looking embarrassed. 'That's all this lady's got. I swear it. I gave her a lotion our apothecary makes. The spots are going down. She has no fever. This isn't what they think.'

'Wrong,' the doctor said. 'It's the same malady we've had everywhere. A plague of panic and ignorance. Men! Get these boards down. Let these people out.'

A few minutes later the young friar stood outside, the girl with him. Her man had turned up looking a little shame-faced. She tried to hug him, not that he was ready for that.

'I want them red crosses off my place,' he said. 'We won't be finding business with them on. I got good food coming soon too. Local speciality.' He licked his lips and rubbed his hands. 'Mule stew. Don't suppose you lads want some? I can give you a special price.'

John looked around and asked, 'Where did you find the mule?'

'Some fool left the poor old thing tethered up here. Lame as anything. I took her out back and did her a favour. Give me my butcher's knives and a couple of hours in the kitchen—'

'Mine. She was mine.'

The girl glared at him. 'If the thing was knackered and tied up in our yard he wasn't to know, was he?'

'So how am I to get home?'

'You're a Franciscan, aren't you?' the man replied. 'Do like your saint did. Pick up your things and get walking.'

The soldiers laughed at that. John started down the lane. After five minutes he'd reached the road, fifteen miles back to Verona one way, ten the other to Mantua.

A liar and a deceiver to the left. A murderer to the right.

'The liar it must be then,' John muttered, and set off down the dry and dusty track.

* * *

The Marangona bell struck one. Then two and three and four. In the palazzo of the Capulets the hours scarcely mattered. Grief and anger reigned, as wide as the oceans, as fierce and relentless as the burning July sun.

By mid-afternoon Luca Capulet was dead drunk, roaring around the palace teary-eyed bellowing at cowering servants, full of fury and despair in equal measure. His wife had retired to Juliet's quarters, to sit in a chair by the bed where they'd found her, listening to the muted sounds of men clearing away the tables in the garden, removing the half-cooked hogs, the gazebos and rose garlands. The musicians had gone, after much wrangling over their money. Not a single serious note they'd played. Still no birds sang. Bianca Capulet wondered if they ever would again.

Count Paris had returned to his mansion near the Duomo feeling robbed of the most cherished transaction he'd sought in years. There, with a more modest reserve of chilled wine than Capulet, he brooded in the dark of his study.

When a kitchen servant came through with food he demanded, 'News, boy. Have they buried her?'

'Tomorrow, Count,' the cowering youth replied. 'So the friars say. In the cemetery where her cousin got laid to rest yesterday.'

Paris grunted at that. 'And now?'

'Now she's in the Franciscan's charnel house, where the dead wait on their funeral.'

'You're from this damned city. May one visit?'

It was all the boy could do not to shiver. 'I doubt that. Not unless you're family.'

'I would have been,' Paris growled.

'Who'd want to look at a sorry sight like that? Besides it's nearly night and they lock the place up then. Robbers. Don't want robbers round there, do you?'

'Not stealing what is mine by right. Fetch me those two Roman cut-throats I used when we had that little argument in Milan. You know the ones?'

The servant gulped. 'That pair live down in Sottoriva now. Alongside all those dubious ladies. What should I tell them?'

'That tonight they'll do my bidding. Be off then!'

At that roared order the lad vanished. Paris supped, lost in festering dark thoughts. The ring was still in his pocket. He took it out and ran his fingers over the soft, worn gold. It felt much as it had that night he'd worked it from his mother's cold hand. Once again he read the faint lettering inscribed inside. A promised bond. A vow to be honoured.

'What god ordained,' he murmured, 'I will obtain.' He drank. 'I will...'

* * *

Across the city, in the subterranean crypt of the cemetery chapel, on a chill marble slab where centuries of corpses had awaited interment,

Juliet lay in her shroud sleeping, a hair's breadth from death itself, dreaming of a creaking rose window, a distant lover and the moment she'd wake and see his face.

Not that misery belonged to the privileged alone. In her tiny room along the corridor from Juliet's quarters Donata Perotti, who no longer thought of herself as Nurse, nor would answer to that name again, wept and wept and wept. Cursing her own stupidity. Her rash willingness to go along with the secret marriage to Romeo. And now her cowardice to speak of it to anyone, even Friar Laurence, the man who surely bore as much blame as she.

Yet they weren't alone. The Montague boy had sought her out. Juliet, sweet Juliet, had beckoned him with arms so welcoming only a fool would refuse entry into that sweet harbour from the bitter world beyond.

Seated on her narrow bed, staring at the little room where she'd lived for nearly seventeen years, the woman muttered, 'I should have said no to her more often. It's no good giving them a taste of freedom when all that happens is someone steals it from you later. Like they always do.'

She screwed up her eyes, trying to stop the tears. This dark day had changed them all. There'd be no going back. They didn't deserve it.

With a shrug she found a sackcloth bag and stuffed it with sufficient belongings as she thought she might be able to carry. Money, clothes, the jewels from Juliet's room and a single bracelet that had become too small for the girl a while back. That she'd taken secretly. Not stolen, just... kept. It was a memento, a marker of the way the girl was changing, from sparky, argumentative child, to bright and questioning young woman. Her own daughter, had she lived, would never have gone that way. She wouldn't have been so clever for one thing. And Donata Perotti wouldn't have allowed it. Her kind had to know their place.

Towards the end of the afternoon she tried to creak open the door as quietly as possible. Without success. Bianca Capulet heard and came out from Juliet's room, pink-eyed, outraged when she saw the bag.

'Where are you going?'

'To find somewhere that needs me, Mistress.' She could see beyond into the room, the bed, the painting on the wall, that bright-eyed girl, face not quite right, hair a different colour, the charcoal drawing held up with such pride. 'You've no use for a stupid old woman any more.'

Juliet's mother walked out into the corridor and came to face her. 'How do you know? If you don't ask?'

'I don't need to ask. I let her down. You, too.'

'In what way?'

Such a big question. One that seemed pointless. It annoyed her.

'By not tempering my love for her with firm counsel. Allowing her charm to rule my head. As she did with everyone.'

There was a fixed, hard look in Bianca Capulet's eyes. 'Firm counsel was for her parents. Not her servant.'

'Aye. I believe that's true. Not that she got it there either.'

It came so quickly the blow seemed to surprise them both. Her mistress's thin arm came out, a bony hand slapped Donata Perotti's flabby cheek, hard enough to leave a red weal rising on the skin.

Silence then. After a while she said, 'I deserved that, Madam. Probably deserved a lot more over the years. I... I...' The tears were coming again and they were nothing to do with being struck. 'I so wish I could have talked to her. Just once last night and...'

The same skinny arms came and embraced her then. The two women clutched at one other in desperate grief.

'I am so sorry,' her mother whispered. 'I never meant... It was the fury and the anguish... nothing else. Lord knows that I should take it out on a gentle soul like you.'

She released the large woman from her grip and peered into her bleary eyes.

'You were a better mother to her than I ever was—'

'Do not say that, Lady! She loved you. And her dad in her own way, like he loved her. She adored this place. For the life of me I do not understand how she could leave it in... in such a fashion.'

The tears came again, for both of them.

'Oh, loyal Nurse,' Bianca Capulet sighed. 'Don't blame yourself. Or anyone. There's a gulf between us, young and old. As if we were... different creatures. They've no notion of what it's like to be us, weighed down by duty, worn away by worldliness and age. And we've forgotten how it was to be them. Fired with life and spirit and hope, never knowing that one day all those bright flames will be extinguished. Too soon. Too soon.'

This moment of intimacy felt awkward on both parts. Neither met the other's eye.

'We could find you work in the kitchen, Donata.'

She laughed at hearing her name. 'Thank you. But I burn things. And them I miss always come out underdone.'

'Somewhere in this house... there's a place for you. I'll make one.'

Donata picked up her simple bag. 'A place in someone's heart is all you need. I'm happy if I have that.'

'Stay till the gates are open. The plague...'

'There was no plague. Didn't you hear? It's all about the streets. Someone went down with a rash out near Vicenza. The rest of them panicked the way men do. Nothing more than chickenpox. A little illness for kiddies. That's all. The restrictions are gone till next time. I can be in Garda by nightfall if I find a farmer going back home who'll take me.'

'No plague?'

'Only the usual ones. Life and death.'

They walked down the long winding stairs to the hall. This was the last time she would descend those familiar steps into this grand interior of stucco and gilt, velvet and glass. Another world beckoned. Peschiera. A decent village cottage of her own. Pike from the lake, cheap coarse wine from the hills. Family again. They had to be there somewhere.

Bianca Capulet insisted on giving her money for the journey. She took it. With the gifts of recent days, all carefully secreted inside her sackcloth bag, she'd be a woman of substance once she got home.

Would that help?

Probably not. The shining, living image she had of Juliet in her head would not leave easily. More likely the memories would follow her all her days. That sweet, infuriating child who seemed so full of life, and left it with one final mystery Donata Perotti felt would always be beyond her comprehension.

The bell was tolling five when she walked out of the palazzo courtyard. No looking back. That way lay misery.

* * *

It was late afternoon by the time Balthazar reached Mantua. The address Romeo had given him was for the apothecary's shop in the rotonda. Nico was there, berating his African neighbour for the dusty objects he'd placed on show to attract trade. A stuffed alligator, skins of lizards and fish, cakes of rose petals, dried bunches of wild garlic.

'If you want a quack, there's your man,' the apothecary announced as Balthazar climbed the stairs.

The African threw up his arms in mock outrage. 'I never had any complaints, Nico.'

'Probably because they're all dead. An alligator? I ask you…'

'I'm from Verona. I seek Romeo.'

Nico took him into the shadows of the shop. The smell of exotic spices was so overwhelming the young servant felt dizzy. 'I'm the brother of Friar Laurence. Did he send you?'

'No,' Balthazar said with care. 'Though I heard the friar this morning. In circumstances…'

'What circumstances?'

'I must see Romeo. This is for his ears first. If afterwards…'

'Very well,' the apothecary declared. 'Then I'll shutter my shop once more. God, my brother will ruin me before this escapade is done, I swear it…'

Five minutes later the little store was locked up. The African smiled and saluted as a grumpy Nico stormed off down the rotonda stairs, Balthazar at his heels.

Outside, Mantua was busy. An odd and fanciful town it seemed to the young man from Verona. Almost like a painting, or a backdrop from one of the plays travelling troops performed in the Piazza Erbe from time to time.

Unreal.

Like the day itself.

Like the news he would soon impart to his master.

* * *

Romeo was lying on a hard wooden couch reading Virgil when they returned to Nico's chambers. He cried out in joy at the sight of them, then leapt up and happily took Balthazar's hand.

'I dreamt there was good news on the way, friend. And here you are to deliver it.'

'What happened in your dream, sir?' the servant asked warily.

Nico found wine, and downed a long draft himself before pouring some for them. He had an inkling whatever news had come from the north was not welcome.

Romeo took a glass and grinned. 'The nonsense you get from supping this apothecary's magical inventions.'

'Well, here's to good ones,' Nico said, raising a toast. 'Though dreams come from something more than drink.'

'Aye. Your fears. I dreamt I was dead and Juliet found me. Then breathed me back to life with such kisses. And so I was revived.' He waved his cup high. 'Turned from a corpse to a king. That's love for you.'

Balthazar didn't touch a drop. Romeo hadn't noticed. Excitedly he went on, 'So you've news? Are there letters from the friar too? How are my mother and father? Most of all...' The smile had left him. 'How... how is my Juliet? Nothing can be wrong with the world if she is well.'

'I wish I could say she was well and nothing wrong.'

Nico pulled up three chairs and had them sit.

'Speak, friend,' Romeo begged. 'You didn't ride all this way for a cup of wine.'

The young servant blinked and wouldn't look him in the eye. 'Your Juliet is dead, Master. I saw her bier leave the Capulet palazzo this morning destined for the crypt. Father Laurence was with the coffin...'

Romeo reached across the table and grabbed him by the collar. 'Dead?'

'Oh, pardon me for bringing this grim news. You said it was my job...'

The apothecary intervened. 'Let the lad go, Romeo. We must listen. You're sure?'

'I saw the coffin on the bier! I asked one of their servants. The fat one who wanted to stick us last Monday...'

A church bell sounded. Someone started shouting in the street: fresh pies for sale. A bluebottle buzzed round the room. The world seemed both ordinary and strange.

'She can't be dead.' Romeo shook his head. 'I left her well and happy. We agreed. I would come here. Work for us to be reunited. She *can't* be dead. Unless...'

Balthazar gulped at his cup and didn't meet his eye.

'There's something else,' Romeo demanded.

'It was just gossip I heard on the street. There was talk she was to be married. To Count Paris. Today. They had musicians, feasting, all manner of things planned. And then a coffin.'

Nico looked at them in turn. 'Here's what's to be done. Balthazar. You return to Verona. See my brother. Give him a letter from me. Then ride back tomorrow with what he says. We'll understand the full position and then consider–'

Romeo got to his feet. 'I'm going back there. Whatever's happened–'

Balthazar took his arm. 'They will kill you! I heard those soldiers when you left. They have orders to execute you on sight, anywhere within the territory of Venice. Those men said...' He shuddered at the horrid memory. 'They promised they'd garrotte you. Till your eyes popped out and your tongue turned black.'

Romeo found his jerkin and the bag he'd brought. 'It'll be dark by the time I get there. I can make my way into the city unseen.' He paused, trying to think it through. 'I'll find her. Discover what we may do. Then…'

'Then what?' Nico asked. 'This is madness. You risk your life for no good reason. Wait until tomorrow…'

'My wife may be in a coffin! You think I have no good reason?'

The apothecary stayed silent.

'I must know.' He put some money on the table then held out his hand. 'This is for you, Nico. For your treasured advice and welcome friendship.'

'Keep your damned coins. I've done nothing for it.'

'Nothing yet. What Balthazar says is true. If I'm found they'll garrotte me. In public like a tortured animal.'

'Don't go then…'

Romeo's eyes strayed to the bottles by them, blue and green and red. And a few pitch black with painted skulls on the side. 'Take the money. Give me one of your black vials in return…'

Nico's eyes grew wide. 'I try to save lives. Not take them.'

'If you won't do as I ask I'll go to one of the others on the rotonda and ask there. I doubt they'll have your scruples.'

Balthazar shook his head and went to the door to look out on Mantua's Piazza Erbe. The light was waning. It would be dark before they got close to Verona's walls.

'The plague rules are over,' he said. 'The stable man I left my horse with told me. He'd heard it from a messenger. You may take my papers and get free entrance so long as no one recognises you. I can talk my own way in.'

Romeo reached out for the nearest empty black vial and thrust it at the apothecary. 'I won't take it unless I have to. But I'm not going to die like a dog in the street. How long will you need?'

Nico looked at his collection of compounds, the jars and ornate bottles of mixtures from all over the known world. 'Give me a few minutes. I had a farmer order some poison for the morning. You'll take a letter for my brother, too.'

'In Greek, I imagine.'

'You imagine right,' Nico muttered and scribbled it out there and then. The potion took a little while and he grew more taciturn by the minute.

He wouldn't come down to the street to see them go.

'Live, Romeo,' he said, taking him by shoulder when they reached the door. 'It's hard sometimes. But I've seen much more of the alternative than you and I know this: if you breathe there's hope. Stop and…'

The older man shrugged and wouldn't go on.

Balthazar broke the awkward silence between them. 'We need to be moving. The later the hour, the warier the guards.'

The sun was down behind square. Night was slowly stealing towards Mantua. Two fresh horses beneath them, Romeo and Balthazar found the straight road north.

* * *

An hour after sunset, the weather began to change. Thick clouds tumbled down the Alps to Garda, caught the strong westerly wind building from Milan then gathered in squally clusters against the moonlit sky. It was dark by the time Friar John tramped wearily back over the Cangrande bridge. The same guards who'd taunted him the night before were there.

'You got chickenpox, then?' the sergeant called and that made the others laugh. ''Cos if that's the case I'm turning you back, boy.' The man came and blocked his path.

'No, sir. I had it when I was a child. No chickenpox. No plague. Nothing that should prevent my return to Verona.'

'What happened to your mule?' one of the soldiers asked. 'Them saddle bags packed with medicine?'

And letters too, John thought.

'Stolen. By vagabonds. I merely set out on my orders, thinking I was doing a good turn for my fellow men.' He took his hands out of his pockets and made a gesture: nothing left. 'And for that here's my reward.'

'Aww.' The sergeant patted him on his head. 'Poor lad. He's learned the world's a hard old place. Specially if you go out there with nowt but a lame nag and a bible by your side.'

One of the men came up and nudged his arm. 'Best thing you can do is chuck away that habit and sign up with us, son. More fun to be had soldiering than hanging round a monastery, that's for sure.'

'We get girls,' the third soldier said with a sly and lascivious wink. 'Well, sometimes anyway. It has been known to happen.'

John gestured at the gate. 'Perhaps I will. First I must talk to my master, Friar Laurence. May I?'

They threw a few more jocular insults in his direction then waved him through. Feet aching, exhausted, hungry, thirsty, he made his way to San Francesco al Corso. Laurence was in his cell, fast asleep on his cot.

'What ho, my brother,' John said loudly then found himself some wine and slumped into a chair. The steady patter of rain began outside. An owl hooted close by, as if offended.

Laurence came to, rubbing his eyes. 'I hear the voice of Friar John. So soon back from Mantua? What did Romeo say? Do you have a letter from him?'

The wine was welcome.

'For pity's sake, speak, son.'

'Of what? Of pestilence that turns out to be chickenpox? Of saddlebags that contain deceit and trickery alongside medicine for a plague that never was? Of passing my precious robes to a murderer to wear in my place?'

Laurence took a deep breath.

'Tell me,' he ordered.

John did, everything from the inn to the woman in it. How he'd opened the letters, found one beyond him, the other, to Romeo, too strange to believe.

'I did not put on this habit to become a messenger to murderers. Nor to be part of whatever game it is you play.'

'Quiet, boy! Oh, sweet Jesus…'

John stayed silent. He'd never heard the older man curse.

Laurence struggled to his feet, stretching from the slumber. 'What are we to do?'

'We?' John asked. 'In the morning I'll shrug off this robe and find my own way in the world. All the years I've spent here…'

'You were an orphan, lad! Destitute. It was either that or beggary.'

John finished his water and glared at him. 'I'd rather be a beggar than a fraud. How could you play these games?'

'Because they demanded it! Because…' That bloody day in Otranto would never desert him, nor the guilt it left behind. 'I thought it might bring them happiness and end the idiotic violence between Capulet and Montague. Now…' He looked around the cell, with its bottles and potions. 'I realise I'm nothing more than a fool, too unworldly for these tangled designs.'

The young friar got up to go. Laurence came and put out a hand to stay him. 'The girl. Juliet. She's not dead. She's trapped inside that crypt, drugged, asleep. I thought the letter you bore would have brought Romeo to her and the two of them could flee.'

John stared at him, appalled. 'Not dead?'

'It was a trick. To allow Romeo to get her out of the city unseen.'

'It won't now. Will it?'

'No. But sometime soon she'll wake.'

'Oh, Lord…' John whispered.

'In that dread place. Alone. What have I done?'

Laurence got up and opened the door. The rain was coming steadily down. The clouds blacked out most of the moon. John joined him.

'It's night. They lock it up, Laurence.'

'I know. I need a crowbar and a torch. If I can get her out of there and back here…' He looked around the little cell again and sighed. 'I've already done enough to put my neck in a noose. There's no call to add your name to the charge sheet. If you can just find me the means–'

'We will do it.' John gripped his shoulder, looked him in the eye. They were equals then. It was the first time. 'Together.'

'You don't need…'

'There are tools in the huts by the garden. I'll get them.'

Ten minutes later they reached the cemetery and the chapel at the end of the long drive, flanked by tall cedars. There was a single gate for entry and high walls to keep out robbers seeking any gold or gems that might be buried with the dead. The thought of her, a girl of sixteen, waking there alone filled both men with horror.

Laurence strode up to the gates. They were closed, as he expected, but two men, tall and burly, swords out and eagle-eyed, stood there.

'Excuse me, sirs,' he said as he hid the crowbar beneath his grey habit. 'This is a place for grief and mourning. Not arms.'

'And who the hell might you be?' the first one demanded.

'Friars from San Francesco al Corso,' John told him. 'Here to do our work. If we're allowed.'

'Work?' the man asked, waving his blade in front of them. 'No one buries folk after dark, do they? This bloody city amazes me sometimes. Stinking rainy night and all people want to do is visit a cemetery.'

'Please…' Laurence looked around him. There was no other way into the little chapel and the crypt beneath. 'Sirs. We have duties…'

'Aye! And we've got duties too. To our master who visits his lost bride. That's what happens when you fall for a girl around here. He should have stuck to Florence.'

The two friars glanced at one another.

'Your master?' Laurence asked.

'Count Paris. A great and noble man who thought this day to be his joyous wedding and instead comes to scatter flowers on his sweetheart's cold corpse.'

There was a light in the chapel. A torch. A figure moving there, close to the altar.

'We could comfort him,' Laurence whispered.

The man sneered. 'Not the way he is right now. No one could. Be off, little men. Before your arses feel a slap of this blade.'

Friar Laurence nodded weakly. 'Very well, sirs. Come, John.'

The young friar didn't move. 'But…'

'Come! Come! We've no place here. These… gentlemen say so.'

There was a roll of thunder somewhere up in the hills.

Paris's men pulled their jerkins around them and grumbled as they tried to take shelter against the cemetery wall.

'Away with you!' the first one cried. 'Bugger off somewhere and have a good pray.'

The sky opened as they retreated back to the lane. Sweeping, gusting rain came down, drenching them. The two raced beneath the thick branches of a chestnut tree beside the path. John swept his cloak round Laurence to give the older man some protection against the downpour.

'If that poor girl wakes…'

'I am aware of this,' Laurence snapped.

'We cannot stay here, either. Not if there's lightning on the way. So what…?'

A forking flash broke from the cloud across the river and sent two dazzling spears down towards the water. The burst was so bright Laurence's eyes hurt at the power. The sky rocked with thunder. John tried to tug him from their perilous position beneath the tree.

'No further,' Laurence said. 'We wait. We watch. There's nothing else to do.'

* * *

Cold, she felt. Cold and frightened, lost in a darkness that ran forever, no stone clocks in it, no deathly martyrs whispering in her ear. She couldn't move, couldn't see, couldn't even feel herself breathe. But she could taste the steely compound running through her veins and, with its spiky power, hear so clearly… rain running down the sodden walls, rats scuttling across the stones, the low and surly growls of distant thunder.

A day, Friar Laurence had said. And then she'd wake. But even he was vague, perhaps more than he'd allowed himself to show.

With all the strength she could muster she willed herself to move a single finger. Then an eyelid. Nothing happened and all that effort did was stir her racing imagination even further until it began to build a fearful picture of that small, dark subterranean room Laurence had shown her.

The damp, worn limestone. The tiny chamber in the earth into which a line of tracery windows had allowed a little of the evening sun. That time there'd been two plain wooden coffins stacked to one side, next to the stone slabs where she surely lay.

Perhaps there were corpses close by. A gory rag from Tybalt's shroud. A pool of blood from dead Mercutio. Whispers of fading ghosts.

The smell...

Damp and incense. Bodies and decay. She thought she might go mad before she woke, then meet him screaming, never fit to be sane again.

Romeo. Where are you?

The picture of him in her raging memory was wrong somehow. Indistinct and hazy, as if he was the one who toyed with death, not her.

Romeo...

Another refrain came then, one that seemed to wish to haunt her through this never-ending nightmare.

I am me and only me and I am me and only...

She knew what it meant now and the realisation chilled her. Perhaps he was dead already. And if so, it was her challenge, her burden to go on.

Then there were new sounds, a sign of hope perhaps. Footsteps, distant, echoing, from the chapel above. Loud and restless pacing. After that a voice too indistinct to recognise though it sounded rough and furious, rent with a sorrowful despair.

Romeo, she whispered. *Come for me. Do not be angry. For it was your violence that put me here, just as much as did your love.*

Then the voice sounded again, clearer this time. Too hard and old for him.

'Wife,' a half-drunk Paris bellowed. 'Where is my *wife?*'

* * *

The plague rules were abandoned. So Romeo and Balthazar had approached by the shorter, easier route, through the southern gate of the city where the guards were too drunk and lazy to step outside their huts into the pouring rain. Waved through, they were in the heart of the city within minutes, leaving their horses at a stable near the arena.

Hoods up against the weather and recognition, they walked on until they found the cemetery. Two heavily-built men were guarding the locked iron gate. Balthazar went ahead and spoke to them, then reported back their threats and orders.

'They're villains by the looks of them. They say no one's allowed in till daylight. They'll stop any man who tries to cross them.'

'Why?' Romeo wondered, as they hid beneath a tree.

'They won't say. Perhaps if we went to your father's...'

Romeo grabbed him by the jacket. 'I must see her!'

'So you say. But what can we do? Not fight these men for sure. Your father's a wise man. He'll know how to proceed.'

'I know myself! I'm not a child. I'll break in somehow. Find a window...'

The two guards were watching from the gate. The nearest yelled, 'Oi! You two. Didn't you get the message? We don't want you lurking round here. Now bugger off.'

Romeo dragged his hood more tightly around his head and set off for the river side of the chapel. There had to be a way...

'Sir...' Halfway along the path Balthazar took hold of his arm. 'This is madness. If we return to your palace and see your father then—'

Romeo put one hand on the hilt of his rapier and with the other pushed the young servant hard against the wall.

'Either you help me now or go, Balthazar. I'll take no defiance.'

'This is not defiance! I wish to help...'

'Upon your life I'm telling you. I don't care what you see, or what you hear. Do not stand in my way.' He pointed at the chapel wall, the tracery windows near their feet, too small to allow a grown man entry. 'Somehow I'll descend into this nest of death and see her. If...' The fury rose in him, fired by the swift, cruel memory of her face. 'If you return to pry on me by heaven I'll tear you limb from limb and strew this hungry churchyard with your bones.'

The young man struggled in his grip, frightened, offended, appalled.

'I do not deserve this fury, master. I've only tried to serve you. I...'

'I'm no man's master. Not fit for it. Tell my father I love him. And my mother, too. Here...' He pulled out his purse and thrust it in the servant's hands. 'Take this for thanks.'

Balthazar shook his head. 'I receive a wage already. Nothing more is needed.'

The heat came back. 'I warn you! Don't linger in this place. Or interfere with what I do now—'

'No, no,' the lad cut in with a bitter nod. 'I heard the first time. I will remove myself from your presence. And wish you well in this sad venture.'

He waited for an answer. 'Goodbye then.'

'Just go…'

Romeo watched him trudge off through the rain. There was a tree with a long, thick branch overhanging the chapel's low roof, close to a window set at the back, for a side room perhaps. Struggling for purchase against the slippery bark, he climbed the trunk and edged along towards the terracotta tiling, slick and wet with rain.

One glance back. No sign of Balthazar. He reached the roof and edged carefully on to the tiles, feeling them give beneath his weight.

With damp and uncertain fingers, Romeo reached out and found the window frame, tugging on the rotting wood. It shifted. He rolled towards the growing gap. From somewhere inside he heard noises…

Someone moving and a fractured, grieving voice mumbling, 'My wife…'

* * *

Again Juliet tried to lift a finger, an eyelid, to raise the slightest sound in her dry and aching throat. Once more she failed. But in this dark place, eyes still blind, she knew something was stirring.

There were footsteps coming down the staircase, heavy and stumbling. Too ponderous for Romeo's light tread.

Then she heard that voice again and for the first time since she'd swallowed the black liquid, felt her body make the slightest tremor, though it was only her frozen heart, leaping in fear.

A slurred Florentine voice croaked about her, 'Oh, dear flower. My sweetest. With these lilies our bridal bed I strew…'

Paris. Full of wine, she guessed, from the self-pitying timbre of his words.

Something formed in her head. A single syllable. *No.* Her lips struggled to shape it, her throat to speak.

Then the sound of him came again, closer still, and she felt the faintest sensation in her face, a welcome one until she realised what it was.

'These precious flowers fall on precious cold skin...'

He was dragging the shroud away, head to toe, exposing her entirely.

'This is the greatest woe a man must have to shoulder. To see the loveliest creature in the world. To have her in his grip. Promised for his bed this very night. And then...'

Furious curses flew around the room. He wailed and ranted, cursed God and heaven. And – her heart leapt once more – Romeo more than any other.

'That haughty banished villain! Who murdered my love's cousin and drove her grieving to this dread deed.'

Oh, she thought. *If only I could speak.*

That was still beyond her. Yet there was a scent now, strong, sweet and familiar. Lilies. Then the gentlest rain of petals on her cheeks.

Her eyelids shunned her will to open. But she could feel them now, leaden, aching. Soon, she thought. *Soon.*

Something hot came to her ear. His breath, the stink of wine. And then a whisper.

'Oh, woe! My darling Juliet. My beautiful child. The canopy of our marriage bed is nothing more than dust and stones.'

I am mine and only mine. Not yours. Not any man's...

'Nightly I'll come to your tomb with flowers. With rosewater to sprinkle over your grave. But only...'

Closer now. She thought she gasped but wasn't sure. And that he'd touched her, and she didn't know where.

'Just one single night… I crave it…'

Something hard and rough she felt, like sandpaper against her skin. It took a moment to realise what it was. Then a scream began, so loud inside it stilled her thoughts, yet silent to the world.

The beard. It was his prickly bristles on her face, her mouth, her lips, her neck.

Wake up. For pity's sake… Wake up…

It hurt so much she'd have cried out if she could. But all her strength went into that single effort.

In one brief moment Juliet's eyes opened, blinked. She glimpsed his drunken, licentious leer as he bent over her neck, slavering with his kisses.

He never saw, just whined, 'This is a dream. A nightmare. And I will see it to the end.'

The panting returned, with it his feverish fingers and the dark.

Then another voice came through the darkness. Three short words.

'Leave her, sir.'

The bristles vanished. Then her wakefulness.

* * *

By the light of a sputtering torch at the foot of the stairs Romeo halted and wondered at what he saw. Paris was there bent over her, a crumpled shroud at his feet. Half-covered by a flimsy shift Juliet's still frame lay on a marble slab. Lily petals the colour of her skin were scattered across her sculpted neck, her slight and naked shoulders.

The count heard his words, looked back, face full of guilt and hatred. His eyes narrowed, his hand went to the hilt of his sword. The black bottle sat in Romeo's jerkin pocket, neck exposed, the dark potion ready to be drunk. Perhaps there'd be no need of it at all.

He stepped out into the yellow light of the torch. The sight of her motionless by Paris, pale flesh exposed, stole the breath from him, and his reason.

'Montague? *Montague*?' Paris muttered as he pulled himself away from her. 'What kind of creature are you? To disturb a place like this?'

He began to adopt the stiff and martial pose of one about to fight. Romeo came a step closer.

'I might ask that of you. In the circumstances.'

'She was mine!' His furious bellow echoed round the crypt. Then, more quietly, 'Promised. Paid for. My bride tonight. My bed. Mine for all her life. It was... ordained.'

'By whom?'

The answer came in a cantankerous drunken slur. 'By me. By her father. By God.'

Slowly Romeo edged between him and Juliet on the slab. The nobleman rushed forward and with a bunched fist punched him hard in the gut. Then, as he fought for breath, bent over, gasping, the count brought up a knee beneath his chin and sent him rolling back towards the steps.

'This evil work of yours is done. The child is dead because you murdered her cousin.'

'Not so,' Romeo whispered, struggling for breath.

Paris wasn't listening. 'You think you can pursue this vengeance against her house further than the grave?'

Blood in his mouth, the salt taste of it on his tongue. Romeo got to his feet and said, 'I merely wished to see her. Like you. Though from a true affection. Not—'

Paris struck again, a quick and cowardly kick to his shins. 'I'll not take such insults from a foul villain. Banished from this town. Escalus can deal with you. I'll bring you to him myself.' The sword came out. His eyes shone with self-righteous fury. 'Do as I say and leave with me now. Tonight you die. One way or another.'

'Aye.' Romeo nodded. 'That's right. Tonight I do.'

'Come with me. Or encounter this—'

The weapon was a military blade, wider, longer, than a rapier. It cut through the musty air. Still Romeo stepped forward.

'Death is why I'm here. So I beg of you... do not be so foolish as to tempt a desperate man. Be gone. I want no further blood on my account. There's sufficient there already.'

The long sword waved at him. 'Up those stairs, boy. It's the scaffold for you.'

'I am no boy. Not now. For God's sake go. Live and tell those you find that a madman's mercy urged you run away. Not meet this red—'

More swiftly than he'd expect of a drunken man, Paris flew at him, his aim quick and straight. The point nicked Romeo's shoulder. Pain, then, and it was welcome, like the blood running in his mouth.

'Throw down your child's rapier and submit to me. Then I'll take you to Escalus and put the noose around your scrawny neck myself.'

Not meet this red rage, Romeo meant to say.

He raised his weapon. Paris lurched at him. They parried. Three times.

The liquor gave the man courage but took away what speed and skill he possessed. A flurry of moves. A feint, a riposte, a remise.

Then with one hard and well-aimed lunge Romeo's blade found

Paris's breast and entered there, as easily as a sharp butcher's cleaver slicing meat.

* * *

The count's shrieks carried through the tracery windows, out into the rainy night. The friars had returned to berate the guards once more, with Balthazar now by their side.

'You hear those dreadful howls!' Friar Laurence cried. 'There's light in the crypt.'

'True,' the big man said. 'Our master. Like we told you. Bidding a sad farewell to his bride. It's just him blubbing…'

Balthazar tried to push past. The men held him back.

'Romeo must have found the count,' the lad said. 'When I left he was intent on getting inside. Some way around the back. Juliet was his love.'

The first guard shook his head. 'No, no, son. You got that all wrong. She was betrothed to our master, Paris.'

Grim-faced, Laurence shook his head. 'You're the one who's mistaken. She was Romeo's wife. If the two of them should fight over her–'

'We have our orders…' the second said feebly.

There was another scream then, a terrible cry of pain and fear.

The first one looked worried. 'I'm off to fetch Marshal Escalus. It's his job to deal with felons like that murderous Montague. You're not getting me in there with that bloody villain.' He nodded at his mate. 'You coming.'

'Dead right I am. Not staying here with these nutters and…'

Laurence was past him, hurtling down the chapel path as fast his legs would take him.

'Saint Francis be my speed,' he whispered as he ran. 'How often tonight do these old feet stumble at fresh graves?'

* * *

Waking once more she heard two voices, one familiar yet angry and full of violence. Then Paris, wheezing, pathetic, frightened. Still she couldn't move, couldn't speak.

'Oh, I am slain!'

Slumped against the wall, the count clutched at his belly, the blade hilt up against his ribs.

'That you are. I warned—'

'Be merciful, man. Have them lay me in the tomb with my sweet Juliet.'

Romeo wanted to laugh. 'If the lady could speak, sir, what do you think she'd say?'

'She'd wish to be with her groom—'

'For sure.'

Roughly, with one quick and violent pull, he dragged the rapier out and didn't look to see what followed with it. Paris bawled in pain and fear, a terrible sound, and then the man was gone.

A short curved dagger with an Arabic ivory hilt gleamed on his bloody waist. This was a night for Queen Mab and the red rage. Not sly and easy poisons. Romeo reached down, took the weapon from the dead count's belt and felt the sharpness of its edge. There were sounds outside. Men's voices, yelling. Time was short and for that he was glad.

First, though, he would see her once more.

He fetched the torch from the wall then returned to the slight shape upon the slab. Her face was young and perfect, eyes closed, skin so pale, features fair and tranquil.

There were noises above. Men had entered the chapel. No seconds to waste. He placed the rising point of the dagger beneath his rib cage. The hilt he leant against the stone to give him purchase and take him out of the world in one swift thrust.

He looked down at her, reached out with his spare hand, touched her cheek. 'I'll stay with you, my love, and by your side depart this palace of grim death. Let worms be our chambermaids. Here our everlasting rest. One look.' He leaned over to see her better. 'One final embrace,' His fingers ran fondly against her neck. 'One last...'

The blade went in, cold and relentless. He stumbled against the slab. 'And final... kiss...'

He tried to reach her. But the light was fading, with it his life.

A drop of blood fell from Romeo's lips and stained the pale linen loose around her shoulders. Dying, stumbling, his knees began to give.

There were anxious voices in the crypt, a clatter of feet closing on him.

Then, as breath failed him, an ultimate cruel torture.

Fetched up against the stone he looked and wondered: was this real? Or the last act of Queen Mab's cruel trickery?

As the cold began to creep on him and the light to dim, she seemed to turn her head and open her eyes so slowly, greeting the half-light above her with a shadow of a welcoming smile.

'Dead Juliet,' he gasped in the softest of whispers. 'Dead Romeo greets you. But the hour's late. And this our race is run...'

* * *

Awake.

Her throat was rough as sand, her eyes bleary, her mind racing.

The friar's fractured voice came to her, full of shock and agony. 'Oh, sweet Jesus, what blood stains this sepulchre? Why are these gory swords inside a place of peace?'

One hand she got to the cold stone and gripped it, coughing, trying to focus.

'Laurence?' Her voice was a croak, her head full of dreams and strange elusive images. 'Where's Romeo? I remember well what we agreed and I am where I should be. This…'

One arm moved. She managed to raise herself on a bare elbow. The shroud they'd put on her was gone. All she wore now was little more than a slip and that half off.

Two figures lay beside the slab, slumped and bloody on the clammy tiles. The brother's arms swept round her, trying to hide the sight of them. There were more shapes now, pouring into the chamber, groaning, sighing at what they found there.

'Romeo…' she whispered, pushing the friar to one side.

Laurence took her cold arm and tried to pull her away. 'I must get you out of this hellish place. A greater power than ours has entered here and ruined all our intentions.'

She shoved him to one side, rolled her legs off the marble, took a tentative step on the cold tiles. Then stood up, swaying, trying not to fall. 'God's too busy for little fools like us. This is our own doing. Where is–?'

The words vanished. She could see him now.

'Your Romeo's dead,' Laurence said. 'And Paris, too. This is a frightful vision, too grievous for you to see. Come! I'll take you to a sisterhood of holy nuns. They'll care for you. The watch will be here soon and who knows what they might think?'

With all the returning strength she possessed, Juliet broke free and fell to the floor, there to kneel beside him, hands running through his matted, sweaty hair. Romeo had died slumped against a pillar, dagger in his guts, those calm and gentle eyes staring out at nothing, mouth open, dripping blood. She reached for the blade. Laurence was too quick. With a fearful cry he dragged the weapon clean out of Romeo's flesh and threw it in the corner.

'No,' he said. 'I've seen you reach for a dagger once before. Not again. There's death enough in this grim place. I'll not allow more.'

She barely heard. Juliet stayed beside him, unable to take her eyes off this strange, unnatural sight. Just a handful of days had passed since that first night in the garden where she'd snatched the apple off the tree and kissed him, feeding its sweet flesh and juice between his parted lips. Now Romeo was gone and there was nothing in his place except this still, cold corpse. From life to death in such short order.

'Give me the knife,' Juliet muttered. 'Or I swear I'll find one somewhere...'

'Come, child...'

His hand grasped her naked shoulder. Still she didn't move.

On Romeo's leather jerkin, above the slow-streaming blood, something glittered in the yellow waxy light of their brands. She reached for it and had the thing in her fingers before Laurence or any of the others now milling round could intervene.

A bottle. Black. Bigger than the one she'd stolen into her bedroom a day before. On the side in white paint was a skull, empty eyes staring straight at her.

'I will have that...' the friar declared and leapt to seize it.

Too late. She turned from him. The stopper was out, the thick and stinking liquid within rolling down her throat.

'I die standing,' Juliet whispered as she got one hand to Laurence's leg and began to raise herself. 'I die...'

Whatever lay in Romeo's vial, it wasn't the friar's weak and cunning liquid. This potion had a strong, disgusting taste, of liquorice and metal. Before she was upright an icy venom was racing deep inside, freezing her blood as it ran furious through her veins.

I am me and only me and...

Laurence took hold of her, seized the bottle, stared at it, sniffed the neck, horror in his face.

'Juliet...'

Her fingers trembled. She raised them, reaching for his cheek. They never found him. Instead came a rising roar, a grating of ancient stone.

She looked down and knew what she would see emerging at her feet. It was the marble rose window of San Zeno, the Wheel of Fortune stirring into motion, groaning, waiting like a millstone hungry for fresh grain. All the figures on it, happy and sad, were staring at her. Holding their stone sides, weeping stone tears, laughing at what they beheld.

Juliet of the Capulets watched them for a moment then felt the cold ground beneath her vanish. Arms flying, hair waving in the unreal wind, she fell headlong down towards the grinning faces and the grinding jaws, wondering at the dark that lay beyond.

* * *

If this was death it came with lots of noise.

Plainchant. Birdsong. Low men's voices, sad and thoughtful. With them, briefly, the hammer of a chisel on stone.

Juliet woke with a sudden shock and found herself on a hard cot, a wicker panel in front of her. When she moved the screen she saw she was in a spacious, shady room crammed with furniture and equipment. There was a strong, familiar smell. Chemicals and potions. This was Laurence's cell. Someone had put a loose black habit around her, the serge fabric scratching at her skin. A bleached white cotton nun's scapular lay on a stool beside the bed, folded ready to wear.

She took two tentative, unsteady steps towards the door. The single window at the front was shuttered, but rays of strong sunlight peeked through the cracks. The voices and the chisel sounds were coming from there. Her father, calm for once but pained, and another, old too and equally disconsolate, accompanied by the measured and cautious tones of Friar Laurence.

She raised her right hand in the gloom and flexed it.

'Yet still I breathe,' she murmured, watching her deft fingers move to her command.

He'd said she might wake from the first drug feeling refreshed, as if she'd enjoyed the best of sleeps. The nightmare in the dead house had been so brief she'd no idea whether that was true or not. But now... hunger nagged at her and thirst. Her mind was sharp and clear. She'd never felt so alert and alive, though she couldn't begin to guess how she'd travelled from the grime and cold of the crypt to this quiet and fragrant place.

Greedily she drank water from a pewter jug set next to the scapular by the bed. Then she walked to the friar's preparation table. There was a knife and a pair of scissors by the bottles and jars and the alembics.

Memories of those last few moments in the crypt returned. She picked up the blade and thought of Romeo, dead on the chill damp tiles. Blood and a black bottle in the dark. His face, his voice, his touch remained part of her, alive in her mind yet distant already, part of a past that lay behind. The world seemed different now and so did she.

The sharp cold edge of the blade moved against her skin and found the raised veins there.

Then from outside she heard her father's heartbroken voice.

'My daughter... my beloved daughter. Cold stone. Grey marble. Is this all there is to be of her?'

Curious, she placed the knife on the table and tiptoed to the shutters, then softly prised them open until the crack was wide enough to see outside, into the dazzling day.

* * *

Luca Capulet wiped the tears from his eyes and retrieved a pouch of coins from his jacket. Andrea Montague stood by his side, shifting awkwardly on old, tired feet. This was the first time they'd spoken in earnest since they were called to the grim scene in the cemetery. Three corpses, two bloody, one with black stains on her lips. Gone now, with only a monument to be decided. A joint one, for Capulet and Montague. Their wives had insisted upon that.

'You should have seen her in life,' her father declared, rubbing his sleeve across his face. 'No statue will do her justice.'

The stonemason with them held a piece of salt-white stone in one hand, lumps chipped from it to show the quality. In the other a preliminary sketch for the memorial: two young figures holding hands, beatific faces upturned to heaven, angel wings on their backs.

'I do believe you,' he agreed. 'But flesh dies and marble lives forever. Though…' He eyed the pouches. 'Immortality does cost.'

'You get half the money up front,' Montague told him, adding a pouch of his own. 'The rest will stay with Friar Laurence. Is that agreed, Luca?'

Capulet stared at him, as if seeing Andrea Montague anew. Or perhaps the way he was when then were childhood friends. He pointed at the sketch, grimacing, shaking his grizzled head.

'Her hair. It should be longer and fuller than this. With no parting or any ribbons. My daughter preferred it plain and natural. No need for ostentation. Her cheekbones were higher and finer, not the flat things he has here. And her brows.' He grabbed the mason's charcoal and scribbled an amendment to the drawing. 'She was the loveliest child a man could ask for. And deserved a father wise enough to tell her that, not an ignorant, selfish idiot who… who…'

His voice faltered and he began to choke on this sudden return of grief. There were tears in the cloister, tears behind the shutters of the cell.

Embarrassed, the mason said he would follow their every wish then took the sketch from the friar's hands and left.

Montague bent to speak to Capulet. Their words were gentle now, for the first time in two decades. 'Luca. Our shared tears could fill an ocean. But when the dead are in the ground one's thoughts must turn to the living. Their legacy. Our wives. The memory of those two sweet children is best served by peace between our houses. Through charity and tenderness. Not constant sorrow. For pity's sake… no more bitter and pointless enmity.'

Capulet wiped his rheumy eyes and took him by the arm. 'Here's to that. We're two old fools and they're the ones who paid the price. If I could take your son's place in that cold tomb…'

'And I your Juliet's. But we can't. I will endow a school in her name. One that teaches the poor to read. Bianca said she wanted that.'

Her father nodded. 'She did, not that I listened. Then in Romeo's name I'll provide a scholarship for poets. That I pledge. I cannot stop wondering at these lost years of hatred between us. Why it took two innocent deaths to teach us the stupidity of that pointless feud. Forgive me, Andrea.'

Montague gripped his fingers and shook them. 'If I'm forgiven in turn.'

'And me, sirs?' Laurence asked quietly.

'My lovely girl would have killed herself in any case, Friar,' said Capulet. 'Rather than marry Paris. I drove her to that. No one else. That's my cross to bear. Don't try to ease the burden of it.'

Montague concurred. 'Your part was small, Friar. We made their lives impossible. It's time to live with our regrets and do our best to learn from them.'

'Well put,' Capulet said and put his cap on, ready to go. 'Besides, that old bastard Escalus pardoned you. Who wants to argue with him?' He thought for a moment and glanced at the frail man beside him. 'It's a long time since I shared a glass of wine with a boyhood friend of mine…'

'It is,' Montague declared. 'Only if I'm buying and it's Garganega.'

Luca Capulet smiled at him, remembering the days when they were young, inseparable, convinced the future ahead was bright and full of love. 'Then I will try your Trebbiano. Which I always liked if I'm honest. Perhaps we should combine them one day. See if two might make a better sale than one.'

'An idea,' said Montague, 'worthy of exploration.'

They wandered off, chatting earnestly. The friar waited until they were out of earshot then glanced anxiously at his cell. Two glittering eyes watched him at the shutter, a face full of questions.

* * *

'Why do I live?'

'Because God willed it.'

His voice was low, his manner oblique. They stayed in the shadows of the cell, seated round the table where he'd married them.

'God won't tell me. You can.'

It was an hour since Juliet's father and Montague had ambled back to the city. Laurence had immediately removed the knife and the scissors from the table then given her more water, something he called tonic, found spelt porridge and boiled eggs for her to eat. She'd fallen greedily on the food. Her body felt alive and tense, her mind sharp and active, almost too much so. The time she'd spent in the crypt she'd dreamt and dreamt. This second strange interlude was different. It was as if she'd died for a while, entered a black state of unconsciousness, then returned renewed, to see the world through different eyes.

His explanation was short, a narrative of accidents mostly, of inadvertent calamities, innocent in themselves, fatal in unison. As he recounted the litany of mishaps she could only think of the dream figures on the rose window of San Zeno, the horror in their eyes as the Wheel of Fortune turned against them. This was life in all its asymmetrical fickleness.

Then Laurence concluded his tale with the disclosure she craved most: an explanation of why she lived. Romeo went to Mantua carrying a letter meant only for the eyes of Nico, Laurence's apothecary brother there. When the second message, telling of the scheme to feign her death, never reached him, he returned to Verona, thinking Juliet dead. But Nico had given him a letter in Greek, too, for his brother. The friar had recovered the parchment from Romeo's tunic before he was buried.

'In my message to Nico I warned him that his visitor was a decent lad at heart but rash, impulsive and, on occasion, prone to violence. In his to me...' He picked the letter out of a sheaf of papers on the table. 'He said he believed Romeo was returning to kill himself by your side. That he'd demanded poison for that purpose. If Nico refused to oblige he'd find another apothecary who would.'

The same black bottle she'd found in the crypt now sat by the pouches of money Laurence had taken for the stonemason. He picked it up and turned the thing upside down to show that it was empty.

'My brother would never give a man a potion designed to take a human life. Instead Romeo left with the same kind of compound I gave to you. An opiate to render him insensate for a while. Stronger, since he was larger in frame. Happily, Nico listed the elements for me...' He leaned forward, touched her face, lifted her eyelids like a physician, then felt her pulse. 'To think I believed you a feeble girl,' Laurence muttered with a shake of his head. 'And wondered if you'd live.'

'This...?' she asked, pointing at the black serge gown.

It was two nights since the fatal sword fight in the cemetery crypt. A day since Romeo was interred in the Montague tomb, and a coffin bearing her name carried into that of the Capulets.

'When I realised you still lived, Friar John helped me remove you from that place. We brought you here. In your coffin we placed a young sister from the nunnery. Her heart had failed that morning. God forgive me.'

She felt the fabric, her eyes growing wide.

'It was meant for her,' he said quickly. 'She never wore it. We gave her your shroud and shift. In turn...' He blushed. 'I'm sorry. We could think of no other way. If I'd told your father and... you never woke. To think his daughter dead a third time would have destroyed the man completely.'

'Then dead Juliet is. And this rift with Montague...?'

'Didn't you hear? It's done with. Escalus insisted. Not that it was necessary.'

He picked up a flask and poured himself a glass of clear amber liquid. Wine. She could smell it. Her senses seemed so finely tuned.

'I thought the marshal might be sending me to the scaffold. But he seemed to think I was a... decent, holy man. Your father begged him on my part too.'

'My mother?'

The friar could barely look at her. 'Heartbroken. Naturally. Though...'

When he didn't go on she asked, 'Though what?'

'There are stations of grief. Anger. Blame. Regret. Then... acceptance. Death comes. Life goes on. As Andrea Montague said. Though when they see you... this miracle...'

She didn't speak. He waited. Finally she rubbed the rough serge of the nun's habit between finger and thumb and said, 'Fetch me fresh clothes.'

'If you're not ready to face them... I could find you breathing space with the nuns.'

'These robes are not for me.'

He laughed. 'This is a community of friars. We have no women's clothes.'

'Then fetch me those of a boy.'

Laurence thought for a moment, finished his wine and said, 'Very well.'

'Tell no one. Promise me, Friar. No one.'

'And will you promise in return you'll do yourself no harm?'

'I did already,' she pointed out. It was the first question he'd asked when he came in from the cloisters. 'Do you not believe me?'

'I wish to,' Laurence said. 'Yet still?'

'Clothes,' she insisted. 'Please.'

* * *

A little while later the friar returned, in his arms a young man's tunic, simple britches, boots, a plain shirt, a cap. The cell looked empty. Hanks of golden hair lay scattered on the tiled floor.

'Juliet! Where are you? What is this? You promised…'

Then a voice from behind the screen said, 'And kept my promise. Leave the clothes on the stool, if you will.'

He averted his eyes as he did what she demanded then went back to the table and waited. After a few minutes she came out so changed he could hardly believe it. Her long hair was gone. The yellow locks left were cropped roughly, tight to her head. In the modest cheap clothes she might have been a fresh-faced servant boy or girl of fifteen.

'What have you done?'

Her face was calm, her manner tranquil. She walked to the table and picked up one of the pouches of coin.

'Juliet. Your father. Your mother…'

'Juliet's dead. You said so.'

He wrung his hands. 'In good time they will be overjoyed to see you…'

Her sharp eyes glared at him. 'Time's rarely been good to me. And if I did as you wish... what then? Do they put that nun's habit back on me for shame? Or find another suitor who'll ignore my... wicked past?'

'They're your parents. They love you...'

'And every time they see me I'll remind them of the pain I caused.' More quietly she added, 'That they caused me.' She raised the pouch. 'I'll take this and put it to better use than gilt on a statue to a myth.'

'But *where*?'

There was one abiding memory from that last trip to the city on the water, when her mother had taken her to see the Carpaccio paintings, hinting heavily at the wedding to come. It was the glorious afternoon they rode lazily across Saint Mark's Basin in a gondola, half-slumbering to the rhythmic movement of the single oar. In the distance lay the grey and empty horizon of the Adriatic, vessels on it, heading out to the unknown world beyond.

'East. To Venice. To begin with...' She took some coins out of the pouch and threw them on the table. 'Find me a horse. I need... papers.' She scratched the new short hair. 'Don't I?'

Laurence shook his head then went to the desk and found quill and parchment. He wrote a letter of introduction to an apothecary he knew, a Turk who worked in a storehouse on the Grand Canal. A man who would give her lodging and ask no hard questions. Then a similar missive to a fellow in Vicenza. Venice was two days' ride. She would need to halt there along the way.

When that was done he looked at her and said, 'For matters of passage you need a name. A new one. I think... Ursula. A holy martyr. The patron saint of orphans—'

'Who didn't exist.'

'Then perhaps it's appropriate. Since you're not an orphan after all.'

'I baptise myself. Call me Eve.' Then she touched her cropped blonde hair. 'Write another for Adam. I'll choose the one that suits.'

He grunted but all the same he wrote two documents of passage as she asked, stamped them with the monastery seal, found an old satchel and placed the papers inside. Her last name he put as Esposito. Exposed. It was what the monks called foundlings left abandoned outside their gates for care.

By now it was almost midday. She could be in Vicenza before nightfall. Venice the day after.

'A horse...' she repeated.

'That I'll do. But you will not travel alone. There's another who can join you. For safety. For company—'

'Friar...'

'Go with him willingly or I swear I'll take you straight to Escalus myself. Let him hang me afterwards. I probably deserve it.'

She smiled then and a little of her previous charm returned. 'Poor Laurence. We brought you such misery. When all you wanted was to spread a little peace.'

He struggled to his feet and said, gruffly, 'Aye. I'm not made for subterfuge and monkey business. The day moves on. The road is long. Which will it be? Escalus or Venice?'

* * *

The afternoon was cooler than she expected, with a soft breeze running from the mountains to the north. By the monastery gates, on the path to the river stood a young man in clothes much like hers. He held the reins of two Bardigiano mares. Small, hardy animals, sure-footed, the kind she'd once ridden with her father.

'This is Friar John,' Laurence said.

'Just John now.' The young man kept staring at her. 'As for names...'

She took the better-looking horse, checked the bridle, the straps, the stirrups. The friar embraced her one last time, said farewell with a few words she barely heard, then wandered off to the herb garden.

'What do I call you?' John asked.

I am me and only me...

'"Girl" will do for now. Or "boy" if you like. Does it matter?'

He laughed at that and started to check his mount much the way she did, though clumsily as if he'd no idea where to begin.

'We leave by the graveyard,' she said, climbing into the saddle and, without waiting for him, stirred the horse to go.

John was at her side by the time they reached the cemetery. Dusty monuments stood in tidy lines, fresh earth like giant molehills between a few of them, two burly sextons busy with their shovels among the cypresses. By the Capulet tomb a small mountain of garlands was stirring in the midday breeze. She asked which was the Montague monument and he pointed out a Gothic structure. Grand in its own way, but pale and grey, a memorial to shadows and memories, not the brief bright and vivid spark of life that was Romeo, flesh and blood.

Once she'd have avoided this place for anything, haunted by visions of the corpses beneath the ground. Now she didn't dread them. She knew: it was life that she'd shrunk from, not death at all. An age seemed to have passed in this strange, short week of joy and horror, love and hate. The agony of his passing would never leave her. Yet in their too-brief time lay such discoveries, of passion, warmth, devotion. A sense of freedom too. That was Romeo's gift, though it came at such a cost.

John was struggling with his mount as they trotted past the gates towards the cobbled path that led to the Adige. The animal grumbled at his clumsiness.

'Never been on anything but a mule before,' he admitted. 'This beast's a lot harder than they ever were.'

'I suppose.'

The bend of the gleaming river emerged ahead, fishing boats idling on the surface, tethered cormorants like dark upright hooks in their bows.

His animal bucked again and he murmured a gentle curse.

'What will you do in Venice, John?'

'I thought I'd find a ship. Provided I don't get seasick.'

'If you struggle with a little mare the high seas might be a bit...'

She didn't finish. He doffed his grey cap and grinned.

'Aye... lady... lad... whatever you are today. That's true. Best I find something else then.' He took the reins more firmly. 'And you? I don't wish to be too bold. But what's done is done. Maybe there's a fine husband waiting amongst all those rich Venetian gentlemen. We all need someone. Can't go through this grim world alone.'

Her mother's voice came back to her. 'We'll see.'

He was watching the way she handled the horse. 'You're all right with that animal, aren't you?'

She turned for one last look at the city. The spiky line of battlements rose behind her, that glorious crown of thorns. Ahead the sparkling water beckoned, and the long flat road to the east.

'I'll cope,' she said and didn't think then, just lightly tapped the Bardigiano's flanks with her ankles. No spurs needed for a horse like this. The little beast couldn't wait to run, almost as much as she.

With a happy bray the mare tossed its head and set off down the track, hooves rattling into a gallop, eyes firm on the way ahead.

John, they left behind, as the horse flew on, bold and wild and wilful.

Down to the winding river, on to the boundless sea.

Acknowledgements

I'm deeply grateful to the many people who made this book possible. Steve Feldberg of Audible US set the wheels in motion with the original project as an audio performance, bringing Richard Armitage on board to narrate. Richard, as well as doing an amazing job, gave me innumerable and generous insights into the story which helped when it came to the substantial rewrite of the audio version as a novel. Katja Reister and her colleagues in Audible Berlin also gave me very useful fresh perspectives when the work was adapted as a full-blown drama in German. And during my several visits to the wonderful city of Verona I was always grateful for the amicable, enthusiastic and selfless assistance I received from the many locals who helped me learn there's so much more to the place than 'Juliet's House' and a few, oversubscribed tourist locations. Finally to Rebecca Lloyd and her colleagues at the Dome Press who took on the task of helping me adapt this adaptation of an original drama into the form of a book. Many thanks to you all.

David Hewson

Author's note

Two households, both alike in dignity,
In fair Verona where we lay our scene,
From ancient grudge break to new mutiny,
Where civil blood makes civil hands unclean.
From forth the fatal loins of these two foes
A pair of star-cross'd lovers take their life;
Whose misadventured piteous overthrows
Doth with their death bury their parents' strife.

So begins *Romeo and Juliet* with Shakespeare making the unusual decision to summarise the play to come in the space of eight lines of verse. In the beautiful but hot-tempered city of Verona two warring families renew hostilities. Their unfortunate offspring become lovers and kill themselves. With their deaths, the vendetta between the two houses ends.

Violence, ancient hatred, hot-blooded teenagers, doomed illicit passion and redemptive suicide… Ingredients enough for a tale that has become the most famous romantic tragedy in the world. But, despite his interpretation's fame, the story itself was not the creation of Shakespeare.

The first recorded version of what was to become *Romeo and Juliet* appeared in a collection of Italian romances published in 1476. It was then set in Siena and the lovers were called Mariotto and Gianozza. The names of Giulietta and Romeo didn't appear until an adaptation by a Venetian writer in 1531. This was elaborated upon further by a later Italian author, Matteo Bandello, as part of a story collection which may also have inspired Shakespeare's *Much Ado About Nothing* and *Twelfth Night*, as well as Webster's *The Duchess of Malfi*.

In 1562 Bandello's work was translated into French. That version was turned into an English poem by a little-known writer called Arthur Brooke. Shakespeare used Brooke's version as the source material for his play.

Brooke copies Bandello in stating that the story really happened, ending his poem with the claim that the tomb of Juliet and her knight still stood in Verona and was much admired. Like the tale itself, this is pure fancy. There is no record of any family with a name like Capulet in the city. One called Montecchi – perhaps an Italian Montague – did exist, but they were expelled in 1229, long before anyone began to write about two star-cross'd lovers.

Romeo and Juliet are fictional characters through and through. None of this stops millions of tourists visiting modern Verona to see Juliet's so-called house with its pretty balcony (erected by a canny tourist office in the 1940s) or taking selfies by her supposed coffin in the former monastery (which strictly speaking was a convent, though the home to monks) of San Francesco al Corso.

Stories are sometimes made as much by the imaginations of audiences and readers as they are by a playwright or author. If enough people believe a myth to be true, is it really still a myth? It's impossible to separate the tale of Juliet and her Romeo from this ancient city in the Veneto. So, from the start, I took the deliberate decision to set much of this narrative in places you can still see today.

Verona's historic centre, set behind its walls in a bend of the Adige river, is recognisably the same as the city of five hundred years ago. The social centre is where the first scene takes place – the market square, once the Roman forum, now the Piazza Erbe, where the servants of Montagues and Capulets are spoiling for a fight. Another key location is the imposing basilica of San Zeno, one of Verona's most impressive sights. The embalmed corpse of the saint, which so appals Juliet, remains there sixteen centuries on from his death, visible in red robes in a glass casket. Above the doors is the famous rose window with its Wheel of Fortune characters around the circumference.

Sant'Anastasia, the Capulets' parish church, is little changed, though its extraordinary Pisanello fresco of *Saint George and the Princess*, with hanged men in the background, has suffered over the years. Around the corner runs the low colonnaded street of Sottoriva where Romeo has his fateful meeting with Tybalt.

Back towards the Piazza Erbe lie the central monumental buildings of the city and the curious raised tombs of the Scaligeri clan where Romeo meets Mercutio and Benvolio before the Capulet banquet. The statue of Cangrande above his sarcophagus, grinning on his horse, a dog's head mask on his back, is a copy. The original you'll find in his castle, the seat of Escalus in this version. Today the fortress is known as the Castelvecchio, the old castle. But to the players in this tale it wouldn't be old at all, so here it's called simply Cangrande's castle. The red-brick swallow-tail bridge over the Adige which Romeo rides across is a popular place for evening excursions. The building itself has been converted into a museum and art gallery – the painting of the girl with her charcoal drawing of a stick figure, seen in Juliet's bedroom, can still be found there. The Roman arena, where the three youths meet after the banquet, is no longer a haunt for prostitutes and vagabonds but a major tourist attraction used for operatic performances that attract music lovers from all over the world.

The tragic event that shapes the lives of both Friar Laurence and his brother Nico – the massacre of the martyrs of Otranto – was all too real. In 2013 Pope Francis canonised the 813 victims of the Ottoman slaughter in the southern Italian city. Many of their skulls make a grisly public memorial behind the altar of the town's cathedral.

The nine canvases of Carpaccio's *Ursula Cycle*, which have a frightening resonance for Juliet, now live in a room of their own in Venice's Accademia Gallery. The contrasting versions of Adam and Eve which she's nagging her mother to visit in Florence remain on the walls for which they were painted, the Brancacci Chapel in the church of Santa Maria del Carmine.

Shakespeare doesn't state when his tale is set, though usually it is assumed to be in the early fourteenth century. I've placed this version very deliberately in July 1499, a time when Italy was in a feverish state of excitement due to what we now call the Renaissance.

This was the era of Machiavelli and Da Vinci, the discovery of unknown continents and the questioning of age-old ties to religion. A new century was just a few months away, and with it the start of the second half of the millennium. It seemed an apt moment for a story about two young people who wish to shrug off the stifling world of their parents and explore the brave new one emerging around them.

Juliet, here, is not the winsome shrinking violet she's occasionally portrayed as on stage. Nor is she in the play, in truth. In the balcony scene, for example, where Romeo wishes to swear by the moon she throws him by objecting, 'O, swear not by the moon, th'inconstant moon, that monthly changes in her circle orb.'

Being an intelligent, sensible girl she's making the practical point that it's odd to swear by something so irregular. This side of her — rational, argumentative, stubborn — contrasts nicely with Romeo's obviously dreamy, impulsive and poetic nature. It also jars with one of the stranger alterations Shakespeare makes to his source material, declaring quite explicitly that she is only thirteen years old. I've gone back to the Italian originals here and made her a more believable sixteen, two years younger than Romeo, though perhaps a touch more mature.

I've added much that's new or changed, including a different ending from Shakespeare's rain of corpses, the traditional close for an Elizabethan tragedy. Why? For the same reason that he and many other writers have departed from their source material over the centuries. Because that's what adaptation entails. This isn't Shakespeare translated any more than Shakespeare was a translation of Brooke or Bandello.

Nor is it a simple love story — or, as Juliet has it here, a story concerning love. This is a narrative that portrays the gulf between generations, the persistence of hope in a time of promise and peril, and the consequences of feuds and hot-headed teenage violence. Its principal subject, however, is Juliet herself, a precocious young woman desperate to throw off the shackles of family, to be free of a society determined to force her into an unwanted marriage.

A key to understanding her predicament lies in the most quoted — and misunderstood — line in the play, 'O Romeo, Romeo! Wherefore art thou Romeo?' She's not asking where her lover can be found.

'Wherefore' means 'why'. Juliet's broader question is: why should she and Romeo be deprived of their love simply because of the names they both bear? What defines us really? The labels family and society wish to place on us? Or that mysterious, elusive thing inside we call 'self'?

Love-struck Romeo may not understand her point but he's only too eager to meet her wishes. 'My name, dear saint, is hateful to myself, because it is an enemy to thee. Had I it written, I would tear the word.'

Fate denies him the opportunity to tear the word. But this Juliet, a stronger, smarter character, deserved, I felt, the chance.

David Hewson